Fated Conflict

CONSPIRACY OF FIRE

Michael T. Sanders

freak ash
BOOKS

Published in the United Kingdom in 2006 by Freak Ash Books, a trade name of Freak Ash Ltd.

www.freakash.net

Cover design by Simon Burn

The cover art comprises the following images:
'Manor House', © Matthew Collingwood,
'Single Tree', © Oxana Prokofyeva,
'Sunsets', © Tadija Savic;
images from BigStockPhoto.com,
and 'Lucy' © Simon Burn.

A CIP catalogue record for this book is available from the British library.

ISBN 978 0 9553403 2 1

Printed and bound by Trade Print Europe Ltd, London.
72 New Bond Street, London, W1S 1RR

DEDICATIONS

For Mr Simon Burn, who has been good enough to edit this book twice now, as well as taking on the momentous task of being my business partner,

Mr Robert Smart, for years of advice and criticism that have developed this project into what it is today,

Miss Elizabeth Shine, for taking care of me when I am dying from overwork, and for supporting us through the long and arduous process of setting up Freak Ash,

Miss Verity Burke, for her help with the second stage of editing of this publication, in addition to very kindly providing us with the front cover,

and Mr Peter Waters, whose infectious enthusiasm has made a great deal of all of this possible.

CONSPIRACY OF FIRE

PART ONE

A red bike tore through the streets of the People's Freedom Society, diving across lanes and weaving between cars during the early morning rush as he darted recklessly towards work. Its rider wore a red helmet with tinted visor, the bright headgear contrasting with his dark green leather jacket and black trousers.

On a normal day he wouldn't even consider attending work for another few hours yet, but today was no ordinary day. For a start, his pager had gone off an hour ago, telling him to get into the office quickly. He had, uncharacteristically, already been awake, as a phone call half an hour before that had warned him to get ready to be called in.

His name was Colonel Liam Cabot, of the Civilian Guard. He had fought in the people's war for independence against their oppressors, ten years ago, starting as a lowly sergeant and ending up, two years later, a Colonel in the guard, responsible for a large portion of field operations.

He swung the bike onto the motorway's off-ramp and drove into the Civilian Guard Headquarters car park. He parked in his personal space and stepped from the vehicle, pulling his helmet off as he did so and slinging the long case strapped to the side of the bike over his shoulder.

Cabot was of slightly above average height, with a muscular build and short black hair, spiked up with gel. He strode confidently through the front door of the Civilian Guard building and went up to the front desk, producing his ID card from his jacket and handing it to the receptionist.

"Welcome back, Colonel Cabot; it's been a while."

Cabot never returned to the Headquarters unless he had to, his superiors preferring to keep him in the field, where they felt his eccentricities could cause less damage.

"It has indeed. Thank you." Cabot accepted his card back and made for the lifts. He got a little way before a large man in dark green uniform stepped into his path.

"Colonel Cabot, I don't know how you handle things out in the field, but here we consider it good manners for you to deposit your weapons before entering a government institution." The man indicated the case on Cabot's back.

"They stay with me." There was a sword and a pistol on the man's belt, Cabot noted, his hand wrapping around the silver box in his pocket before he thought better of it.

The man in his path nodded to two guards, who started to move in on him.

"What do you think you're doing?"

The guards shrank away as a newcomer approached. Colonel Sophie Paris was the head of base security, being deemed far too important for field work because of her position as one of the Society's social elite, the 'Old Crowd'.

"Colonel Paris."

"Colonel Cabot." She graced him with a stiff nod. "Come upstairs, they're waiting for us; do you feel like leaving your weapons with these guys?"

"Not especially, no."

"So be it then."

The two colonels stepped into the lift and rode it to the top floor of the building. The doors opened again onto a large conference room, around which were a series of small groups of people.

"The gang's all here," Paris said.

"Must be something quite important," Cabot remarked. Around the room, chatting and helping themselves to doughnuts, was every member of the Guard over the rank of major, none apparently certain of what they were here for.

"Ah, Colonel Cabot, Colonel Paris; we can begin." The head of the Guard, Cayley Tufnell, stood at the end of the large conference table, around which the various guardsmen were gathered.

"This morning four bodies were discovered around the PFS; each mutilated in a different way, but there are some similar themes running between the murders. The victims were apparently unrelated; a senate aide, a coffee shop assistant, a young boy of six, and a researcher for the Marine Biology institute." Tufnell paused, letting them take in the enormity of this situation; four murders in one night in a society which barely had ten a year.

"The Chancellor and Lord Protector have issued announcements saying that the murderer needs to be caught at all costs. This means that the army will be racing to beat us to the catch—they must not be allowed to do so. For the honour of our organisation, we must be the first to bring this murderer to justice."

Tufnell paused once again to flick to the next page of her notes.

"Colonel Cabot."

Cabot looked up.

"I am assigning you to this task; you will have the full backing of this department. Assemble whomsoever you need to get this done; and do not fail us."

"Of course, ma'am."

"Very good; you are all dismissed. Help Colonel Cabot with his enquiries if you can, and keep on the look out for anything suspicious, or for members of the army."

The assembled council stood up and began to move for the doors. Cabot remained seated. Granted, he was head of field activities, but he wasn't actually a homicide investigator, so he was a rather odd choice for the job. However, he had his suspicions about why he had been chosen.

"Ma'am." He ran up to Tufnell.

"Yes, Colonel?"

"You know I don't have access to the Covenant Database any more, and Cooke Hall hasn't contacted me in six months?"

"The Hall contacted you this morning, Colonel." Tufnell spoke quietly now, so nobody else in the room could hear.

"No they didn't," he lied.

"Don't be so foolish, Liam," she snapped. "We have your phone tapped; we know that McInnes contacted you this morning to tell you we were about to call you."

"What if he did? There's no crime in that!" Cabot countered defensively.

"True, but the Senate believes you may be able to use some of your old contacts to solicit information."

"The Senate can think what they like, of course. Regardless of whether they're right or not."

"That's not the point; Chancellor O'Hare wants you on this case, so you're on it. Get to work, Colonel." The General began to walk off.

"Yes, ma'am."

Cabot left the building, nodding courteously to the guards on the way out, and rounding the corner. He got onto his bike and quickly and turned the key he had left in the ignition. The fuel metre showed he had almost a full tank and he smiled. He revved the engine a few times then tore off, back onto the motorway.

Two grey Jeeps pulled out of the car park after him, following him at a distance of about two hundred yards. He saw them in his mirrors and accelerated, darting through the heavy traffic. He could not evade them forever, but he could at least buy himself some time to contact those he would later need.

In his pocket was the familiar, smooth shape of his mobile phone, still something of a luxury in the Society, and one with which he would not be gifted, were it not for his sponsors. He pulled the earpiece and microphone from his pocket with one hand as he swerved to avoid a car, and clipped them to his ear.

"Call Terry," he instructed the phone and it began to dial. After two rings the phone was answered.

"Hello, Liam."

It was Terry McInnes, head of the Weapons Technology Development Department. The WTDD, as it was commonly known, was one of the most influential divisions of the Society's government, with its mandate ranging from designing and distributing weaponry to the Society's various armed forces, to policing their use and ultimately serving as loyal allies of the Society's leader, Lord Robert Stanford.

"Terry!" Cabot smiled, reassured at the sound of his old comrade's voice. "They know you contacted me earlier, my phone's bugged; is this line still secure?"

"Yes," McInnes told him confidently. "They want you to investigate the murders, I presume?"

"Shockingly, yes; I think they expect you to help."

"Not unless it's a matter of some importance."

"You *did* call me, Terry; that's usually a sign of extreme importance, is it not?"

"Touché, Colonel; the Council has assigned us to oversee the investigation, subtly—"

"The Council?" Cabot asked, doubtfully.

"The office of the Lord Protector."

"Very well; I'll contact you when I've got something, okay?"

"So be it." The phone went dead.

"And so it begins," Cabot sighed, pocketing the earpiece and microphone. Whenever the Lord Protector called upon the Engineers for aid it meant that bad things were afoot; that he had great fear for the welfare of their Society. Why did this always happen to him?

Because you used to be an Engineer, he thought; they trusted you, they trained you. You owe them this much.

1

Robert Stanford awoke at eight-thirty and rolled over to face his girlfriend, Emily Johnson, as she lay still dozing beside him. He reached across to her and brushed a strand of hair from her face, then rolled out of bed and went to the bathroom to take a shower.

As he went through the mundane morning ritual he began to wake up and thoughts started coming freely. The murders last night were a rarity—the Society had very little crime—but they were not entirely shocking. Since the citizens of what was now the Society had freed themselves, their history was marked by violence and bloodshed, culminating in a coup a year after its foundation by one of Stanford's political rivals, Samantha Kensington. Stanford felt a pang of guilt crossed with sadness at this thought; he and Kensington had carried on a two year affair behind the backs of their respective partners, right up until the war which had torn them apart, and which had ended with Stanford killing Kensington in a duel.

It was amazing, he thought, returning to a slightly lighter topic, that all of this had gone on without outside intervention or even influence; the PFS existed behind a security cordon in the south-west of Britain, erected twelve years ago after the nearby nuclear power station was believed to have melted down, posing a certainty of death to anyone trapped within the area after the cordon was in place.

Stanford had been about among the oldest of those left behind, aged fourteen at the time. He had watched as the oldest, aged no more than nineteen, had saved the other children from death by taking charge, only to turn quickly into the slave drivers that they had been when the revolution had happened; the outside world remaining blissfully ignorant of proceedings inside the area, unaware that there was no fallout, and that the power plant continued to work smoothly, powering the homes and offices of the PFS even now.

He stepped out of the shower, and wrapped himself in a large grey towel, using it to dry off while staring idly into the mirror.

Twenty six years old, and ruler of sixty thousand people; all that was left of the original hundred after poverty and war had been overcome. His black hair, kept short and tidy, was beginning to show signs of thinning under the stress of his job, but the face that smiled back at him in the mirror every morning was still youthful and unjaded by the rigours of office.

By the time he had returned Emily was awake, sitting up in bed. He dressed into the black suit he was almost forced to wear as part of his job and sat on the end of the bed next to her.

"I have to go," he told her. "Something happened last night."

"I know," she told him. "Your shower only takes that long when you've got something on your mind."

"Hmm," Stanford replied, the something in question still

on his mind. "The traffic's going to be bad this morning, I doubt you'll make it to work on time. You should stay here and get a lie in."

"Okay," she agreed. "I'll see you at the meeting then?"

"Of course." He smiled at her and walked out of the room. Stanford had three homes; quite a shift from the Kensington Coup, when he had forced himself to live in a small, two room apartment in the fortress-city of Walshton. His first, favourite home, was his mansion about four miles from his current location; the New Command Centre, or NCC, built in the aftermath of the Coup after Walshton had suffered critical damage. He also held this apartment, two floors down from his office in the NCC, where he and Emily spent their nights during the week, when Stanford was frequently called to work at unholy hours in the morning, and then Stanford's final home, the small area partitioned from his office in which he had all the amenities necessary to keep him alive, if not particularly comfortable, for when he couldn't leave the office due to a crisis but had a few precious minutes of downtime to rest his aching head.

He wandered into his office about ten minutes after leaving the apartment and took his seat. He looked at the huge pile of papers on his desk and span his chair to face the window. The window of the Lord Protector's office was huge, occupying an entire wall, the curved glass giving a perfect view of the Society as the curvature of the glass made it vanish from sight.

From here he could see the soft Gothic features of the Senate building, the cold brick surface of Walshton Fort and, in the far distance, just straining his eyes, he could see Cooke Hall. The Hall was home to the WTDD, and was guarded by the most sophisticated technology in the Society, watching over it during its denizens' often prolonged periods of absence.

He had a meeting with the Council at ten o'clock. The Council, of nine members, himself included, were the supervisors of the Society, representing the various functions of the government; the legislature, Housing, infrastructure, administration, the military, intelligence gathering, Sciences, the health service and weapons development.

He was obliged to meet them once a week, under the terms of the constitution, supposedly so that the running of the Society over the next week could be coordinated and educated. Stanford knew better, however. The Council was there so that people unafraid of arguing with Stanford would do so and try to sway his mind, though they were ultimately obliged to follow his instructions with regards to the running of their departments. Not that they did, of course.

He turned back to the ominous pile of paper and sighed deeply. He picked a thin folder from the top of the pile with the riveting title of *Potential Agricultural Prospects within the lower section of the NFFRT (Near CC6)*. Ben Chiswick's department sent him, on average, five hundred folders like this a week, of which about eighty percent could be filtered out through his staff, lurking two floors below in their smaller, windowless offices, but that still meant one hundred folders worth of time spent on an activity about as interesting as an eternity in the universe of eternally drying paint.

He opened the folder and his pager beeped. He unclipped it from his belt and looked at it.

Bored yet?

He chuckled at the message and put the pager back down on the desk. He read through the document slowly, absent-mindedly underlining all of the spelling mistakes and then ticking off things that went against his policies. He got to the end of the document and wrote two numbers in the bottom right hand margin, the same as he had done for every document since taking up the job. The number on the left was the number of spelling mistakes, the number on the right was the number of statements or implications against his policies. He then mentally divided the right number by the left and came up with an answer. If this document came out with a result higher than one it would be sent back, and the author chastised by Chiswick; if less than one, then the document would be sent back for spelling corrections, but otherwise passed without complaint.

And so it had gone, for six years now, Stanford ticking off folder after folder based on these two criteria and their ratios, while secretly keeping a tally on a sheet in the bottom drawer of his desk of the number of one-plus folders, happy in the knowledge that if it ever rose above one hundred he would fire Ben Chiswick. He was now in his mid-twenties after six years and the rate of returns was decreasing every year.

Stanford wrote the two numbers at the bottom of the page and did the division in his head; 0.8, excellent. He stamped the folder with his big red approval stamp (a Christmas present from Emily two years previously), and laid it on the out tray on his desk.

♦

At noon he stood up, the two piles now roughly equal in height, and set off towards the Council Chamber, a large conference room on the far side of the floor.

That this entire floor was under heavy guard, Stanford had no problem with, because it meant that the imposing, navy-blue suited figures of his bodyguards weren't following him around all the time. The guards reported his progress through the floor as he walked down the serenely decorated halls.

He reached the Council Chamber and opened the door by placing his index finger onto the print scanner and pushing the door open as it pinged at him.

The room was dominated by a long, black marble conference table, with nine seats set around it. There were viewing galleries surrounding the room, accessible most of the time by external staircases to the press and members of the public.

Stanford looked up as he moved towards his large chair at the head of the table. Today the galleries were empty; this meeting was private. The guards around the sides of the room had gone, relieved of their duty by one of the eight other councillors, he didn't doubt; they weren't the sort to just leave him unguarded without direct orders, and even then it was doubtful. His phone began to ring and he answered it.

"Stanford here."

"My Lord."

"Hello James," Stanford greeted James Cooke, the former head of the WTDD. "What do you need?"

"Tufnell has taken the bait. All things are now in play; the thorn may be driven out." Cooke spoke in the agreed code.

"If you say so, James," Stanford replied, feigning exasperation with his old friend. The phone went dead and he snapped it closed before pocketing it. He took his chair, a large red-leather office chair which completely dwarfed him, despite his impressive height of six-foot four, and turned it to face the door.

The door opened and Ben Chiswick, the district commissioner entered with Laura Andrews, the representative from the Senate. Chiswick looked at Stanford with mild impatience as he passed, the small, mousy man peering out from behind a pair of thick spectacles with his beady eyes, and Stanford noted, not for the first time, that Chiswick either reused the same suit every day or, more likely, he reasoned, owned a number of identical grey suits, each as ugly as the last.

Mary and Danny Sharp-Thomas were the next two through the door, hand in hand. Mary was a tall woman, standing six foot two, and extremely muscular, as was befitting her position as head of the army, with medium-length brown hair and wearing her maroon military uniform. Her husband, Danny, was four inches shorter than her and significantly less muscular. His short, bright ginger hair was gelled messily. He grinned cheerfully at Stanford as he approached the table. Once the four of them had taken their seats, the two newcomers without paperwork or formalities, three of the remaining members of the Council arrived, filing into their seats. Doctor Bryony Willows, chief of the Society's health service entered with Johnson, who ran one hand along Stanford's arm as she passed before she took her seat at his left hand.

The final member of this council was Michael Chiswick. Black satin clothing marked him as an assassin, leader of the Special Services division, the not-so-secret police of the Society, the all-powerful force that ensured the laws were kept and monitored the monitors; or so they would have everyone believe. The man standing before him, a slightly broader version of his elder brother, showed no trace of anything save for absolute confidence and condescension.

Yet underneath this guise, Stanford knew that Chiswick's operations were hampered by the hatred possessed of his men by the CG and the Army, and by the residents of the Hall's reluctance to give him carte blanche over his own activities.

There was no seat for the head of the SS here; following his death six years ago and a bizarre series of incidents involving technology now outlawed, his personality had been stored within the computer files of the PFS's central memory system, allowing him to be projected anywhere within his own base or the NCC as a hologram.

"I see the representative from the WTDD has once again deemed himself beyond our meagre levels of government," Michael Chiswick remarked scathingly, turning his glare on Stanford. "Or do they simply not deem this recent rash of murders to be important enough for their attention?"

"I assure you that the WTDD is most concerned about the recent happenings, Councillor, and their absence will, I have no doubt, have a worthy reason—"

"You mean a plausible excuse, my Lord," the elder brother leapt in now. "Repeatedly we are snubbed by these scientists; what importance do they hold? Surely not equal to my office, or those of the Councillors Sharp-Thomas." Chiswick kept his eyes on Stanford, knowing that the look on Johnson's face could have killed him.

"With respect, Councillors Chiswick—"

"And where is the respect to be shown to us by the Councillor from the WTDD? Do you not believe as we do that your office and ours are worthy of such respect?"

"Need I remind you, Commissioner Chiswick, that Master McInnes played far greater a part in getting us here than you; as did many other *scientists*." Johnson stressed this last word very carefully.

"All in the past, Councillor; the future is in the sea and the sky; with you, not in weapons, with McInnes."

"Do not speak of the future; you have not the wit to foresee it, sir." Terry McInnes strode into the room, garbed in the white lab coat of his office. The man was a passive giant, standing at six foot six inches with messy, curly black hair. The Engineer had the power in one hand to lift a man of Stanford's size four feet into the air and throw him across a room, yet seldom was this ability used; he far preferred oratory to any other method of victory.

"Do you claim to be prophetic then?" Michael asked.

"Surely not; were he able to see the future he surely would have been here on time." Andrews put in her first statement and McInnes rolled his eyes.

"The future is not for man to see, though we may sometimes catch a glimmer, out of the corner of our eye. I apologise for my tardiness, but I have come to you now not a moment too soon, it would appear, for the Senate have launched their investigation into these murders most foul." McInnes took his seat with some flourish at Stanford's right-hand side, producing a small notebook from the depths of his lab coat.

"Yes; Colonel Cabot has been assigned to the task of bringing this murderer to justice," Andrews said, stating what most of them already knew.

"Are we even sure it was just one murderer?" Mary asked. "I've just glanced over the report, but these murders seem a long way apart and quite unconnected for just one assailant."

"I'm sure that our inquiry will find out soon enough," Andrews assured her.

"Of course, yes; *your* inquiry." Mary was quiet for a moment. "We are, of course, running our own investigation into this incident."

"That is your prerogative, General."

"Thank you, Senator. I know what my responsibilities are," Mary snapped back. "I will provide the Council with information of our procedures tomorrow morning, if that is acceptable."

"I'd like a draft this afternoon if possible, but the general announcement can wait until tomorrow, sure," Stanford told her. "I don't think we have any other pressing agenda today, so unless anyone has anything critical they want us to discuss that'll be it." He looked around the faces of the Council, confirming that all were silent.

"Then we are adjourned for the day. Master McInnes, if you could follow me, please?"

"Of course, my Lord." McInnes stood up and followed Stanford out of the door.

"What do you think of all this?"

"I fear that once again our petty power struggles will fail to bring to light the identity of the murderer, as happened before the last war."

"Do you believe the two events are linked?"

"I am... uncertain." Terry paused, choosing his words carefully. "They are both definitely examples of serial killing, but the only thing we can be sure they are connected through is the forces at work at bringing the perpetrators to justice; all the departments will struggle to try and find out who it was before the other. Much information may be lost through the conflict."

"As ever your words are veiled, Terry, though I see more from them than perhaps many might."

Terry smiled.

"How is Master Cooke?" Stanford asked.

"He regrets being still unable to leave the house, but is otherwise in good spirits."

"I may visit him soon, if things aren't too hectic."

"He will be most pleased, my Lord."

"Thank you, Terry."

2

The road to the Senate building was more or less empty at ten AM as a jet-black S-Class Mercedes tore along the road, its tinted windows hiding its driver from the view of the outside world and its blank license plate rendering the driver impervious to the jurisdiction of the law.

"No, no, you're misinterpreting the bill and now you're misinterpreting me; the language says 'under situations of extreme danger as defined by appropriate mediums', which is taken to mean, under new-clause eight, that the issue must first be decided on by the judiciary, and then us, before the effects are bought into play." The driver spoke into the headset mounted on the side of his head as he drove. "Hold on, I'll be in the office in a moment; I'll come and find you. Bye." The call ended as he swerved into the car park and sailed smoothly into his allocated parking space.

The door to the Mercedes opened and Senator Tim Greenwood, Senate leader of the Democratic party, climbed out. He wore a black Armani suit and a pair of Ralph Lauren sunglasses, carrying in one hand a leather folio.

He entered through the front door of the Senate building, nodding to the two security guards as he passed.

"Mornin' Senator."

"Good morning, Jerry," he replied politely.

The woman behind the desk gave him a nod.

"Good morning, Diane."

"Senator Greenwood," she greeted him. "It's a lovely day, isn't it?"

"Ask me again after the vote, Diane." He handed over his ID card and she swiped it quickly through the machine on her desk.

"Thank you, sir." She handed the card back.

"Thank you, Diane." He put the card into his pocket and walked to the lifts. Senator Tim Greenwood, he thought; who'd have imagined it? He had held his seat for nearly eight years, since the beginning of the Society, one of only a handful of senators to do so, and had slowly made his way through the ranks of the Democratic party until he was made leader two years ago.

He stepped into the lift and hit the button for the third floor. Today was the day of the Executive Powers Bill, a piece of legislation three-thousand pages in length, the longest document since the original People's Law. The purpose of the new bill was to allow the Society, when faced with a huge calamity which required speed of reaction, to pass over the power of the Senate temporarily to the Lord Protector, granting him the ability to do whatever he or she deemed necessary to save the Society.

This was the third vote on this bill, the past two incarnations having been declined by the Senate by five and four votes respectively. This, the third version, was distinctly tamer than the past two, but it was no less controversial. Party lines had ruptured, senators from all parties falling on both sides of the line, so those that had planned to abstain were being swept up as the two ideologies crashed into each other each day in the Senate Hall with the force of two freight trains, ploughing in opposite directions down the same track.

Greenwood went to his office on the third floor and sat down in his chair. Senators were not allowed to do very much to their offices insofar as decorating went, except for bringing in personal items for their desk, and so his office didn't reflect his wealth as his car and suits did.

He took a deep breath to compose himself and then rose to his feet again. He exited the office and headed down the corridor. On his way he passed the cafeteria and helped himself to one of the cups of coffee that were free to senators. He nodded to the waitress as she passed him and carried on his way.

He reached the door of Senator Hannah Thatcher, always open, and stepped in.

"Morning Tim," she greeted him, looking out of the window from her high-backed chair.

"Good morning, Senator Thatcher."

"Hannah, Tim; my name is Hannah. We've known each other since long before either of us had these silly titles."

"Silly, maybe, but it's never good to forget what we are now," Greenwood answered her, looking around the walls. The Confederate Senator, a member of the cultural oversight committee, had covered every available space on her walls with paintings of various styles, the signature on each reading HT.

"I don't understand why they'll let you move these things in but they won't let me strap a sword to my wall."

Thatcher sighed at the re-emergence of a familiar argument.

"I am on the committee for culture, Tim."

"And I'm on the defence subcommittee; you can hardly say it's not related to my job!"

"Yes, but no weapons are allowed in the Senate building

except for ceremonies."

"Ah, touché." He paused for a moment before continuing with the more pressing matter of his visit. "So you've changed your mind on the vote today?" he asked.

"Not changed it, per se. I'm just a little uncertain." She turned her chair to look at him. She wore, as was the trend amongst Confederates, distinctly casual clothes. Her suit jacket was slung over the back of her chair and her pink shirt had its sleeves rolled up, held in place by clips. She wore no tie, but still she managed to pull off an air of respectability and smartness, despite not being dressed for the part.

"Hannah, you've been behind us from the start; you can't seriously say you're going to vote no now?"

"Well Winter raised some good points yesterday, Timmy."

"Simon Winter, need I remind you, can twist words into any form that suits him."

"He is a member of *your* party, Tim."

"Yes, and when he's on my side I'm glad of him, but right now it's annoying. I thought you'd be above falling for the subtleties of Winter."

"And I thought you'd be reluctant to sign any document that so much as set precedent for giving Stanford more power; or could it be that the influence of the Hall has gotten to you?"

"Stanford will not always be Lord Protector, Hannah, and I will not always be a Senator."

"Ah, of course; I forgot your morals entirely. Then again, you *are* a Democrat."

"Yes, Hannah; I am—" His pager went off and he took a glance at it. "I have to go now; please consider what I've said, okay?"

"Of course, Timmy," she smiled at him at the same time as her deep blue eyes pierced him from behind her burgundy-rimmed glasses. "Goodbye."

"Bye-bye, Hannah."

He left the office and flicked out his phone.

"Hey, it's Tim Greenwood; I just got a page?" He listened for a second. "Okay, I'll be right there." He turned and walked back down the corridor.

The Senate in the PFS consisted of four parties; the Democrats, stringent holders of the right; Liberals, who held the left; Republicans, who were positioned somewhere between centre and right; and the Confederates, who averaged out as being centrists. At their more extreme they could be further left than the Liberals or just as far right as the Republicans. This Lord Protector, Lord Stanford, was a Confederate, elected with sixty-five percent of the votes in 2009, the year of the first Senate and Executive Branch. The Chancellor, the leader of the Senate, was Rebecca O'Hare, a Liberal whose party held fifty-four of the one hundred seats in the Senate. Greenwood had found himself, a Democrat—the smallest party in the Senate—being one of the ringleaders of the group of senators keen to pass the bill. With him was Adam Kant, leader of the Confederate senators, and Senator Andrea Berkley, leader of the backbench revolt for the Liberal Party.

Greenwood stepped into the lift once more and pushed the button for the second floor. The third floor housed the area for the senators' everyday work, principally their offices and the cafeteria. The fourth and top floor housed the apartments in which some of the Senate resided. The ground floor held the Senate Hall itself, as well as the security stations and the Chancellor's chambers, and the second floor, where he was headed now, housed the committee halls, where the various committees in the Senate would meet to discuss the motions to be put before them.

Greenwood slowly opened the door of committee room number three and stepped inside. Senator Simon Winter, of the domestic policy committee, was waiting for him.

"Hello, Senator Winter," Greenwood greeted him. The man sat in the position of the committee chair in a black suit with a silk tie in blue, the colour of the Democratic Party.

"Senator Greenwood," the man's voice was one of distinction and intelligence, with an underlying hint of practised sarcasm and contempt. "I see you're still busy trying to convince people to yield their power to Stanford?"

"Not to Stanford, no; to the Lord Protector during a crisis."

"Stanford will rule until he is thrown from office; a crisis is bound to occur in that time and he will never hand the power back."

"You're a cynic, Winter."

"I'm a realist."

"You say potato."

"Oh whatever, Tim. I'm here on behalf of the party."

"I assumed you probably would be, Simon."

"Then do you have the foresight to know what I'm going to say next?"

Greenwood stood silent.

"I thought not. I'm calling for a vote of no-confidence in your leadership of the party, to be held after this dreadful bill is finally finished with."

"So you're saying that if the bill passes you're going to vote me out?"

"No, I'm saying that I'm going to vote against you no matter what happens—the bill will affect the others, not me, so you really have to decide what you're going to do with the time you have left in your seat."

"So be it, then, Simon." Greenwood left the room quickly, backing up against the wall outside and taking a few deep breaths before he continued. He was not, by nature, a violent man, but years of working with Democrats, each apparently more concerned with personal glory than with the Society or the party, had occasionally given him call to throw breakable objects across a room.

He went back up to the third floor and drank another cup of coffee slowly in his office. The bells would go in a matter of minutes; it was too late now to change anyone's mind, though he guessed by the senators dashing back and forth outside his door that not everybody thought so.

The bells rang; a single burst, about ten seconds long, high-pitched screaming at the senators. They emerged from their offices, all one hundred. The Democrats moved quickly, as did the front-bench Liberals, but there were still some of them willing to hang back and wait a little while for things to die down around the three voting rooms on the bottom floor.

Greenwood walked slowly, skimming his hand along the walkway's rail as he looked down two floors to where the press and the senators were moving about on the bottom floor. He caught Winter's eye as the man left the committee room and made for the lifts, the only senator on the second floor.

He heard his name called and turned to face Thatcher, bounding along, diving between senators to get to him.

"Hey Timmy, cheer up! It isn't the end of the world."

"You say that now," he smiled at her.

"Don't worry about it, Timmy; it's all just a game. None of it matters."

"But it does, Hannah, how can you not realize?"

"Ah, how can *you* not notice?"

"Not notice what?"

"Exactly Timmy, poor dear; so clever, yet not very bright." She reached up and patted him on the head before darting into the lift, leaving him standing alone and confused.

He caught the next lift down. It was filled with Liberals, none of them known particularly well to him. The lift doors opened and he made his way to the door of the leftmost voting room; for those voting aye. Most of the senators were gone from here now, assembling in the Senate Hall itself, but he just caught a glimpse of Thatcher's back as she darted from the room into the chamber.

He quickly scribbled his vote onto a piece of paper and dropped it into the ballot box before rushing through into the Senate Hall.

He took his seat in the front row of the Democratic Party's minimal seating area, about as far from the main podium of the Speaker as possible. He strained to look as the Speaker stood up.

The Senate Hall was decorated with cream seats. Along the rafters above were several hundred immensely powerful lights, and cameras for the press covering Senate proceedings. At the near end of the hall were a set of huge oak double doors, always locked except when the Lord Protector wished to use them. The Senate's seating was some thirty feet above the floor, allowing them to look symbolically down on the Executive Branch leader when he entered. At the far end were two large podiums, reachable only by lifts in their bases. The two large cylinders held the seat of the Chancellor, Rebecca O'Hare, who sat still as a statue about level with the rest of the Senate, and the second, higher plinth belonged to the Speaker, dressed in his dark green robes of office.

"Ladies and Gentlemen of the Senate," Stephen Olivier, the Speaker, began. "The votes are in for the Executive Powers Bill, and the votes are as follows." He paused for dramatic effect. "The votes Nay, those against the Executive

Powers Bill: forty eight."

There was a hushed silence; this was the first time the Nays had lost a majority.

"The votes Aye, those in favour of this Bill..." the Speaker continued.

Greenwood sat further forward in his seat, waiting, sensing that something big was about to happen as the tension in the room began to grow exponentially with every passing second.

"Forty eight."

A sigh went up from the Confederate ranks, where most of the senators supported the bill. The bill was drawn, and a wave of whispering broke through the senators. "That concludes your service for today, thank you for your time," the Speaker declared.

The senators began to make for their exits.

Greenwood sighed; back to the drawing board, it seemed. No doubt the Confederates would be rewriting the bill as best they could to make it different and more appealing to the masses, or at least to the four abstaining senators, and in the meantime he had things to do, people to see.

3

War raged across the city of Bristol. Killian McBride
crouched with his back to the wall next to the second storey
window of a house. A squad of enemy troops were marching
down the street outside, and he had to hold them off or his
entire unit would die.

He checked the clip of his MK. 7 staple rifle. Eighteen
rounds left; enough to stop them, if he was lucky. He leaned
out of the window and put two shots through the forehead of
the sergeant. As the NCO toppled McBride was answered by
a volley from the guns, blowing chunks from the window
ledge as he swung back into cover.

He leapt to the nearby door and rolled quickly down the
stairs, rising to his feet and firing a few more rounds at the
men coming through the door. He moved so that he could
see the entrance and put a couple more shots into the unit,
killing another man and making the others turn. The door
couldn't be closed, the bodies of the fallen attackers blocked
the way, and he couldn't reach their weapons. He checked
the gun again. Six rounds left, and about eight men outside,
mere seconds from coming through the doorway and killing
him. He had his sword strapped to his belt, but he doubted it

would be any use to him against that many targets with guns.

He got to his feet and backed quickly up the stairs as the soldiers entered the building. He emptied the rest of the clip into the first man through the door and then discarded it, turning around and running to the top of the stairs. He drew his sword and leapt out of the back window of the house, rolling as he hit the lawn in the back garden. He rose to his feet again, swinging the sword across the chest of a soldier. He ran through the back gate, around the corner, leapt over the fence of another house and stopped for a moment, snatching up the radio from his belt.

"Daniel! They've got past me; repeat, they've got past me, about six of them."

"Affirmative Killian, I can see it; thanks." Dan Carter looked over the giant holographic map of Bristol and at the little holographic troops moving around it. They called it a game, but it felt so real. Killian and the others were strapped into the holographic machines, the devices putting them into the game, each of them trying to follow Carter's orders to protect the PFS's troops.

The third company of the CG was taking heavy fire and was pinned down at St. Paul's, and the battalion he had sent to back them up was stuck in Knowle west. He sighed; the CG would almost certainly be done for now that Killian had failed to cover their advance.

In Winterbourne he had two more of his people, David Short and Annie Davies, waiting to intercept the troops and hopefully slow the attack on his main emplacements, but he held out little hope. The crux of the mission was to take out the enemy's command centre, about a mile from his front line in the heart of the city, but it was guarded by two full companies of men and surrounded by snipers.

A move too late is worse than none at all, he thought to himself.

"Short; take two hundred men from Winterbourne and march headlong at their attack," he instructed.

"Carter?" Short's reedy voice came over the radio.

"You heard me, Short—try and draw out their strength from their main base."

"Yes, sir!"

"Annie, I need you to make your way across the rooftops to Knowle west; get to Killian and help him, then the two of you need to find a way to get through their defenses and destroy their command centre. You'd better take some extra guns with you."

"Okay, Dan; you got it," Davies said cheerfully. Carter watched as the holograms representing them, coloured red against the insipid blue background of the map, began to move to do their tasks.

"Killian, reinforcements are on their way there."

"Excellent."

Carter looked at the map again. There were eight real people down there, and one thousand of his original two and a half thousand troops remained to fight an enemy who outnumbered them and who had tactics far superior to theirs.

"This is going to be the end," he muttered. "One last play."

The door behind him opened and the light from outside the room passed through the holograms, making them flicker.

"Carry on, Mister Carter." Doctor Siobhan Bishop of the WTDD closed the door behind her. "How goes the battle?"

"Not particularly well; Killian was outnumbered and had to concede some ground, so my CG are going to go unreinforced, and the relief force will be fighting on two fronts."

"Ah," Siobhan smiled at him warmly. "I assume this is the first time you've done this?"

"I was on the inside for your trial by fire, but that was a bit different."

"Quite; I presume you're sacrificing all your troops so you can complete the objective?"

"Yes, I really can't see any other way."

"There isn't one, to be fair," Siobhan told him. "But you won't be able to achieve it with two people attacking them; Killian and Annie will be dead before they get within three hundred yards of the perimeter."

"The thought had crossed my mind."

"You have a plan then?"

"Not really, no." He looked at the hologram. There was an enemy unit separating Davies from McBride, and McBride himself couldn't move as a platoon of soldiers was walking past his concealed location. His base would be breached within ten minutes, Carter estimated, if the CG fell, or if Short was unable to hold the attack.

♦

David Short drew his sword as the enemies came into view at the end of the street. He had two companies behind him and his instructions in mind; he wasn't about to fail.

"Charge!" he yelled, and his forces poured forward, surging towards the front line before them.

...Davies leapt across the gap between two roofs and landed, cursing as she dropped to one knee, the strength in her left leg spent...

...McBride stabbed a man in the chest then spun, decapitating a second with an angry swing. He had been seen by a squad of men, and now he didn't stand a chance...

In the midst of the troops in his command centre Dan Carter appeared, a sword in his hand. He wore a black leather jacket and his short brown hair was spiked up with gel. There was nothing more he could do now on the outside, so he had strapped himself back into the machine, joining his troops for the last battle.

Troops rounded the corner; all that was left of Short's men, their leader perished in the game and so waking in the real world. Carter stood his ground, waiting for the line to get close enough. He could see individual people amongst the mass of enemies closing now, individual faces, the simulated anger in their eyes, and he struck. He brought the sword around, striking a man down, then lunged out. The sword was bashed aside by a rifle and a bayonet brought to bear; he closed his eyes, shielding his face with his arms...

His eyes snapped open and he pulled off the helmet of the device. The others stood in front of him now, and gave him a quick round of applause.

"Pretty good, Dan; we lasted quite a while," McBride congratulated him.

"Not good enough though; I'll work on my tactics for next time, guys."

"Alright then," Davies stood up. "Now, let's go get a drink."

Davies led them out of the room and into the ballroom it was once the anteroom for. This place was Cooke Hall, the home of the WTDD and their servants, the last refuge of the academic in the society. McBride, Carter and Short were part of the twenty-strong class of apprentices, each learning the ways of the WTDD under McInnes and Bishop.

They made their way across the ballroom to the stairs leading down into the cellar. The wine cellar of the Hall was huge, but before the war the Hall's former owner, now absent, had converted it to hold a modern bar and a vast fridge capable of storing more fashionable drinks.

Davies leapt over the bar and took from this fridge four bottles of beer. The other apprentices had vanished into the library or some such place to study; a philosophy of hard work and dedication not shared by Carter and McBride as they began to drink.

♦

Terry McInnes and Siobhan Bishop sat at a wooden table playing chess. They had been playing this game for three hours now and neither of them had made any significant headway over the other.

"This is going to be a long game."

"Really? How can you tell?" she asked.

"You're angry about something, or agitated; it's always harder to beat you when you're irrational."

"I'll take that as a compliment, I suppose." She moved her queen three places to the left.

"Feel free." He moved a knight without looking down. "What do you think of the new guys?"

"They're okay; they've settled in nicely and Carter's already having a go at the trials."

"Passed any yet?"

"No, but for a guy who doesn't study and spends most of the day making eyes at Annie he's not doing too badly."

"Carter's interested in Annie?"

"Most of them are, Terry; she's the only, how would you

32

put it?" Bishop paused for a moment to consider the best choice of words. "*Active* female in the house."

"I see your point; they'll get over it soon enough."

"Especially when they realise they can't get close to her."

"That'll be the beginning of it, certainly; but not the end, I fear."

"She cannot continue living here indefinitely, Master."

"Master Cooke will be the one to answer that, and since his friendship with the girl is significantly older than with you I wouldn't be the one to raise it with him, if I were you."

"You could always do it; you are the head of the WTDD now, Terry."

"Siobhan, you know that's not true."

"He's dead, Terry! The guy died six years ago and you're still bowing to him about everything; do what you want! Throw the damn abstinence if you want, throw anything, you're in charge now, can't you understand that?" She moved the pawn.

"I understand that very well, Siobhan." His knight swept down to take the pawn. "But you know, as well as anyone, that my position on almost everything, especially abstinence, is exactly the same as the position held by my predecessor."

"Alright." Bishop calmed down and moved her queen across, sweeping into his knight and knocking it from the board. "Check," she announced triumphantly.

McInnes, without looking down, moved his second knight down to take the queen.

"Nice try, Siobhan."

"Master McInnes," Killian McBride spoke up from the corner of the room.

"Killian?"

"Senator Greenwood is on the driveway, sir; also Lord Stanford is on his way here with Colonel Empter. Senator

Thatcher wants an audience with Master Cooke at some point soon; we've also got a couple of calls from Liam's people looking for information from us."

"What kind of information?"

"The location of Doctor Bishop."

"I'm here," Bishop told him.

"Yes ma'am, we know, but we don't take calls from aides; only from people on the list and people who actually have a title. Those are the rules."

"Thank you, Killian." McInnes stood up, took his lab coat from the back of his chair and threw it on. "We'll finish this up later, Siobhan."

She nodded to him and picked up her own lab coat.

"Greenwood, then Stanford?" she asked. "That's pretty bad."

"Potentially, yes," McInnes admitted.

"Would you like me to get Master Cooke, sir?" McBride asked.

"I think he knows what's going on."

The holographic projectors in the roof kicked in and the lab-coated figure of Master James Cooke, former leader of the WTDD, who had died during the Kensington Coup, appeared in front of the others.

The hologram's gaunt, pale face and overlong brown hair identified him as being in his early twenties, but grey streaks in the brown, and the confident, distinguished way in which Cooke carried himself made it clear that he had experienced far more, and possessed greater wisdom, than many of his age.

"Apprentice McBride," he said, "put a cup of coffee on; the Senator will take his black and without sugar."

"Rob's on his way here too, you know?"

"Yes I know, along with Alan. Hannah Thatcher is going to be leaving her offices in about ten minutes to come here."

"Since when have we been the most popular organisation in the Society?"

"Since everything went wrong."

♦

Greenwood climbed out of his car and handed the keys to McBride as he ran down the stairs. "Put it out of sight, would you?"

"Certainly, Senator." McBride slid into the driver's seat.

"Senator Greenwood; I feel almost reluctant to welcome you in such dire times as these." McInnes came down the steps after McBride and shook the hand of the Senator.

"I wish I didn't have to come, Terry, but it seems as though I do, and so here I am."

"Of course, Senator; James is waiting for you inside."

Greenwood walked in through the door, removing his navy-blue overcoat and hanging it on the coat stand just inside the main entrance.

"Good evening, Tim; I regret not being able to shake your hand, but that can't be helped as yet." Cooke bowed at his old friend as he stepped through the door.

"Good evening, Master Cooke."

"I trust the stresses and strains of political life are not proving too great for you?"

"Some days I do envy your lateness, James."

"I don't doubt; the vote was a draw?"

"Yes, another vote will be held in two weeks time; we were wondering if you could sway any senators."

"All those who have come to me for counsel have been told my view, but I cannot swing any more senators without exerting an unfair influence."

"Senator Winter is the running boy of the SS, James; he is exerting unfair influence upon several senators. Anything you did would only be by way of leveling the playing field a little."

"The playing field need not be leveled any further; I understand your job is currently hanging in the balance based on this bill?"

"It is, yes."

"Then you must decide what to do; to turn the tide once more against, or to carry on and allow us to risk the possibility of losing a great senator."

"What would you counsel? Or any of you, for that matter; the wisdoms of your council are not to be underestimated." He looked around the three assembled Engineers.

"I would have you act prudently, Senator Greenwood; mind yourself against the possibility of granting Winter leadership of your party," McInnes said. "Our enemies may be difficult to see, or even fictitious, but if any of them are to strike they will doubtless get the approval of Senator Winter should he lead the party."

"That may be inevitable anyway, and by acting prudently we may be neglecting the one chance we have to stay the power of the enemy if they ever rise to a position to strike," Bishop replied, facing off against her master. Greenwood found it unfathomable how they could be quite so clearly geared up for debate and yet still be so calm, so separate from their egos and emotions.

"As for myself, I will offer you no wisdom for now; some darkness has revealed itself in the past day in the form of these murders; this may yet lead Cabot to the assailant who struck before the Coup, and hence negate our worry about Winter."

"What do I do then?"

"Work at getting people in a position to follow your lead; keep the votes you need in the house, but be prepared to let your people out of the headlocks if need be," McInnes told him. "That's what we'd advise, anyway; we want you to do what you believe best."

"You've never led me astray thus far."

"We haven't really had much of a chance to, though."

"Well, true..."

"Sir," McBride appeared once more in the doorway, "Lord Stanford is here now; what would you have us do?"

"Tim, I must beg your pardon; would you be so good as to follow Killian to the library? I will return to you in a moment, once we have seen what Stanford wants." Terry went back through the door outside as a motorcade pulled up; Stanford stepped onto the gravel driveway.

"Master McInnes; is there any word of Cabot's investigation, or of our own counter to it?" Stanford greeted McInnes quickly and they headed inside, Stanford's guards remaining on the driveway.

"Neither investigation has gotten properly underway as yet, sir; Cabot is still trying to cut through the red tape to get the people he needs for his operation."

"Red tape? I thought Tufnell had given him full permission to use whatever he needed?"

"Tufnell did, yes; unfortunately, members of the committee responsible for CG activities are refusing to hand over transfers," McInnes explained.

"How is that possible? Surely the Senate want to beat us to this."

"Most of the Senate do, but there are forces at work to slow the army too; it is most puzzling."

"Most puzzling. I trust you'll investigate this immediately?"

"We will turn our attention to it tomorrow morning, yes."

"And what of this evening?"

"We are going to be in attendance at the Senate Ball; as will you, no doubt?"

"Of course; who invited you guys?" Stanford seemed snubbed by this, as if sharing the hall with the Engineers was a slight on him personally.

"The Liberal Party leadership."

"The Liberals?" Stanford's expression contorted once more to a look of shock. "O'Hare?"

"Her office, yes; we do some business with them."

"Some business?"

"They, like everyone else in the Society, buy their guns from us, my Lord." Cooke strode across the floor to where they were standing. "We've been friends longer than we've been paranoid revolutionaries, Rob; a little faith would be nice."

"It would be, no doubt; and I have every faith in you, in Terry, and in Siobhan. Experience, however, has taught me not to trust institutions."

"Ah; you trust the cogs but not the machine, then?"

"Yes." Stanford looked into the eyes of the hologram, such as they were, and burst into a warm smile. "How's it going, James?"

"Can't complain sir. A few glands would be nice, but I'm not desperate for them; you?"

"I have all the glands I need, thank you, James."

"Of course, sir; and how is the good Councillor Johnson?"

"She's fine as ever; she sends her love."

"Give her my regards, would you? I'm still trying to find a way to leave here, but as yet nothing has presented itself as immediately obvious."

"I'll do that for you."

"Terry says the brothers are getting ever more argumentative?"

The others had left them now, and the two friends walked together through the hall.

"That's an understatement; they're getting riled about the least thing, and they just don't stop."

"Since when has Ben ever shown restraint with regard to his opinion?"

"Well true, but he's getting worse; and that damn guy in the Senate, what's his name... Wintrose?"

"Senator Winter?" James suggested.

"That's the one. He almost brought a couple of our guys around on the Executive Powers Bill: Kant's going to have to fight him every step of the way."

"I know. I presume Alan's absence can be explained by this?"

"He's meeting with the Senate leaders on our side, then taking lunch with a couple of Republicans; he's desperate to get this bill passed."

"As are a great many people on all sides; and now the house is split." Cooke paused in thought for a moment. "What about the abstainers?"

"Liberals to a man; none of them will move," Stanford explained. "I suppose I should go? Emily will get most upset if I don't spend an hour getting ready for this shindig tonight."

"I also expect she would be most upset to hear you call it a shindig, my Lord; it is the Senate Ball."

"Will you attend?"

"I fear not, Lord; I cannot leave this hall even to get into the NCC any more, I dare not for fear of Chiswick."

"Michael? What can he do?"

"He is a virus, our programs are written such that they can infiltrate any other; he is much more masterful at the use of this ability, and I fear that if I leave this place he will take from me the wisdom and the knowledge hard fought for by the Engineers, in a second he would become unstoppable, and the peace you have made for the people will be extinguished in an instant."

"You fear him that much? I thought you two were friends, once?"

"That is hard to say, my Lord. I must bid you leave now; the Senate Ball awaits you and I fear no force as much as the wrath of your beautiful girlfriend, sir."

"You and I both, Master Cooke, you and I both." Stanford looked at his friend. "You will find a way out, some day?"

"Of course, my Lord."

"Then goodbye, for now; I will return soon, I have no doubt."

"Thank you, my Lord." Cooke vanished and Stanford left the hall. He took his seat in the back of his limo and turned to his Press Secretary, Katie Hardy.

"I'm going back home; go in one of the other cars and tell Colonel Empter that I won't be in until nine tomorrow morning, understand?"

"Yes, my Lord," she nodded respectfully as she left the car and closed the door behind her.

♦

Alan Empter looked at his watch and sighed deeply.

"Marie!" he screamed at his secretary. "Call Senator Kant and tell him we're done for the day, the Senate is going home early and so are we."

"Why is the Senate going home early?"

"That they may go to their precious ball and be merry for an evening as the Society falls apart around them."

"And why aren't we going?"

"Because we weren't invited," Empter told her.

"Alan..."

"Okay, because I dislike the Senate and their little social

events; they just get on my nerves, and they don't even serve regular beer."

"Always a reason not to attend, but you could have taken me!"

"So you can show off the ball gown you bought yourself but are planning to take back tomorrow?" he asked.

"Well, yes," she admitted.

Marie Hampton was, Empter would be among the first to admit, significantly smarter than her employer, and almost always better dressed. Empter's suit was awful and cheap, when he could ever be bothered to wear it, despite the modest sum he inherited by the death of Cooke, whereas she was dressed exquisitely, tastefully, in a much more expensive, much better fitting suit that she had quite clearly been born to wear.

"So let's go!"

"And drink wine with bubbles in it?"

"Yes."

"That's hardly my idea of fun, Marie."

"Yes, but I work eighteen hour days for you, and I think it's time I got something in return."

"You do! I pay you quite reasonably!"

"You know what I mean: I haven't taken a vacation since you took this job, neither have you; you need to take time off!"

"Oh alright, I'll see if I can talk to the right people..."

♦

"Senator Hannah Thatcher; what brings you to our humble home?" Dan Carter and Killian McBride bowed before the Senator as she came up the driveway. Like Thatcher, they were Confederates, and unlike Greenwood, she was a very attractive woman, which explained the distinct difference in the levels of respect granted.

"I seek Master McInnes; he who is leader of the WTDD and master of this house." She walked up the stairs and past them and they did not rise from their bowed positions. The Senator wore a dark blue cloak—secured by a leaf-shaped broach—the hood of which hung behind her. She entered the house through the door and almost collided with Annie Davies in her haste.

The girl in front of her was one year her junior and two inches her inferior, but quite clearly in control of the situation. She was dressed casually, as always, in a white top and black trousers, with her straight black hair coming down around her chest.

"Master McInnes is not master of this house; that title belongs to Master Cooke, Senator."

"My apologies for the error: where I may find either of the two?"

"They are both located in the gym; third door on your right down that corridor." Davies pointed down the long, snaking corridor to Thatcher's left.

"Thank you." Thatcher strode through the corridor to the door in question and entered. McInnes was involved in training with Siobhan Bishop, both armed with five-foot fighting staves, and neither being gentle with their blows.

McInnes leapt over a low swing and struck at Bishop. His former apprentice narrowly managed to block the staff and pushed him back.

"Hold." The calm voice of Master Cooke spoke up from behind Thatcher. "Welcome, Senator Thatcher; with what can we aid you?"

"I require escort to this evening's ball. I come to you all now in search of that escort."

"You wish for Master McInnes to escort you, I presume?" Bishop asked, leaning on her staff.

"That would be ideal, yes." The Senator turned to McInnes.

"Far be it for me, a humble servant, to decline the wishes of a Member of the People's Senate; I shall be with you momentarily, if you would care to wait?"

"Thank you." Thatcher smiled, and Bishop made a face behind her back as she watched McInnes leave.

"Self control, Doctor Bishop," Cooke murmured to her as she made her way past him and out. "You can wait in the sickly green drawing room, if you wish ma'am; Terry will be ready soon."

♦

Stanford closed the door to his own mansion and caught an enthusiastic Emily in his arms. "You're home!" she announced chirpily, planting a kiss on his cheek.

"That I am." He kissed her back and set her down on the floor. "We have a party to go to. Did you think I'd forget?"

"To be perfectly honest, yes I did," she admitted. "I got your tux ready in case I had to send a courier to you with it, and my gown is ready."

"Which one?"

"The blue one you like; I thought you'd have had a hard day, what with the murders and the vote and all."

"Yes; but that's behind us for now; tonight we dance, we pretend to be riveted by tales of Senate procedure, and we generally have a good time!"

"It's been a while since you've been this..." She struggled for the right word. "Alive. What's happened to change your mind?"

"Does it matter? All that matters is that we will make the most of tonight; we will go change, then I will take you for a drive before the ball."

"Sounds good." She kissed him again. "Whoever did this, tell them thank you from me."

He led her upstairs and they changed into their clothes, Rob into his white dinner jacket and black bow tie, and her into her blue ball gown.

"Who else is going to be there?" she asked.

"The Senate, the Council, some of the WTDD; a few of Alan's people maybe. I'm not sure other than that."

"Alan's going to be there?"

"Not likely, but Katie may be, and her boyfriend."

"What of that funny little boy; Liam Cabot, the apprentice of James?"

"He is busy investigating the murders, my dear."

"A shame; he was a little odd, but quite amusing, in small doses."

"Yes, Emmy; would you like me to have him called from duty to be your jester for the night?"

"Don't be patronising with me, Rob."

They looped arms and made their way down the stairs.

♦

Stanford's limo pulled up outside the Halls of Audience, the venue in which all large events of this nature were held, at seven-fifteen. The door was opened by a valet and the Lord Protector stepped out in his tux, reaching out behind him to help Emily out of the car. They went inside, hand in hand, and went up the stairs.

"This is the best part of my job," Stanford said and turned to a stout Senate aide in evening dress with a dark green cumberbund.

"Hello, George."

"My Lord," the aide answered respectfully.

"Tell the Senate I would like to see them."

Two men on the far side opened the double doors and George stepped in. He grasped the balcony and a little further away trumpeters played a fanfare.

Rob and Emily began to step into the room as the fanfare ended and George's voice, deep and booming, commanded the attention of all present.

"Ladies and gentlemen of the Senate, honoured guests, Mister Speaker; the Lord Protector, General Robert Stanford, and Councillor Emily Johnson."

There was applause from below as they glided down the stairs together.

Stanford looked around. The hall wasn't packed, for it was far larger than it would ever need to be by design, to make the room more intimidating, but it was distinctly busy with couples who would soon be twirling and spinning on the floor. Stanford looked to one side and saw Ben Chiswick and Laura Andrews sipping cocktails together, looking disdainfully at those in the crowd immature enough to actually be having fun. He looked across the hall for the white flash of a lab coat, but saw none; could it be that McInnes had not deigned to come after all?

Of course he was here, Stanford thought. He doubted even McInnes would wear his lab coat to such a function, despite the respect it bought. He finally caught sight of the huge Irish Engineer dancing a little way off with Senator Thatcher and smiled to himself; he wouldn't disturb him just yet then. The room was full of people, all of them known to him, but very few of them friendly; Senators, even the Confederate ones, disliked the Executive Branch for the raw power it represented. If only they knew that he was buried under even more bureaucracy than they, then they would resent him his position all the less.

"Ladies and gentlemen of the Senate, honoured guests, Mister Speaker..."

There had been no fanfare this time; Stanford looked up to see who it was.

"Miss Siobhan Bishop."

Bishop strode down the stairs, gliding like an angel on a cloud, her silver dress shimmering in the light from the chandelier above. Her hair was tied back loosely, a single wavy brown strand dangling before her pale face, and around her neck an emerald hung, supported by a chain embedded with diamonds.

Faces turned, the senators suddenly agog, wondering who this girl was. She bore none of the marks of her profession, and were it not for his knowledge of her Stanford would have thought her some kind of temptress.

"Excuse me one moment," said a deep voice next to him and McInnes cut through the crowd. The senators parted before him, knowing who he was as he had been introduced. The nature of the Engineers was to hide in shadow, never to strike with their full strength, or even to be seen, unless it was absolutely necessary, yet still McInnes commanded the respect of almost everyone he met, especially those who had seen him fight. He reached Bishop as she came to the bottom of the stairs and offered her a hand.

"Doctor."

"Master." She took the hand and began to dance. The other occupants of the room went back to their own amusements as the two of them moved around the floor, years of training in martial arts making their actions light and graceful.

"How much of your inheritance did you blow on that?" he asked as she came close.

"It was in one of Annie's cupboards; we simply adjusted it," she told him.

"And the rock?"

"That cost money, yes," she said.

"How much?"

"I can't entirely remember; very pretty though, don't you agree?"

"Can't say I observe such things," he said coldly, spinning her out.

"Oh really? And what of the good Senator?" she asked as they came together again.

"She needed a date."

"And she could have had any of the residents of the house; why you?"

"Why not me?"

"Don't be evasive, Master; we may be sworn to celibacy but almost all have had... indiscretions."

"I am Master of the Engineers, Siobhan; what are you implying?"

"The rules are awfully vague as to what is allowed and not allowed, Master, and that is all I am saying."

"Of course it is."

A hand tapped Bishop on the shoulder and she turned to face a young man, dressed in a black suit and purple cummerbund.

"May I cut in?" he inquired, looking into McInnes' eyes coldly.

"But of course. Until later, Doctor." He turned away from Bishop and she began to dance with the man. He found Thatcher in a corner, sipping pensively from her glass of champagne.

"Senator."

"Master McInnes." She turned to face him, taking another sip as she did so. "How is Doctor Bishop?"

"She's fine," McInnes replied. "She thinks I have some ulterior motive behind coming here with you rather than alone." He offered his hand.

"It's always nice to have company; or is the good Miss

Bishop a perfect little Engineer?" she took the hand.

"She's good, but she is known for her indiscretions."

"Indiscretions?" Thatcher asked. "Oh, of course; your oaths of celibacy."

"Yes, those."

"Ever regret taking them? I understand one of your number left rather than take them."

"I have never regretted it; we serve the greater good, and the evil that can be unleashed by our desires is too great for us to go about fulfilling them," he said, honestly.

"Bishop looks ravishing, don't you think?" Emily asked Rob as he held her.

"Hadn't noticed," he lied.

"Oh really? Your eyes were as big as saucepans, Rob; you should know better than to lie to me."

"Oh, all right, she looked good; for an Engineer."

"That's a bit harsh."

"Whatever. How's the Nautilus coming along?"

As head of the Marine Biological Sciences Department, Johnson was in charge of supervising the development of the Society's first submarine, the Nautilus.

"Ahead of schedule; we're ready to mount the weapons to the hull now, then it's just a case of fitting her out."

"Excellent; how fast is she?"

"Thirty-two knots submerged, thirty-seven surfaced."

"You're using the new engines?"

"Yes: they're really quite excellent. If it weren't for the new metals and these engines I doubt the Nautilus would even be able to move."

"The metal certainly is helpful."

The Society had the good fortune to own a large group of mines in the Middle East, primarily concerned with the extraction of precious metals and stones, until a year ago, when a large quantity of a new, previously unseen element was discovered by the deep excavation teams. Some had theorised that it was from a meteor impact long ago, but whatever the reason, it was there, and in vast quantities. It had been easy to extract as it was almost completely unreactive, and so separate from its surrounding rocks, but once it was out! The metal was stronger than steel, to a magnitude of almost twenty times, and the same amount lighter as well; the Society had found itself a metal of extreme value, and nobody else knew of its existence. Over the past year around eighteen tonnes of it had been excavated. A large portion of that was in the Nautilus' armour, around ten tonnes worth. Six tonnes had been used to reinforce the outside of the NCC, and the other two tonnes were waiting for a use to be found.

The WTDD, as the most experienced in dealing with such matters, had samples handed over to them for examination, but the new metal, adamantium as they called it, completely defied description or comparison to anything that had come before it; they were having to significantly alter conventional thinking about metals in order to let the new element into a group on the periodic table.

"Do we have any clue as to how much is left?" Johnson asked.

"Nobody's certain; estimates are ranging from a hundred to a million more tonnes."

"Ah; so there's some down there, but they haven't really got a clue what?"

"That's the gist. And we're still no closer to understanding it at all; all we know is it's useful and we've got it and nobody else seems to."

"That seems like an advantage worth seizing, doesn't it?"

"And so we seize." He sighed deeply. "I'm going to sit this one out; do you mind?"

"Of course not, I'll just get my kicks from somebody else." She smiled and kissed him on the lips. "I'll see you later."

"See you later." Rob took a glass of water from a waiter and found a seat at the side of the hall.

"Ah, court intrigue; always amusing to watch, isn't it?"

He looked around at Senator Simon Winter and gave what he hoped didn't look like a forced smile.

"Senator Winter," he nodded curtly.

"Lord Stanford; enjoying the evening?"

"Yes, you guys have really excelled yourselves this year."

"You're sat here by yourself, my Lord; is Lady Johnson at home?" Winter asked in his normal condescending manner.

"No; I just felt flushed, so I sat down for a moment," Stanford explained. "And it's Councillor Johnson; we're not married."

"Oh, bad luck old chap."

"I am not a chap, nor am I old, Senator Winter. Where's your date?"

"I came unaccompanied; I have yet to find someone capable of matching my wit and intellect."

"Did you look in your compost heap?" Stanford muttered. "I suddenly feel much better; if you'll excuse me, Senator?"

"Of course."

Stanford vanished back into the dance floor and quickly found Emily.

"I saw you talking with Winter back there; is everything alright?"

"I hate that man."

"Yes, I know."

"No; there're people like Ben, who I merely dislike intensely, or even Michael, but that man is... terrible."

"He's the hand of the brothers in the Senate, you know that."

"Everybody knows that," Rob said.

Or rather, he thought, everybody who gets briefing books from Alan once a week knows that.

"I suppose. It's nice to see everybody at least pretending to have fun for an evening; if Ben drinks enough of those cocktails he might even dance."

"And if Laura drinks enough she might let him," Rob admitted.

"They're on their third each now?"

"Something like that; Laura's already worse for wear."

Rob glanced over at the Senate Councillor and saw that she had begun to lean on a buffet table for support.

♦

A young woman approached the rear entrance to Cooke hall, a doorway rarely used and one of the few to be kept locked by the Hall's residents. She wore a cloak, fastened with a dragon-shaped clasp, and carried a black umbrella to keep off the rain, the latter of which she leant against the wall once she was in the lee of the building, and opened the door with her key.

The doorway led directly into a spiralling staircase, up which she climbed slowly, pensively, eventually reaching the top, which ended in a brick wall. She pushed it and the secret doorway slid open, admitting her to a dark room, illuminated only by the pinpricks of electrical power lights.

She looked around, marvelling at the gadgetry which bedecked most of the horizontal surfaces, interested by the clash of the antique furniture and cutting edge technology, and again the array of weaponry on the walls.

The room's main door, which led out into a hallway, closed slowly by itself, and she heard the bolt slide across, locking it. She smiled gently, not scared at being trapped; she felt safer here than in her own house.

The lights kicked in, a series of art-deco lamps poised around the room offering a mid-level orange glow to the room, and letting her see, at the far end of the study, a table, with two chairs and a chess board. Of course; he wouldn't do anything so passé as dinner.

"Good evening, Senator Robbins." Cooke greeted her, his hologram appearing behind her. She turned and smiled.

"Master Cooke, thank you for inviting me." She gave him a warm smile.

"I have to say I'm surprised you're not at the ball with the rest of civilised society. And don't call me Master Cooke; it's James to you, it always has been."

"Then I am Julia, and not Senator Robbins; I barely feel like one most of the time; the rest of the Senate are a little too tied up with their social niceties and extravagant parties for my liking. I prefer to think of myself as an elected civil servant."

"Very good. I'd offer to take your coat, but you know..." he waved a hand through a computer screen to demonstrate.

"I completely understand." She undid the clasp and removed her cloak, draping it over the back of one of the chairs. With the cloak gone, he could see that she wore a pair of blue jeans and a conservative, long-sleeved top. She was just as he remembered her; tall, slim-figured and elegant, her chiselled facial features and bright green eyes lending her a refined appearance. Her shoulder length brown hair shone in the orange light and she smiled at catching him looking at her, a slight sorrow in his eyes.

"How long has it been?" she asked, sitting down in her chair and quickly admiring the ebony and ivory pieces laid out on the board.

"Almost two years," he told her, taking his own seat.

"Too long," she commented, picking up and moving one of the white pawns before her.

"Much," he agreed. "How's the Senate treating you?"

"Not bad. I shouldn't really complain, I guess, I get everything I ever dreamed of, and I love my work; it's just sometimes like bashing my head against a brick wall."

You've been working with Tim on the Executive Powers Bill?"

"Yeah," she acknowledged.

"What do you make of him?"

"Interesting guy, intelligent, dedicated to public service. I'm glad you met him when you did though; there's a very real concern that he might have turned out more like Winter if it weren't for your influence."

"My influence?" Cooke asked, questioning.

"I suspect your unwillingness to cut moral corners may have rubbed off on him," she explained. "Only in a good way, of course."

"Of course," he smiled. "So you like him?"

"He's alright... for a Democrat."

"I'm glad you think so. He'll be LP one day."

"When Stanford retires, perhaps; but that won't be for a long while yet."

"Indeed not; Rob loves his job even more than you."

"I'd imagine. How about you; how's the Engineer life going?"

"I'd hardly call it a life," he joked, and she felt a pang of guilt; it was all too easy to forget that one of the graves in Cooke Hall's mausoleum was that of her current host.

"But seriously, it's difficult at the moment; I'm not sure about any of the apprentices, and obviously I can't train them myself. These murders are most troubling. Seven years ago I'd have rushed to investigate them, but now I have to sit back and let Cabot deal with it."

"Ah yes, the good Colonel Cabot. Has he grown any more respectful these past years?"

"Alas no." Cooke smiled. "Still as youthful and exuberant as ever."

"Still got a girl in every village?"

"So rumour has it." He laughed, then stopped, looking pensively down at the board. "How about you?" he asked.

"I have girls in very few villages, I'm afraid," she replied, trying to keep the tone light.

"I meant..."

"I know what you meant, James." She looked at him, the same sad expression in each of their eyes. "And you know the answer."

"You're telling me no young senator has taken it upon themselves to sweep you off your feet?"

"I'm telling you that I haven't been swept," she corrected, "and it's the truth. I haven't been swept in a long time. A little house in Tockington, during the convention, I seem to recall..." She trailed off.

"I'm sorry, Julia..."

"Don't be sorry, James; I understand everything, you know that, as you must understand my reluctance to be swept."

"I understand."

She looked down sadly, and extended her hand across the table to rest upon his own. It slipped through the projection of his skin, and she felt sadness grip her. "That's always been the problem for us, hasn't it, James; intangibility."

He smiled. "In one way or another, yes." He waved a hand, and one of his pieces moved, taking another of hers and placing her king in peril. "Check."

"Indeed," she acknowledged, moving her king to a safer location. "Will the Executive Powers Bill pass?"

"There's increasing pressure from the public, and Winter will have to back down eventually; puppet of the brothers that he is, he's still subject to the court of public opinion."

"That man is a nasty piece of work; with him and the brothers working together, I'd be worried if I were you. They'll stop at nothing to get what they want."

"I'm aware of the danger," he admitted. "I haven't left the safety of this Hall in the longest time, for fear of what might happen if I did, but there will come a time when these walls will not protect me."

♦

"Senator Winter; are you lost?" one of the civilian guardsmen on the doors asked the Senator as he opened a door.

"No Tom, just looking for the loos."

"They're over there, sir." The guardsman pointed at the opposite door.

"Ah, thank you." Winter's hand slid from his pocket, holding a silver box about three inches square. He tapped the side and it opened into an 'S' shape. He pointed it at the guard, whose back was now turned from him, and pressed the small button on the top.

Blue hands of electricity flew from the Taser, striking the man in the back and rendering him unconscious Winter opened the door he had been entering originally and went through it, sliding the silver box back into his pocket. He moved quickly now; the guard would wake up soon, and he couldn't risk being discovered. He closed his eyes to glance at the map he had memorized earlier that day and stopped. He turned to the door on his right-hand side and tried the handle; it was locked. He reached into his pocket again and removed the box once more, using it to disarm the electronic lock. He pushed the door open and went to the bureau against the room's wall. He opened the bottom drawer of the desk and began rifling through it purposefully.

He pulled open the second drawer, then the third, until he found what he was looking for, and put it into his pocket. Winter went out, leaving the drawers open and the door ajar. He ran back down the corridor to where he had knocked out the guard, and put his hand in his right pocket. He activated the Taser, then fired two shots. The electricity crackled down his side and he toppled to the ground, knocked out by his own weapon, the box sliding shut as its battery ran empty.

♦

"Ladies and gentlemen, if you can remain calm—"

The senators instantly turned on the guardsman now addressing them, like peregrines on a mouse.

"Why should we remain calm? What cause could we have for not remaining calm?" Senator Migson stepped forward.

"Senator Winter and a guardsman have been knocked out in the foyer; we're going to have to end the party now."

Stanford looked around at Senator Thatcher, who shrugged. He quickly took a mobile phone from his pocket and began to make calls, just as everybody else in the room began to do the same.

"Alan, it's Stanford—"

"I know, I'm at the party."

Stanford span his head to see Empter standing a few feet away, accompanied by Marie Hampton.

"Okay, that's a shock; get on the phone to your people, the Hall will need to be told."

"We're also here." McInnes and Bishop arrived in the huddle. "Somebody should call Liam," McInnes instructed.

"He won't like that at all," Bishop warned, and caught the people staring at her. "Oh alright, I'll call him."

♦

Cabot woke, as always, with a start. The phone in his apartment was ringing, three yards away, and his pager was rumbling on his bedside cabinet. In his trousers thrown somewhere randomly on the floor, his mobile was ringing: there was only one thing that this could signal.

"What's that?" the girl lying beside him, covered to her neck in blankets, asked as she sat up.

"Trouble," he answered truthfully, pulling himself out of bed. He picked up the landline phone and slammed it down again instantly. Pulling his trousers from the previous day on over his underwear, he pulled the mobile phone out of the pocket. "Hey; this is the second day in a row you guys have—"

"Quit the whining, Liam." Bishop's voice came down the line. "Get to the Halls of Audience immediately; Winter and one of your guys have been attacked."

"Winter? Is it serious?"

"He was just knocked out; Taser blast."

"Shame; has he woken up yet?"

"Yes, about two minutes ago."

"Even more of a shame. I'll be there in ten minutes." After closing the phone he kicked his shirt from the floor into his hands and pulled it on. "I've got to go."

"Early meeting?" the girl asked.

"You could say that; you can let yourself out, right?"

"Of course. Maybe I'll see you again?"

"It's entirely plausible;" he paused, and considered this for a moment. "I'd look forward to it, in fact."

She got out of bed and began to dress as he left the room.

He got into the lift and rode it down to the ground floor. He was completely unarmed, he realised, and his coat was still in his room. Damn. It had been a long while since he had left his quarters unarmed, ever since being one of those who failed to pass from apprentice to Engineer just after the Coup.

He leapt onto the motorbike and sped off at high speed towards the Halls of Audience, thinking about nothing in particular on his way there. Masters of ancient and modern philosophy had taught themselves how to empty their mind of all thoughts, that they could ponder the secrets of the universe better. Cabot had learnt to do it simply for a bit of peace and quiet from time to time.

He pulled up outside and leapt from the back of the bike quickly, dashing inside.

"Okay, what do we know?" he asked the Guard Captain who stood waiting for him.

"Senator Winter and Private Wilson were attacked; they were stunned by an electric shock but both are fine now. A door down the corridor has been forced by a similar method. The office was that of one of the senators' aides."

"Which one?"

"We're not sure of that one yet; nothing seems to have been taken though; the drawers were completely filled."

"So, someone broke into the building, knocked out Senator Winter and a guardsman, broke into an office, and didn't steal anything?" Cabot asked. "A touch implausible?"

"Something may have distracted them?"

"I suppose. Have you searched the victims?"

"We can't search Winter, sir; he's a senator."

"Ah, another sign of the corruption in our perfect political system," Cabot sighed. "Very well; write a formal request to search him, little good that it'll do us. Is there anything else?"

"Just one thing, sir; the Senator was found over here, about five metres from the guard; if there was just one assailant then they'd have to have moved pretty quick to hit both men with a Taser."

"Unless they had an air Taser, of course?"

"Impossible sir, neither man had any needle marks."

"So you checked then?"

The Captain nodded.

"Excellent work," Cabot nodded pensively. There was a way to shock someone from across the room, but it was extremely unlikely that...

The Light Assault Taser, a silver box which extended into an effective stunning weapon, such as he kept in his pocket, was highly classified; nobody outside of the Hall and their closest allies knew of their existence.

"I'm going to go and find out if anyone saw anything, Captain; keep an eye open."

"Yes, sir." The Captain saluted and Cabot returned the gesture. The guard turned to leave, then hesitated. "But sir, we've already asked the guests; they've all said they saw and heard nothing. They were all at the party."

"Good work, Captain; I'll be back soon." Cabot went into the ballroom, nodding at the senators as he went, and then stepped out through the open back door onto the veranda. "Doctor Bishop."

Bishop turned to face him, none of her poise or grace lessened by the events of the night. "Mister Cabot—"

"May I just say how lovely you look this evening? I haven't seen you in a dress since... oh, I don't know when."

"Thank you, Liam; what's your expert verdict on the situation?"

"Well, first, you guys dropped the ball, then somebody broke in, shot Winter and a guard, stole something small from the office, then left."

"*We* dropped the ball?"

"Two targets, knocked out by what was quite clearly a Taser of some kind, standing on opposite sides of a foyer; no sign of one assailant, let alone two. What does this suggest to you?"

"Someone has access to the LAT?" Bishop's face fell. "Terry will need to be told."

"Where's he gone?"

"He's taking Hannah Thatcher home."

"Oh, right, well then." Cabot stumbled verbally, confused by this fact. "I expect he's already aware. Michael's guys will be descending faster than you can get a team in here; you need to clear out anything they might be able to use against you."

"Liam..."

"Just go, Siobhan," he urged her.

"Have you searched Winter?"

"No; we can't get clearance for it, why?"

"Because there was something in his pocket about the right size for a Taser," she told him.

"And you know this because..."

"I'm very good at my job, Liam."

"It could also have been a cigar case, a large phone or a trick of the light, Siobhan. Or maybe he was just pleased to see you... Besides," he continued in the face of her disapproving glare, "I don't know whether you've noticed, from behind the ivory walls of the Hall, but I can't easily go up to a member of the Senate and accuse him of being in possession of a piece of technology which he would have to have stolen to possess."

"I know, but if Winter stole this item, Liam, you know what that means."

"The man is in this to his neck; he's not only working for Chiswick but he's working for the SS as an operative. The

Senate will have been compromised. This is why I don't want it getting out, and also why I'm reluctant to investigate it openly; if we go after him and he does have the contacts we think he does there may be another war."

"I know; I'll look into it and get back to you tomorrow when I have info from Terry, okay?"

"Okay, Siobhan."

From the area around them there was the sound of motorbikes and cars stopping, around a dozen of each, from the sounds. As they got closer their lights became visible through the trees.

"Black bikes, eh? These guys have gone up in the world."

"Covert Ops Teams, Liam." Bishop looked out over the car park. "Thirty SS agents, black clothing, as always armed."

She looked up at the balcony above her head and then paused as she tensed. "Not in this dress, I think," she announced, and re-entered the hall. She moved quickly through the throng of dazed senators and unzipped the small bag slung over her right shoulder.

She took out a fairly ordinary three by two-inch blue card and her mobile phone. She flicked it open and dialled the first number in the speed-dial group.

"Hello?" a female voice answered on the other end, slightly drowsily, after five rings.

"Annie, it's Siobhan; wake everybody up, get them into one of the halls and wait for me to get back."

"What's happened, Doctor?"

"Later." Bishop slammed the phone shut and left the building through the front entrance. She ran out of the building and saw Cabot's bike parked to one side. She shrugged and threw her leg over the bike, turning the keys that were already in the ignition and driving off.

A few minutes later, when she arrived back at the hall and leapt from the bike, she announced: "Here's the deal."

♦

"Colonel Cabot," Cayley Tufnell approached Cabot. "Why are you here?"

"I was called," he answered, not looking up from the bureau as he sifted through the papers.

"By whom?"

"Someone."

"The Hall?"

"Why would the Hall call me? None of them could possibly have access to information that quickly; you're paranoid, ma'am." He picked a piece of paper out of the drawer and looked at it.

"McInnes was here."

"Yes, with Senator Thatcher; he's also left now. If he called me do you not think he would have the courtesy to be here when I arrived?"

"Alright then. What have you learned?"

"This room has no owner; it hasn't been used since twenty-twelve."

"What?"

"The room isn't assigned to anyone."

"So whatever the assailant was looking for has been here for quite a while?"

"That's what I thought, but these documents were dated within the past week."

"Somebody's been using this room without anyone noticing?"

Cabot got up and faced his superior officer. She wore a low-cut ball gown in dark green satin, he noted; she had been a guest at the ball.

"That'd be my conclusion."

"That's impossible."

"Is it?" Cabot tilted his head to one side. "This place isn't guarded during the day and the bureaucrats who run it will not be paying a lot of attention to everybody they see; they're not going to see one face which isn't there every day, especially if it *is* there every day."

"I suppose."

The door opened behind Tufnell and a young officer stepped in.

"General Tufnell; the SS have very nearly finished interviewing the guests."

"Thank you Lieutenant."

The man started to leave but Cabot called him back.

"Lieutenant!"

"Yes, Colonel?"

"Get as many men as you can find in here and empty the contents of this desk into bags. Strap CG Protected Evidence stickers on the side and then take them back to the analysis room. Do it quickly."

"Why are we doing this?" Tufnell asked, holding back the officer.

"So that the SS don't get their thieving hands on the evidence so it can go missing."

"Do it." Tufnell let the officer go. "How's the investigation into the murders going?"

"I can't get time with the pathologists, they're being held up by reports for Senate Armed Services."

"When were those announced?" Tufnell asked.

"About five minutes before I arrived to request autopsies on the bodies," he told her. "Something's going on outside of your jurisdiction, ma'am."

"The Council, or the army?"

"No, neither of them could have swung this, and from

what I hear Sharp's people are having just as much trouble as we are. Someone in the Senate is doing this to us."

"The Senate? But why?"

"I don't know that yet, ma'am but I'm going to find—"

Cabot stopped as the door opened and several guards came in with clear plastic bags. He and the General left the room, heading down the corridor. The doors from the foyer opened and two women walked through. They both wore loose black clothing, with holsters strapped to both sides of their belts.

"Ladies," Cabot took a step towards them and they carried on walking, apparently oblivious to his presence. "General, your sword."

"Do you really think that's necessary?"

The SS agents barged past the General, spinning her as one of their shoulders collided with hers. Cabot reached out his hands to touch either wall of the corridor.

"If you'd be so good as to stop?"

The women stopped.

"Now, hand over the guns."

They looked at him blankly for a second.

"Please?"

"You have no jurisdiction over us."

"This is a public institution, and a crime scene. Your weapons are illegal here; hand them over."

"No." The women drew themselves up to fight and Cabot sighed.

"Stand down."

The two girls turned to face a third woman, taller than them and wearing the same uniform, only without guns in her holsters.

"Sergeant Houghton!"

"You are not above the law just because you wear the black of the SS; you will surrender your guns immediately or you will remove them from your colon before your court-martial," Sergeant Rachel Houghton of the SS snapped at the two girls. "*Now.*"

The girls reached down and drew their pistols, handing them butt-first to Liam.

"Thank you for your co-operation." He flashed them a smile and heard the door opening behind him. Three guardsmen, carrying a plastic bag in either hand, walked down the corridor away from them.

"What's going on?" one of the SS asked.

"We're taking evidence for analysis," Cabot told them. "As per our job; why're you here?"

"A senator was attacked, we're here to clear up your mess."

"Whatever," Cabot turned and walked away. "You can pick up your guns from the CG building tomorrow, if you want them," he called back.

"We have other guns, you know!" one woman shouted after him.

"Suit yourselves," he went into the next corridor and turned to face the mass of guardsmen assembled there. "Could anyone, perchance, give me a lift home? I suspect that my bike has been appropriated by higher forces."

♦

Two men in plain clothes walked the streets of the city of Bristol, making their way calmly but purposefully towards a house in the centre. They carried no identification papers and no warrant, though they had institutional backing for their operation.

The men were SS operatives, among the best; responsible, since their employer had been suddenly spooked a week ago, for re-acquiring certain items for him.

They didn't know the use of these items, they didn't know what crimes the innocents they had taken them from had committed, and they didn't care: they had been given a mission to complete and that was moral justification enough for their actions.

Behind them, stalking across the rooftops, a single figure in grey moved silently, observing the two operatives as they closed on the house. He knew what needed to be done, he even knew why—indeed, he had more knowledge about the SS's mission than the men in the street.

The men turned a corner down a residential street and their rooftop stalker continued to watch as they approached a house and knocked on the door. It would be soon now; all he had to do was stop them from getting one of the keys, and it would all be over for them.

A young woman opened the door and one of the two men shot her twice in the chest with a silenced pistol before both stepped into the building over her flailing body, beginning their search of the house.

The man watching them from the rooftop drew a pistol from the recesses of his outfit and aimed it at the door, awaiting their return. He felt a hand upon his shoulder and turned, shrugging off the grip and punching out.

The woman behind him writhed out of the way of the fist and countered with a kick, the blow finding its target and knocking him back from the roof. He landed, crouched, on the pavement below, and looked up as the woman started to fire with her pistol, leaping aside to avoid her fire and snapping two shots upward in return.

The woman landed beside him, lashing out with both fists. He quickly blocked the blows and took a step back as she struck again; he was surprised to find himself needing all his concentration to turn back the torrent of attacks, combined with impressive speed and accuracy, that she was throwing at him. He leapt backward, gliding through the air with a practiced grace and taking his favoured offensive stance, prepared to start the fight afresh, without underestimating his opponent.

Before he could react, she slipped a box from her pocket and waved it at him. Two pins impacted in his skin, which suddenly grew warm, a second before he collapsed, the Taser energy quickly incapacitating him.

The woman turned back and headed back to the house, but she was too late; the owner was dead, and the SS operatives had already left.

♦

"The Society sleeps not peacefully, my dear."

Rob sat on the bed, sipping a mug of cocoa, as Emily emerged from the bathroom in her nightdress.

"Does it ever?"

"More peacefully than this, usually. I have no idea what's going on out there; the others are dealing with it now, but I feel I should be involved, that I should be making a difference to this somehow."

"You can't make a difference if you're too tired, Rob." Emily got into bed and pulled the covers over herself. "Now sleep."

"Alright." He got in too and she curled up beside him.

"Goodnight."

"Goodnight." She kissed him and closed her eyes, falling instantly into a deep and peaceful sleep.

♦

Senator Winter got home at just gone three in the morning and threw his jacket onto his armchair. He had a busy day tomorrow downstairs in the main Senate Hall, but he could afford to wait a few more minutes for his guests to arrive. He crossed to the shotgun mounted on a rack on the wall and took it down. He pulled the slide back and released it to load one round into the chamber, then sat in the armchair facing the door.

There was a knock on the door and his finger tensed on the trigger.

"It's unlocked."

The door opened and a man garbed in black entered. Winter put the gun down on his side table.

"Hello Jameson."

"Senator; you got the package?"

The Senator reached into his pocket and removed an ordinary-looking key.

"Thank you, Senator." The man, identified as a sergeant by the silver stripes on his sleeve, took the key from him and put it into a small silk bag.

"What's so valuable about a key?" Winter asked. "Cabot's people said the office wasn't even supposed to be in use."

"If I knew that, Senator, I wouldn't just be a sergeant. All I know is that Councillor Chiswick wants these keys badly, and is willing to do anything to get them."

"Sergeant Jameson?" Another agent had appeared in the doorway.

"Yes, Mister Evans?"

"The guards will be here in a few moments, sir." The newcomer told him, a hint of anxiety in his voice.

"Thank you, Ewan." He nodded to the Senator and the two men left.

4

"Good morning. What is our agenda for the day?" the chairperson of the Senate Armed Services committee opened the meeting.

"Today, it is an agendum." Cabot was sat in a spare seat around the horseshoe table.

"What?"

"It's the singular form of agenda; you have only one thing to consider this morning."

"And what, Colonel, is that? Explain yourself quickly, lest I grow tired with your whimsy and call guards to take you away."

"There has been a devastating series of murders. Senator Winter, a member of your brother committee, was attacked yesterday, and two members of the SS were also attacked. I need pathologists and I need them before what little warmth is left in the trail vanishes."

"You think we are holding back your pathologists? What makes you think that?"

"Members of this committee have ordered members of the CG into reviews for the next three days; all of my pathologists have been taken, as well as my forensic examiners and a crime scene specialist. I need them back now."

"You realise, Colonel, that this committee is not responsible for the actions of its individual members?"

"Yes, I realise that, Senator; but I'm here to tell you all while you're here to drop the reviews—or at least postpone them—or I will be ordering an independent review of the activities of senators within this committee."

He glared at them, making eye contact with each of the senators around the table.

"Did you just threaten us, Colonel?" Charles Migson, of the Democratic Party, asked.

"No, Senator; I just threatened several members of this committee; not all of you, and not you personally, sir."

"Very well; we will take this under advisement, Colonel."

Cabot nodded to the senators and left the room, content that his work was done for the morning.

"Colonel Cabot!" Sophie Paris shouted at him from across the walkway. Cabot crossed to her slowly.

"Colonel Paris? What brings you here?"

"Do I need a reason to be here?" she asked elusively. "Last time I checked we have the same rank; if you can be here then surely so can I."

"Except for the fact that you're assigned to a desk job and aren't supposed to leave the CG headquarters without escort."

"Actually, General Tufnell would prefer me to stay in my office, because if I died she'd lose her job. However, as a member of the Old Crowd, I can do basically what I wish."

"You carry a sword and a gun?"

"Yes."

"Nobody tried to take them from you?"

She shook her head.

"I feel I really missed out on something, training with Cooke rather than Walsh."

"You wouldn't have been Walsh's kind of person." Paris laughed hollowly. "You're too promiscuous, and you enjoy jumping around too much."

"I'm too prolific?" Cabot's face became suddenly stony. "I may only have been in the care of the WTDD since after the war, but I know that Walsh was hardly without blemishes on his record."

"What?" Paris took a step back. "What are you saying, Liam?"

"I'm saying that Walsh took no less than five partners between the beginning of the war and his death; I don't know who they were, but I know that much."

"How did you know?"

"You think the Crowd was the only group of people around him every second protecting him? Danielle's people were there, much more discretely, every second of the day; nothing happened to him they didn't know about."

"They were spying on him?" Paris was getting angry now.

"No, Sophie; they were protecting him, just like they did for Stanford during the Faction War, as ill-acknowledged as they were for that, while you guys tried to establish where your loyalties lay."

"You speak against the Crowd, Liam."

"Forgive me, ma'am, but I do not; I just object to everybody labeling me as prolific and a philanderer simply because I take partners from time to time, unlike my former comrades."

Sophie was passified by this. "Accepted, and my apologies for the insult. The Crowd are meeting for lunch today; I thought I'd come loiter down here beforehand."

"Where do you guys eat out? I can't imagine that any normal restaurant can accommodate the security."

"There's a place in downtown, the Beijing Dragon; they clear the place out for us and the Secret Service stand outside in a mob."

"Interesting; James' guys just use Clapton's, down by the Marine Biology Institute."

"The same Clapton's as was used for the second Tockington conventions?"

"New venue, same friendly service."

"Ah, James' guys? You mean the WTDD?"

Cabot nodded.

"I was under the impression Cooke hadn't left the hall, otherwise he would be dining with us this lunchtime."

"He's one of the Crowd?"

"Yes, you didn't know? There isn't some sort of rule saying you can't be master of the Hall and member of the Old Crowd at the same time, is there?"

"Well, no, but the Crowd are all high profile people; everyone recognises you on the streets—"

"No, everyone in the CG, PA, SS and WTDD, as well as all the members of the Senate and Executive Branch recognise us all on the street; the same is true of Cooke. He's just less noticeably one of us because the lab coat he wore when he was alive tended to camouflage him."

"Alright then. I'm surprised I never noticed this, but okay; wanna get some coffee while you wait?"

"Sure."

They went upstairs to the café and sat down with two cups of coffee.

"Any leads on the murders yet?" Paris inquired.

"Not yet, no; I haven't been able to get access to the people I need yet. Something's holding them back."

"What?"

"If I knew that, I wouldn't be sitting here drinking coffee with you so much as I'd be breaking noses somewhere in this building."

"You think it was somebody in the Senate?"

"Nobody in the committee is on the influenced party list."

"Influenced what?"

"It's a list kept by my office; it tells me everyone who receives donations from the halls of Chiswick or Cooke; armed services aren't an area of particular concern for either of them."

"So somebody on the committee is doing it off their own back, or being influenced by someone outside of the SS and WTDD?"

"Yes. Also outside of the Crowd." Cabot floated this remark gently and took a sip of his coffee, watching Paris as she let the words run off her back.

"Colonel Cabot?" came a new voice.

Cabot looked around at Senator Winter and rose from his seat. Paris remained seated, nodding coldly at the Democrat.

"Senator Winter; you're feeling alright?"

"Yes, thank you Colonel. I just came over to thank you for the assistance rendered me by you and your staff yesterday."

The Senator put his right hand forward and Cabot's mind flared up, moving with the speed that had gotten him appointed to this position two months after starting as a Lieutenant; the Senator was offering to shake his hand, he was wearing the same coat as last night, a black overcoat. Winter was influencing people for Chiswick, that much was clearly true, but how far dare Cabot go? What if the Senator was more than just a pawn? What would he do if he found out that Cabot was investigating him?

Fuck it. Liam reached out with his hand, grasping the Senator's firmly and shaking it as his left hand darted out unseen.

"You're welcome. Senator; I'm only sorry we haven't yet been able to catch your assailant."

"Oh, you'll find him eventually, and whatever he took."

Liam let this lie, carefully ignoring the clumsy statement.

"Well, we'll try sir."

"I'm sure you will; thank you again, Colonel."

"Thank you, sir." Cabot sat back down and faced Paris again. The girl sipped her coffee and nodded to him once Winter was gone.

"Why didn't you pick him up on that? How was he to know that anything had been stolen; even we're not sure about that!"

"I didn't need to question him, I've found all the proof of his involvement that I need." Liam lifted his left hand. Held in place by a clenching of the peripheral muscles was a small silver box, roughly three inches in side length.

"An LAT? Where did he get that from?" Paris, as one of the Old Crowd, also carried a Taser in her pocket, access to unofficial technologies granted by her unofficial privilege.

"I haven't got any idea, but he shouldn't have it, no matter where it came from."

"Unless he's working for both Terry and the SS?"

"Terry would rather die than place so much as one secret in the hands of Senator Winter; they're not in allegiance."

"Okay then, so where did it come from?"

"I haven't a clue; I'll send it to the Hall for analysis, but I doubt anything will turn up, not unless we get really, really lucky."

"And that doesn't happen often."

"Have you noticed something strange?" Cabot asked.

"Like a distinct rise in the members of the Secret Service in here in the past few minutes?" Sophie asked and he nodded.

"Always happens; one of the others is here. They're probably looking for me now."

"Colonel Paris; Miss Kesner requests that you join her on the ground floor," a Secret Service agent said, looming behind the Colonel.

"Tell her I'll be down in a moment," she instructed without turning around. "Well, thanks for keeping me company, Liam, and good luck getting staff."

"Thank you, Colonel Paris." Cabot stood up as she did and she left, two members of the Secret Service lurking close behind her. He sighed and picked up his phone.

"Joan; call the pathologists, tell them they're free until I tell them different and that they're to begin conducting an autopsy on the bodies immediately. Then hold all calls to the morgue or forward them to me if they're important; do not let them leave the morgue until they're done, do you understand?"

"Yes, sir; I'll get to that right away."

"Thank you Joan." Cabot slammed the phone shut.

♦

"And they attacked you?" Colonel Michael Chiswick stood above Private Ewan Evans, watching the man's face intently as he was interrogated.

"Yes. Two of them, only they were both knocked out by a third person before we could do anything." Evans described the events of the previous night after he and Jameson had left Winter's apartment.

"A third person?" Michael asked.

"Yes. A woman, good figure, dressed in black but not like us, or like the others; like a lot of bandages."

"Ninja dress?"

"That's one of the ways of looking at it, yes."

"And she defended you from the men in cloaks?"

"Yes; then she hit me in the neck with something and I passed out."

"From Jameson's testimony it sounds like that was a Taser; apparently they took the package from him."

"Will we be able to get it back?"

"I don't doubt it; there are only a few women who would be up to such a task."

"May I request permission to be assigned to the team that goes to get her, sir?"

"I'll think about it; go home, get some rest, and come back tomorrow morning."

The guards on the door let Ewan go before leaving the room themselves.

Michael Chiswick closed his eyes and his clothes changed instantly from the black silk of an SS agent to a grey hakama, the dress worn by samurai. He opened his eyes again and thought. They were moving for the first time since the gaff that had been the Coup, that meant they were after something, and it didn't take a supercomputer to work out what that was.

He could get them. It would be quite easy, given access to all his resources, but after last night that was looking increasingly difficult. They knew what he was up to and they had sent people to get the key back from Jameson and Evans; no doubt the two men would have been killed if it weren't for their mysterious rescuer.

Of course, that was another problem; he had some benefactor, who had saved the lives of his people but taken the key—someone who knew its true value? Or perhaps someone less informed but who hated the SS enough to try and foil their plans regardless. They were certainly very talented though, whoever they were...

◆

"Bethany!"

"Sophie!" The two women exchanged a brief hug. Bethany Kesner had been the first member of the Old Crowd to leave military service, and had become *the* star of the PFS's new movie industry; refusing to direct, but starring in and financing quite a number of the movies the Senate Cultural Oversight Committee were firmly supporting in their endeavour to create culture in the juvenile society.

The two friends walked out of the Senate building together, climbed into Beth's chauffeured Jaguar and set off for the restaurant. Downtown in the PFS was little more than a shanty town; a collection of buildings hastily constructed after the Coup to house the population surplus as Walshton was turned into a Fort instead of a city and most of Bristol, already besieged once during the first war, was now barely standing. Slowly downtown had emptied of permanent denizens as they had moved into either the NCC or the huge structures of the Civilian Centres; large blocks of accommodation for the masses, of which there were now twenty-three scattered around the Society, and so downtown had flourished as a new business and eatery district.

The two of them got out of the car as it stopped outside the Beijing Dragon. The Secret Service agent in the passenger seat of the car climbed out and stood beside the door as they went inside. There were no agents in the restaurant itself, and no patrons, except for at a table in the centre of the room, around which five people were sat, perusing menus.

"Hey guys," Stanford greeted them as they walked toward the large circular table, grabbing chairs from nearby tables as they walked up and depositing them where they wanted to sit. The group of friends were eclectic in their appearances and interests, but were linked by a common bond of experience and power; around the table was a Colonel in the Civilian Guard, a member of the Council, the Council's leader, the Chief Justice of the Society's Supreme Court, and a movie star—after the war those that remained of the once two-dozen strong band of friends had either been elected or appointed to positions of authority; these occasional lunches being accepted as part of the functioning of the government.

A waitress in a kimono came to the table. "Can I take your orders?"

"Okay," Stanford looked around the group. "We'd like four sweet and sour porks, two kung po chicken, three chicken chow mien, three Peking ducks, six bowls of wonton soup and twelve spring rolls."

"Right away," the girl bobbed slightly and dashed into the kitchen.

"Do we know her?" Clare Fox asked and the others shook their heads. "I thought there weren't supposed to be people we didn't know." After the death of so many of their number, the most recent of which being Cooke, in the dying hours of the Kensington Coup, some members of the crowd had becoming suspicious and untrusting.

"There always will be, Clare; turnover happens," Nick Kelvin told her. "And I doubt that a sixteen-year old is out to get the seven of us."

"Younger people have been." She reminded him, and there was a general hushed agreement from the others.

"Nick; are you guys getting ready for the murder trials?" Stanford asked, trying to change the subject.

"A panel of judges have been arranged, if that's what you mean, but beyond that we're a little tied up since Coates has been dragged before the bar."

"Coates? What did he do?"

"Not a damn thing."

"Then why—"

"Justice Hurley has called an inquiry."

"Hurley again? How did we let that guy get through the Senate?"

Justice Hurley was the only Democratic member of the PFS Senate, nominated by Senator Winter and Senator Migson and then bizarrely confirmed by the Senate in a practically empty session.

"Kant's guys dropped the ball; it's happened before and it'll happen again, but we now have a man elected to position of Justice for the rest of his life whose sole purpose and pleasure seems to be dragging Confederate and Liberal members of the bar before inquiries."

"I'll see if I can do anything to—" Stanford began.

"No you won't; the powers are separated for a reason, Rob," Paris spoke up. "The Senate'll get jumpy if you start invoking executive powers on the judiciary."

"I suppose—"

"Suppose nothing; it'll happen, and then we'll have far bigger problems than Hurley."

The table went silent for a moment and their food arrived, carried through on large trays by four waiters who deposited empty white plates in front of each of them, then placed bowls full of the other dishes in the centre of the table.

"Bon appétit." Beth raised her glass of water.

"Carpe diem," Kelvin inchimed.

"To old friends," Stanford paused before finishing the toast, "and those yet to come."

The glasses clanged together.

♦

"Any word from the pathologists yet?" Cabot asked Joan, walking into the NCC station of the CG.

"Nothing yet, no sir."

"Okay, but they're definitely still there?"

"I placed a dozen guards on the doors, sir; they're not going anywhere without killing anyone."

"I'm not sure whether to be comforted by that."

Cabot walked past the rows of desks and into the room his unit was based in. The murder investigation squad for this area were not known to him, and also not experienced or insightful enough for his liking, so his staff had moved across town to be here. In the middle of the room there was a map with red pins in it. Each of the red pins denoted a murder site. Each of the pins had a series of pieces of string looped around it and stretching from one victim to the next, to the next.

"Assuming that our murderer moved from one victim to the next by the shortest possible route, performing, essentially, a deadly round-robin, what sort of distances would they have had to have travelled?"

"The average distance between murders was seven miles; that makes it a twenty-eight mile round trip."

"Right," Cabot stopped for a second, "all we have at the moment is displayed on this map, correct?"

The others nodded.

"Okay then, I'm going out to tour the murder scenes. I presume our people are there now?"

"Yes sir, but they're under instructions not to touch anything."

"Excellent work; I'll go check things out and report back in about three hours, you guys keep doing what you can from here, and for God's sake keep track of those pathologists!"

"Yes sir," they droned dully; these people had been working with him for between three and five years and were fully accustomed to his redundancy.

♦

Cabot arrived in Titherington and pulled up outside a building cordoned off by tape.

"Excuse me; you can't come in here—"

Cabot pulled out his wallet and flashed them his ID badge. "Colonel Liam Cabot; I'm leading this investigation. What can you tell me?"

"Sorry sir; just you're not wearing uniform."

"No, I never do." Cabot smiled brightly at the man. "What transpired?"

"Well, the victim, identified by his *girlfriend* as Mike Hobson, was found dead this morning by the milkman—"

"His milkman found him?" he asked. "How?"

"The door was ajar and the late gentleman was lying on the inside propped up against that bookshelf." The officer pushed the door open, revealing an oak bookshelf with a stain on the bottom two shelves.

"Ah; do continue."

"Well, the milkman called us immediately and we arrived shortly thereafter. Initial examinations of the deceased led us to the conclusion that he had been shot twice through his breast bone at close range with a staple weapon of some description."

Cabot looked inside the door and peered at the lock.

"Do you notice this damage to the lock?"

There was a split running down the wood of the door, passing through the locking mechanism.

"Yes sir. It's quite a split, no doubt, but not enough to open the door; I came to the conclusion that the attacker tried to force the door, but was unable to, and then as he was thinking of a solution to the problem the deceased gentleman opened it for him, investigating the disturbance, and his attacker shot him twice in the chest."

"Interesting hypothesis, but it does have a flaw or two."

Cabot stepped into the house, quickly scanning the entire hallway.

"Oh yes, sir, and what might those be?"

"Ah; there is no blood either on the door or the wall behind it; either the weapon was a collapsible impact staple, in which case you would surely have found the munitions by now, or our unfortunate friend was not shot here. Secondly, the corpse was sat upright against this bookshelf here, is that correct?" Cabot asked.

"Yes sir, but I hardly—"

"If you sit down while drunk against a bookshelf you invariably have a hard time keeping yourself upright. Now, having never been shot to death myself, I can only imagine that the dizziness and disorientation that comes with such an event as losing several pints of blood is comparable, and yet our gentleman was perfectly upright."

"You believe that he was propped up by the attacker? Why?"

"So that he could be shot, of course."

"Why not on the doorstep then?"

"Because the staple gun is, whilst a relatively quiet weapon, not completely silent, and hence if you don't want anybody to notice you shooting you do it indoors. Also, those two shots as you described them were accurate; take out your pistol."

The officer did so, offering it to Cabot.

"No, no; keep it by your side," Cabot told him. "Okay, so you're standing there with your gun in your hand, now— *point the gun at me!*" He snapped the order and the man hesitated, eventually bringing the gun up, but his hand was still shaking.

"If you wanted to kill me, you just missed your chance; even if I was slow enough in my reflexes for you to shoot me, the shots would never have been as accurate as two shots through the breastbone. Our man tried the front door, but it didn't work. They then found another entrance, but the man was already on his way downstairs; he subdued him, most likely with a Taser as you noticed no trauma, and then he propped him up against this bookshelf and shot him twice."

"Very neat."

"Except for waking up the victim, yes; I expect the plan would have been to shoot him while he was in bed. The door, fortunately, was made of stouter stuff than our suspect expected."

"Not fortunately enough for Hobson though, sir."

"Well quite. I have three more of these scenes to look at this afternoon; you have my authorisation to begin looking for new evidence. Make sure everything gets bagged and sent to the lab; write a report and send it to *me* not to the Guard Headquarters, okay?"

"Yes sir; have a good day, sir."

"Not gonna happen..."

Cabot began to walk back to his bike when a thought crossed his mind. The man had said something before, something that had seemed out of place at the time but which he had forgotten.

"What do you mean *girlfriend*?" he asked, turning back.

"Sir?"

"You said girlfriend as if you had your doubts; you think she was something more?"

"No sir; something less. The girl is known to be..." the officer took a few steps towards Liam and spoke quietly so nobody could hear him. "A lady of negotiable affection."

"And you didn't take her into custody because..."

"It's not a crime, sir; the law doesn't ban such activities, and the Senate merely frowns upon it."

"Ah yes, of course." Cabot nodded. "I keep forgetting our legal system is a piece of crap," he muttered to himself and climbed onto the bike. "I'll probably be around again."

"We'll still be here like as not, sir."

Cabot kicked the bike into motion and tore off.

♦

The second murder scene was quite a change from the first. He parked the bike in the car park of Evolution, one of the very few clubs in Bristol still running, and stepped inside. The lower floor of the club was still preparing for tonight's flow of consumers; the people of the PFS being so used to death and destruction as the various conflicts had raged on their doorsteps that a murder would barely put a dent in the clientèle of a club.

"We're not open till six."

Cabot sighed as he took out his wallet; while there was a distinct cool-factor in not wearing the uniform assigned him by the Senate, there were times when it would be nice not to go through all of this.

"I'm Colonel Liam Cabot of the Civilian Guard; I'm here about the murder."

"Your bloody people have been here all morning, busy-bodying about; they even threatened to shut down my club!"

"Well sir, murder is a serious crime. I can assure you we won't be taking up any more of your time than absolutely necessary; we would hate to damage the business of one of the Society's most respectable entrepreneurs."

"Well good." The owner seemed contented by this. "The body's still upstairs."

"I'd just like to ask you a few questions before I go up, if you don't mind?"

"Certainly, what do you need?"

"Was the victim a regular of the club?"

"Yeah, I guess you could say that; was in here twice a week. Nice guy. Shaun, his name was, Shaun Clarkson,"

"And did Mister Clarkson have any enemies that you knew of?"

"Not that I knew; decent enough bloke, a bit obsessed with his own image, but who isn't these days?"

"Quite; who was working last night, on your staff?"

The owner began to list the people there the previous night. Cabot caught a glimpse of movement in the kitchen and turned. A girl with tanned skin and black hair stood there, staring at him. Cabot blinked, and the girl was gone, nothing more than a memory.

"Who was that girl?" Cabot asked, interrupting the owner.

"What girl?"

"The one in the kitchen, dammit."

"There was no girl in the kitchen, Colonel; only myself and my bouncer are here at the moment, and he's in the cellar."

"Alright." Cabot shook himself. "I must just be imagining it. The job does that to you after a while; you start jumping at shadows."

"I know how you feel."

No you don't, Cabot thought.

"I'm going to go upstairs to check out the crime scene; thank you for your help sir."

"Just doing my civic duty, Colonel."

"Of course; if you think of anything that might be important, anything at all, don't hesitate to call me on this number." He produced a business card and handed it to the man.

"Okay, Colonel."

Cabot made his way up the stairs to the lounge area. The large room was furnished with a lot of soft silver sofas and three strobe lights were hung from a rig on the ceiling.

"Somebody, what've we got?" Cabot asked the crime team present.

"Victim's white, early twenties, death by repeated stab wounds to the torso and face," a sergeant spoke up.

"When you say repeated—"

"About thirty, sir; this was an attack of some savagery."

Cabot nodded. The cushions of one sofa were torn from repeated strikes, presumably from the murder weapon, and were stained red, as was a large area of the ceiling.

"Can we be sure it wasn't just an amateur with a chainsaw?"

"Yes, sir; we've found the murder weapon, a kitchen knife, heavily sharpened, which I guess is good for the victim, but it could be found in any home."

"Killer; male, female?"

"By the looks of the wounds, probably male, but a strong woman could have done it."

"Ah, so our suspect is a human being?"

"Who owns a fairly generic kitchen knife."

"An open and shut case then?"

"There's another puzzle, sir."

"Oh good, another one; what is it?"

"There's only one way into this room, and everybody's searched for weapons on their way in; even our weapons were taken, so how did a kitchen knife get all the way up here?"

"The kitchen, perhaps?"

"That's what I thought, but I already checked; they use a different type of knife from the murder weapon."

"Oh, goodie."

"It could be the Invisible Man," the sergeant suggested.

"Of course, yes, that makes perfect sense," Cabot responded dryly, but a voice in the back of his head coughed gently.

"I still have two other murder scenes to check out; I want your report in the scene on my desk within two hours."

"Certainly, sir."

The officers in the room saluted and Cabot left.

♦

Cabot exited the club and instead of getting on his bike took a walk along the side of the river. Ducks quacked at him from below, having come to associate pensively walking humans with food. He looked down at them and reached into the recesses of his mind. He closed his eyes, scrunching them up with concentration, and opened them again. The ducks scattered, flying away from him, and he heard the alien voice in his head offering advice.

Invisibility isn't entirely impossible, you know, his reflection spoke back to him.

"No, it's not, but those who practice it are long since dead."

Mendelson?

"She wasn't good enough—"

Six years ago, maybe; but what about now?

"You think she stayed out of my way for six years and now decided to go on a modest killing spree?"

That's for you to decide...

The voice fell silent, and Cabot knew that it would offer no more illumination on this subject.

5

"Good morning, apprentices."

The twenty young hopefuls, selected from the cream of that year's classes at the Civilian Guard and army training schools, stood around the edges of Cooke Hall's dojo, a large room with weapons racks on the walls and bamboo flooring; one of the additions Cooke had made to his ancestral home since the war.

"Today," Bishop continued, standing in the centre of them, her lab coat exchanged for a more comfortable tracksuit, and her long auburn hair tied into a tight bob to keep it out of her face, "you will be learning self defence. This may seem like a somewhat weedy subject, given that your training includes the use of a sword, among other weapons, and five hours a week of Kung Fu with Master McInnes, but I warn you now; this is far from an easy course."

The apprentices remained silent, but Bishop knew from experience that they didn't believe her. It mattered little to her; they would soon learn their error.

"It is at this point that we identify the two apprentices making the most progress so far in their martial training;

now, bear in mind that this is by no means definitive, but it is an indication of who we believe to be training hard enough, and who we do not."

This bought about an ambience of anxiety in the room as the apprentices waited for the announcement; the competition among them for the two positions as fully-fledged Engineers was fierce.

"Killian McBride and Daniel Carter," Bishop announced without any great ceremony. "You will therefore have the unrivalled joy of assisting me in this lesson."

The two lucky apprentices, confidence buoyed by their success, stepped forward.

"Mr McBride; you go first. Your goal is to land a blow on me," she ordered him, and, still confident, he moved forward, pivoting on one foot and bringing the other around in a high roundhouse kick.

Bishop's arm jutted out suddenly, blocking the blow around McBride's shin. To the watching apprentices, it looked like barely a tap, but the blow rang through his leg, spinning him around, so fast that he was only just able to keep his balance.

He moved forward again, swinging out with his fist. With one hand, she caught his arm just above the wrist, and with her other hand, knocked him to the ground.

"Mr Barton." She nodded to the second apprentice, who ran forward and jumped into a flying kick. Bishop dodged the kick and struck him with the back of one hand. Carter hit the ground and rolled, bouncing a little way before halting, aware that he had just been tossed across the room like a doll.

"Nice try, gentlemen." Master McInnes stood in the doorway, then turned to address the other apprentices. "In future, I expect you'll all think twice before sniggering at Doctor Bishop. I hope you all enjoyed the demonstration, but remember combat is only one section of the trials. You must complete the trial by fire, in which you must fight a partner determined by us; the trial by steel, in which you must create your own sword; and the lengthy written examination to fulfill all of the requirements of this course. You are dismissed to go practice."

The apprentices ran out, leaving Carter and McBride left in the room together.

"Nice try," McBride congratulated Carter, "she's bloody quick though..."

"Yeah; think how good McInnes must be."

They pondered this for a moment.

"Do you think we'll ever be that good?" Carter asked.

"Well, we seem to be doing alright in the training program, so hopefully someday."

"So, what do we do in the meantime?"

"Well, we could get drunk..."

The two of them looked at each other for a second. "I'll get Annie, you go request funds."

"Got it."

They both darted from the room. Dan ran into the library, finding Doctor Bishop and Master McInnes sitting at their chessboard again, their original game not yet finished.

"Master," Carter gave a stiff bow as he approached the table. "McBride and I intend to go into Bristol for the evening, sir; we request transportation and access to the safe to retrieve some of our money."

"You don't want to be wasting your money on drinking, Mister Carter."

Carter took a deep breath, preparing to launch into a defense of his plans, when McInnes reached into his pocket. The master produced a brown envelope, took a brief look inside, and threw it to the apprentice.

"That's two hundred pounds," he told Carter and threw a

ball of metal at him which Carter recognized well: McInnes'
car keyring. "Take the Aston or the Jag; the Merc needs its
oil changing. Bring it back in one piece."

"Uh, Master; may I ask why we have been afforded these?
Have we done anything to deserve them?" Carter's mind
raced as he tried to work out what was going on, as even
Doctor Bishop, who was usually relatively in tune with
McInnes' thoughts ,was looking decidedly confused.

"No, just you've been working hard, and the training will
get harder from here on in; it's a good time wind down.
Have fun at Evolution."

Carter's eyebrows lowered as he frowned, then rose as
realization dawned.

"Of course, sir, thank you, sir."

He backed out of the room, bowing as he went, and
re-entered the foyer where McBride and Davies were
waiting.

"Did you get permission?" McBride asked as he
straightened his tie in the mirror beside him.

"Slightly more than permission." Carter held up his hand
and McBride turned sharply at as the keys clanged together.

"You got the keys to the Aston?"

"I got the keys to the Aston," Carter repeated. "We're
going to Evolution, and we have two hundred pounds to
spend; also compliments of the good Master McInnes..."

McBride's grin didn't sink at all as he realized what was
being asked of him. "He wants us to look around in case
there's another murder?" he asked.

"Looks that way."

"So we get to drive the cool car, go to a club, paid for
entirely by the WTDD, and there's a possibility of a fight to
the death?"

"That pretty much covers it, yes."

"Let's go then."

They stalked through the corridors, side by side, confident, walking past other apprentices training in the gym and a few of the doctors still up burning the midnight oil on their weapons projects, until they reached the door to the garage. McBride and Carter pushed open the door and stepped inside, Davies following close behind.

The garage housed around thirty cars, a modest collection of vehicles, from bikes to minibuses and Jeeps, but on the far side of the garage were McInnes and Bishop's cars, as the ranking members of the WTDD and the major beneficiary of Cooke's will.

McInnes owned three cars, an Aston Martin DB7 Vanquish, an X-Type Jaguar, and a large custom-built Mercedes, whereas Bishop's parking spaces held her Audi TT, Porsche Boxter and her bike, the same model as Cabot's, only white in the place of his red.

They crossed quickly to the coat stands beside the cars and took their identical black leather trench-coats from the pegs, throwing them on and feeling the reassuring bulk of their concealed pistols sitting inside webbing.

"I'm driving on the way there." Carter slid onto the leather seat behind the car's steering wheel and turned the key in the ignition. The car's engine roared into life and Carter pushed the button mounted on the dashboard to open the garage door in front of them.

The door rose into the roof as McBride and Davies climbed in, McBride in the passenger seat and Davies dejectedly taking the backseat, aware that she had just been usurped by a large piece of metal.

♦

McBride, Carter and Davies got out of the car and made their way to the club's entrance, oozing confidence.

"Sirs, we'll need to search you for weapons." The two security guards on the door, large men with shaved heads and black glasses, looked down at the three apprentices.

"Actually, no." McBride produced his wallet and flicked it open, showing the card identifying him as a member of the WTDD and licensed to carry weapons regardless of other legislative stipulations.

"I'm sorry sir; go right in."

"Thank you." The three apprentices exchanged grins as they stepped into the club.

Strobe lights and lasers darted around the club, disrupting the darkness only slightly as Carter and McBride peered around the room. The club was crowded, as always, and the three of them made their way to the bar through the throng of bodies.

McBride ordered drinks and leaned against the side, surprised to find himself looking straight at Liam Cabot.

"Cabot's here..."

Cabot saw a familiar figure in the crowd and walked towards it, stopping behind his quarry and tapping her on the shoulder.

"Sergeant Mendelson."

The girl turned and froze, mid snarl.

"Liam!" she smiled. "Long time no see!"

"Is that a fact?" He tilted his head slightly. "It wasn't you here earlier?"

"Well, okay, it was; I was just checking out the murder scene. I'd been here the previous night and I wasn't sure if... I thought there might be something I could do."

"Was there?"

"Not really; whoever did this was a pro," Rose Mendelson was silent for a second, thinking to herself. "Chiswick's been doing a lot of things lately I disapprove of; I thought he might have had a hand in this."

"Are you convinced otherwise?"

"Not entirely; not after Winter was visited by two SS agents last night."

"SS agents?"

"Evans and Jameson; they were sent to see Winter after he was attacked."

"Oh, thank you for telling me—"

There was shriek of horror from a few meters away and Cabot turned to see the crowd parting. A figure in black robes was making for the door, barging through those spectators who had not moved.

"Shit." Cabot pushed aside the man in front of him, forcing his way forward. A girl was lying in a pool of blood, a black knife sticking from her chest. "Stop that man!" Cabot cried, making to pursue, barging through partiers. He looked behind him and saw Mendelson following him.

"Someone's been killed," McBride told Carter. "Let's go."

"It's too crowded; we'll never catch them." Carter looked across the room full of panicking clubbers, all too stunned to get out of the way quickly.

"That's not the right kinda attitude, Dan." McBride reached inside his trench-coat and drew two pistols, pointing them at the nearest people to him.

"WTDD! Let me through!" he bellowed and people sprang apart to get out of his way. The two apprentices,

Carter's guns now drawn too, ran through the gap in the crowd, following Cabot.

♦

Cabot leapt onto a bin and from there onto the roof, his own pistol in his right hand. His quarry was twenty meters ahead of him, wearing black on a dark night, and Cabot didn't want to risk shooting and missing. The man leapt from one roof to another and Cabot followed, feeling that he was catching up.

Carter and McBride sprinted through the streets below, looking up at the rooftop chase as it unfolded, planning their strike.

"He's cutting left," McBride announced and made for a fire escape, landing atop the first horizontal railing and carrying on up the ladder. Carter followed him up, snatching the railing and swinging himself over in a single move.

Cabot was behind the two apprentices now, looking on as they both fired their pistols at the running figure in front of them. He sighed. Apprentices were so headstrong; had he ever been like that? Yes, he remembered, and he still was. He leapt the next roof and a second cloaked figure came at him from the dark.

He used his pistol, swung across the body, to deflect the knife veering toward his abdomen, and fired two shots towards his assailant, who contorted, somehow avoiding both staples, and palmed Cabot in the chest, hurling him across the gap between two buildings.

McBride looked back at Cabot's yell and turned, firing both pistols at his cloaked assailant as he dashed towards it, emptying both clips in the second before he got there. Another figure, an unhooded girl in a white robe, appeared in front of him—presumably having leapt up from the alley below—and struck out at him.

He caught the fist in his palm but fell to the floor, his hand burning as if on fire. The girl seemed illuminated, despite the dark, as she looked down at him.

Carter caught his quarry, leaping between buildings at the same time as the target and landing, reaching out one hand and placing it on the shoulder of the robed figure.

"That's quite enough of that."

The shape within the robe changed, shrinking into a more feminine form, and it turned, hood flying back to reveal the face of a woman of nineteen, black hair flowing down into the rest of the robe and a pale, melancholy face. The eyes flashed, though illuminated by no external source, and she seized Dan by the arms, throwing him backwards, into the alleyway below.

The girl reached down, her palm hovering a few inches from McBride's forehead and his fear of her now gone. If she had wanted to kill him he would be dead already, he knew.

"I am sorry," she said, and extended her index finger to meet his forehead. "This gift was not meant for you—"

She stepped back suddenly, an arrow having pierced her arm. She looked over at the black-cloaked figure, then stepped back off of the building, into the alleyway.

♦

Apprentices, woken by the commotion downstairs, got out of bed and made their way to the Hall's foyer, anxious to find out what the Civilian Guard van had dropped off outside.

By the time they had arrived, Master McInnes and Doctor Bishop were looking at the three people laid on their porch, and Davies was standing to one side being comforted by Doctor Sofia Lyons.

"Get these three to the infirmary immediately. Mister Mason, take Annie to the kitchen and make her some cocoa," McInnes ordered and six apprentices moved forward, two carrying each of Carter, McBride and Cabot into the main building and along the corridor to the infirmary.

The three of them were rigged up to a series of monitors displaying their vital signs and other bits of information impossible for the apprentices to decipher. Cooke appeared beside Carter's bed and blinked at the screen a few times, changing the data being shown.

"Terry, take a look at this."

McInnes came to Carter's screen and looked at it.

"It's an EMF diagram for Liam, James."

"No, Terry; it's for Dan."

"He's..."

"Yes, Terry; he's..."

McInnes turned, facing the crowded room. "Everybody out below Council level!" he bellowed and the others left quickly, though reluctantly, to return to their beds, leaving just McInnes and Bishop standing with the three unconscious men and the hologram.

"Siobhan; Dan's electromagnetic field has changed. It's at the same level and frequency as yours and Liam's."

Bishop was silent for a moment, knowing what this could mean.

"Call Gary," McInnes instructed her. "He'll want to be here for this."

"He has no experience dealing with this, Terry. We've concealed this from him for this long, we may as well continue until we're sure what it means," Bishop argued.

"I think it's obvious what it means," Cooke interjected. "Somebody like Lucy is at play, and may possibly be the murderer Liam is after. The Council must be warned; Michael may be able to stop it."

"We have no evidence of that: we have no evidence that Lucy caused this in the first place, it may simply have been a coincidence that she was around at the same time as we contracted the problem!" Bishop replied. "We need to keep this the way it's always been; quiet. If Chiswick got hold of this, if he knew what we'd been hiding, he'd go spare."

"Alright, we keep it secret, but let's check to see if anything else has happened."

Bishop nodded, went to McBride's screen and tapped the buttons. "That's odd..."

"What is?" McInnes went to the screen.

"Killian's EMF is completely changed; it's unlike anything I've seen."

Cooke peered over her shoulder. "I've seen it before."

"What does it mean?"

"I don't know. That in itself should worry you—move Dan and Liam to rooms upstairs, I'll sit with Killian."

"What's going—" Bishop began.

"Go, take them and stay with them; see that they aren't disturbed. Dan'll need you when he wakes up."

McInnes nodded to Bishop and the two of them wheeled the gurneys the boys were on through the halls.

Cooke looked at the wave pattern on the screen. It was different to the one he knew, the one that he himself had been plagued with carrying before his death, but it followed the same kind of form, complex fractal patterns existing within a series of seemingly random fluctuations of the electromagnetic field.

"How is he?" an oddly familiar voice asked. He turned to face a figure, a girl in white, strangely illuminated, as if the lights hitting her were somehow different from those hitting everything else.

"And you are?"

"Oh, the many inconveniences of erasing your memory," she sighed and waved a hand at him. Suddenly, he knew who she was.

"Eleanor; you've returned?"

"Yes, I've returned," she smiled. "The boy; how is he?"

"Stable; he fell from a building, and one of your guys touched him."

"I know." She paused guiltily for a second. "Me."

"Oh." He looked as if he was trying to decide whether to be angry or not, and then spoke again. "He'll be okay, physically, but as for mentally..."

"I know."

"Can you remove it from him?"

The girl shook her head sadly.

"Why not? You removed it from Gray."

"He was not meant to have it: it was orchestrated by Lucy rather than by us. I'm not even sure if I can, let alone whether I should."

"Then we have to train him; he'll succeed me one day?"

"Yes. You must train him; Terry won't understand."

"Very well. I'll need more than I have though; even what you gave me last time won't get me out of my current predicament."

"So be it. This is bordering on the extremely illegal, but..."

She extended her hand and he placed the holographic form of his just next to it, their fingertips touching. He felt, despite the absence of any glands or nerves, the energy flow into him. The very building blocks of life; this energy was power beyond measure, surging through him, taking on form...

♦

McBride's head swam with arguments, battles of consciousness and will. The part he dimly recognized as himself was young, younger than he had ever realized before, and he was fighting an enemy infinitely older, wiser and more subtle than he could ever dream.

He jerked awake, snapping upright in a moment and snatching a scalpel from a nearby table in a single motion. He saw the girl standing a few meters from him and threw the scalpel at her.

He swung himself off of the bed, reaching for a pistol that wasn't there and looking around.

"Where am I?" he asked, staring blearily at Cooke.

"You are home, Killian; you're in the infirmary at the Hall."

Killian saw the girl, standing with the blade embedded in her ribs. She took the handle genteelly between two fingers and pulled it from her chest, the wound and the hole in her robe closing up instantly behind it.

"What is she doing here?" he asked, spinning and pointing an accusatory finger.

"She's here to help you—"

"She did this to me, didn't she? It burns my mind."

"I know, Killian; it will subside. For the time being I recommend you be still before you burst a blood vessel."

"Okay." He sat down on the gurney. "Now will you explain what's going on? She attacked me, I'm not so addled as to forget that."

"I was trying to defend you," Ellie told him calmly.

"That's hard to believe."

"Had you fought them I have no doubt you would be dead right now."

"I could have taken them. Who are you anyway?"

"Her name is Eleanor Giles. I fought alongside her in the battle for house three."

"House Three?"

"One of the bloodiest battles of the war; a hundred of us were surrounded by ten thousand troops. We couldn't retreat, or the entire army would be doomed. We held them as long as we could, ultimately destroying the building and buying Walsh enough time to muster a defence, but the cost was immense. Lord Stanford, Terry and I were the only survivors."

"But if you were the only survivors, doesn't that make her..."

"Dead? Yes. I don't know how to explain this to you..." Cooke trailed off, then began to tell the apprentice what he could. "You've got a disorder, an extremely potent psychological one. You can hear the voices now, feel them in your mind; they are you but not you. They get easier with time, I promise you: it's possible you're talking to an angel right now, but it's possible you're hallucinating the whole thing, or maybe a mix of the two."

"So it could be a dream?"

"No. You're definitely awake."

McBride's eyebrows creased. "So I might be hallucinating, or this might actually be happening, but I'm not dreaming?"

"Yes. All you really have to know is that she's here to help you; regardless of whether or not she's real she knows a lot."

"No doubt." McBride blinked, his focus consumed with fire once more, and when he opened his eyes, Ellie was gone.

"What—"

"That's up to you to decide; I never came to much of a conclusion on that myself."

"Right."

♦

"This doesn't entirely make sense to me."

Carter was talking to Bishop, three floors up. "You're telling me I've now got some psychological disorder, maybe because of a fight, maybe not, and that I have to live with it because there's no cure, and I can't tell anyone because it's a deadly secret."

"Yes."

"Why?"

"Which bit?"

"If I knew that it'd be a start," Carter sighed. "I think I need a drink."

♦

McInnes, Bishop and Cabot arrived in Cooke's study at four AM, having just put Carter back to bed.

"What's wrong with McBride?" Bishop asked, taking a comfortable armchair.

"He'll be okay. Carter?"

"He's got the same as us; he'll be fine, Siobhan will take him as an apprentice. He's guaranteed a place now, we can't let someone with our curse out into the world, it could be horrific."

"Yes," Cooke paused. "I think it's best if I take over the tutelage of McBride after his trials."

"You? It's hardly as if you can actually teach anybody; you can't even touch a sword!" Cabot remarked jokingly. In answer, Cooke leant over to a rack on the wall and drew the sword resting on it from its sheath.

"Uh—" McInnes rose from his chair, drawing his pistol by reflex.

"You like?" Cooke smiled. "It's an android, I've been working on the designs for three years and it's finally complete; all I had to do was transfer my programme into it." Cooke lied; he had constructed it over the course of the previous fifteen minutes, using the knowledge Eleanor had given him in the infirmary.

"What's it made of?" Cabot walked around Cooke, peering intently at it.

"Adamantium, mostly; I've appropriated some from various sources."

"How much have you appropriated, James?" McInnes had been around for quite a while, and had known Cooke since long before the revolution, and had known the extent to which his old friend would bend the rules in the interest of scientific research.

"About three tonnes: the estimates are all wrong, by the way, there's about thirty in the Society now."

"And you have ten percent of it?"

"Yes."

"And what have you been doing with it?"

"Absolutely nothing." He looked at the disbelief in McInnes' eyes. "You have my word." He paused and smiled. "Though I fear we may have to start moving quite quickly with it."

"Why?"

Cooke picked up a piece of folded paper from his desk and handed it to McInnes, who opened it and read it.

"We've been summoned to the Council Chamber tomorrow," Cooke summarized the message.

"Summoned?"

"I suppose subpoenaed would be a better word."

"They want to ask us questions?"

"Yes, all of us; tomorrow afternoon."

"Then we'd better be there, I suppose."

6

Stanford awoke in his mansion, about two miles from the hall, as his alarm sounded at five AM. He looked groggily at the black box, read the time, hit the snooze button and rolled over.

Eventually he forced himself to get out of bed and got ready for the day. He emerged from the bathroom at six, fully dressed in a suit and jacket, and flicked open his mobile phone.

"Alan, it's Rob; send someone round with my files in about two hours, and cancel all my appointments this morning. I'm working from home today."

"Of course, my Lord; you know there's a Council meeting this afternoon, and Senator Thatcher has an appointment with you?"

"Call Thatcher, tell her to come to the mansion; I'll be at the Council meeting too. Is anything important enough to need me there?"

"No sir; we've got it covered."

"Excellent; keep up the good work." Stanford went downstairs. The house was empty, Emily in the NCC for an early meeting, and he had never had much truck with servants, though he had to admit that the odd one or two would be nice when you couldn't be bothered to make your own breakfast.

He sat down with a pot of coffee, a mug, and some of the files he had lying around his house, poring through the documents on military intelligence and promotions; his particular area of expertise as a former general.

♦

"Lord Stanford?" Senator Hannah Thatcher asked tentatively as she pushed open the door to Stanford's mansion. Putting her briefcase down by the door she progressed into the house. The huge staircase leading up the first floor loomed to her right as she looked around. On the wall frames were hung, each containing a picture of one or more of the Old Crowd, and centrally, above the fire and opposite the staircase, was a huge photo of Tom Walsh—founder of the PFS—taken the day the war with the teachers began, below which was hanging a sword.

The weapon was crude, a sword at its very basest; a sharpened bit of curved metal for killing people. It had once been Walsh's sword, made for him by McInnes before the war, and it had passed to Stanford when the General had fallen in battle on the last day of the war.

"Senator Thatcher."

She jumped, heart rate spiking at the noise, and turned to face Lord Stanford. The Society's leader was dressed casually in jeans and a black-and-blue patterned shirt. The Lord Protector wore no tie, carried no sign of office; he looked like any other man of his age.

"My Lord."

"Call me Rob, Senator; I am not Lord of the Senate, as Councillor Andrews so enjoys reminding me."

"But surely you are Lord of the Council of which she is a member?"

"As I so enjoy reminding Councillor Andrews."

"Besides, if you are not Lord to the Senate then surely I am not Senator to the Protectorship, and you should call me Hannah?"

"Excellent point Senator." He smiled and hugged her. "I have missed you, Hannah."

"And I you, Rob."

"How're things in the Senate? They keeping you busy on the committee for culture?" he asked, leading her through into the kitchen.

"Busy enough, I suppose. The others are still acting as though we've got to hate each other just because our views are different."

"Tell me about it." Stanford flicked the switch on the kettle to start the water boiling and Hannah genteelly took a stool. "There's an air about both branches that the other is the enemy, that we're supposed to be set at loggerheads, rather than working together for progress."

"There are many who believe so. On both sides," she said gently.

"Yes," Stanford took two mugs from the cupboard and put them on the work surface. "White, two sugars?" he asked.

"That's right; impressive recall, too. It must have been a year since we had coffee."

"Fourteen months," he told her. "My job requires me to remember an awful lot about everything I do or read, so the habit kinda sticks into my personal life." He poured the boiling water from the kettle into the mugs.

"What was this meeting about, by the way? Your secretary didn't say and personally I doubt it was because you wanted to chat about old times."

"The murders, of late; and the Executive Powers Bill," she told him. "Our branches have a history of not communicating; I wanted to come and see you about it to clear up what the hell is going on."

"I think, in that case, that we'd better skip the coffee and head straight outside." He led her out to the small stables adjoining the back of the house.

"Is this about the bill?" she asked, stroking the mane of a cream-coloured horse. "I didn't think there was going to be much new."

"This isn't about that." Stanford opened the door to one of the compartments and climbed onto a horse.

"Then what?" She mounted the horse she had been stroking and they rode out onto the grounds of the mansion.

"The murders."

"Oh," Hannah sighed. "You want Cabot to back off?" she asked.

"Quite the opposite!"

She looked at him quizzically.

"Not everyone in the Executive is dedicated to winning. Cabot has the full support of myself and of Cooke Hall, under my instruction. The army's investigation is moving very slowly for a reason, Hannah; I want it to be Cabot who finds the perpetrators."

"Then why is there a problem?"

"The autopsies will be inconclusive, they will yield no information about the criminals, and nobody will come forward. This was no crime of insanity or passion, we know that much."

"You think there is a connection between these crimes and the deaths of the senators before the Coup?"

"Yes."

"Is there any evidence to back this up?"

"No there isn't, but the SS are moving in secret, patrolling at night again, just like they did before the Coup. They think something's going to go down."

"This is classified information, isn't it?"

"Yes," he told her.

"You could get in trouble for telling me this?"

"I could go to jail for telling you this, but that clearly isn't going to happen."

"What do you want me to do?" she asked. "I don't see why you're asking me about this."

Stanford looked back at the house and drove his horse forward into a run.

Thatcher pulled at her reins, driving her own horse forward after him. She had once been a great rider, and quickly caught Stanford, despite her lack of practice. He had entered a small orchard, and a few leaves brushed against her as she caught up with him.

"So what's—"

She felt something hit her, painful at first, and then spreading into an all-consuming numbness.

Stanford looked back as the Taser strike knocked Thatcher from her horse and the animal slowed to a walk. He brought his own horse to a stop and slid from its back, drawing the pistol he kept in the rear of his jeans.

A knife hit the tree beside him and he looked at where it had come from; a female figure, halfway up a tree and dressed in camouflage, climbing higher. She leapt and hit the ground, about fifty metres from Stanford, and began to sprint away. He squinted down the barrel of his pistol and snapped off two shots, both flying just wide. He swore and put the pistol away.

"Hannah?" He crossed to where she lay on the ground.

"My Lord," she said wearily. "What happened?"

"Never mind that; are you alright?"

"I'll be okay, just a bit bruised. I'll live to fight another day."

"I'm glad to hear that," he smiled at her. "Can you walk?"

She sat up, slowly, and took a deep breath.

"Yeah, it seems to be wearing off quite quickly."

"It tends to." Stanford had been irritated by the speed with which assailants got back up after a Taser strike in training, and so had asked for his Taser, currently in his desk, to be modified to give it a little extra punch. "We're going to go back to the house, then I have a Council meeting, so I'll leave you with the guards. They'll look after you until you feel fit enough to go home, okay?"

"Okay, Rob."

♦

"Sorry I'm late." Stanford entered the Council committee room, the tables arrayed in a horseshoe facing the three Master Engineers sat in one corner. "I was attacked."

"You were attacked?" Ben asked with genuine shock. "By whom?"

"Don't know."

"Did your bodyguards not stop them?" Michael asked.

"They weren't there."

"Do you not have a panic button?" Michael spoke of the small black box on each of their belts which, when activated, summoned around a dozen bodyguards to them.

"Of course I do; don't be a cretin, Michael."

"Then why didn't you activate it?"

"I wasn't panicked." Stanford took his seat at the head of the table. "Ah, I see today we're interrogating the masters of the WTDD." He glanced at the top of his notes. "Who summoned them?"

"I did, sir," Michael spoke up.

"What a shock," Stanford muttered under his breath. "You may begin the questioning then, Colonel Chiswick."

"Master McInnes," the hologram began eagerly, and rose from his seat to walk around the table.

"Yes, Colonel?"

"There are a great number of people within military service who feel that the WTDD is peering over their shoulder the entire time, and that your lack of approval can be hazardous to their career. What do you think of that claim?"

"We provide weapons to every organization in the Society, Colonel Chiswick. We do not have any position greater than that, and to suggest that we peer over people's shoulders is to suggest that we have operatives who move covertly and who are not answerable to anyone; a task aptly performed by the SS, I believe," McInnes replied, calmly.

"Objection!" Ben cried. "The actions of the SS are not under investigation here; I demand that the mention of them be struck from the record."

"I'm going to allow it." Stanford nodded to the girl taking the minutes, who continued typing.

"Then I request that my request that it be struck from the minutes be struck from the minutes."

"No, I'm going to let that stay in too." Stanford smiled thinly. "Do continue with your questions, Colonel."

"With respect, my Lord, I do not believe that it is possible to continue my questions when they may all be directed back at myself, sir," Michael remarked, quietly.

"Yes; heaven forbid that the legal process be just and accountable," Johnson returned snidely.

"Strike the last two from the minutes," Stanford instructed the woman. "Continue, Michael, we don't have all day."

"Very well, sir." Michael looked at his notepad and flicked over a few pages. "I have but one remaining question then, my Lord, since your time is short."

Bishop and McInnes turned slightly to face Cooke, the android face a picture of serenity, revealing none of the emotions that must have existed beneath.

"Master Cooke."

"Colonel Chiswick." Cooke nodded to his counterpart, smiling slightly.

"You are, if I may say so, dead; is that correct?"

"Yes."

"And when you died your not inconsiderable funds were divided among a variety of different people; the beneficiaries in your will?"

Cooke nodded.

"That is correct?"

"Yes."

"There was quite a significant sum of money involved, I presume?"

"Yes."

"How great a sum of money?" Michael waited a second for the answer.

"Around two and a half billion pounds sterling, at the time; about three billion now, allowing for interest and inflation."

There was a hushed silence; other than Stanford and McInnes nobody knew just how rich the WTDD head had been.

"Divided between?"

"One hundred million for each of the Old Crowd, of which there are seven members, two hundred million to each of Terry, Siobhan, and Liam, thirty million to Tim, ten to you and your brother—that's about one-point-three-five billion thus far, if you're keeping track. Six hundred and fifty million to the WTDD, to keep them in business for a while, ten million to establish and maintain the Mortuary for Fallen Friends, one hundred million is set aside for the next two people to become doctors, and the remaining four hundred million is divided between about forty people, my friends."

"And for what reason were all of these people chosen?"

"They were important to me; I wanted to be sure they could be okay when I was gone."

"But you *aren't* gone, Master Cooke." Michael tilted his head. "You are looking very well indeed, and yet sums of money which are not insignificant, by any means, have been given, by you, to a great number of people in positions of some authority; the leader of the Democratic Party in the Senate, the head of the SS, the District Commissioner, the Chief Justice, the Lord Protector, the head of the Institute for Scientific Research and Discovery, two Colonels in the Civilian Guard, and the head of the Secret Service, to name but a few of the more prominent—is this correct?"

"Yes."

"It could be seen by some, if not by all, as a deliberate attempt on the part of the WTDD to manipulate, coerce or influence every branch of the Society's Government; what do you say to that, Mister Cooke?"

"Don't be so ridiculous, Michael."

"I don't think he is being ridiculous, James." Ben rose to his feet. "And you no longer sit on this Council so answer the damn question; what do you say?"

The lights of the building flickered slightly, then died completely.

"What's going on?" Ben asked, already on his feet, as the rest of the Council leapt up. Weapons were drawn hurriedly, the Council all being comrades-in-arms at one time or another.

"There's been a power cut," Michael said. "My generator is intact, everything else has gone down."

"The doors to the executive wing will be locked, as will those to this room; we'll be fine," McInnes said, having designed the building's security.

"I wouldn't guarantee that," Michael said. "I'm going to get help." The hologram vanished. The lights flickered on and a girl, covered by black bandages, stood in front of them.

"You have to get out of here," she said, "they are coming." She looked at the Engineers, winked, and vanished.

"Who was that?" Ben demanded as Cooke went to the door. "What are you doing?"

"Getting us out of here," Cooke said, trying the handle.

"The door is locked, and the lock is made of adamantium. As is the inner layer of the door, in fact."

"Let me handle that."

"Handle that? There is no handling; we're stuck in here, and I frankly don't have a problem with that. We're safer in here than out there if someone is coming to get us."

"I wouldn't be so sure." Cooke took a step away from the door.

"I told you it was too—"

The android struck the door with his right palm, tearing it from its mountings.

"Oh."

"Quite," Stanford stepped over the fallen door and out into the corridor, pistol in his hand.

"For the record I think we're inviting our own death," Chiswick announced as he followed them down the corridor. "I think shadowy figures in black can hardly be trusted as a reliable source of information."

"Yes Ben, but the SS are built into the constitution, there's nothing we can do about them," Rob replied. "Mary;

we're outside of the area now."

Sharp-Thomas took her mobile phone from her pocket, flicked it open, and dialed one of the speed-dial options.

"Colonel, This is General Sharp-Thomas, Authorisation Six Fifty-Two Monkeys. Initiate a lock down of NCC corridor Green Seven, section B." She paused, listening. "Certainly, hold on a second."

She threw the phone to Stanford, who held it to his ear.

"Ready? Authorise General Sharp-Thomas' order, Authorisation One Eighteen Peekaboo—thank you."

Stanford flicked the phone closed.

"Peekaboo?" Johnson asked.

"Would you have guessed it?"

"I guess not."

Behind them huge steel doors slid into place, locking down the area of the building they had been in.

"Steel?" Chiswick asked.

"Adamantium plated, yes."

"It should hold them, so long as they don't have any interesting tricks up their sleeves."

"My Lord..."

The Council turned to face McInnes.

"Has our purpose here been served, or would you like us to remain longer?"

"Remain!" Chiswick began to protest.

"Of course you may go, Master McInnes; thank you for your assistance, you are dismissed."

"Thank you, My Lord." McInnes walked away, making sure he was out of earshot before he issued his orders to Bishop.

"Find Mendelson."

♦

The apprentices, with wooden training swords—or bokkens—in hand, moved across the gym floor in unison, each making the same sweeps and strikes at their non-existent opponents at the same time. Kata training, as this was called, was one of the more boring aspects of the day, and Doctor Gary Mortimer, supervising them, knew it. Unfortunately mindless, unrelenting practice was part of the doctrine every Engineer had to live by if he wished to survive out in the real world, where the SS would more than happily pick a fight with anyone in a white lab coat.

Of course, the only thing less interesting than doing kata was watching others do it, flawlessly except for one or two mistakes on a few of the more complicated strikes, but the apprentices corrected their own errors, knowing exactly what they were supposed to be doing.

Mortimer's hand went into the pocket of his coat, the bottom of which had been cut out so that the hilt of his katana, strapped to the inside, could be accessed without opening the coat.

Something had piqued his interest—someone was moving quietly on the balcony above. They moved lightly, like an assassin, but there was no ill intent. No matter, trespassing on this land was punishable at the discretion of the senior Engineer present and for now that was him. He slid his hand down the katana's hilt gently, his eyes still focused on the apprentices as they span to perform the kata towards the other end of the hall.

His fingers found the small throwing knife, four inches long and a centimeter wide, concealed within the sword's scabbard, and he eased it out between thumb and forefinger.

He span, arm darting forwards and releasing the knife. It whistled through the air and he began to run for the stairs, not stopping to see if his throw was effective.

McBride and Carter looked at each other as Mortimer ran from the room, a powerful will rising in each of their minds, and nodded. They broke into a run and leapt onto the top bars of the weapons racks, then from there up the ten feet to the balcony, landing beside each other. They looked across at a girl in black robes, her face concealed by her hood.

"Can we help you?" McBride asked.

"I'm looking for McInnes," she hissed at them.

"He's not here right now—is there a message you'd like us to pass on?" Carter asked. There was burst of motion and the girl loosed Mortimer's knife at Carter.

Carter blinked. The tip of the knife was reverberating just in front of his nose, stuck through the side of McBride's bokken.

"Very good," the woman hissed again.

Mortimer ran up the stairs behind them, his katana drawn. The woman reached for the curved sword attached to her belt, McBride and Carter taking up stances. Both apprentices felt themselves take a back seat in their own bodies, some much more powerful consciousness seizing control.

The girl took a step away from the apprentices, her sword not yet drawn. "More Touched Ones?" She shouted something in a language none of them could understand and leapt off of the balcony, into the midst of the other apprentices.

The eighteen of them dashed in to fight her, swords swinging. She ducked the first sword coming at her, both hands heading for the boy's left hand side. One hand planted on the shoulder, the other swinging at his face, the shape within the robe changing, becoming taller and more muscular as it struck, breaking the apprentice's neck. The intruder span, palm-striking Dan Short and hurling him into the wall.

The doors to the gym burst open; McInnes, Bishop and Cooke ran in, lab coats billowing.

"Step aside." Cooke looked at the robed form as the apprentices parted before him. "Identify yourself, or I will kill you."

"Really? How can you kill someone who's already dead?" The robe changed shape again and she pushed back her hood.

"Lucy?" Bishop took a step back.

"Surprised?"

"Not unduly. What do you want?"

"The death of all those who opposed me. You were first, Cooke; you and your beloved Dalton. You will all fall, one by one, and now it's time for McInnes."

She leapt, drawing her sword; an ancient scimitar, Arabic engravings all along both sides. She glided for a few seconds, a picture of grace, until she bounced off a barrier; some invisible wall preventing her from getting any closer.

She staggered slightly, taken aback by this. "What sorcery is this, Cooke? You stopped me once before, but not like this."

Cooke shrugged and closed his eyes. "Go now Lucy, but be assured, I will hunt you down and kill you and all that support you."

Lucy put her hood back on. "I look forward to it." Her form changed and she leapt, over their heads and to the door.

"What was that?" Bishop asked. "She's not dead!"

"So it would seem," Cooke muttered. "Terry; you know what to do?"

"Of course."

"Then I'm going to speak to Annie. Say three hours?"

"Okay."

♦

Annie Davies had once been the girlfriend of William Cooke, heir to Cooke hall, and while he had only wanted her for one thing, she had loved him, and still occupied the room the two of them had shared after the Revolution.

She sat on the edge of her bed in a dressing gown watching TV as the door opened. The TV blinked into darkness and she smiled, not turning around.

"Hello, James."

"Hey." He sat down beside her. "One of the apprentices has just been killed, I thought you might like to know."

"Oh. Which one?"

"Jackson."

"I didn't know him that well. Still, a terrible shame; who killed him?"

"Lucy."

"From the Faction War?"

"Yes."

"I thought she was dead?"

"So did everyone. She hasn't aged a day though; it's very mysterious."

There was a knock at the door and Cooke turned to it.

"Come in," Davies shouted and Carter and McBride entered.

"Master McInnes sent us up to see you, sir; he said you might want to ask a few questions."

Cooke tilted his head, not understanding, and caught the look in their eyes. "You fought her?"

"Sort of."

"Okay. Annie, I'll come speak to you again later. Will you be okay for now?"

"I'll be fine, don't worry."

The three men left the room.

"What happened?" Cooke asked once they were in the corridor.

"We saw Doctor Mortimer heading for the balcony and went up there. When we got to her she said she was looking for Master McInnes, sir, then she threw a knife at us, which Killian blocked with his sword, and she leapt into the crowd, and killed Jackson."

"Okay, there are a number of things you missed there, Mister Carter, so I'm going to ask you some more questions."

"Go ahead."

"How did you get onto the balcony?"

"We, uh, jumped, from on top of the weapons stands."

"The barrier must be ten feet up from there, Daniel; you'd have to jump twelve feet to be able to get a handhold. Does this not seem at all odd to you?"

"We had been seized sir, the recessive parts of our personality you and Doctor Bishop warned us about."

"Before Lucy jumped she said something about 'Touched Ones', and something I couldn't understand; she seemed to know what had happened to us," McBride reported. "What is she?"

"I don't know," Cooke told them. "But she will have to be held accountable. We'll be meeting in about two and a half hours in the great hall; I'd recommend being there. This is a secret; don't let anyone else know, not even Annie."

"Okay sir; what shall we do until then?"

"Your time is your own, but don't leave the house."

◆

Thick black smoke poured from the side of the NCC; smashed glass lay across the ground. Who planted the bomb was uncertain, its exact nature as well, but where it had been and what it had been for were guaranteed.

An attack had been made upon the NCC and the Council, their meeting chamber destroyed by the bomb hidden under the floorboards. The shockwave had been stopped by the lock down barriers, but several rooms had been gutted and three innocent people killed in the blast. Stanford was in his office, surrounded by security guards and aides trying to convince him to go home.

"The Society hasn't ground to a halt, so we can't either," he told Empter as he picked up another of the folders that had accumulated during his morning off.

"With respect, sir, we have no idea what's going on or who is trying to kill you or why; nothing's making any sense and we can protect you a lot easier at the mansion than here. Take the paperwork with you if you want, sir, but we need to get you out of here. At least until the bomb squad has finished checking everything over."

"Oh, all right." Stanford got up. "Ellie!" he shouted and his secretary dashed in.

"I'm going home for the day; you're done here, okay?"

"Thank you, my Lord. I'll see you tomorrow?"

"Certainly."

She curtsied and then left the room.

"Okay; Captain Delaney, have your men move him out to the mansion and secure the place. I want guards everywhere and all the security measures triple checked, got that?"

"Yes, sir."

♦

Tim Greenwood found himself wandering the halls of the Senate building aimlessly. He wore a navy-blue overcoat over his suit, his pistol slung on webbing inside. He regretted nothing more than having to wear a weapon, hated nothing more than their proliferation and those responsible for it; those members of the SS clever enough to reverse-engineer bits and pieces of the WTDD weaponry, and who had sold it on the black market to their informants who had, in turn, sold it on to even less friendly characters.

And so it was that he, Senator Greenwood, was forced, during times of need, to wear a gun in his coat, to protect him from the criminals who had been armed by the people who sent him the memo telling him to carry a gun to protect himself from the criminals. He sighed quietly, and carried on walking.

The Executive Powers Bill was scheduled for another vote in a month's time, and the debates were already going on, Senator Kant currently holding the floor in the chamber, according to the screens dotted around the building, providing information about goings-on.

"Hello Timmy," the cheerful, high pitched voice greeted Greenwood and he turned as Senator Thatcher collided with him, smiling. "Too bad about the vote, Timmy; better luck next time."

"If there is a next time."

She skipped off and he followed her, keeping pace with his long strides to her short, energetic ones.

"Of course there will be; you love this bill."

"Winter says I'll lose my job, and we have to ask if it's important enough to warrant that."

She was leading him outside, he knew; she always did. She pushed open the doors that led into the park and began to walk sensibly, taking on what she felt was an appropriate air of responsibility and respectability for a senator, but there was still a distinct spring in her step.

"Winter's an ass, Timmy; he's all boring and conservative and Conservative." She pronounced the capital letter on the second Conservative perfectly. "He'll never amount to anything like what you are, Timmy."

"He'll succeed me as leader of the party, Hannah; I've only got one term left, max."

"Don't be silly, Tim. Your position in the party isn't who or what you are. There's more to life than the Senate, than this Society and the seriously screwed up things it does to people."

"I don't understand what you're talking about, Hannah."

"Of course you don't." She looked mournful for a second. "It'll come with time, it always does." She skipped off a little way, down a side path between some bushes.

He followed her cautiously, into a small side garden, encircled by a ring of tall hedges, inside which a maze of paths created by flowers of all kinds grew, centred by a large circular bench, a statue in bronze standing in the very centre, looking over everyone who entered the garden.

"Tell me," Hannah seemed suddenly serious, "what do you see, as you look around this garden?"

"Bushes, flowers, a bench, a statue of the late Colonel Kensington; generally garden-like things. Why?"

"Do you not see it as a thing of beauty? There is so much life here, so much hope."

"Despite the garden commemorating a woman who tried to tear the Society apart."

"The actions of the person do not prevent a garden, or even a statue, being beautiful; a box is not shaped by its contents, after all."

"But humans are, Hannah."

There was a soft crunch on the path leading up to the garden and they both span from the argument, facing the newcomer.

He wore baggy trousers and a hooded fleece, making him out of place among the smart clothes of the Senate hall, compounded by his unkempt curly brown hair and vague smile.

"Senators, my apologies for disturbing you," he spoke calmly and held up his left arm. On this signal, a bird from one of the trees flew to his hand and stood there, placidly.

"What can we do for Senator Robinson today, Mister Gray?" Tim asked.

"I come not from my employer, but rather from he who is master and yet is not served; you are needed urgently, Senators."

"The Hall is calling?" Hannah asked.

"Yes, ma'am." Gray glanced at the bird and it flew off.

"Then we ride," Tim smiled, quietly removing his car keys from his pocket.

♦

Rose Mendelson stood in an alleyway a little way from the NCC, the smoke billowing from the side still visible to her as the firefighters struggled to extinguish the potassium-fueled blaze. She let her concentration lapse, becoming visible again, and began to walk down the alleyway. She was an assassin by trade, a sniper by calling, and the Council's best friend by choice. She threw the duffel bag containing her equipment into a dumpster as she walked.

Everything about her, from her confident striding walk to the calm, level tone of her voice, to the cool yet sexy way she dressed in a black suit, to the minuscule pistol contained within, seemed to scream SS to everybody in the know, and to be fair, she had once been one of those who walked in the shadows and claimed to be saving the Society.

But she had seen things, far too many things, that discredited and dishonoured the SS and its motives, and now she hid from their agents wherever they sought her, and undid as much of the evils they caused as she could.

"Sergeant Mendelson."

She turned, looking at the man now obscuring some of the limited light to come into this alleyway.

"Would you be so kind as to come with me?"

She drew her pistol, leaping towards the man and firing its two rounds. He leapt backward, landing two metres in front of her, two pistols of his own drawn.

She took a step toward him, her left arm flicking up to snatch the gun from his right hand. She span the gun on her hand, turning it on him as he struck back, snatching the gun back. Both of them moved rapidly, neither of their guns staying in their hands for much longer than a second before the other snapped it away.

A few shots fired into the walls of the alleyway and Mendelson focused, snatching a gun and completing the thought. She vanished and stepped to the right, pressing the gun against her assailant's forehead.

"Identify yourself," she instructed.

"Doctor Gary Mortimer; WTDD. I'm here at the request of Master McInnes; he wants you there."

"The Hall?" she asked.

"Yes."

She span the weapon so that the grip faced Mortimer and he took it from her.

"Then lead on, Doctor."

♦

McInnes' bedroom faced out towards the driveway of the Hall and he looked out over it as the area directly in front of the house filled with cars, each of which was slowly driven away by one of the apprentices.

"Master McInnes."

"Hello Kim." He lingered at the window, not turning into the room.

The woman stood in the doorway holding a clipboard nervously across her torso, her long auburn hair falling about her shoulders messily, as though she had just run up three flights of stairs—which was, of course, the case.

"What can I do you for?"

"Everybody's been summoned." Kim Horowicz spoke half in statement, half in question.

"Yes." McInnes' tone was level, his voice quiet as he spoke to her, one of only three of those under the protection of the Hall to be made so by himself, rather than by Cooke. "The Crowd are not coming, but the others will be."

"Thirty of us? Here? I thought we were supposed to be less than open about being friends with the Hall after Palmer."

George Palmer, a middle-level aide to one of the Liberal senators, had died two years ago. The autopsy had been largely nonspecific, cause of death being a blunt trauma, most likely sustained while having fallen from a three-storey roof into the river below.

It was ruled to be suicide, but there were those, mostly among the number gathering in the great hall below, who believed that the circumstances surrounding the death were less than innocent; that shadowy figures had struck him down for being under the protection of Cooke Hall.

"That was a long time ago, and now we may have bigger problems than death," McInnes said. "We're going to all be in this pretty deep."

Something about what this meant snagged in Horowicz's mind.

"Terry. We're all supposed to be in the hall by now, and

yet you still aren't even making the effort; what're you going to do?"

"You've always been good at reading people, Kim." He turned to face her now for the first time.

"I do get paid rather a lot of money to do so," the psychiatrist remarked.

"You should really get downstairs, Doctor Horowicz."

"Terry—"

"You don't want anything to do with this, believe me. It's probably best if you believe I'm downstairs in fact."

She looked into his eyes for a brief second before turning to leave.

"Just see to it you come back, okay?" she asked.

"Haven't failed to yet, have I?"

◆

As Horowicz entered the great hall the others were finding their seats around the huge dining table running straight down the centre of the room, and a large number of people were also filing out. The apprentices, for the most part, had provided everybody with drinks; they were now leaving, along with a lot of the doctors. Horowicz took a seat next to Senator Greenwood, whom she recognized from the papers, and poured herself a glass of water; her eyes, like everybody else's, fixed on the end of the table where Cooke sat quietly, hands held together.

He glanced up at the clock on the wall for a moment and then back down to the table, still silent and perfectly motionless.

In the compartment behind the clock, able to see but not be seen, McBride and Carter stood patiently, waiting for the talking to begin.

"My friends," Cooke spoke quietly, "never before have I

summoned you all here at the same time, and for good reason; this Hall, despite the friendship and protection it has afforded each of you, is not immune to the games played outside of its walls, and has garnered for itself—mostly due to my actions—a great number of enemies, most notably those within the SS, who are above no act of terrorism."

There was a general mutter of agreement from around the room and Cooke paused to allow it to subside before continuing.

"Lately, however, a greater threat has risen against us; Lucy is not, as we had so long hoped and believed, dead, but stands against us again. What her plans are we cannot yet be certain, as her very existence was only made clear to me a few hours ago, but we can be certain that her intentions are as they always have been; to destabilize the PFS and to destroy its fragile unity."

He paused for a moment, as if for effect, as his mind flew through the systems of the PFS mainframe, finding where it was needed and applying just the right pressure.

♦

McInnes stepped into the lift, Bishop and Lyons following him in. All three wore leather jackets, white as their lab coats but heavier and less identifying, given the situation.

"There will be eight guards," McInnes spoke authoritatively, "they will be armed with MK. 8 staple rifles, and that puts us through the door to the building. There will be five more officers between the entrance and what we are looking for, on the top floor; all will be armed with enough pistols to significantly slow us down, and we can't afford to let that happen. Don't stand still, not for even a second, or we will fail."

"What is it we're after?" Lyons asked as the lift ascended.

"That's not your concern; just worry about covering me," McInnes told her. "I don't want anyone dead, so Tasers only and no craziness." His eyes fixed on Bishop for a second before he continued, not long enough for Lyons to notice, but long enough for Bishop to get the message. "We're going to the fifth floor; the lift will work for us, if everything goes to plan, but we can't let them sound the alarm or no degree of skill will get us out of there alive."

"I'm not entirely certain I know what's going on," Lyons told him as Bishop silently checked through her weapons.

"None of us are, no-one on our side has ever known exactly what's going on; whoever or whatever gives Cooke instructions hides stuff from him, and he hides stuff from us —for our protection, I guess—and then we do what he says and so far we haven't died," Bishop responded.

"Except Palmer," Lyons reminded her.

"Yes, except for Palmer." Bishop looked down mournfully. "But that was an exception, and a lot more good has been done than bad, so we don't complain." She slid her two Tasers into the inside of her jacket and the lift doors opened.

They had ascended in the lift to the top of a hill, flattened out to form a concrete plateau, leading to a hemispherical white building directly in front of them.

"Sofia," Terry prompted softly and the doctor walked out of the lift, the other two keeping out of sight.

Lyons looked along the steel path to the building as the walkway led her towards the archway of the metal detectors. There were two guards behind her now, two more by the archway, and four more on the far side; the complex being about a hundred yards distant.

"What is this place, anyway?" Bishop asked as they waited, McInnes keeping an eye on Lyon's progress.

"This is the place the Society keeps its dark secrets; facts about the past that cannot be destroyed or undone, truths that we cannot forget but which are too dangerous to be free. It is such a truth we have come to retrieve for James. They call this place the Ark; it houses the Covenant Database, and is the only point from which the most heavily encrypted files can be accessed; files which reveal what darkness men are truly capable of." McInnes stopped as Lyons got to the metal detector and it pinged at her urgently, stopping the walkway with a slight jolt.

The guards moved quickly—part of the Secret Service, they answered to none but Stanford—and anybody who came here with metallic objects had no right to be here; they were to be killed. Guns were raised, the four guards nearest her holding her within the square they formed, and she closed her eyes for a moment. Why not Bishop? She was always so much better at this than Lyons was.

Two Tasers slid down the sleeves of her coat, into her hands as the boxes opened, firing shots at the two guards in front of her. The guards behind her fell, bands of Taser energy striking them as McInnes and Bishop sprinted down the path. On the far side of the archway the guards were reacting, two running down, firing rifles, and the other two making for the entrance to the building to sound the alarm.

McInnes and Lyons broke off, running at the two heading for the Engineers as staples flew around them, chipping the concrete. Bishop dashed down the centre of the plateau, holding fire with the Tasers as they were out of range. She reached into the back of her mind, letting herself slip, while keeping as much of a hold on the reins as possible as the darkness rose. McInnes looked on, swearing to himself, as Bishop leapt, gliding forty yards with a single jump and landing, firing Tasers at the two guards before they got through the door.

McInnes walked to the main entrance, knowing the guards inside couldn't see out, slipping the spent Taser batteries into his coat pocket. The door stood in front of him, solid white steel; he could not force it with anything short of a cannon, and he had none with him.

McInnes waited, staring at the door before him, waiting for a few moments before the door slid open, into an illuminated silver corridor, stretching into the building.

♦

"We can only assume that Lucy, and the organization she represents—either from being part of or leader of it—are out to do what they always have been; to destabilize the Society, to bring us into the eye of the forces that dwell outside our border. Such an occurrence would almost certainly bring about our demise."

Cooke paused again.

"You are the best and brightest of the Society, you have the greatest minds, the greatest physical ability, the greatest souls of anyone I have ever met, and I am honoured that you all return to me when I call, but this force rising against us may well be beyond my power to stop alone; it will require each and every one of us to stand against it, and I have to tell you that we may still fail and that some will almost inevitably die."

In this pause there was no restlessness from the others, sitting silently and waiting for Cooke—who seemed suddenly to be far older than ever before—to continue speaking.

"A great evil is rising; one we may be unable to hold, one that may tear us to shreds, but one which may be averted, if all of our people work together."

"With respect, James," Greenwood spoke up, "friends in this Society cannot pull together, let alone several departments and political parties."

"I know." Cooke sighed; something extremely difficult to do when considering that he wasn't actually breathing. "I need to speak with Chiswick—"

This time there was no silence, merely outcry.

"He cannot be trusted," Greenwood snapped.

"The Senator's right; he killed Palmer, he's still hiding so much from us over these murders, and the support he offers the Society is far less now than it ever has been," Cabot remarked.

"Things are getting worse, not better," Horowicz summed up, proud of her contribution.

"We must stop this. As much of a misguided bastard Chiswick is, he must understand what's going on; better than us perhaps. I believe he can be helped, convinced to save us."

"He won't listen to you." Mendelson stood up from where she had been sat at the end of the table, but the others could have sworn that she hadn't been there previously.

"Why not, Sergeant Mendelson?" Cooke asked, turning pensively to the girl.

"He's a stubborn, arrogant man; he will reach into your program and take from it everything he needs, everything he wants, and he will destroy those you support. He hates nothing more than this Hall, its power and its influence, and he will crush you in a second."

"He must be approached, Rose; we cannot let our resentments get the better of our desire to protect the Society."

"The Society is an idea that has been corrupted and mutilated by those who seek to improve their own standing."

"But an idea it remains, and a good one; one I have died to protect, Rose. I will confront Chiswick tomorrow."

"Very well. What would you have me do?"

"You have contacts who know what the SS are up to, or what they have been doing over the past few years?"

"Yes."

"I want you to find out from them what the hell's going on; why they're hiding so much from us and why they are being such a hindrance. Start tomorrow; you'd better stay here tonight. You'd all better had, actually."

◆

McInnes stepped through the door into the building, his walk becoming a sprint as he made for the lift, followed by Lyons and Bishop.

Lyons opened fire as a man poked his head around the corner, swatting him with the third Taser blast. McInnes carried on sprinting, holding his Tasers in front of him as he moved towards the lift. Bishop darted off down a side corridor towards the guard station while Lyons remained by the door, prepared to hold it open, should the need arise.

McInnes got to the lift; it wouldn't open without authorization from the guard station.

Bishop ran two steps along the wall, emptying her Tasers into the two guards outside the station. There was one left inside, turning to look at her with panic in his eyes; he raised his pistols and fired a burst at her. Bishop span, diving behind the wall. She knew he would be going for the alarm, the big red button in the corner of the room, but he would be moving cautiously, in case she leapt out. Not cautiously enough for her to reload her Tasers though. She slid her pistols from her coat and struck, cart-wheeling out as her staples sprayed across the room. She landed on her feet, finishing the clip in her right hand into the alarm box, neutralizing it. She stepped through the door; the man fired a staple over her shoulder and she broke the arm his gun was held in before rendering him unconscious with a swift kick to the head.

She went to the desk and flicked the switch to activate the lift before holstering her pistols again and leaving the decimated room.

McInnes stepped into the lift and pressed the button for the fifth floor, patiently checking his weapons as it rose. The doors opened into a single room, its roof curving to the top of the hemisphere. The entire room seemed to hum, like the noise made by a computer but amplified several thousand times so that it was extremely audible.

In front of him was a white desk, standing out against the chrome of the wall, like an altar; four objects sitting atop it. On the left was a key, fairly nondescript, but somehow important enough for it to warrant being placed within this building. On the right hand side of the desk was a large notebook, A3 in size, containing around five hundred sheets of thick paper, with a pink plastic cover. McInnes pocketed the key and took a black plastic bag from the webbing of his coat, flicking it open and inserting the book. He looked at the last two objects, occupying the centre of the table. One was a black stone, perfectly egg-shaped, polished, bearing no symbols. He snatched it up, not overly shocked to find it warm, despite the cool room, and dropped it gently into the bag.

The final object was wrapped in a case of purple velvet, that failed to conceal the long thin shape beneath as it balanced neatly on its stand. It was not to be removed by anyone but its rightful owner. McInnes paused, his hand hovering over the case for a moment, before he turned without taking it and stepped back into the lift.

♦

Piano music wafted through the corridors of the Hall, complex cadences intermingled with chords of beauteous simplicity. The music had no name, had most likely not been played before, and would most likely never be heard again. The grand piano in the great hall played on, the fingers of Tom Gray dancing across its keys.

"I've been meaning to learn how to do that for years." Cooke turned from the piano to face McBride. It was five PM and the apprentices were cooking the evening meal for the Hall's now much expanded array of residents, who were dispersed throughout the house, leaving the great hall free.

"Sir," McBride said.

"You can feel the darkness in the back of your mind?"

"Yes, sir."

"What does it look like?"

"Sir?" McBride's face contorted to one of confusion.

"You have been taught how to use the memory palace?"

"Yes, Master."

"Use it now."

McBride closed his eyes, delving into the recesses of his mind, running through the corridors of his memory palace; a medieval castle he had visited once when he was young, one that had stayed in his mind with details so perfect that he had been able, during his training, to put every other memory within a brick of the castle.

"What am I looking for?"

"Nothing; it will find you."

McBride looked around, still jogging along, and turn to face himself, dressed in grey, a sinister look on his face.

McBride sensed that this phantom was both himself and not himself; the dark fire he sensed fighting to seize his mind whenever he was alone, when he was weakest. He drew the sword attached to his belt.

His counterpart drew his own sword, practically identical to McBride's broadsword, only with a slightly darker tint in the metal. McBride swung, leaping forward, and the blade clanged heavily from his opponent's. He tried a few more strikes and the other man simply laughed as he parried them with ease. The sword would not avail him, McBride realized and turned, running as fast as he could through the corridors.

His eyes snapped open, unbidden, and he looked at Cooke.

"He's me?"

"A hybrid of yourself and Eleanor, yes."

"How is that possible?"

"We're not sure," Gray told him. "We have very little information on what happens; all that we know is that it does, and what its symptoms are. We know it's caused on some level by contact with someone like Ellie or Lucy, and that it appears to be transmittable from human to human when a Touched One is in contact with one of them—that's what happened to me eight years ago."

"You're a Touched One? I can't sense anything about you like I can with Doctor Bishop or Colonel Cabot."

Gray and Cooke tried to hide the glance they shot each other and Gray carried on.

"That's because I am no longer a Touched One; the darkness visited upon me by Lucy was removed by Ellie at the end of the Faction War."

"Removed? How?"

"I subdued him, then Eleanor took it from him," Cooke began to explain as much as he knew, "we don't know how.

She says she can't remove it from you though; whether that's because the darkness Tom had wasn't supposed to happen—wasn't part of the Path as she calls it—or whether it's because it was just a mirror of my own abilities rather than a true touching. We can't even remember properly what happened."

"You can't remember?" McBride questioned sarcastically. "I find that a little hard to believe."

"The memories of basically everyone involved were altered. Rob believes Danielle died raiding the Republican Special unit base, and that she killed Lucy; he has no memory of Eleanor, and no memory of Lucy's rather extraordinary ability. He wouldn't recognize the scimitar. His knowledge of the events, like everyone's—even Siobhan and the other Touched Ones—was changed."

"Then how can you remember any of it?"

"When she came back Eleanor returned my memory to what I have to believe was more or less its unaltered state, leaving a few gaps for things I'm not supposed to know."

McBride turned to face Gray. "Then how does—"

"For several months our minds were interlinked, what one thought the other became instantly aware of, making the battles of the Faction War alarmingly complex. While we no longer share the same level of connectedness, we are still linked in the effects of such things as is controlled by hardlight."

"'Hard light'?" McBride shook his head. "This is all going a little too fast; all this talk of Ellie and Lucy, the hint at the supernatural, at living theology, and now 'hard light', or some such thing? Can we slow down a little?"

"Certainly." Cooke and Gray backed away from McBride somewhat, Gray moving his mug of coffee from the piano onto the main table. "Where would you like to start?"

"Okay; 'hard light'. What is it?"

"In its most simple form, power."

"Care to elaborate?"

"During the Revolution I designed some quite interesting devices, including an energy shield, which was far more advanced than anything available outside, powered by a source of energy I found to be abundant and naturally occurring. It required a very fiddly and complex process to tap into, and once I had done so I was barely scratching the surface, but it was still more than enough to serve my purposes. The energy used, I learnt during my first encounter with the angels, was the energy that makes each of us each of us; the energy in the universe which essentially promotes everything staying in the form it's in right now, instead of a pile of carbon atoms; the energy that maintains gravity and also alters it—"

"The power of God, essentially?" McBride asked.

"If there is indeed a creator out there, monitoring us all and seeing to it that something happens, then it is through this energy that his work is done."

"*If* there is a god?" McBride asked. "There are dead people walking around, psychological shit being transferred by touch, energy shields and people jumping far too far for physics; what other possible explanation could there be? And that's before we even factor in the presence of bizarrely huge quantities of energy keeping everything in shape!"

"There may well be another explanation, but the belief in the divine does seem to be a lot more justified than before we knew all of this," Cooke confessed. "Now; this energy is lower in some objects than others, and hence changing things into other things becomes slightly easier depending on what they are made of."

"Are you telling me it's possible to turn something into something else?"

"It may well be—all I was able to do when I was alive was turn something into a pile of dust, or turn something into a lot of energy."

"You could do it? Not just Ellie?"

"Yes, I could do it."

"And you were Touched like I am, not like Dan is?"

"Yes; the others seem to have less advanced abilities, though it's possible they just haven't tapped into them out of fear of what will happen."

"But what you're saying," McBride stated emphatically, giving this some thought, "is that I can turn stuff into dust?"

"Well, yes."

"Me?"

"Yes, Mister McBride, you."

Gray span, pointing one finger at the clock on the wall, which obligingly crumbled. "And me, but I can't do it so easily; most of my power is gone now."

"How do I do it?" McBride asked.

"Okay, you have to remember it won't work on organic stuff, like people, or wood; there's too much energy in things which are or were alive. Stones, metal and ceramics, stuff like that, however, should be quite simple."

"So what do I do?" McBride asked impatiently.

"Well first, apprentice, be calm; we cannot have you bursting a blood vessel. If you strain yourself trying you will be no more likely to succeed than if you only push very gently."

McBride nodded, clearing his mind.

"Look at the mug in front of you."

He looked at the mug Gray had placed on the table.

"Now, that mug is made of atoms; you know this?"

McBride nodded again.

"Try to visualize the atoms of that mug, trillions of them, bonded together; can you visualize it?"

"Just about; it's a bit complex."

"It will be at first. Now; each of these atoms, each of these bonds, has energy pouring into it, forcing it to remain a mug, controlling its destiny."

"Yes."

"The energy is huge and intangible, but at the same time you know you can reach out and stop it, with your mind. Reach out; cut off the energy."

McBride felt himself extend one hand to point at the mug and felt the energy flow through him, energy he never knew he possessed, flowing from him and into the mug...

The mug exploded in a shower of ceramic and hot coffee, erupting towards the three men. Cooke held up one hand, holding the fragments still in mid air for a second, and then retracting them into the fully formed mug again, none of the cracks visible.

"Impressive," he remarked.

"Though not something you want to be doing too often. You can't do that kind of thing to metal, or to rocks; I'd get out of the habit quite quickly, if I were you." Gray added.

"I recommend you practice as much as you feel able to until you can reliably reduce a mug to particles, rather than exploding it, then we'll move on."

The door to the hall opened and McInnes entered.

"You can go now," Cooke told McBride, "enjoy your evening."

"There's so many more questions—"

"And we can't answer them all, but we will answer those we can. Later, Mister McBride."

McBride bowed slightly to Master McInnes and left the room, making his way quickly to his quarters.

"You got the stuff, Terry?" Cooke asked, turning to McInnes.

"Yes." McInnes set the bag gently down upon the table. "I left the other item; it didn't seem right..."

"Thank you, my friend." Cooke slid the notebook from the bag and flicked open to a random page. "Such promise; such great evil and such great good could be wrought by this book. It is good that I died, or I fear it would have fallen to me to decide its use."

"Who does it fall to then, if not you? This book, the technology within, good or bad, is your book, your technology; who could judge its use better than you, who lived and died in fear of what you might have unleashed?"

"Well, you, Terry,"

"It is too great a task for one as weak as me."

"We have all lost loved ones, Terry. Mel died a long time ago—"

"That's not what this is about."

"It is, Terry. Everything since the Faction War has been about that, everyone you've protected, you've been trying to find something like what you felt for her. Despite your rather futile attempts to pretend you guys felt nothing for each other and were content being just friends, you've gone after people similar to her, but none of them have lived up to your expectations—"

"She shouldn't be dead. I see her every day, I see where she should be in our lives, James; she wasn't supposed to die."

"That's all very well, Terry, but she did, and we have to live with it; you are strong enough to take charge of the book, because you have to be."

"Very well. What are we going to do about Chiswick? This isn't going to be anywhere near enough to take him down."

"The key being in our possession will slow him, at least, and we have no interest in removing him from his position. After all, he is still one of us."

"One of us? How do you come to that conclusion?"
"Well, he hasn't killed us yet."

♦

"Sirs, this investigation is growing in size and its nature becoming more clouded under the auspices of the Civilian Guard and Colonel Cabot." Simon Winter stood before the Senate committee for internal defense and security.

"That is without a doubt, Senator Winter; what is your point?" Senator Wyatt, leader of this committee, spoke up.

"My point is this; I simply request that control of the investigation be handed over, at least in part, to the Special Services division, who are better equipped to deal with this kind of threat to the Society and bring its perpetrator to justice." Winter looked up. There was nobody in the stranger's gallery watching the proceedings, Cooke had no friends on the committee; the day was his.

There was a general murmuring about the committee and Wyatt spoke again. "This committee will grant the request of the Senator. Word will be sent to Colonels Cabot and Chiswick, informing them that this investigation is now the jurisdiction of the SS and not of the Guard; are you happy with this, Senator?"

"I am pleased with the decision of the committee, and am confident that the murderer will be bought to justice."

"Let us hope so."

Winter looked into Wyatt's eyes and caught something he didn't particularly want to see; a look of anger at the decision of her fellow committee members. He stalked from the chamber, his victory spoilt by the knowledge of what was going to happen next. There was a small chance to rectify it, but there was only a very small window of opportunity. He took out his mobile phone and dialed Chiswick's number.

"Michael; you have authorization, but you must move quickly. Wyatt will warn the guard you're coming."

"Very well. Excellent work, Simon."

♦

Cabot's phone rang and he snatched it up. "Now? How do you know?" He listened to the response. "Okay, well done for calling me; get the autopsy reports and the location reports you guys did originally and get them ready. Burn bag everything in my desk... Everything, okay? I'll be back tomorrow morning, alright, I'm just following some leads. Bye."

Sitting on the other side of the chessboard to him Bishop raised her eyebrows.

"Winter just got the defense committee to hand over the investigation to the SS; we've been back-benched, so I've ordered my people to destroy everything of any value to the Chiswick."

"Ah." She idly moved a pawn. "We've finished the analysis of the Taser you took from Winter, by the way; it was definitely one of ours, but it's been tampered with. The energy drains from it far too fast. The general thinking is that it was dropped or discarded by one of our people and so broke, then the SS picked it up."

"So Winter's the only one of them with a Taser? I can't see that happening."

"If the others have one, they backward engineered it. That Taser was registered as destroyed, but all the others are with us and accounted for."

"Alright then, that's progress; can we get Winter on anything?"

"Unfortunately no; the law says the WTDD isn't allowed to stockpile technology without officially declaring it, which we haven't, and you took it from the Senator by picking his pocket, which is also illegal."

"Got the job done, didn't I?"

"Yes, and we're grateful, but we can't prosecute Winter with it."

"How about just kicking his ass?" Cabot moved his knight to take her pawn.

"Unwise, Liam."

"What, the move, or the kicking Winter's ass?"

"Both." Her rook slid down the board to a square his knight had been covering the previous turn. "Checkmate."

"Ah. I think it's unfair for you to win; I'm startled by your dazzling beauty."

"Cut the crap, Liam; you lost because you suck."

"Well there is that, I suppose," he sighed. "Should I tell the others about Winter?"

"Yeah, I'd say so..."

♦

"I didn't know the Senate could do this kind of thing Alan," Stanford sighed as his Chief of Staff briefed him over the intercom of the mansion.

"Well, sir, it was right there in that law you signed—"

"Meh meh meh, I'm Alan, I know what the law says. What can we do to stop it?"

"Uh, nothing, sir; the Senate is outside of our jurisdiction." Alan reminded him. "That was in the law too."

"Does it say anywhere in the law I can't kill senators just because they're annoying me?"

"Uh, yes, my Lord."

"Alright then. I don't suppose Liam will have left them anything they need to incriminate all of us in a huge conspiracy: does the Hall know?"

"I can't imagine them not knowing, really."

"True, it is the kinda thing they usually tell us about."

Stanford thought for a second. "I have a meeting with the Nautilus design team tomorrow, right?"

"Yes."

"Any chance I can cancel it?"

"Uh, no; you've already postponed it five times."

Empter was well aware of his employer's reluctance to meet with scientists, and could understand it as a friend, but as the guy responsible for chivying the Lord Protector along, he couldn't allow him to be influenced by anything so trifling and unimportant as his own judgement.

"Alright; call the guys from Justice in tomorrow afternoon and try and find a way to take Michael's legs out."

"Yes, my Lord."

"Okay; I'll see you tomorrow."

"Have a good evening, my Lord."

"Yeah, you too; bye."

◆

By day, Cooke Hall was an impressive building, but by night its size was staggering, the mansion dominating the landscape for miles around. Walking across the roof, McInnes could see half the Society, but, such was the design of the building, he could not see either side of the Hall itself. Beneath him were enough rooms to hold three hundred guests in comfort, a collection of studies and laboratories to match any in the Society, in addition to the enormous dining hall, great hall, dojo, and three libraries.

McInnes liked to come onto the roof sometimes, when the wind wasn't too strong, and look out over the countryside, hoping to catch a glance of the invisible, to sense that which could not be sensed, but once again he failed.

There were footsteps from elsewhere on the top of the Hall; not from the guards who were supposed to stay up here, concealed, but from someone else, someone moving cautiously across the flat sections of the roof, scared that the wind would strike.

"Hello Kim," he said when the figure got close to hand.

"Terry." Horowicz had never had much truck with titles, never referring to anyone by them unless they were there, and only very rarely then. It made a nice change to McInnes, who had grown reluctantly accustomed to everyone calling him Master; to be referred to by his real name was something only a very few did these days, and even then they somehow implied the word they didn't say. "You never told me you came up here."

"I don't often."

"You're lying, Terry."

The girl was insightful, he knew, but still had no idea about what was going on in his head.

"Why do you come up here?"

"I have to keep watch over the grounds, make sure there're no intruders—"

"In the building with the highest security in the society, second only to the NCC?"

"I think the SS would argue their building is a little more secure than ours."

"Yes, well Chiswick was always an arrogant son of a bitch," she spoke bluntly and checked herself, aware she had spoken out of turn. "This place puts people at ease; it's strange."

"Strange?"

"Cooke Hall is the centre of so much hatred, not to mention the general insanity possessed by most of its denizens, and the fact that what you do here is create weapons—"

"What we do here, mostly, is a lot of good, and the place is secure. If we like you you're safe here, though I fear that may be about to change."

"Why?"

"I just have a feeling that something's going to go terribly wrong."

"I think you're probably just being paranoid, Terry."

"I don't know. My predictions tend to be fairly accurate; I just hope James knows what he's doing."

"He probably does. He's lasted this long."

"True. He just hasn't *lived* this long."

♦

McBride moved quickly through the moves of his own improvised kata, his bokken slicing the air silently, then stopping abruptly before he moved on.

"You need to practice."

He turned, bringing the sword up to meet David Short's neck.

"What're you doing here, Short?" He looked at the thin case in the other apprentice's hand. "You completed the trial by steel?"

"Yes McBride, I did." The case slid down as Short released it, revealing the dark-blue scabbard of the sword.

"Katana?"

"Of course; they are the weapon of choice for Engineers."

McBride smiled to himself; the boy was totally unaware of Doctor Bishop, standing quietly on the balcony.

McBride had no doubt that the boy was here to challenge him; and that if challenged he would be forced to accept, armed only with a bokken, entering combat against a man with a sword. No matter.

"I presume you know why I'm here?" Short asked.

"I can take a guess."

"Let's do this then." Short drew the sword, throwing away the scabbard and then falling to the floor as the hilt of McBride's bokken struck him in the chest, bowling the small framed boy over.

He swung out at McBride's legs, just missing, as he tried to rise, before the bokken struck him in the back of the neck, putting him back on the floor.

Quickly McBride stamped on one of Short's hands with his foot and flicked the blade up into his hand.

"No fair." Short lay there, submissive for now. "You cheated."

"I fought the battle so that I could win."

"By playing against the rules..."

"No, Mister Short." Bishop glided down from the balcony into the squash court McBride used for practicing. "It is you who is at fault."

The apprentice leapt to his feet, snapping to attention painfully.

"Never, never, draw your blade unless you intend to kill your opponent."

"Ma'am, with respect—"

"You *do not* draw unless you intend to kill someone, or at the very least are willing to do so."

"I've been practicing, ma'am; I think I can probably take McBride."

"Then do so with bokkens, apprentice. You do not argue with me."

Short snatched his sword back from McBride.

"Put it away, and go to your quarters; your challenge of Mister McBride will be carried out in three days time, God willing and if the Masters authorize it."

"Yes, Doctor." Short bowed and left the room.

"You need to practice, apprentice," she told him.

"I have been practicing, ma'am."

"Not with a sword, there is more to combat than your weapons; your body is a powerful tool, and it can easily overcome a man with a sword or a gun if used properly."

"My training does not require me to learn unarmed combat, ma'am."

"No, but your duties as a Doctor most likely will; take up your stance."

McBride adopted a defensive boxing stance, both fists held ready to block in front of him.

"Now strike me."

He punched, aiming for her stomach, and felt his fist make contact, but only briefly, as her muscles seemed to roll out of the way, deflecting his punch and sending a sharp jolt of pain up his arm.

"How can you do that?"

"Practice. Try again."

He punched again, alternating between fists now, and all the strikes were quickly deflected by the doctor. He tried a kick and her leg moved up, countering the strike by pinning his foot to the floor with hers.

"Impressive; you have strength and speed, but there's more to fighting than that."

She ducked a punch and placed a palm in his chest, pushing him back a couple of feet.

He prepared to strike as she leapt, planting three kicks in his chest while still in the air.

"What is there then?"

He blocked her fist and it rolled across his arm, reaching his shoulder blade and squeezing. He twisted away, punching out, the blow going wide as she span aside.

"Grace, fluidity of motion, understanding of your opponent."

She leapt, over his head, and he found his moment, kicking her in the stomach. She began to fall, and he smiled. Her leg flicked out, haphazardly it seemed, but suddenly arcing around, taking his legs from under him. He fell to the ground, reaching out for the air, and finding himself stopping, his body all but laid down at an angle of thirty degrees to the horizontal, perfectly suspended in the air.

"Interesting," Bishop muttered and he swung up, coming forward into a flying kick. She kept her feet, preparing to strike back.

The alarm on her watch went off and her arm halted, mid-swing.

"Someone's breached the perimeter," she told him, snatching up a bokken from the racks outside the door as she sped out.

"People come and go regularly, ma'am. We have operatives in the field all the time, apprentices take nights out; what makes this any different?" McBride asked, following her.

"No-one's out at the moment, and all the cars of our people are marked."

"Maybe it's a squirrel?" he tried.

"Not big enough to trip the sensors."

"A bear then?"

"Unlikely, but a possibility, I'll admit."

"It's not a bear."

They turned to face McInnes, coming down the main staircase behind them. "Justice just gave Chiswick a warrant."

"For here?"

"Yes, for here."

"Then we kill him, clearly."

"That's not an option. Everything we have to hide is hidden too well for him to find."

"But he'll know that all the others are here, surely?"

"They've been moved into the servants quarters; the warrant doesn't cover the entire property, and if he tries to gain access then he's ours."

♦

The gravel on the pathway crackled underfoot as the two dozen operatives made their way toward tentatively towards the Hall. Chiswick, hologram maintained by a projector in his Jeep, gestured for a few agents to move off to either side.

He went through the front door and found the Engineers waiting for him.

"You were tipped off," he stated; this wasn't a question. "You'll know we have a warrant then?"

"I'd like to see it, if you'd be so good?"

Rachel Houghton handed over the piece of folded paper and McInnes read it, slowly. "It's most definitely binding. You may conduct your search, Mister Chiswick: we have nothing to hide, we have committed no crime."

"I'll be the judge of that."

A radio crackled into life.

"Sir, we need assistance; we're in one of the drawing rooms."

Chiswick shot a glance at the Doctors as this message was relayed.

"Killian?"

"Carter and Annie were playing Cluedo, sir."

"Oh God..."

The card table in the vile green drawing room was tipped over, playing pieces spread across the floor, some landing near a downed SS operative, lying still but alert, his nose broken, looking down the barrel of the staple pistol at Daniel Carter.

His friend, who had called for assistance, was pinned to a bookshelf by a knife through his sleeve and was also confronted by another pistol.

"Stand down, Mister Carter." McInnes entered the room, speaking calmly to the apprentice. "They have a warrant."

"Then why're they coming through the back door?"

"Good question; Colonel Chiswick?"

"We anticipated resistance, and thought that by catching you off guard we would be able to do this with a minimum of fuss."

"It seems you were mistaken—I said *stand down*, Daniel."

The guns span into the apprentice's jacket and he smiled.

"Of course, Master McInnes."

"Thank you, Dan. You may continue your search, Colonel."

"Good; you will wait outside until we have finished."

"Very well; move out, guys."

The other Engineers followed him out of the back door and onto the patio, where they sat on the lawn tables silently for a few minutes.

"We could have stopped them, Master," McBride finally said. "Taser Chiswick's generator, slice and dice the others..."

"That time may come, but it is not upon us yet. For now our place is to maintain the peace, and we're doing that."

"We could at least make them regret—" Carter began.

"Oh, they will; Chiswick more than the others."

♦

Michael Chiswick stalked into Cooke's study, a hexagonal

room with no windows, the only source of illumination coming from the observatory above, reachable by a staircase to one side of the room.

The technology in this room was more advanced than anything else in the house, from the holographic projection pad on the floor to the weapons lining the racks and the supercomputer sitting at the solitary desk amid the bookshelves.

He reached the holo-pad and paused, a sudden feeling of dread penetrating him. He should never have come here, never given up the home field advantage to a mind that was already greater than his.

The force hit him like an iron bar and the room changed, huge white walls now towering away from him, sourceless light illuminating everything, the only element of colour being the chess board atop a table in the middle of the room.

Cooke appeared in front of him, unarmed and dressed in a white monk's habit.

"What's happened to you, Michael?"

Chiswick moved to sit down by the chess board and a chair appeared.

"Nothing's happened to me." He looked down at the white pieces in front of him and moved the king's pawn two spaces forward. "You're the one who's betrayed all the principles of the PFS."

"We were friends once, Michael."

"We were never friends, Cooke; we've always hated each other."

"That's not true. We shared information during the Coup, we fought together in the first war, you backed my proposals during the Faction War negotiations: what's changed?"

"Well, we both died."

"That doesn't seem to have affected our career paths very much."

"There has been a determination; our paths changed after the Coup, yours to protecting yourself and mine to protecting the Society."

"Interesting; that's how you justify paying off Winter, is it?"

"I don't justify what I don't do, Master Cooke, and since I have a warrant to search your premises I think you should be less resistant, or at the very least, less accusatory..."

♦

"Get Justice on the phone." Rob Stanford kicked through the swing doors of the NCC, making his way to the office of the Executive Branch. Empter followed him, keeping pace with the Lord Protector as his aides dropped off behind.

"Get Justice on the phone, Alan; I'll handle the rest."

"But the Council..."

"Without the WTDD the council is split; Andrews and the Chiswicks will vote to overrule any action I make or support any of their number, Mary, Bryony and Emily will vote with me, Danny's never here; the Council is tied."

"The Council is purely an advisory committee, my Lord; they can't actually affect what you do!"

"Not directly, no, but if the majority of the Council votes on diminished capacity then my decisions are subject to the Senate's approval."

"Aren't they already?"

"I can order us to invade Bristol."

"But you're unlikely to succeed without the CG."

"Well, actually, I'm likely to succeed because I'm ruler of Bristol and my friend owns about half the property, but that's neither here nor there..."

They entered the outer office, staffed by a single secretary, one whose name Stanford could not quite remember as he barreled through into the office of the Executive Branch.

The rooms upstairs, the council chambers, his office, belonged to the Lord Protector; the leader of the Council, mediator, politician and generally part of the Council. This office was bigger, a huge rectangle of cream-painted walls with comfortable sofas, a huge oak desk and, on the plush cream carpet of the room, the seal of the Lord Protector of the People's Freedom Society: this was the place the power of the Executive Branch was manifest. Councillors were not allowed to come in here except if subpoenaed to give testimony down the hall; senators were to be found here, summoned by the officials of the Chief of Staff's office on a regular basis to discuss and argue on key matters for the administration. This was where the power was.

"Get Justice on the phone, call Thatcher and get her here, and Colonel Paris from the CG," Stanford instructed and Empter sighed, leaving the room.

"Good evening, my Lord," an aide poked her head in through the door. "Can I get you a drink, sir?"

"Sparkling mineral water, ice, no lemon; thanks Susan."

"Thank you, sir." She left.

"Justice is on the phone," Empter shouted from the outer office.

"Who at Justice?" Stanford asked.

"Uh, Sammy Bradshaw; associate DC Counsel."

"Okay, I can deal with him." Stanford picked up the phone and took Bradshaw off hold. "Sammy, hi; it's Rob Stanford here—I need you to tell me how I can invalidate a warrant taken out for the search of premises."

"Is this the warrant handed down to Cooke Hall?"

"Yes." Stanford confessed.

"It's pretty watertight; Senator Greenwood's office faxed us a copy, but we're working on it. We may have something for you in a few hours."

"What good to me is a few hours?"

"Well, you can call in every member of the Senate committee on internal defence and security and the SS to find out why they did what they did; the senators won't get back up, they'll just roll over and accept being thrown out of office, and you could use it as an excuse to restrict the power of the SS—"

"Alan!"

The Chief of Staff entered the room again.

"How secure is this phone line?"

"Not at all, sir; you want the cell?"

"No no, I think I've got everything I need; thank you, Mister Bradshaw."

"Any time, my Lord."

♦

"You're only thirty-two moves from checkmate, you know."

Chiswick looked up from the board as his adversary spoke.

"Is this the game, or out there in the real world?"

"I couldn't say in the real world. Why're you doing this?"

"Because I have to, James. Something's going to happen and I need every edge I can get to stop it."

"Is that why you're going after the keys?"

Chiswick's face became wooden.

"I have no idea what you're talking about."

"The keys: nine objects which unlock the encrypted parts of the Covenant Database, cast out among the Society to protect the secrets..."

"I know what they are. They're too spread out for anyone to get hold of them now, even if they knew what they were looking for. And even if I could find them all, what would I use them to do? The doors they unlock have no military ramifications; you saw to that."

"Yes I did. Who're the guys in the robes, Michael? You have to tell me."

"I really don't; when my guys find the weapons here, or evidence you've been usurping me at every turn, or something else—anything else, really—you'll be deactivated and your supporters imprisoned."

"What makes you so certain you'll find something incriminating here?"

"I'll plant something if there's nothing to be found."

"Well, thanks for being honest."

♦

It was a gloomy night, Nathan Jenkins reflected as he sat on his bed in the asylum, staring morosely out through the room's tiny portal to the outside, a barred opening ten feet from the ground.

He leaned over forwards, straining his strait-jacket to take a brief sip through the straw in his beaker of water. They were out there still, he knew. People thought he was crazy, thought that the darkness existed only in his mind, but he knew different; he knew that they were out there and were still after those who were holding the keys.

There was a muffled thump from outside the thick door to his cell, such as might be made by the guard being palmed into it.

He stood up and made himself as presentable as possible as he heard the light fizzing noise coming from the door. The explosion that came was quieter than the ones he had made when he had been sneaking into places and blowing the doors off, but the door fell into the room nonetheless.

Rose Mendelson stepped daintily over the fallen door, a pistol in her hand.

"Sergeant Jenkins."

"Sergeant Mendelson." He nodded cordially.

"Turn around."

He obliged and she drew a knife, making a quick series of sweeps that freed his arms from their restraints.

"Thank you. Why are you here?"

"You know why."

"They're moving?"

"I have reason to believe so, or at the very least that your life may be in some kind of danger; Chiswick's taking back the keys."

"Ah; you think I have one? Or simply that he believes that I do?"

"One of the keys resides with Cooke, one with me. The SS has six now; the ninth must be around somewhere, and I'd suggest that you got to it before they locked you away."

"Now why are you really here?"

"You were preaching about dead people walking around and starting the Coup, Nathan. You were one of the best of us; we figured the stress of the job got too much for you. Then you started blaming Chiswick for it, saying he knew about some secret organization and we knew, just *knew* you'd lost it, that you had to be taken in."

"The CG arrested me, not the SS; I don't hold you responsible."

"You think the CG could take you out?"

"I was surprised, and there were many of them—"

"They didn't shoot, they went for an arrest, they ignored the first thing Stanford taught them, the first thing Cabot taught them..."

"If you want an SS agent down, put them down; shoot them, stab them, but don't expect to beat them in combat unless you cheat," he recited.

"Exactly. They couldn't surprise you; you killed three of them before they took you in, and there was no good reason for them to be able to. Maybe they had help?"

"Chiswick sent you to assist in my arrest?"

"No."

"Then what?"

"I sent myself; I decided you were a threat to the Society and was on my way to take you in myself when the call was made to the CG. I facilitated."

Mendelson's normally confident features were now softened by guilt and self doubt. "I'm sorry."

"No need for it; it's all in the past: I want to know about the present."

"Cooke Hall is being searched by Michael's guys, and he's after the keys, but none of us know what they're for. Chiswick's trying to stop some people, they wear black robes, and that sparked a memory of you."

"Hardly surprising." Jenkins paused. "Is there anywhere we can go? I don't particularly want to be interrupted by some nurse coming to bring me medication."

"Of course." She led him along the corridors, both of them slinking silently through the shadows of the empty building until they got out.

The asylum was situated alongside the River Severn—the principal estuary in the PFS—and they walked down it for a few hundred metres before coming to Mendelson's car, a jet-black BMW, and drove off.

♦

Outside the Marine Biological Research Building, place of employment of Emily Johnson when she wasn't sitting on the Council, was a restaurant, a diner of the American style, with bright red plastic and chrome making up a substantial portion of the décor and with a huge fish tank across one wall of the restaurant.

Mendelson entered first, through the saloon-style swing doors, and nodded to the proprietor, Sarah Clapton, an old friend of Cooke and his allies.

The place, in a different incarnation, had held the negotiations that had played a part in the ending of the Faction War, and since had become the preferred eatery of those protected by the Hall, a form of sanctuary unto itself.

"I need a private table, Sarah; no questions."

Sarah nodded and led the two of them to a secluded table, some distance from the main bar, located so that from there the doors could be monitored, but the people sitting at the table would be practically invisible to anyone else in the restaurant.

"A coffee for me and a dry Martini for him," Mendelson ordered and handed over the money.

"Thank you." Sarah left the table.

"Who're the robed guys?" Mendelson asked.

"They call themselves the PPA, or at least they did, during the Coup. It stood for People's Protection Agency; a group of vigilantes, of which there were at least four principal members. They manipulated everybody in power in 2011, brought everybody closer to war, played Kensington like a fiddle; she wasn't really to blame for the Coup at all."

Mendelson sat silently for a second, letting all of this settle in.

"What makes you think Michael knows about them?"

"He formed the group."

"He did what?"

"The PPA was part of the SS, originally intended to be like America's National Security Agency, but they went behind Chiswick's back; they forced the Coup."

"Why did they do that? Did they want power for themselves?"

"I'm not sure; even Kensington didn't know who they were, so she couldn't have given them money or power. My guess is they just hate Stanford, and that's why they're resurfacing now; to get rid of him."

♦

Three men, all in white robes, stood around a complicated diagram, marked out by a raised pattern on the marble floor, the centre of which seemed fluid despite being totally stationary, as if it was somehow different to the stone outside of the symbol; like a pentagram with added enthusiasm.

They turned at the sound of the door to the room opening and saw a figure in black running towards them. Concentrated spheres of hardlight energy, crackling green, appeared in their open hands as they turned, and they released all three toward the runner.

A sword was drawn; a long, curved scimitar, and the balls vanished as they touched it. A fourth energy ball flew quickly from the hand of their assailant and struck one of the men, knocking him back.

Lucy's hood flew off as she ran, spinning the sword to decapitate the first man, who fell to the floor, his body evaporating as he did so. She span on one heel and threw another slightly larger energy ball at the second man, knocking him to the floor this time as her sword atomized the third. She looked at the seal on the floor before her, about five feet across, and began murmuring under her breath, an almost constant stream of words in a language she couldn't understand.

The particles within the seal span through the air like a whirlwind full of sand, then came together into a single form. A young woman stood on the seal, dressed in tattered brown robes.

"You are a hisa-me?" Lucy asked.

"I am." The girl spoke gently. She looked no more than twenty years old, yet radiated the arrogance of millenia. "You have summoned me?"

"Yes: the first seal has fallen."

"I heard nothing of it."

"The Morningstar doesn't know."

"How is that possible?"

"I have a sword, I was sent up a few years ago and took a host when I was defeated: I'm going to take this planet for myself, and you can help, or you can go back."

"You're taking the planet for yourself?"

"Yes."

"How is that possible? He'll stop you."

"I can close off the staircases, and hold all the seals. Then no-one can get in or out without me summoning them."

"But the fallers—"

"Will all die. What do you say?"

"I think you're insane, but preferable to eternal damnation—count me in."

Lucy muttered something else and the seal glowed for a second, allowing the girl to step through to the other side, taking on a certain degree of reality as she did so, as if behind the seal she was somehow not truly there, but was merely a projection.

"Now for the others..."

♦

Cooke's queen fell to a knight, the offending piece quickly removed by a well-placed pawn.

"Who outside of our organizations knows what the keys are for?"

"No-one. There are conspiracy theories about the Covenant Database, but they think we're hiding a superweapon; interestingly, they tend to think you've got something to hide. You know, McInnes, and Siobhan, of course, and me."

"And that's it?"

"Well, Jenkins also..."

"The crazy one?"

"Yes. He found out before he was arrested, went rooting through files, made a lot of stuff up but came across the files on it."

"You keep files on the keys? That's extremely foolish—"

"Firstly, we *kept* files on it; they were destroyed as soon as the Jenkins incident happened. Secondly, you're hardly in a position to lecture me about foolishness; you've told your whole council."

"I died once, Michael; I am unwilling to let this knowledge be lost when we eventually pass away."

"I thought you were in favour of all we know being lost? Wasn't that why the keys were scattered in the first place?"

"No, the keys were scattered so *you* couldn't use them, to be perfectly honest. I knew where they'd gone."

"You knew..."

"If you'd come to me and told me what was going on then I could have helped—"

"The hell you would have! The SS will stop this; we don't need your help."

"You bloody do, Michael. You're attacking the Hall."

"*Searching*, James, we're searching."

"Whatever; you're here without my consent because whatever enemies you're fighting are too big for you to manage."

Cooke looked up sharply in confusion. "Now what's going on?" The whole room faded, returning them to the study.

"What was that?" Chiswick asked.

"Somebody else is here."

"The room's empty though."

"No, downstairs. Someone else has arrived within the perimeter; someone like you."

"I haven't got anyone scheduled to come down here..."

The intercom on the wall burst into life.

"James; the perimeter's been—"

"I know Terry: get the others into the foyer immediately and try to get Michael's people down there as well; I would assume it to be our mutual friends..."

"Got it."

♦

Mendelson looked up as someone approached the table, their form disguised by their black robes. Both the agents rose to their feet, Mendelson's pistol now back in her hand and pointed at the newcomer.

"Can we help you?"

"Sergeant Rose Mendelson, I am arresting you on a charge of freeing a convicted prisoner, treason and the murder of Nathan Jenkins." A knife was thrown and Jenkins fell, the blade between his ribs.

Mendelson's gun was taken from her before she could even pull the trigger. She leapt away, making for the entrance; past the bloodied corpse of Sarah Clapton.

She turned, focusing as she vanished and struck at her opponent. The fist was blocked in mid-air and rolled back at her. She caught a final glimpse of her adversary as they too vanished from sight.

♦

When Cooke and Chiswick arrived in the lobby where the others were gathered, five women stood in the doorway to the Hall, the hoods of their black robes pushed back. They were very beautiful, McBride noted subconsciously, but their faces were odd; almost perfectly symmetrical, and they all looked almost exactly the same, as if they had been constructed, not born.

"James?"

"Michael."

"Any tricks up your sleeve for this one?"

"Perhaps..."

"James Cooke. You should be dead," one of the girls hissed. "She killed you."

"Lucy sent you?"

"Yes," all five said at the same time.

Bright, glowing spheres appeared in the hands of the women. They smiled, and threw them at those gathered around Cooke. The android extended one hand and several pieces of furniture took to the air, flying into the path of the projectiles and disintegrating on contact, protecting the Hall's residents.

"Impressive. Not good enough, though." One of the girls stepped forward, putting herself directly in front of Michael. She thrust a hand into his chest and he fell, the holographic field around him rippling as energy surged through it. Cooke knocked her aside, only to have a fist put him on the floor.

McBride stepped forward as an energy ball was thrown by one of the other women, reflexively raising a hand to protect himself. The energy ball stopped on his hand, held in place somehow, and he threw it back, knocking down one of the women.

McInnes looked around: Carter was already down, and the girl who had attacked the apprentice was now heading towards him. The world assumed the treacle-like quality it always did when McInnes fought and he ducked a punch, rolling his stomach to avoid the second. The girl kicked and he blocked it with an open palm, striking back with his right fist.

She caught the fist a few inches from her neck and he delivered a swift kick to her knee. She fell but began to get back up, though not fast enough to stop his knee colliding with her face. She stood in front of him. She wasn't bleeding, though the blow was strong enough to have broken her nose. She wasn't even breathing heavily.

"You have the sight," she breathed, an energy ball appearing in her hand.

"Leave them. Go back to your mistress and tell her you've failed." Ellie stood on a staircase, her ancient scimitar in her hand. The girls looked at each other and left through the front door, not running but leaping, taking bounds of around thirty feet at a time.

"That isn't going to be the end of this." Cooke was back on his feet. "They'll come back, whoever they were."

"I think *whatever* is a slightly better word." McBride helped Carter to his feet.

"They were hisa-me," Ellie said, "low level servants of the other side. They are known in Japanese myth, they are assassins of Touched Ones; Lucy will have summoned them to deal with you."

"Oh, okay. Nice to know we're being taken seriously then."

"I don't think she's fully aware of how many of you there are here yet, but it's only a matter of time."

"The weaknesses of Stanford are clear." Lucy turned to the members of the PPA, sat around the hall where they met in secret, none of the members aware of who everyone else was due to the black hoods. "He, like the majority of his kind, is corruptible by attractive women. The Coup would have been less successful had it not been for his affair with Kensington. It is clear to me that if he can be seduced, he can be destroyed."

"This hardly seems like a task any of us can complete: we're all regular citizens of the Society, and we don't have access to the LP," one of the hooded figures spoke up.

"True," Lucy spoke quietly, so that only those in the first few rows, the most senior members of the Agency, could heard her, "however I may be able to find just the person, but we will have to strike quickly, take out all of our current targets one after the other; we can't afford any slip-ups."

♦

Cooke led McBride and Carter into a small dojo in the Hall's servants quarters; it wasn't as grand as its counterpart in the main house, but it had the advantage of being more secluded.

"Mister Carter; the universe, what is it made of?" he asked, rounding on the young apprentice.

"Particles, mostly."

"And you are made of mostly hydrogen, oxygen and carbon?"

"Yes, Master."

"And these are quite prolific elements?"

"Yes."

"So what's the difference between them coming together to form you and them coming together to form a cloud?"

"Uh..." Carter stopped, his knowledge falling short.

"Hardlight energy," McBride said. "The energy tells Dan what form to stay in; like how the holo-games work, by projecting the image of yourself which you see?"

"To a certain extent, yes, Killian. Now, as a result of this, since people touched by darkness and hence possessed of light have more control on their own energy levels than people like you, Killian, they can fluctuate the amount of energy in them at any one time..."

"What are you saying, sir?" Carter asked.

"That your form isn't permanent. You can change it to a certain extent; become a cloud." McBride answered for Cooke.

"Exactly."

"That's impossible!" Carter exclaimed. "Things can't just change their form as and when they wish to; there'd be no sense in the universe, why would things not just change all the time? Why stay a planet when there's a perfectly good goose you could be being right now?"

"Not everything can, just people with enough energy to overwrite their body's natural shape for a moment."

"That's crap—"

Cooke's arm snapped up, holding a pistol, and the Master Engineer fired a shot at Carter.

Carter felt a sensation like being buffeted with wind, while Cooke and McBride watched his body explode in a shower of barely visible particles, forming a cloud that hovered for a second in the air before snapping back into Carter's form.

He felt something rise up in the back of his mind as he reformed, a dark, angry presence that surged forward and took control; suddenly he was furious with Cooke.

"Unfair," he hissed and struck out. The android caught his fist.

"Let him go." Cooke spoke authoritatively, his artificial green eyes staring at Carter.

The presence eased back, the eyes softened and the muscles around the face relaxed.

"Most things are possible, Mister Carter; you just have to learn where the tricks are."

"Yes, Master."

"And as for you," Cooke turned to McBride, "you already know that, don't you?"

McBride nodded slightly. "Energy is infinitely versatile and malleable, all you have to do is learn how to form it..."

He held out his hand and a ball of energy, flickering green and incandescent, formed atop it.

"Good."

The slim figure of Doctor Bishop appeared in the doorway of the mausoleum.

"Liam is in trouble; he needs our help."

"Where?"

"Bristol."

"Can you guys handle it?" Cooke asked Carter and McBride. "He'll be easy enough to find; take two of the bikes."

The apprentices nodded and left the building.

◆

Cabot walked the streets of Bristol as he did every day, happy to be alive, feeling the sun on his face. It was going to rain later, but he didn't really care; it was a nice for now and with the WTDD behind him he'd have the murder solved long before Chiswick.

The streets were busy, as they always were around noon, and he moved seamlessly through the throng of bodies, sensing the life in each of them as he passed. The crowds parted to one side of him and he saw a man sat on the floor, his clothes scruffy and torn. The man looked up at Cabot and an expression of recognition came over his face.

The man hurled himself forward, snatching Cabot's arm and clinging on.

"They are coming for you, for the Sighted One: you must stop them!" he wheezed into Cabot's face, his breath stinking of alcohol.

"I think it's probably best if you keep quiet, citizen," Cabot murmured to him. "Would you like to come with me…"

There was a muffled squelch and the man toppled forward, bleeding from a staple entry point in the back of his skull.

Cabot looked up at the figure on the roof holding a staple pistol and leapt out of the crowd, landing on the roof of the building and facing his assailant.

"Mister Cabot." The voice was feminine and somehow familiar as the woman assumed her stance.

"And you are?"

"Of little significance."

172

Cabot smiled, slinging the black case from his back and drawing his weapon, a five foot graphite staff.

"Oh excellent," he said and span the staff experimentally through his fingers with dazzling speed, settling in an offensive stance. "Another melodramatic faceless enemy behind the black robes of doom, eh?"

"I think that's a touch condescending Liam."

The voice really was familiar.

"Who *are* you?"

She struck, kicking out with her right foot. He blocked with the staff and she brought her left leg up, neither of her feet now on the ground, hooking them both around the staff and tossing it from Cabot's grip as she landed, having been in the air for far longer than gravity should allow.

He tilted his head, confused, and her palm hit him in the chest, hurling him from the building and into the crowd, which quickly parted. Cabot smashed into the wall, dust and bits of masonry flying around him as he tried to get back to his feet.

The girl landed in the street in front of Cabot, his staff now in her hands. There was the roar of an engine and a motorbike flew from the roof above, crashing into the ground, its rider leaping back from the seat, landing between the assassin and her quarry.

"And you are?" the assassin asked, looking at the boy standing in front of her, barely twenty years old, garbed in a long white lab coat.

"My name is Killian McBride; I've been assigned to protect Colonel Cabot, and I have every intention of doing so."

The crowd had reformed now, a few metres from the fight, out of harm's way but close enough to see and hear everything.

"I don't think that'll be much of a trial for me, little boy—"

An energy ball hit the ground by her feet. "Interesting; you're one of new Touched Ones."

"That I am."

She vanished from sight and McBride hurled another energy ball, straight towards where she had been. The crowd ruptured rapidly, something fast-moving and unseen colliding with people as it struggled to get away, fighting quickly through the crowd. McBride burst into a run, following the disruption of the crowd before it got a chance to fully close in front of him, unwilling to throw an energy ball and risk harming innocents.

Cabot looked up as a second man in a lab coat arrived, offering him a dark green leather jacket.

"You brought my coat, Mister Carter."

"Doctor Bishop suggested you might need it."

Cabot put the coat on. He felt the reassuring weight of his sword—the one he had made for his own trial by steel—hanging on the inside, the formerly maroon scabbard painted black upon his moving out of the hall, no longer part of the WTDD.

"Let's go."

"Where?"

"Down this alleyway here, acting as casually as you lads can manage, and hope nobody follows us." Cabot was walking with an almost forced nonchalance; enough to make Carter start to look around, but he was shot in the back by a Taser.

Cabot turned to face the five men coming down the alleyway, aware that he had now backed himself into a corner.

"Hello, boys. Chiswick send you?"

"We were looking for leads on the murder, but since you're getting into fights and causing an affray—"

"A ruckus, even," Cabot suggested sarcastically.

"We thought we might as well see to it that justice was served."

"How civil-minded of you."

"Hand over the sword."

Cabot hesitated, his training at the WTDD, though long since repressed, still with him.

"Now."

He unclipped the katana from its belt and handed it over, quickly glancing to see how wide the alleyway was.

"Nice sword." The man held the weapon horizontally, one hand on the scabbard, the other moving to the hilt.

"Don't do that."

"Don't do what?"

"Draw the sword," Cabot spoke softly.

"What are you, Cabot? Some kind of ninja?"

"Ninji did not value their swords and lives equally; they were simply a means to an end."

"A samurai then? The sword's curved right."

"The word you're looking for," Cabot tensed, "is ronin." His right hand sprung up, snatching the hilt of the sword and drawing it, the scabbard still held within the hand of the SS officer. He drew the sword back, across the throat of the man.

The SS began to fire their pistols and Cabot leapt up, taking two steps along the wall and swinging the sword down to slice the hands off another man. He stabbed straight through a neck, astounded, as he always had been, by the strength of the blade—light in his hand—and the fragility of the human body.

"Go home to Chiswick; tell him the time of the SS is over: if he sends anyone after me again it's his head I'll have." Cabot snapped, staring down the two remaining men.

♦

Senator Simon Winter walked smugly through the corridors of the Senate building, straightening his silk tie as he went. He reached the office of Senator Greenwood, the door strangely closed, and knocked three times.

"Come in," came the answering call. He entered.

"Good morning, Senator Greenwood."

"Good morning, Simon." Greenwood seemed tired, more so than usual, an empty coffee mug sat on his desk, practically invisible within the huge pile of paperwork.

"I see the Executive Powers Bill is back on the table for a vote in three days time?"

"It is."

"I take this to mean you've come to a decision about my remarks after the last vote."

"Yes."

"Could you tell me what your decision was?"

"Certainly." Greenwood paused for a moment. "You're gonna vote in favour, you're going to speak in favour at the debate this afternoon, and you're going to free up everyone you've bullied into voting your way."

"Actually, Tim, I don't think that's going to happen—"

"Oh, I think it is."

"Why?"

"Because if you don't you'll lose your seat at the next election, if you even get nominated."

"There's no Democrat stupid enough to run for my seat."

"True, and we're pretty stupid. But there is Joe Scott."

"He's a Republican."

"And a war hero, he's practically identical to you, policy wise."

"Better the devil you know; I'm not worried about my seat being taken by Scott."

"But he will take votes from you. The naval barracks on the Severn is in your constituency and I can see them turning up to vote for Scott; he was an Admiral, after all. At the very least he'll take your votes, and give the Confederates more of a chance."

"You're threatening me, Senator? You'd seriously encourage a Republican candidate out of spite?"

"I'd do you one better, I'd openly endorse him, and here's why: you're a son of a bitch, Simon. You're why Empter didn't want parties, so people wouldn't go getting partisan, so that people could bring about change and reform without getting stuck behind groupings and labels and their pride. You're the reason we're the smallest party, the reason we haven't got a chance at the Protectorship for the next few decades—"

"And the fact that you jumped in bed with the Confederates from day one—"

"Shut your mouth, Winter. I'm still the head of this party and while I am you take don't get to talk like that to me. Vote with me and get rid of me afterward, or vote against me and lose your seat: the choice is yours. Good day Senator."

"Tim—"

"Good day, Senator."

◆

"Time stands against us, an ever-flowing tide of malevolence created by humanity and maintained by their own self awareness."

"Time has always been against us, Terry."

The two masters sat around the table in the small lounge off the kitchen, the early evening light shining through the large windows all around them.

"Liam will handle it, he usually does."

McInnes went over to the kettle in one corner and set it to boil, then took four cups from the top shelf of the cupboard, putting instant coffee into three and a teabag into the last.

"I don't think the murders are quite the important part of the issue here, James: something's afoot, the SS are hiding something."

"Something's always afoot and the SS are always hiding something. In fact, it's a pretty good day if it's just one thing."

"We need to send an operative into their building, take back the keys they have and find out what the hell they know."

"I think it's more Chiswick than anyone who knows something."

"Can you take over his program?"

"Yeah, because that's not an ethically grey area."

"It's ethically black, but you can't pretend that they don't deserve it."

"If we did this we'd deserve it too." McInnes reached across to the kettle, his hand wrapping around the handle the second before the light turned off to indicate it had finished, and poured water into the mug with tea and two of the coffee mugs.

He passed one of the coffees to Cooke and set the other down in front of his own seat, passing over the sugar.

"You know I can't drink this, right?" Cooke told him.

"You can smell it?"

"Yes."

"Then it's worth it." The back door opened and Cabot entered quietly with Dan Carter, setting his sword, now back in its sheath, down on the table.

"The SS interrupted my escape," Cabot told them. "Chiswick isn't listening to you. I was attacked before they arrived though; a woman who could defy gravity and make herself invisible. Master Cooke; I'm sure I recognized her voice," Cabot explained, not daring to voice his suspicions openly.

"You haven't called me that in a while," Cooke smiled. "Chiswick is the more immediate concern; we have to warn Stanford."

"It's too late for that," McInnes told him as Cabot took the teabag from his mug and threw it into the bin.

"It's what?"

"Too late for that."

"Master?" Carter cocked his head.

"Oh God." Cooke was out of the room, running, before his stool hit the ground.

♦

District Commissioner Ben Chiswick strode through the door to Stanford's mansion, his bodyguards right behind him.

"Good morning," he greeted the Secret Service agent on the door and carried on into the house.

"That's quite far enough." Another agent stood between him and the foyer.

"Let me past."

"Nobody gets in without an appointment."

"I'm the District Commissioner: don't make me remove you."

The agent had his gun in his hand, drawn from the holster inside his navy-blue suit, before Chiswick could do anything.

"I'm afraid that's not going to happen, sir."

Chiswick's men went for their guns.

"You sure you've got enough rounds in that gun?" Chiswick asked.

"Oh, almost certainly enough, sir."

The guns were now in the hands of Chiswick's men.

"Put them down, then raise your hands, gents. Point the guns at anything other than the floor or take a step forward and I'll shoot you."

"I'm the District Commissioner, damn you!" Chiswick snapped petulantly. "What's the big deal?"

"You're bringing armed guards inside the mansion. My job is to protect the Lord Protector; you represent a threat to him."

"He's my friend!"

"And rival, sir."

"Fuck you." One of the men moved forward and a small explosion reverberated around the cramped space.

The body hit the ground, blood draining into a puddle around the back of his head, like a dark red halo, at the same time as spurting upward in a fountain from the hole through the bridge of his nose.

"Put the weapons down, and step away from them; put your hands in the goddamn air," the agent snapped.

"No," Chiswick replied. "Get Stanford."

"Certainly," the agent spoke into his sleeve. "This is Burton; DC Chiswick is here to see the Lord Protector. He's got armed men with him."

He listened to the reply in his earpiece.

"He'll be right down."

Chiswick's guards were getting edgy, the agent's staple pistol still pointed at their employer.

"Good," Chiswick responded coolly.

♦

Lucy chanted once more, incorporeal shapes flickering within the seal for a few seconds before the human form appeared. The woman in the centre was crouched, her brown hair messy and large chunks of it missing. She wore what may once have been a uniform in dark green, torn to the point of being barely recognizable as clothing, her arms uncovered, with deep cuts— blood still seeping from them—present along the whole arm.

"Welcome back."

"What?" The girl looked up, a once beautiful face contorted by agony and abuse. There was a long cut, like a blow from a rapier or foil, from her cheek to her ear. "This isn't happening."

"It is."

"Send me back."

"We both know I'm not going to do that."

"Send me back. Now."

"No."

The woman behind the seal stuck her hand through the barrier, incandescent energy pouring from her arm. The girl toppled, back to her crouched position, nursing fresh wounds.

"I have one last task for you."

"In exchange for which?"

"I will kill you. Properly this time; you won't have to do all that again."

"Lower the seal."

"I want your word first."

"How much good is a promise to someone like you? All you are is empty words and lies."

"Not a promise. Your word, there's a difference."

"You have my word I won't attack you."

Lucy nodded and the seal glowed...

♦

"Benjamin. I presume you're here to try and kill me."

Lord Stanford came to the bottom of the stairs, two other Secret Service agents with him.

"Of course not; just in these times I believe it prudent to have protection."

"You have a Secret Service detail, Ben; these guys are gonna have to put down the weapons if they want to come in."

"I don't really think you've brought enough guards with you, old friend, if you're thinking about taking us by force."

"Three against six; I don't have a problem with our odds."

"Not very prudent, Robert."

"Nor is bringing armed guards to initiate a coup."

"At least I'll pull it off, unlike Kensington."

"Such confidence."

Another explosion and Burton fell, a staple through his shoulder. He fired twice on the ground, taking out the kneecaps of one of Chiswick's men as the remaining agents struggled to get in front of the Lord Protector, firing their pistols at the bodyguards.

The shooting was over quickly. Burton was lying on the floor, losing blood fast; Stanford and Chiswick stood opposite each other, everyone else dead.

"Just you and me, Ben; wanna leave this now and forget it ever happened?"

"You won't do that; you'll have me killed the second I leave this place. I know how this sort of thing works."

"No, you know how these things work for your brother, you know how the SS do business. Not me. I'm more than happy to forget the whole thing; I have an excellent selective memory."

"Hmm." Chiswick kicked up, a gun lying on his foot flying into his hand and he pulled the trigger.

The staple stopped in mid air, suspended by electromagnets in Stanford's suit, a defense mechanism built in compliments of Cooke Hall.

"Did you honestly believe I was gonna let you kill me?"

Stanford reached into his jacket and produced a staple pistol. "The Council is based around trust, Ben."

He looked at the gun in his hand mournfully.

"You have breached that trust, destroyed what the Council stands for. You can leave; you won't be killed, but I want your resignation by the end of the day."

"Yes, my Lord."

Chiswick left, his head bowed and his smugness gone. Stanford sat down on the stairs where he was, too mentally exhausted to cry or scream or blindly fire the gun in sheer rage. He had been sat there three minutes when the doors in front of him were smashed open by someone running headlong through them.

"He's gone, James."

The android stopped, looking at the bodies lying in the hallway.

"You let him go?"

"What else could I have done?"

"Well, killed him, I suppose."

"That wasn't an option and you know it. This is the second time this has happened; how can we be sure it won't happen again?"

"It will," Cooke told him what he didn't want to hear. "So long as there are leaders there will always be those who want the power; and some of those will go to these lengths, especially in a Society like this one, founded on a war, built in fire."

"Yes," Stanford admitted. "See to it that Chiswick resigns, and get someone to talk to Empter would you?"

"Certainly, my Lord." Cooke bowed low.

"You're not going to try and take power, are you?"

"I am your servant until the end of all worlds and plains, my Lord, and besides, I have more than enough power where I am." And with that he left.

♦

The club was packed that night, the lull in business caused by the murders now well and truly worn off. Three men, dressed casually, walked across the room to the bar, eyeing up the women as they went. You could tell by the confidence of their gait and the way they scanned the room that they were at home in this environment, probably helped by the flick-knives in their back pockets.

They got to the bar and ordered their drinks, looking around, when all three spotted the same person at once, and were struck dumb. The woman danced in the middle of the floor, running her fingers through her long brown hair. She wore a red tank-top and a short black skirt, flattering her impressive figure. Men were dancing all around her, all keen to go home with her, and she entertained a few for maybe a minute a time, dancing close up with them, enticing them, but ultimately leaving them.

These were not the kind of men to dance with a girl and be cast aside. They drank their drinks, still staring at the girl, allowing their minds to wander to other topics, all related to her in some way. Eventually the girl left as the club closed, making her way through the dark streets alone without a hint of concern or nervousness, as the three men followed her together, their intent now clear within their minds on some unspoken signal.

She reached a dingy apartment block in downtown and went inside. They followed. She went upstairs to the rooms she was renting and opened the door. The first man jammed his foot in the gap and pushed it open, forcing entrance to the room. He grabbed the girl and slammed her against the wall, tearing a part of her tank-top off as he did so.

He leaned in and kissed her as his two associates entered the room, astounded when she kissed him back, biting his lip so hard that he felt the salty taste of blood within his mouth.

She pushed him back and he made forwards again. She grinned at him and seized him by the throat with her left hand, lifting him from the ground.

"You are mine now, fool."

One of the other men made to help him and she thrust out her right hand, putting it through his chest with a splatter of blood and pulling out his heart. She tossed the first man onto the bed and turned, hurling a sphere of light into her third would-be rapist, killing him outright, and turning back to the bed.

She walked toward it, taking on her natural form as she did so, the beauty of her host impossible to outdo as the clothes formed from her mind vanished and she leapt, pinning down her first assailant...

◆

The girl in the red tank top departed from the building fifteen minutes later, leaving alive only the first man in a catatonic state; his heart beating, his mind ticking away, but something indescribable gone.

Samantha Kensington looked around her, feeling power flow through her, its intoxicating effects almost outdoing the knowledge of how she had gotten it, what she had done to attain this high. It was nice to be back in the world, the signs of her recent residence vanished from her skin as she walked through the streets, feeling the cool breeze on her flesh for the first time in six years.

You still have a target to kill, girl.

She heard Lucy's voice in her head, despite the lack of proximity between them.

"I will."

See to it that you do.

"I need a host."

Why?

"I think I, who he killed after I raised an army against him, will probably have a hard time bedding him."

You did it before.

"That was a long time ago." Sam smiled to herself; Lucy seemed to have no grasp of time and its effects on human relationships.

Kensington stopped and admired herself in a shop window; she was a little older than when she had last been in the world, but was still very beautiful, aware that her long, smooth legs and ample figure would be enough to win her most men, but not her target. Someone else, she thought; like me, not like that stick insect of a girlfriend of his, a real woman.

She gave a low sigh, remembering the time she had spent with Stanford before the Coup. But that was over now, she had no choice, she would kill him.

♦

"I think," Cabot said, "that we're going to have to consider taking down the SS." He was sat around a table with McInnes, Cooke, Bishop and the two apprentices.

"I think your chances for that are limited; their new enemy will probably have them down before we can act," McBride remarked, drinking the coffee from the last of the four cups.

"If only we knew who they were."

"I may be able to shed some light on that issue."

They looked up as Rose Mendelson came through the back door from the garden.

"Rose."

The others got to their feet. The assassin was clearly one step from collapse.

"There's quite a bounty on your head; they say you freed and killed Jenkins."

"Half right. I freed him; he knew about Michael's enemies, they killed him before he could finish the story."

"Rose, tell us everything you know." Cooke took on a sudden sense of urgency.

"Steady on, James; she's clearly been through a lot, she needs to rest!"

"No; thanks for the consideration, Terry, but I'd rather tell you guys this before I do anything else."

"Okay, sit down. McBride, make her a drink."

"Brandy please, straight up."

♦

There was a hammering at the door of a woman's apartment in the city, waking her from her slumber.

"You get it honey," her boyfriend groaned at her and she pulled herself out of bed, putting on a silk robe and tying it closed as she made her way to the door. The hammering resumed, louder this time.

"I'm coming, I'm coming. Hold on!" she shouted. She undid the first three locks, leaving the chain across, and opened the door slightly.

"What do you want at this time?"

"*You*," the voice on the other side replied.

"What? Go away!" She slammed the door closed and put the locks back in place, returning to bed quickly. The door exploded inward as she made her way back to the bedroom, the hinges and the locks torn from the wall.

Samantha Kensington stood in the doorway, staring at the woman. She opened her mouth to scream and Kensington leapt towards her, her form disintegrating as she came into contact.

She felt, for the briefest of instants, as if someone had splashed water on her, then a sudden numbness in her mind was the last thing she was aware of.

"Jenny?" Her boyfriend appeared in the doorway from the bedroom, bleary eyed and drowsy. "Who was it?"

She turned to face him and hurled an energy ball into his chest.

"Let's see..." Kensington went into the bedroom and admired her new body in the full length mirror. Nice body; and the former occupant had clearly taken care of it. Still, she thought, inspecting the curves critically; she preferred her own.

♦

Rob poured himself a martini from his drinks shaker and took a sip. He never had been altogether that tolerant of alcohol, and despite the notable cool factor of martini hadn't really taken to it. Emily was in the bunker tonight, as well as a number of other key figures in the government. He had a copy of Chiswick's resignation from the Council on the desk in front of him.

"Hello Rob."

He looked up at the figure stood in front of him; the body of Jenny, inhabited by the mind of Kensington, still dressed in her night gown.

"How did you get past the guards?"

"Subtlety and guile." She smiled at him and his heart fluttered.

"Why did you come here?"

"I think we both know the answer to that."

She was walking towards him slowly and he found it odd that he wasn't at all uncomfortable.

"Emily's in the bunker; you must be so lonely."

"Well, a bit..." he tried, amazed at how unconcerned he was.

"What will you do?" she asked, untying the robe as she advanced.

"Uh... I was just planning on having a drink then going to bed." He considered averting his eyes from the now undone robe, but the fog that was rapidly overtaking his mind prevented him.

"That doesn't sound like any fun at all; imagine all the other things you could be doing."

Stanford nodded mutely; he'd given up trying not to imagine the other things.

The woman, this total stranger, shrugged off the robe and leapt at him. She kissed him, a hungry, passionate kiss, Kensington making up for lost time, her tongue finding his as her hands found the buckle of his belt.

♦

"We're going to need to open the Ark," McInnes said when Mendelson finished. "We need to know who these guys are; we need to know how to stop them."

"I can't help but concur," Cooke replied. "We'll need to go into the SS building to get their keys."

The SS building was located in Bristol city centre, the third incarnation of the building being a small office complex, a generally unimpressive looking building, below which a labyrinth of offices and tunnels were sprawled like the root system of a very strange plant. The building was infinitely approachable, being in the middle of a city, but getting in was difficult. Getting out was impossible for all but the SS.

Eight figures, in black robes, appeared out of the fog that seemed to perpetually surround the building, even in the height of summer. They walked with purpose and confidence and eventually reached the front entrance.

They walked through the door and into the building, two turning to the security cameras and immediately putting them out of action as the others directed their attention at the unit of guards inside.

A backpack was dropped in this room as they departed, moving further into the SS building, guns blazing for brief seconds as they encountered members of the organization.

They blazed a path quickly through the building to Chiswick's office, then halted, watching the corridors surrounding it as a ninth member of their group walked down the path they had cleared and pushed open the door to the office.

"I think the robes are a little superfluous now, Lucy."

The robes became almost fluidic, reforming and changing colour until she stood before Chiswick in a denim jacket over white top and white trousers, her old canvas sword case slung over her back and her long brown hair now visible, the cloak's hood vanished.

"Hello Michael."

"So this is my comeuppance?"

"No, you will be tried before a higher court than I, though I wouldn't recommend holding out your hopes."

"Well quite," he sighed mournfully, still the fourteen-year-old boy he had been when all this had started, somewhere underneath the black of his garments and mind. "We might as well get it over with."

"As you wish." Lucy raised her hand to him and he contorted, his shape twisted violently, reforming when he was on his knees, screaming.

"Why," he breathed after the agony had subsided.

"You believed I would let you die painlessly?"

And it began again.

♦

Sex wasn't supposed to feel like this, Stanford thought, his senses returning to him at the most bizarre moment, as he looked up at the woman's face. There was no physical ecstasy, and none of the thrill he associated with the danger of an affair. He was simply numb, almost just watching events as they happened.

Suddenly the numbness subsided, feeling sweeping back through him, and the girl he was with changed just as suddenly as she had arrived, and he looked up into a face he had not seen in years.

"Sam?"

She tilted her head and leapt off of him, scowling.

"You see me?" she asked.

"Damn straight."

He pulled on the robe he kept by the side of his bed.

"Explain yourself." As an afterthought he grabbed the gun he kept under his pillow.

"How?" she scowled again and he jumped back as a ball of light appeared in her hand. With a flick of the wrist it was loosed towards him, spelling certain death until, mere inches from his body, the ball evaporated, disintegrating into the air.

"Right."

He tried to act as if he had even the vaguest of clues what was happening. "What the hell is going on?"

She turned and leapt, straight through the window and into the grounds below.

Stanford snatched up the phone beside his bed and dialed hurriedly, not willing to waste even one moment.

♦

"Okay, Rob; we'll have some people there soon." Cooke put the phone down and turned to the apprentices. "Rob's just been... Rob's just... something's happened at the mansion; I need you guys to get down there."

The door to the library burst open and Doctor Mortimer followed it.

"Something's happened in Bristol," he said, gasping for air as he leant against a bookshelf.

"Do you think you could take the time and oxygen to be little less vague?"

"The SS building; it just exploded."

"A fire?"

"No, an explosion, the kinda thing caused by a bomb or thirty," Mortimer told them, catching his breath.

"The SS building has fallen?"

"Yes, we have reason to believe that Michael Chiswick is dead."

"The others," McBride muttered so that only Cooke could hear. An hour previously Cabot, Bishop, Mendelson and Lyons had been dispatched to the Ark to gain access to the files on the PPA there, opting to use an alternative to the keys in the form of highly advanced, highly illegal hacking software.

"I know: we need a strategy…"

♦

"Is this going to take much longer?" Cabot asked irritably, sitting with his back against the dais on the penultimate floor of the Ark and his gun pointed at the lift.

"About thirty seconds longer, we're in; we just have to access the files."

"Well surely that should be quick?" Cabot asked.

"Well it would be, in a normal PC, but we have about three thousand terabytes of *compressed* information on this thing, it may take a while to find the file we're looking for." Bishop was typing frantically on the keyboard of her laptop, trying to find a needle in a very large stack of needles.

"Okay, I suppose it'll be no worse than waiting three hours for you to finish doing your makeup."

"That was ten years ago."

"You say potato…"

"We're in." Bishop brought the file up.

"Excellent; what does it say?"

"Oh God."

"Oh God?" Cabot asked, looking over her shoulder at the list of names on the screen.

"Oh God," he concurred. "We need to warn the others."

♦

"I think it's clear we're next on the list," McBride said.

"So we stick together, make sure nobody gets left alone."

The phone began to ring, they ignored it.

"Nobody gets left alone..." Carter said quietly. "Where's Master McInnes?"

"He's in the conservatory."

"Go!" Cooke yelled. Carter erupted, forming into a cloud and pouring through the keyhole, followed by McBride barging through the door.

♦

The wind blew the conservatory door open and McInnes put down his book to go and close it. He locked the door behind him and turned into the room.

"Terry," a woman greeted him coldly.

"Mel?" He stared into the eyes of his old friend, unwilling to panic despite the gun in her hand. "You're dead."

"No," she replied. "Never died, just vanished." She became invisible for a second then reappeared in front of him. "Much like the others."

"Ah." Realization dawned for McInnes. "Lucy sent you to kill me."

"Yes, and the Touched Ones."

"Oh." A cloud of dust fell through the glass roof of the conservatory and reformed into Daniel Carter, standing beside Mel.

"Bad idea, Dan," McInnes warned. She gave a brief head kick and Carter fell to the floor.

"So are you going to kill me, or stand around and talk about old times?"

Killian McBride, already in mid flight, crashed through the glass door to the conservatory and into Mel, bowling her over. She flipped to her feet as he got to his.

She loosed a stream of metal, a dozen or so throwing knives, in his direction and he waved his hands quickly toward each of them, atomising them in a second.

"Nice trick."

"I've got better."

She somersaulted backward, narrowly avoiding an energy ball and he tackled her, pushing both of them through the plate glass and onto the grass outside.

McBride pinned her down, one hand held in front of her face with an energy ball in it, ready to kill her.

"Don't," McInnes' soft voice spoke from inside the building. He went to the prostrate assassin and placed one hand on her forehead. She closed her eyes, trying to fight at first but then becoming suddenly looser, more relaxed.

"Undo the darkness of corruption, free the servant from this evil."

She opened her eyes.

"Let her go," McInnes instructed.

"Who is she?" McBride demanded.

"Mel Kingston; she's with the PPA. Now let her go."

"Are you mad?" McBride asked. "She was sent to kill you!"

"All of us, in fact."

"And I'm supposed to feel better about that?"

"Just do as he says." Cooke appeared in the doorway and McBride unpinned Kingston, keeping his palms open, ready to strike if necessary.

She got to her feet and looked to McInnes.

"What did you do?"

"I freed you from the illusion Lucy was putting you under; you are now who you once were."

"I'm free of her?"

"Yes."

Kingston threw her arms around McInnes and Cooke raised an eyebrow to his friend behind her back.

"There is little time, still; we must warn Stanford of what is to come," Cooke told them.

"There is nothing to be done; what has been set in motion must be allowed to continue. Our only chance is to strike after what is inevitable has finished, and what is avoidable has begun," McInnes corrected him.

"Meaning?" McBride replied, puzzled.

"Stanford will go before the Senate tomorrow; we must be there to save him," Kingston said.

"Ah."

♦

McBride went upstairs to bed. It had been a long day, after all, and the names on the list provided by Bishop and Cabot were really outside of his area. He got to his room and found Annie there waiting for him.

"You saved Terry?"

"Well, I rendered some assistance—" Killian was interrupted when she kissed him, suddenly.

"Stop being so modest!" she told him. "You're just being silly; well done, we'll talk in the morning."

"I have an early morning, we have things to do."

"Alright then, I'll see you in the afternoon?"

"Most likely late morning, yeah."

"Okay then; night." She kissed him again and left the room chirpily.

"That's a little odd," he said to himself, and went to bed.

♦

It was three AM, four hours before Stanford was scheduled to be on the Senate floor, when a small house in Alveston was attacked. The two women, practically identical in their appearance, opened the unlocked doors to the house and went inside. They made no noise as they walked up the stairs and into the house's only bedroom, before emptying clips from their pistols into the bed.

Blood began to seep through the covers and they smiled to themselves, content that their job was done.

"Hey."

The two woman turned, glaring at the young girl suddenly stood between them and the door. She looked barely more than fifteen, but she glowered at the pair angrily.

"Missed me," she announced.

The faster of the two quickly threw an energy ball that struck the girl, who flinched slightly but turned back to face them. She grew in height, changing from teenage girl to mid-twenties woman with short brown hair, a pale complexion and a body covered by a long white robe.

A wave of her hand was all it took to dispatch the two assassins and she looked around her bedroom with a curious smile; it suddenly seemed so much smaller. The woman sensed something and quickly her form reverted, becoming once again the teenage girl, a moment before Eleanor appeared before her in long white robes.

"Verity, are you alright?"

"A couple of women just tried to kill me," she admitted, "anything to do with you?"

"Ultimately my fault, but there's nothing I can do about that now; I've come to take you home."

"This is my home now, Ellie, the court ruled..."

"It'll just be our little secret, okay?"

"Okay!" The girl smiled enthusiastically. Eleanor took Verity by the hand and both women vanished.

Cooke sat alone in the great hall, thinking, when Ellie appeared beside him, the young girl still in her charge.

"James!" Verity smiled at seeing him. "Why so grumpy?" she asked, a hint of sarcasm in her tone.

"Oh, nothing you need worry about, Miss Robbins: how're you?"

"Some women tried to kill me!"

"Why did they do that?" he asked.

"Because I can do this." She smiled brightly and an energy ball formed in her hands, changing shape from a sphere into a plane, then into a swan, and finally a glowing green rose.

"She's a Touched One?" Cooke asked Ellie, speaking over the girl's head. "How is that possible?"

"I cared for her as a child; did you ever wonder how she recovered after her parents died?"

"I did. I thought it was Tina."

"It was, in part, but I had a hand in it."

"You cursed her like this?"

"She dealt with it from a much younger age than the rest of you; she doesn't really notice the other voices."

"Hmm."

"It's okay, James. I'm home now."

"Yes Verity; you are." He smiled. "Eleanor, I'm gonna need you to—"

"Not yet; there is time enough to worry about that tomorrow," Ellie interrupted him before he could finish his request.

"Alright."

"Now rest."

"I don't need to sleep, Eleanor, I..."

"Sleep and rest are two completely different things," she interrupted him.

"Very well."

8

Robert Stanford walked towards the Senate Hall at six fifty-five, at the same time as the Engineers ran towards the back entrance of the building. With Stanford were the Council, a number of aides, and a large quotient of Secret Service agents, ready with their guns.

The debate began today on the Executive Powers bill, and it needed to be passed. Empter said he should speak to the Senate, possibly make some compromises, hopefully get some votes back; it was a hard sell, but Stanford was confident.

Nobody knew about the events of the previous night, and none of them ever would if he had anything to do with it. The secret died with him. Michael Chiswick was gone, no trace of his program had been found throughout the Society, and Ben Chiswick had been found an hour ago having died from an overdose. Laura's eyes were red with tears as she walked with him now, and he had to respect her for coming. Once more unto the breach, he thought.

♦

Tim Greenwood came to the office of Senator Simon Winter to walk with him to the Senate Hall and saw the Senator lying on the floor in front of his desk, a dozen or so staple holes through the back of his white shirt.

Greenwood turned to run and stared into the face of a black-clad operative. He felt the cold metal of the gun-barrel against his side and took a deep breath before the shot was fired.

♦

Stanford reached the doors of the Senate Hall and pushed them both open with all the strength he could muster, stepping into the chamber.

He never saw it coming; a staple straight through the forehead, and a second through the heart. The Senate wasn't here. Those that hadn't fled during the night were now in custody or dead, and the three snipers in the roof had just completed their objective when Stanford hit the ground. Dead.

The Secret Service exploded with rage, pistols firing up towards where they thought the snipers might be as Emily fell, trying to be close to her love, her corpse falling just beside his.

The doors at the other end of the hall burst open, as well as the doors through which the senators entered, the last remnants of the SS and the WTDD joining the fight. Shots from the Secret Service hit members of the SS, shots from the SS hit members of the Secret Service, and the three snipers continued firing, felling Mary Sharp-Thomas as her guns clicked dry within the first thirty seconds.

"Killian!" Cooke yelled at his apprentice.

McBride fired his pistols into a cluster of SS agents, emptying both clips then discarding the weapons. He looked across at Cooke as the Master Engineer was struck three times in the chest by sniper rounds from above.

"Deal with the snipers, now!"

McBride nodded and leapt, kicking off one pillar about thirty feet up and launching into in the rafters, landing right in front of one of the PPA.

McBride knocked the long rifle to one side and caught the fist heading toward his face. The apprentice squeezed the man's hand and he winced in pain, then fell as McBride poured hardlight energy into him.

Carter somersaulted into the Senate seating area, spraying rounds in all directions as the SS struggled to get close enough to him to aim properly, becoming a cloud whenever he saw one fire a shot that would actually hit him.

The clips fell to the ground as they were expended and he swung the guns around his back to the speed-loader attached to his jacket, ramming new clips in and starting to fire again instantly.

Looking down he put three staples through the back of a robed figure running toward Danny Sharp-Thomas, then was helpless to do anything but watch as the councillor fell to a sniper round from above. Carter leapt at the pillars, kicking away from the right-hand one as he reached it and becoming gaseous as shots poured into him, using the comparative weightlessness to float toward the ceiling, then reforming twenty feet up on the left-hand pillar, shooting down at the SS before expanding again.

He condensed beside the sniper and broke his neck before pushing him from the rafters, down into the fight below.

He heard a voice speaking to him through his earpiece and listened hard amidst the gunshots.

"The Council is dead; it's just SS versus PPA now. We've got to go."

"I'm in the rafters," he spoke into the collar of his lab coat.

"There's an exit on the far left, probably guarded, but it's your best bet. We'll wait five minutes."

The rafters began to creak under Carter's feet and he leapt the thirty feet to the far side of the hall as the sheer weight of staples began to tear apart the structure of the building's roof. He kicked open the door in front of him and found himself in a room with bare-wood walls, with a series of ropes and pulleys slung along the sides; presumably for the use of people who performed maintenance on the rafters.

He kicked open another door and ran down a long flight of steps, firing his guns indiscriminately in front in case any guards appeared to challenge him. He ran through the next room, head bowed as staples flew from both sides, no doubt causing more damage to the gunmen than their target.

He moved through this room, turning left and then right through the last door which shattered as he collided with it, and he burst out into the fresh air, just as the Aston pulled off a hand-break turn, stopping right in front of him and facing towards the exit.

McBride pushed open the door and Carter leapt in, slamming it closed behind himself as the last of their pursuers emerged from the building.

♦

The car, dented and scratched from the firefight, stopped just short of the staircase into the Hall, its pursuers now dead or stopped by other means. The three occupants got out, their lab-coats torn in several places and all of their guns empty.

The two apprentices sighed wearily, though they still ran up the steps into the hall, where Davies and McInnes were waiting for them.

"Was your mission a success?" McInnes asked anxiously as they came through the door.

"Catastrophe," Carter remarked, falling into a chair, exhausted. "The Council is dead, as is much of the Senate."

"Hmm."

"Terry," Cooke spoke quietly. "Now is not the time for us to be pensive; summon everybody in the Hall to me, and quickly. Lucy will be here within minutes."

"Of course."

♦

"You are all my family, my brothers and sisters in arms, my children, my friends, and I love you all." Cooke looked between the forty or so people gathered in front of him. "An unspeakable enemy has taken over the society, destroying all that we have built and that we have sworn to protect. I must ask you now, each of you, something which will be hard for those of you who know me well and return my love to do—"

"We're ready to fight, Master." McBride spoke up from the crowd.

"Yes, I know, and that is why it will be hard for you all to leave here, to flee into the Society, to hide and wait until it is time—"

"Sir!" Carter shouted. "We are going to fight this!"

"You will fight, when the time comes, but there is a chance, however remote, that I may be able to stop Lucy before this gets out of hand, remove the ringleader of the forces arrayed against you and still be with you to destroy the others, and bring back the Society Tom Walsh dreamed of: I have to do this, I have to remain here and fight her, or my chance is lost, and our dreams may go with it.

"Follow Master McInnes from here, go into Bristol and spread out, communicate only in secret, and never show your abilities to anyone; go now."

The others began to leave, McInnes shaking his old friend's hand as he went, and Bishop exchanging a brief hug with him before going.

"Master," McBride began as he faced the android.

"No."

"You don't even—!"

"You can't stay. This is my fight. Yours will come later, I promise you, in a place of far graver need."

"Very well."

They bowed to each other and McBride left, leaving Cooke alone in the hall.

"Never has this place seemed so large, like a house with all the children gone, and I am the old man, left in my big house with nothing but empty memories and half-built dreams," he spoke aloud, as if to himself.

"She will kill you."

"Maybe, maybe not." He smiled. "Tell me everything."

Ellie closed her eyes and the energy flowed between them once more.

"That is it," she said when it was done. "That is all I can do for you."

"There is one last thing." He spoke softly, as he had done whilst alive, when contemplating things of enormous gravity. "You can return me to my original form."

"You wish to live, only to die?"

"Doesn't everyone?"

"Ultimately, yes, but they don't choose to do it for such a short time."

"I want to taste coffee again,"

"Alright then: if it is what you truly want."

"It is, and then you must return to the place you belong, and never look back."

"I can't do that, you know I can't."

"You can at least try though, my dear."

"Very well."

He knelt before her and she placed both hands upon his head, dust swirling around them into a whirlwind as the energy built up.

♦

McInnes led the apprentices through a back alley in Bristol and saw in front of them a man, as tall as himself, and with shoulders just as broad. He was dressed finely— even elegantly—in black and maroon, with a long black cape fluttering in the breeze.

"Turn back," McInnes whispered and the others turned, only to find three dozen of Lucy's soldiers now behind them.

"Mister McBride; take the others out of here, right now. We'll handle this." McInnes shrugged off his lab coat and dropped it to the floor, the man in front of them doing the same with his cape.

"Yes sir." McBride looked at a likely door along the alleyway and shot it open, leading the others through as Bishop, Cabot, McInnes and Mortimer faced the others.

"What's the plan?" Cabot asked.

"You guys take the guards; Siobhan and Liam lead them away if you can. I'll do what I can with that guy."

The man leapt, gliding towards them. McInnes kicked him in the side as he went for Bishop and quickly dodged three punches, drawing a pistol from his braces and shooting him four times in the face before the man tore the gun angrily from McInnes' hand.

♦

"Killian!" Carter shouted to his friend as the other apprentice stopped in the middle of the cathedral, staring up at the stained glass window depicting the Last Supper and then, lower down, the crucifixion of Christ.

"Dan; go."

Carter ran to him and grabbed him by the shoulder.

"You're crazy! You've got to come!"

"Hisa-me are coming. Lots of them. I can hold them off and make my escape later, while you guys vanish; go now."

Carter looked into his friend's eyes and nodded slowly.

"Till happy reunion."

"Till happy reunion," McBride intoned, and Carter left.

McBride knelt on the floor and waited for them to come. When they did, it only took them a few moments to surround him.

"Amen," he muttered, and stood.

♦

"The great Master Cooke: I killed you once before. This time I will purge every trace of your existence from this planet."

Cooke stood in front of his desk, an empty coffee cup near him, waiting for Lucy as she strode forward, stopping a few paces from him.

"No doubt." He hurled an energy ball at her and she shuddered slightly, taking the blow. He hurled another, and another, and another, emptying all the strength he had into her before sagging, propping himself up against the desk.

"Most impressive. I see you've sent your helpers away? No matter, we'll find them and kill them. There's no where left for them to run, no allies left to protect them."

♦

McBride waved a hand at the nearest hisa-me, summoning all the energy he could. Nothing happened.

"Ironic, isn't it; as a servant of the light your powers don't work on holy ground, yet..." The woman opened her hand slowly, and an energy ball appeared in it. "Ours do."

McBride expanded his mind, feeling the air around him. It felt as it always did these days. There was a chance then.

The hisa-me threw an energy ball and he leapt straight up, somersaulting through the air as he made his way towards the ceiling, almost two hundred feet up, and grabbed a rafter. He leapt again, down this time to a balcony a little way away and caught the next energy ball thrown, hurling it back at its owner. A gargoyle beside him exploded as light struck it. He leapt again, praying silently for some kind of intervention as he moved, landing beside one of the women and kicking her down, leaping off again and letting a ball aimed at him strike the girl he had just knocked down.

♦

Lucy slid her scimitar back into the canvas bag and drew a pistol. "I wonder if you can still feel pain in there? Any last words?"

Cooke smiled sadly and opened his mouth.

"Our Father, who art in heaven, hallowed be thy name; thy kingdom come, thy will be done, on Earth as it is..."

The shot reverberated around the Hall, the high-powered staple smashing through Cooke's skull, the Master of the Engineers falling the ground, bleeding from his head wound and soon to be dead.

PART TWO

Two men played a game of pool in a bar, eighteen miles outside of Bristol on a cool summer's night. Around them the other patrons of the establishment watched, sipping their beers.

One player smoothly potted the black and his opponent retreated bitterly, retaking his seat.

"Anyone else feel lucky?" the victor taunted the reluctant audience to play him.

"I'll give it a go."

A man stepped from a shadowy corner. He wore an ankle-length leather coat and had long black hair with hints of blue. He walked to the table confidently, taking one of the cues from the rack at one side and faced the man who had just won three games of pool in a row, entirely unfazed.

"Care to make this interesting?"

"Oh certainly," the challenger replied, dropping a huge wad of notes on the table. "How does two thousand pounds sound to you?"

"It's your money, I suppose; I'll take that bet, and what's more, I'll let you break."

The newcomer smiled the easy smile of someone who

fears nothing.

"Very generous of you." He set up the balls quickly and then walked casually to the other side of the table. He lined up the cue with the white ball and struck.

The ball bounced from the far cushion, rebounding into the clustered balls and knocking them from their positions, sending three red balls rolling gently into pockets.

"You can put that down, by the way." The newcomer nodded towards his opponent's cue as he potted a fourth ball.

♦

It was all over in a few scant minutes, all the balls potted by the mysterious man before the reigning champion had taken so much as a shot.

"Now, the two thousand pounds, if you'd be so good?"

The pub's regulars got to their feet, a variety of weapons appearing in their hands.

"I don't want any trouble, just what I'm due."

"You'll get what's coming to you—"

There was a flash of movement and a long sword was drawn from within the leather coat, slicing off the barrels of the nearest three guns. The newcomer settled into in a defensive stance.

"What are you?"

"Waiting for two thousand pounds..."

♦

The man slept that night in the pub, having been living in such establishments for the last three weeks after all that had happened, his coat and scant few other belongings lying on a nearby armchair.

He woke noiselessly at about two in the morning, feeling a change in the atmosphere of the room. He leapt from the bed, fully clothed, and snatched up his sword, unsheathing it even as he swung at the intruder.

His strike was parried and he struck again, the deflection this time pushing his sword down into a chair, slicing through the wood.

Cabot flicked the light switch and faced his enemy, finding him no enemy at all.

"Master McInnes!" He sheathed the sword and the taller man did the same.

"It's good to see you, Liam."

"It's good to see *me*? Damn, Terry, with you here we stand a chance; I thought I was the only one left outside."

"So did I, until I saw your little game in the bar today."

"Ah." Cabot paused. "I presume you want me to give it all back like a good boy? Not using our abilities for our own good, that sort of thing?"

"Under normal circumstances I'd say yes, but right now we don't have time to be taking the moral high ground."

"Have you heard anything since—"

"He's dead."

"That's impossible! He couldn't have been—"

"We can't ignore the signs, Liam; you can't say you didn't sense it?"

"I did, but that doesn't mean—"

"It happened before, eight years ago."

"That doesn't mean that's what it was! We understand so little of what any of this stuff means at the best of times!"

"Liam." McInnes spoke soothingly to the man who had once been his apprentice. "He is dead. He could not have allowed himself to be taken alive, and yet our victory is not yet won; thus he is dead and the task falls to us."

"Aha, then you have not given up all hope, Master?"

"Never for a second; our friends need help and we can provide: let us do so, shortly."

"Why shortly? Why not take them now, rescue our colleagues from their cells by dead of night, and strike down our foes while there?"

"You have not your wits about you; at night their holders will be most aware, most ready for us, expecting an attack. We strike in two days, after I have some troops together."

"Troops? There are others?"

"You must be aware of Robinson's little force, mustering on the fringes of our territory?"

"I am aware, but I doubt you will get assistance from them in rescuing the others; the risks are high."

"We shall see; perhaps the Hall still holds some power even now?"

1

Killian McBride lurched awake, falling from the small stone bench that was his bed within his cell. He looked at the glass door in front of him, and at his four guards, guns always trained either on him or down the corridor. These weren't the kind of guys to get sloppy, to leave the doors open for a little while by accident, to give him so much as a chance of getting out.

He sat on the bed and picked up a chunk of rock he had found on his first day here. He scratched another line onto the wall, then counted them. Forty days. He wondered what was going on in the outside world; if any of the others had escaped. He only knew one thing for sure, and that was that James Cooke, master of Cooke Hall and mentor to McBride, was dead. He had felt something, like a concussion wave expanding at the speed of light, hit every particle in his body simultaneously. He had been in mid-air, trying to buy the others time to escape as he fought the dozen or so foes sent to take them in by Lucy, and had been knocked back to earth by the blow, leading to his capture and his current predicament.

He sensed Lucy's presence in the world like a lead ball on

the rubber sheet of his mind, distorting everything by her mere presence. The last battle was yet to be fought.

♦

Five men gathered, one at each of the five points of the pentagram, each taking a predestined spot wordlessly, facing each other and looking at the large space in the middle of the symbol imprinted on the floor.

The renegade was out of hand; something needed to be done. Someone would be called and she would be brought to order; she would pay for this.

♦

The best word for what they were was rebels. A small group of people, clustered in a storm cellar built foolishly by someone who lived in the mistaken belief that a hurricane was going to strike the south-west of England at any moment.

They had been in the cellar, some thirty miles from the centre of the PFS, for almost a week now, since their last safe house had been discovered and raided.

There was a banging on the door to the cellar and they all looked up, guns concealed beneath their jackets suddenly brought to bear on a square metre of wood.

"Answer it," one spoke up as the knocking came again. "It might be a friend."

"It might also be the army," another countered.

"I hardly think it's likely, James, that an army has turned up outside our hideout and is *knocking*."

"Good point." The one named James moved to the door the flung it open, gun in front of him.

"Speak friend and enter!" he bellowed into the darkness.

"Friend!" came the reply; a distinctly female voice.

"What is your name?" James Robinson shouted back, uncertain.

"Hannah Thatcher!"

"Let her in," the sarcastic man said and moved towards the door, lowering his gun.

Robinson stepped aside and a figure, cloaked in dark blue, entered the cellar, throwing off her hood and revealing herself to be, as she claimed, the former Senator, Hannah Thatcher.

"How did you find us?" Robinson asked as she took the seat he had vacated to answer the door.

"An old friend gave me directions." She shot a glance at the sarcastic man. "You could at least say hello, Timmy."

"Hello, Hannah."

She smiled.

"She can be trusted," Greenwood said.

"Very well," Robinson put his gun away with a flourish. "Senator Thatcher." He extended his hand.

"Senator Robinson. I don't recall you being quite so civil when we last met." She took the hand and shook it.

"Then we were on opposing sides of an argument. It would seem that now we are allies."

"Or at least that we have a mutual enemy."

"That's one way of putting it." He paused and looked around the room at the others. "Senator Thatcher, meet the other members of our band of survivors. We had many more, until we were attacked. We're not sure how many are left now, scattered."

"Ah," Thatcher said softly.

"Anyway, this is Rose Mendelson, former SS, as is the guy sitting next to her; Ewan Evans, as was—one of the very few survivors of the SS building explosion the day this all began."

"Impressive that you got out: there are others here?"

"Yes, scattered around the buildings near this one, maybe twenty men."

"Ah. So we're not in a position to launch a revolution tomorrow?"

"Give us time; have you got any news from the Society?"

"Most of the Senate is dead, but we already knew that would be the case. The Executive has been taken over by a man named Richard Marlow—"

"That's impossible," Greenwood spoke up.

"What?"

"He was one of the assassins working for the Unity Alliance during the Faction War; he died killing Lucy."

"Lucy isn't dead though, Tim; perhaps the same is true of this Marlow?" Mendelson asked.

"But it makes no sense; they were total opposites, Richard was one of the best martial artists in the Society, a man of honour and decency. Why would Lucy give him power?"

"That's not really important right now," Mendelson told him.

"What is then?"

"Richard Marlow, unlike Lucy, is within my abilities to kill; I want permission to make a hit."

"Not yet. We can't afford for anything to go wrong just yet, not until we have better information and preferably far more men."

♦

The morning after Thatcher's arrival amongst the rebels, members of the former PFS army found themselves again smashing rocks in a quarry. They were unsure as to why they did this, but had no other option: hammers hit rock over and over repeatedly and in time, whilst further convicts scurried about with wheelbarrows, collecting the rubble.

The supervisors, a mix of servicemen who followed Lucy's government into power, watched, their rifles held alertly, scanning the new slaves for dissension or slackness, and were ready to shoot should they sense any.

The leader of the supervisors was a woman; standing tall at five-eleven she was perfectly proportioned, but yet strangely unattractive, the symmetry of her face passing out of beautiful and into creepy.

A guard toppled forward, crashing into the ground and throwing a cloud of sand up. Instantly the others moved to find out what had happened, quickly locating the neat staple hole in the back of his head.

"Good morning, ladies and gentlemen."

Standing on one of the nearby ridges stood a tall figure in camouflage gear, his clothing not concealing him against the grey quarry.

"I'm here to offer you the choice to free yourselves from your current lives and labours, or, failing that, to die."

"They will die either way, and who are you to challenge us?"

Clichéd, Cabot thought as he watched from the wood bordering the quarry, training his sniper rifle on the nearby guards.

McInnes leapt down from the ridge, the blade of his katana swinging; shining steel death for the nearest guard. Cabot and the guards opened fire at the same time, the Engineer's round caving in the skull of his target as McInnes danced quickly around staples, blade flashing brightly as his sword strokes cut swathes through the troops trying to divide their fire between him and Cabot.

The woman rose up in front of the Master Engineer and McInnes stopped, facing her with his sword at the ready.

"I've defeated your kind before."

"Ah yes, with support from your apprentices and the others; now, as you can see, it's just the two of us."

"Make that the three of us." Melanie Kingston appeared beside McInnes, her fists clenched.

"It makes no difference."

Cabot dropped down from his hiding place and began freeing the prisoners, quickly and quietly telling them to run. He looked up as the woman leapt angrily towards McInnes, fists flying through the air rapidly. Cabot fired a shot absently behind him at a guard as McInnes dodged the strikes effortlessly before kicking the woman back.

The woman sprawled but flipped to her feet for a brief second before an arm like an iron bar collided with her and she went down again.

She was quickly back on her feet and swinging at Kingston, knocking the assassin back, the American girl landing on her hands and kicking out with both feet angrily.

As the blocks inevitably came, McInnes landed a fist in her stomach and back-flipped, kicking her in the face.

"Mel, go with Liam; I'll handle this."

"There's no way to finish this: she's immune to our weapons," Kingston argued.

"Really?"

The woman swung at McInnes and he dropped, leg spinning to take her legs out from under her. He drew the sword in his sheath and swung it down through her stomach and into the ground as she tried to rise. She did not bleed or scream, she simply spat at him and continued to try and rise as McInnes smashed his second sword down through her mouth.

She glared up at him over the hilt of the sword, still struggling, and he walked away to where Cabot had assembled the former prisoners.

"We've got maybe an hour before she manages to get out of that and informs her superiors," he whispered to Cabot before addressing his new troops.

"I'm not gonna waste any time telling you all that's happened, because the bits that can be understood you already know. There's a resistance movement a little way from here—Liam and Mel are going to take you there now—and hopefully they'll have food and shelter for you all. Things have changed a lot lately, so don't do anything rash, but we will take our homes back; I promise you."

The assembled men and women prepared to move, picking up their spades and pickaxes, now weapons of freedom rather than tools of enslavement.

"Terry," Cabot said, putting one hand on his shoulder, "why aren't you coming with us?"

"I've got something to do in the city. I'll go to the safehouse when I'm done."

"What? Are you crazy? Everybody will be looking for you: even you can't honestly hope to survive!"

"What I must do will take a few moments; there will be no chance of me coming to harm, thank you."

"Very well, but be careful, Master; God knows what manner of creatures we are yet to encounter."

"I will tread softly, Liam." McInnes chuckled slightly. "It seems odd for you to be counselling me to be more careful, does it not?"

"Every role must be reversed at some point, Master."

"Ah-so." McInnes smiled. "Take care of the others, I will return by dawn tomorrow."

♦

A figure condensed in the centre of the seal; a dark presence vaguely recognizable amidst the swirling particles as human, still slightly translucent but becoming more solid, more real over time.

The shape blurred for a moment, going against the flow, and the five cloaked men around the edge of the seal looked at each other, but continued to chant; their words getting louder each second until the shape was completely formed. It looked slightly different than they had expected; breathing heavily as though out of breath. Its robes, unlike those of everyone else to come through, were grey and untorn; indeed, they looked brand new.

"Who are you?" one of the men asked suspiciously. "Are you the one we called for?"

"I could hardly be here, were I not," the robed figure said, his face hidden beneath his hood. "Lower the barrier."

"What is your name?"

The man they had summoned took a step towards the one speaking, who flinched nervously.

"I asked you your name, creature," he said with false bravado, "answer me or we shall send you back!"

This threat didn't have quite the effect he had intended, as the hooded figure within the seal punched the barrier between the two of them. His hand penetrated the edge of the seal and the blood-stained fingers wrapped around the throat of the man, who screamed at the top of his lungs. Fire glowed around the point at which arm and barrier met.

The hand retracted, pulling the captive up to its waist through the seal. The man screamed again, the energy of the barrier now attacking his stomach. He looked up into the hood, trying to see the face of his captor, but it was impossible; the hood was empty.

"Lower the barrier," the bodiless voice hissed. "If you don't we'll both be sent down."

The man, aware that even now he was beginning to lose his hold on his form, quickly muttered something under his breath.

The seal faded and his captor released him, letting him drop to the ground as the grey-robed man turned on the remaining four, the men gathered around the pentagram summoning what power they had to defend themselves, but not fast enough. Before any of them could open their palms to muster energy they were all dead, the mysterious figure leaving only the first alive before he swept from the room.

♦

The members of the rebellion sat in the cellar, trying their best to amuse themselves and stave off the cabin fever they knew was descending inexorably upon them.

"I'm just going out for a fag," Evans said, standing up, throwing on his leather jacket and leaving. He got outside and lit a cigarette, putting it into his mouth and waiting amid the haze of his own smoke. It wasn't long before a woman in black emerged from the darkness and stood looking at him expectantly.

The former SS agent's shape changed; the leather jacket, jeans and T-shirt becoming now freshly-pressed evening dress; his build taller and slimmer, his facial expressions more chiseled and his hair slicked back with gel.

"That's better." He held the cigarette away from his mouth. "They're planning a hit on Richard Marlow in the near future; the girl Mendelson will be carrying it out."

"This is not a problem; he is quite safe," the woman replied coldly. "Is that all you have to tell me?"

"The girl has talents; she will not be able to achieve her goal, but she will doubtless cause some damage, and she will be very difficult to apprehend."

"I think we're up to catching one little girl."

"I merely report things as I find them; it is, of course, the duty of the new Executive to decide what is to be done with such situations."

"Yes, as little help as you have been. We launched the raid by ourselves; you practically stood in the way!"

"Actually, I did stand in the way. If you'd waited for them to launch an attack I would have warned you and we could have been ready and they could all have been killed or captured. As it is you've given them more publicity, more confidence and they're still on the loose. How do you like them apples?"

"I think being in their form is going to your head: we will stop this Mendelson, and then we will attack again, and you can't stop us."

"I'd watch your tone, and don't start presuming that your wishes are those of our new leader."

"I am here as her emissary; and why should I watch my tone? We are both merely servants, and we both have the same power and status; or we will do, right up until Lucy finds out that you've been insubordinate—"

The trapdoor creaked behind the man and he smiled, waving one hand at the woman to atomise her as he turned, Ewan Evans once again facing the newcomer.

"Is everything okay, Tim?"

"Just thought you'd been out here a long time," Greenwood said softly.

"I was just thinking. I didn't mean to cause alarm, sorry."

"No worries, I guess we're all just a little on edge these days." Greenwood turned back towards the trapdoor. "See you in a bit then," he said, and disappeared into the hole.

♦

Mendelson hadn't had any trouble sneaking out of the cellar, and now stalked the streets of the Society by herself, moving through the crowds, unseen by the dull eyes of the passing men and women. She had not worn the black of her trade in quite some time, she realised, as she walked through the city, amused by what things the mind turned to when it was nervous. In front of her the massive form of the NCC loomed, its metal-plated walls reflecting the flickering orange street lamps.

The Lord Protector's office was on the fourth floor, she remembered, recalling the time when she had been a legitimate servant of the administration. Mendelson checked her equipment nervously as she looked up at the building. It started to rain, the drops falling quickly, and she moved underneath the cover of a shop awning. It was about three hundred meters across Sharp-Thomas Square to the front door, and that was just how she was going to get in: through the front door, guns blazing.

A hand came from behind her, covering her mouth as another wrapped around her waist and pulled her into the shop.

She drew her pistol and was about to fire when she recognized the man who had so suddenly abducted her.

"Master McInnes, in civilized societies people don't go around seizing young ladies and pulling them into darkened rooms!" she said quickly, brushing the rain from her satin clothing, obviously frustrated at having been taken unawares.

"My dear Miss Mendelson; in civilized societies, young ladies do not go around with enough weapons to take on a small army."

"Touché." She sat down on the shop counter, looking about herself at the shop's contents; sweets, toffees, chocolate and chewing gums. "What brings you here?" She removed a thin piece of metal from her belt and began absent-mindedly tinkering with the lock on one of the display cabinets.

"You."

"How so?"

"You're here to try and kill Richard Marlow: I'm here to counsel you to not."

"It'd be a magnificent stroke! A coup de grace for the rebels, a massive sign that we're not to be—"

"It'd be a coup de grace *on* the rebels, having lost one of their best chances of putting up a decent fight!"

"I can take Richard; I used to beat him in sparring matches, and he was one of Danielle's guys."

"Does it not strike you as strange that he, a valiant servant of Robert Stanford, comes back to claim power over a government which you know Lucy is pulling the strings on, eight years after being declared dead trying to kill her."

"It's strange, but no stranger than you knowing exactly when and where to find me, or you what I was here to do."

"But they're all part of the same thing; my bizarre intuition even I don't understand, but you've seen things over the past ten years, things which make Marvel comics look mundane."

"What are you saying? That there's some connection between this woman Lucy and Marlow?"

"I'm saying this woman Lucy *is* Marlow. She's a demon, Rose. Richard Marlow is possessed by a demon. The form he shows externally is no longer the shape of his mind. Lucy was weakened by Eleanor Giles and so took his body to make herself strong again, as well as to bring Mel Kingston, Ellie Hutton and Phillip Rooke around to her side; with that she's pretty much unstoppable, wouldn't you agree?"

"Oh, I'd say so: but there is one crucial flaw in your theory."

"Really? And what might that be?"

"Demons don't exist; you're living in a world of fairy tales, Master McInnes."

"Rose," McInnes shook his head sadly. He drew a knife and made to throw it at her, catching her completely off guard, and she slipped from view as she made for her own weapon.

"You can vanish at will! You aren't using any form of stealth, you are simply becoming invisible! And you deny the possibility of demons? This is the real world and it is full of them, both metaphorical and actual, and Lucy is one: if you go and attempt this hit you will die."

She focused her mind, pulling herself back into sight.

"I'm glad for your concern, Terry, but I think you've lost your mind."

"Said with all due respect, I presume?"

"Of course. Now if you'll excuse me—"

A bright light shone outside the window and it shattered, bits of glass flying inward. McInnes dived for the floor and Mendelson tried to get down, but was too slow; fragments of the glass tore her skin, drawing blood.

A man stepped across the threshold into the shop, an energy ball held cautiously in one hand.

"Miss Mendelson?"

Mendelson had vanished, but he saw the blood on the floor and pressed on.

A foot came from below, knocking his hand up, and the ball into the ceiling. He span, throwing another at McInnes as the Engineer rose, quickly dodging and then striking back, two well-aimed fists putting the man into a cabinet full of toffees.

The man scowled, his clothes swirling into long black robes as he climbed to his feet.

"I've fought worse than you," he scowled, but McInnes had gone.

◆

"What the hell was that?" Mendelson asked McInnes, when he joined her on the roof of the shop, taking a bite from a large bar of chocolate.

"Where did you get that?"

"Stole it from the shop, of course."

"You're *looting* now?"

"I think that's the least of our concerns, Terry; who was that?"

"One of our enemies; quite a powerful one."

"Is he dead?"

"No; I don't have anything at my disposal which will let me kill them."

"You can't kill them?"

"I fought one the night this all began. Emptied entire clips into him; he didn't dodge them, they hit him, and..." McInnes sighed, recalling the fight from his elaborate memory palace, "they were useless; the same will be true if you go up against the guards in the NCC."

"Alright; after what just happened I'm inclined to give you the benefit of the doubt, but if it turns out I wasted a chance to end this I'm going to kill you myself."

"Sounds fair."

◆

The rebels ran for their guns, arming themselves with whatever they could. Robinson gestured to a group of about a dozen and led them outside, weapons pointed into the fog in the direction the noise was coming from.

Figures came through the darkness at a run and Robinson braced himself, ready to shoot.

The leading runner leapt, covering the twenty yards with inhuman ease and knocking Robinson's gun from his hand with a kick.

Three other guns were immediately placed against the man's head and he stopped dead, looking around him.

"I'm Colonel Cabot; I bring you reinforcements with the compliments of Master McInnes."

"Where did they come from?" Robinson asked suspiciously.

"The quarry, where Lucy's people have been holding all the prisoners of war," Cabot explained. "Master McInnes should be here soon; can you accommodate more people?"

"I'm sure we can make room," Greenwood spoke up from the back, and the guns were removed from Cabot's head.

"Much obliged, Senator Greenwood—"

"It's just Tim here, Liam: there's no Senate left."

"Around a dozen senators remain alive. Some of them are serving Lucy: I'm surprised Winter isn't among them, myself; he always followed evil's coat tails to the top."

"Well, quite. In this instant, however, he appears to have backed the wrong horse; he was killed on the same day as Stanford and the others."

"I expected as much. Listen, this place gives me the creeps, can we get indoors?"

"Sure thing," Greenwood led them down the ramp into the storm cellar, Robinson remaining outside with Evans.

"What do you think?" Robinson asked the former agent.

"I think they're up to something; no-one's ever really trusted the WTDD, and I'm sure you know that Greenwood was under their protection?"

"Yeah, that's what I was thinking; keep an eye on that Cabot fellow, would you? I don't trust his sort."

"Certainly, James."

Evans smiled to himself as Robinson went back down into the storm cellar, and took another cigarette from a pouch on his belt, lighting it with a snap of his fingers.

2

Tim Greenwood awoke painfully in the morning and got out of his bunk set deep into the wall of the storm shelter. He walked over to the small washbasin and looked at himself in the mirror. His hair, normally cut short on a regular basis, was beginning to get over-long; his glasses were bent and his clothes were grimy. He lifted his shirt a few inches. The bandage around his waist would need changing again today, he knew, dreading the prospect.

On the day this chaos had begun, he had been stabbed from behind, the blow destroying his left kidney and leaving him grievously wounded. McInnes had found him and saved him, doing what he could to mend the wound, and then brought him to the house where Robinson had been based at the time, hoping the rebels could offer more protection than the few remnants of the WTDD.

He splashed some of the ice-cold water from the tap onto his face, for all the good it would do him, and went into the main communal area of the cellar. He was shocked to find, sat on a chair in the middle of the room, Master McInnes; the Engineer's lab coat torn and stained with blood and mud, his hair unkempt and straggly, though his face was bright.

"Ah, Tim; you look as bad as I feel. Pull up a chair."

It was impossible to resist the instructions of the charismatic Master Engineer, even had Greenwood wanted to, and he slumped into the nearest chair.

"How's your injury?"

"Well, I've felt better."

"It's a shame Tina isn't still with us, she'd have patched you up in a jiffy." McInnes looked to Mendelson, who was sat in the corner, drinking slowly from a bottle of bourbon.

"Are you sure she should be drinking that, Terry?"

"I'm going to need to stitch her up, she's got a bad gash down one arm, and since there's no morphine here, I thought it would be best."

"I suppose." Greenwood looked at Mendelson again, seeing for the first time her injury. It was about an inch deep, caused by a shard of glass. "How did that happen? I thought you were supposed to stay here."

"No harm's done, Tim; let's just let bygones be bygones." McInnes took a small box from his coat and produced from it a needle, attached to which was a long surgical thread.

Mendelson dragged her chair over to him and sat perfectly still, wincing slightly as the needle moved in and out of her flesh, McInnes making the minutest of movements, carefully stitching.

"What's our next move?" Greenwood asked. "I presume that because you're here it means you have a plan now?"

"Yes, I have a plan, but it is extremely dangerous."

"For who?"

"For all of us, Senator Greenwood."

"Oh, good then. What is this plan?"

"We're going to attack the detention facility in the city; rescue all those who were taken."

"They're not coming back," James Robinson said from

one corner of the room. "And if we try to get them, neither are we."

"There is a window of opportunity. They're on the back foot now; we can strike while they're not sure of our strength, and rescue our friends."

"That's preposterous! We don't stand a chance yet, and on a list of people we should save a few civilians and your apprentices are pretty low, *Master* McInnes."

James Robinson was the only person Greenwood had ever met who could say Master in a disrespectful manner, and he started to get to his feet.

"I say, James; that's a little harsh—"

"Shut up, Greenwood; we don't have time for this shit. I recommend that Terry and his chums get ready to leave; they've outstayed their welcome."

McInnes was on his feet as well now, and Greenwood noticed for the first time that the others in the room were awake; Cabot had one hand on the hilt of his sword, and Ewan Evans stood in the shadows, waiting perhaps to see how the others handled the situation.

"That's enough!" The voice was quiet and yet authoritative, and everyone span to look at the woman who had suddenly appeared in the centre of the room, the hands of all but McInnes and Cabot going to their guns. Greenwood looked from person to person and saw that Evans too was unarmed, having taken a stance with both hands palm open, one positioned to block his chest and the other as if about to beckon to the girl.

"Who is this?"

"Her name is Eleanor Giles, James; she's not a threat," McInnes said quickly, moving between Robinson and the girl.

"Bullshit," Evans spoke up. "We should kill her now, James."

"How did she get in here?"

"She's able to..." McInnes searched for an explanation that would make sense to the others in the room.

"Step aside, Terry, I'd hate to have to shoot you," Robinson said as McInnes hesitated, and Cabot began to draw his sword.

"Liam," McInnes said reproachfully and the glimmer of steel vanished into the scabbard once more. "Now James; put the gun down."

"Why?" Robinson's grip on his weapon got tighter.

"Ellie, can you do anything for me here?"

"Like what?" The girl watched at the others panicking with a hint of amusement.

"Oh, I don't know. Just anything, really, to save you being shot at."

"Step aside," Ellie instructed and McInnes did so, aware, as he moved, exactly what was going to happen.

Robinson opened fire, putting two staples into Ellie's torso. She looked at him calmly.

"Right, so she's impervious to bullets. I guess we're gonna have to listen to what she has to say."

"Don't," Evans hissed, but Robinson ignored him.

"Thank you." Ellie smiled at the entire room.

"Lucy is preparing to move against you; she will strike within two days, and there will be foes like me among her army, enemies you cannot kill with bullets. Your only chance lies with those imprisoned in the detention facility—"

"Excuse me, but I think we've heard this before," Evans spoke over her, the only man bold enough to do so. "She's one of McInnes' little holograms, a trick to make us go along with what he wants us to do."

At these words Ellie turned and smashed a fist through the wooden table in the centre of the room. "Satisfied?"

"Not entirely."

Evans stared angrily at Ellie. She caught his gaze and stared back along it, her face emotionless until he broke away.

"Most satisfied, thank you," Greenwood spoke up. "Do continue."

"The detention centre will be heavily guarded, there may well be deaths, but if you fail to act now then you will all die when the attack comes."

"Can you help us?" Cabot asked, hopefully.

"No. I'm not even supposed to be here now; it could be catastrophic if I were to engage in combat."

"Alright; so we attack?" Robinson asked. "Since we seem to have no other choice in the matter."

"Yes; tomorrow evening, just before dusk."

"Why dusk?"

"It'll be dark by the time we get out; the fading light will work to our advantage," Mendelson replied. "It's the best time to make a hit."

"How are we going to divide our forces?" Greenwood asked.

"An all-out attack is likely to be met with overwhelming force, which would have much the same effect as them attacking us. If instead we send a few dozen men to attack a couple of targets, that'd probably be enough to draw attention away from the facility," Robinson replied; having been a colonel in the war that had led to the formation of the Society, he was used to diversionary attacks. "How many do we send to attack the base itself?"

"Two; Liam and I will take the base by ourselves, save anyone else the risk."

"That's suicide, Terry," Greenwood informed him bluntly.

"I think me and Liam can handle ourselves, Senator." McInnes spoke calmly, but Cabot's face showed that he wasn't so sure.

"Alright, but stay in contact, we'll come and help if we're needed."

"Thank you, James; we'd better prepare."

3

The sunlight was fading as guards rushed from their posts to answer calls for aid. A patrol had been pinned down about a hundred yards from Sharp-Thomas Square by dissidents with staple rifles, suspected to be members of the group that had escaped from the quarry only a day previously.

Richard Marlow had dispatched some of his personal guard to the area, only to find that by the time they had arrived the enemy had already gone, and another attack had started about a mile away.

Crouched on the roof of the three-storey building opposite the detention facility, McInnes and Cabot saw the staple fire begin at the second diversion.

"It's time." McInnes swung himself over the ledge and dropped unhesitatingly to the ground, breaking into a run as he headed for the building. The two guards out front raised their guns and two staples from Cabot put them down, McInnes' own staple finding a sniper leaning out of a nearby window.

McInnes went to the doorway and tore off the front panel of the code locking system, proceeding to tinker around with the wires within.

The doors jerked open a few seconds later and he and Cabot entered cautiously, guns held in front of them.

McInnes stalked into the building, moving through the corridors, keeping a pistol at eye level, scanning the walls. The building's blueprints said the holding cells were down the third corridor on his left. He reached the opening and put his back against the wall, getting Cabot to stop with a wave of his hand. He moved his pistol out into the opening and it was greeted by a spray of gunfire. They would be going for the alarm; time to move.

He turned the corner and began sprinting through the building, spraying fire down the corridors; he hadn't time for aiming now. The door to the part of the complex used as a prison burst open before him. Two guards dashed out to meet him, their swords drawn, too late, as he shot the first and batted the second into the wall with his arm.

There were more guards in here; he leapt over them, firing his Tasers into them and landing behind those that remained standing as Cabot followed him into the room. He grinned at the guards as he raised his sword and charged them.

McInnes came to the first cell and shot the lock out, freeing Cayley Tufnell. She nodded appreciatively and followed him as he moved down the cells, his pace quickening as he saved more and more people, until he rounded the corner and two women faced him, their swords already drawn.

"Hisa-me," he whispered to himself, holstering his weapons and drawing his sword.

"The Survivor."

The two women leapt, swords swinging for him, and he ducked, dodged and dived, avoiding their strikes cleanly and elegantly for a few seconds before he brought his own sword around, smashing it against theirs simultaneously. One of the women took a step back and the other swung again, harder this time. McInnes dropped to the floor, rolled, and rose again behind the still-swinging hisa-me, thrusting his sword through her chest and into the wall behind.

He let go of the weapon and ran, aware that the other would be pursuing him, and span out his guns, leaping and turning in mid air, shooting open the doors of the next two cells with one gun whilst sending an almost constant stream of Taser energy hurtling towards his remaining adversary.

The shots that struck her seemed to slow her slightly, but not enough; McInnes hit the ground, continuing to fire lying down. The girl took to the air, hissing as she prepared to strike.

Green light blurred down the corridor from behind her, striking the lower-level demon in the back and reducing her to ash seconds before she would have killed McInnes.

"Mister McBride."

"Master McInnes." The man standing in the corridor gave a bow. "Much obliged for the rescue."

"And I to you for the assistance."

"I hate to break up this little conversation, guys, but we're still well and truly behind enemy lines, and I'd bet there's more of those things around." Dan Carter, who had been in the cell McInnes had opened last, spoke up.

"Yes; and neither of you are in any state to fight an army," McInnes said; the two apprentices were bleeding and tired, and had obviously been beaten during their stay here.

"Let's get going then, eh?" McBride span and led them two down the corridor to where the others were waiting, pausing only to vaporise the second woman as she struggled against McInnes' blade.

McInnes smoothly removed the sword from the wall and replaced it in his sheath, unsurprised that the blade was clean of blood.

Cabot stood by the others.

"Anyone lost?"

Cabot shook his head. "I'm not sure about Robinson's guys, but I know all our people got back out safely."

"Okay, that's something..." McInnes paused, and put his hand to his temple, as if suddenly struck by an acute headache.

"Master?"

"Liam, get the others into a cell and guard them. McBride, Carter; I'll need your help." McInnes drew his sword slowly and the two apprentices readied the ones they had taken from the hisa-me.

"Master, what's wrong?" McBride asked.

"Something wicked this way comes," McInnes warned, and the two apprentices spread out, waiting.

A man in a grey robe came around the corner, his hood up and the cloak held together by a golden dragon broach at his neck. He carried no sword, but it was clear from the way he moved that he probably wouldn't need one. The prisoners were not all yet into the cell Cabot had led them to, and the figure swept quickly towards Verity Robbins, the young girl who had lived with the abilities of a Touched One since she was five.

McBride leapt, putting himself between the man and the girl. "You must kill us all first."

"I have no intention of killing anyone: step aside."

"That's not going to happen; we're not entirely without skill, you know." McBride stretched out the palm of his free hand, forming an energy ball.

"My abilities are beyond those of the Touched Ones. I must ask you to step aside one last time."

"No." McBride hurled the energy ball and the man's body contorted, avoiding it without shifting position. The mysterious figure charged and lashed out with one foot, flinging McBride's sword into the ceiling as Carter struck. His sword was blocked by one cloaked arm and the young Engineer was pushed back into a wall. The man leapt backward, avoiding McInnes' strike and turning. McInnes looked past the figure at the two women now running down the corridor, in a second recognising them as more hisa-me. He swore and began to move towards McBride, but as he moved, the grey figure turned and waved his hands, two energy balls flying down the corridor and into the two women.

"Who are you?" McInnes asked, trying to see into the depths of the hood.

"Let's just say I'm a friend of Eleanor, shall we? I can't say any more here."

The others looked at him suspiciously.

"Listen, you must trust me. There are more on the way; McBride is too weak to fight them and I can't reveal myself. We've got to go now."

"Let's go then," McInnes said, but was still unsure, and nodded to McBride as a warning to keep his eyes open.

They ran from the building, their new ally moving amidst them, everyone with their eyes open and as many people as possible toting acquired pistols and swords. The streets were quiet for the first two hundred yards or so when they came to a mass of people about fifty strong, running away from something.

McInnes grabbed his radio and depressed the button to talk.

"Anyone; what's going on?"

"Terry, it's Tim; the last diversion got ambushed. I managed to get about a dozen people away, but James was surrounded when I last saw him."

"Where?"

"Uh, about halfway down Short Street," Greenwood

replied.

"Carter, McBride; go help out."

"I hate to be a stick in the mud," Annie spoke up, "but where's Verity gone?"

They all looked around, but the young girl was nowhere to be seen.

"Carter, McBride, go; we'll find Verity."

"I've got it," the mysterious figure said and disappeared with a swirling of particles.

♦

Verity Robbins was sat in an alleyway, looking around anxiously for guards, clutching her knee where she had fallen and injured herself. There was a sudden rush of air and everything went black for a moment, and when she opened her eyes once more she found herself on a rooftop, the grey figure standing over her.

♦

Robinson was surrounded, the former army Colonel swinging his sword wildly to keep back the troops.

"You get Robinson out, I'll handle the others; alright?" McBride asked.

"Sounds like a good deal to me," Carter said, nodding, and they ploughed into the circle of guards, Carter making a beeline for Robinson. He used his sword only occasionally, preferring to vanish into a cloud of atomic particles whenever threatened. A blade swung down at McBride and he ducked, lashing out with the palm of his hand as he charged it with hardlight energy, sending his assailant flying back and cutting a path through other enemies.

His sword, stolen from the hisa-me, slid smoothly from

its scabbard, the fluidic motion continuing until it had passed through the neck of another guard. Carter had seized Robinson, McBride saw from across the crowd, and his comrade was now fighting his way out, towards a nearby building.

McBride smiled, hurling an energy ball with one hand at the guard directly in front of Carter whilst simultaneously swinging his blade at the other guards.

But then there were no more targets: Killian McBride stood quite alone on the street, surrounded by corpses. All his living opponents had vanished.

"Uh—"

There was a sudden rush around him, and the street was crowded again, a circle of black-garbed enemies formed around McBride their swords at the ready.

"Shit."

♦

"Are you alright?" the grey figure asked Verity as he bent over her, his face still concealed by the robe.

"I'm fine, but I think Mister McBride is going to need some help."

The figure turned and followed her eye-line to the circle developing around the apprentice, around three hundred yards away. There was a clatter along the nearby rooftops.

"Enemies are coming: can you handle them?"

Verity pulled herself to her feet and opened both fists, two energy balls materialising on her palms.

"I think I've got it, thanks."

The figure leapt, the cloak he wore billowing out around him, and as he reached the zenith of his jump, great leathery wings sprouted from his back, powering him forward and down towards the circle.

The figures paused as the man swooped in, snatching McBride by the shoulders of his shirt and hurling him onto the roof of the nearby building.

"Go back to your mistress; inform her the field is level," he hissed, turning his head to glower at them all from within the hood.

They leapt, but with the same blurring of particles he was gone again.

♦

"Master McInnes, you must return home immediately; only from Cooke Hall may the coming battle be won," the grey figure addressed McInnes when the rebels had regrouped outside of the city.

"That place is swarming with enemies; we don't stand a chance if we try and attack."

"The Hall contains the only weapons capable of narrowing the odds; we must take it back."

"And if such weapons exist, what makes you think that Lucy won't have found them? After all, it's gotta be the top of the list of things she's looking for."

"And how are you even sure such weapons exist?" McBride interjected.

"More importantly, who *are* you?" McInnes asked.

The figure pushed back its hood, revealing a pale, gaunt face, topped by messy brown hair. The man bowed low to them, smiling. The figure was the spitting image of James Cooke, former leader of the WTDD, except that his eyes had changed from green to maroon.

"Master Cooke?"

"In a manner of speaking."

"We thought you were dead."

"The concussion wave," McBride murmured.

"And so I was; fortunately, with the knowledge Eleanor gave me I was able to overcome the barriers blocking me and return."

"Ellie's bosses sent you to help?"

"Not *per se*." Cooke seemed embarrassed, as though he was being forced to relive something he didn't want to remember. "Lucy has been seizing the seals, the entrances to Hell; I was able to slip through the door into this world."

"But if you were in Heaven..." Dan Carter stopped in mid sentence.

"But you weren't in Heaven, were you, Master? They sent you to Hell."

"Well observed, Mister McBride." Cooke paused, shook himself and continued. "We must attempt to take back what is ours. The Hall needs to be taken back; Lucy will not have found the weapons, and they are the only chance we have."

"Very well then; we'll attack tomorrow morning at dawn—"

"No," Cooke said abruptly. "Now."

"James—" McInnes began, trying to calm his friend.

"McBride, Carter and I will take back the Hall from the enemy: be there in half an hour."

"Are you sure that's him?" Carter asked quietly as Cooke stalked away.

"Sure acts like him."

♦

"So, I presume there's some sort of master plan involving a clever use of our knowledge of the Hall and its secret entrances?" McBride asked as the three of them stood facing the cast iron gate that was the main entrance to Cooke Hall; the weakest point of the wall that encircled the building. It had once been left perpetually open, but now the gate was padlocked shut.

"Something like that," Cooke said and reached out, pulling the padlock forcibly from the gate and stepping onto the grounds. The three men charged, sprinting down the deserted pathway. The doorway was close now, and Cooke leapt, extending both hands as his hood rose and his cloak wrapped around him, the door flying open before him. The three men ran into the house that had once been their home and the guards around the main staircase looked up, several going for weapons, while others simply mustered energy balls.

McBride and Carter parted, both dashing for the entrances to different wings while their pistols spat staples at the guards.

Both apprentices had vanished into passageways when the assembled guards looked back around and saw that the man in grey was still there, stood on the bottom step of the staircase.

"Hello, boys." Two thin, pale hands stretched out from the robe, bright points of hardlight energy erupting from each of the fingertips, each bolt striking a different guard. The man leapt into a spin, narrowly dodging two energy balls and throwing two back in response, each hitting and killing an opponent as Cooke hung in mid air for a second, before dropping back to the ground and brushing imaginary dust from his shoulders.

McBride sidled silently through the secret passageway that led to the armoury, watching the four guards outside move around. One of them seemed to sense that something was awry, and was looking down the corridor, his hands positioned ready to hurl an energy ball at a moment's notice. McBride looked into the armoury, finding it empty, and pushed open the passageway's door, built into the back of a sword rack. He slid his right hand down his side to his holster and pulled out a pistol, staring at the sealed steel door that led to the corridor.

He tapped in the code on the relevant panel beside the door and the barrier slid aside, allowing him to quickly place two staples into the back of the nearest guard. He ran for the furthest man, discarding his pistol and not bothering to eliminate the two remaining guards, simply disarming one with a jab to the elbow followed by an abrupt crunch, and putting the other to the floor with a swift kick in the knees.

The man in front of him struck, the blow catching the airborne McBride in the middle of a flying kick in the stomach and sending him back through the door. McBride punched the pad as it flew past his left hand, and the door slid shut, the steel absorbing the energy ball that was pursuing him.

"Right, okay; demon outside the door, energy balls bouncing off it as we speak," he mumbled seriously, then grinned, "piece of cake." He stood aside and focused, directing his mind at the door, focusing on the structure of the metal, ignoring the repeated sound of the energy balls outside.

He reached out with his hand and, with one final surge of focus, the door exploded outward. Shards of hot metal struck the man in the corridor as McBride rushed out, forming an energy ball in his own hand and hurling it down at the fallen man, finishing him and spinning into a complex kick that broke the necks of his two remaining foes.

Dan Carter kicked from wall to wall, guns blazing at guards, the touched apprentice quite content to leave demons standing and humans dead as he burst through the corridors, atomising when threatened and returning to form in a devastating hail of kicks, punches and steel.

♦

The residents of the Hall, old and new, walked tentatively up the staircase and into the building, finding the three men waiting for them. The two apprentices were slumped on the huge sofas in the reception hall while the third man stood in the centre of the room, a thin smile on his face.

"Cooke?" Robinson spoke in astonishment. "We were told you were dead!"

"Not quite; I was simply captured by the enemy. Master McInnes was kind enough to rescue me along with the others."

"Well," Robinson began, not entirely convinced, "that's nice."

Someone swore from behind him and Robinson turned. Ewan Evans had dropped his bags, and lay on the ground just before the threshold, stunned.

"What is the meaning of this?" Robinson demanded.

"I couldn't get through the door, it was like walking into a wall!" Evans shouted, getting to his feet. "Like some kind of trap..."

"Senator Robinson, step aside," Cooke instructed calmly.

"What kind of trick is this then? What sorcery have the masters of the Hall bought to bear against us now?"

"I said *step aside*." Cooke's voice was getting more urgent now.

"Not before you explain what's going on." Robinson turned back to Cooke and the robed figure stretched out a hand, lifting the Senator aside and placing him back on the ground without touching him. He started towards Evans and flew back as an energy ball struck him in the chest. McBride began creating an energy ball in his hand to throw back at the SS Agent, but was driven to the floor by Carter as a sphere flew towards him.

McInnes drew two pistols and began firing them at Evans, but the man barely shuddered as the high-powered staples drove through his chest. Suddenly, two streams of hardlight energy collided with Evans, forcing him through the air and down the entranceway steps.

Cooke followed, leaping through the door and catching Evans' next energy ball as it came flying at him.

"That's a nice trick," Evans commented sarcastically.

"Who are you?" Cooke asked. The two men were facing each other now on the gravel around the entrance to the Hall, their feet crunching on the small stones as they circled.

"My name is Ewan Evans."

The man facing him smiled as the others rushed out to watch.

"Liar." Cooke waved a hand and the impostor crashed into the staircase. The grey robe Cooke still wore blew in the air as an ethereal wind swung around him, several shards of rock taking to the air as he muttered under his breath. The wind rushed away from him, the fragments of stone colliding with the petrified Evans, the form of the man changing to its true self; a tux-wearing demon.

"Impressive," the demon said and leapt at Cooke. He was blown apart in mid flight, an energy ball from McBride striking him in the back.

"What the hell was that?" Robinson asked.

"One of the enemies coming for us now: I would advise you get back into the house, Mister Robinson."

"Hold on one second; where did you guys learn how to do all this lightning-ball crap? And why did you just kill Evans?"

"That *wasn't* Ewan Evans," Cooke told him.

"Of course it was! What the hell are you talking about?" Robinson demanded.

"That was a demon who had assumed the form of Evans; I put an energy barrier around the Hall which wouldn't admit his kind. Good thing I did, really."

"Are you seriously expecting me to believe that demons exist?"

"I assure you; they are quite real," McInnes said in the defence of his old friend.

"Not you as well, McInnes; I know that Stanford had a great deal of time for you people, so I don't mean to be harsh, but I must say that it's a wonder if you spoke like this the whole time."

"James," Greenwood stepped forward.

"Leave him," Cooke said. "He's clearly not ready to believe: he may die ignorant, if he wishes."

"Are you threatening me, Master Cooke?"

"Of course not, Senator Robinson; but if you do not come to grips with the reality with which you are now presented then you will quite quickly perish in much the same manner as Lord Stanford."

"Stanford was a fool; I am no such thing."

"You will not speak of him that way!" Cooke's robe billowed, changing colour until it was a jet black.

"James," Terry said calmly, "now is not the time."

He turned to the others. "I must advise you all to get inside; a storm is coming."

"What kind?"

"That much is uncertain; but the Hall will weather it."

They swept inside, the apprentices who knew the Hall best taking the newcomers to find quarters while Cabot and the senior Engineers accumulated in the great hall.

4

"The future lies shrouded from us; we stand alone and isolated, our friends and allies are scattered or dead," Cooke addressed them all. "Lucy will come; she does not know how many we are, or how powerful, and several of our number she continues to underestimate, but that will not be enough; there will be many more battles to be fought before she can arrive, if we are to win."

"Like what?"

"The stones must be returned here, the hardlight weapons program must be completed, and we must prepare everyone we can for a war they will almost certainly not survive."

"A bit glum, isn't it, James?" Cabot asked. "I mean, we've beaten Lucy before, and the hisa-me are easy enough to kill…"

"They are fast becoming superfluous; Lucy is summoning more and more demons to her cause, each more powerful than the last, and we must be prepared to be besieged by the stuff of nightmares."

"You're saying we're going to have to face giant bunny rabbits?" Cabot looked around at the others and their inscrutable faces. "Maybe just me then?"

"Yeah," Bishop said loudly, ready to move on. "Where are the other stones?"

"One is in the attic, where I put it before I died, another one is buried with Danielle, in the mausoleum; the location of the third I am uncertain of."

"It lies within a place Lucy may not go; it has been placed there to protect us." McInnes said softly.

"How do you know?" Cooke demanded.

"I haven't a clue, it just popped into my head."

"Ah; and the odds once more tip."

"How do you mean?"

"There are a mere dozen or so places on this earth a demon may not tread."

"Surely any holy ground should stop them?" Bishop asked. "That's always what we were taught in Sunday school."

"They can definitely enter churches; that's where they managed to get me. Their power worked there, too: unlike mine." McBride announced bitterly.

"Exactly; the places decreed holy by humans are protected from damage being done to them by His servants, but they are not truly holy in the sense that they are not divinely protected, and demons can still enter and destroy whatever they wish without fear of reprisal"

"That seems like a bad plan, really."

"Well, a little." Cooke paused. "I'll go try and hunt down the last stone tomorrow; we need to get everyone settled in here and armed, ready for the coming onslaught."

"When will it come?"

"I don't know. Lucy will probably try something subtle at first; that's closer to her modus operandi. Once she realises I'm here, though, I should think that she'll try something a little more extreme."

"Extreme?"

"Think army of demons and you won't go far wrong."

"An *army*?" McBride exclaimed. "We can take about one or two at a time; an army will be unstoppable! How do you intend for us to pull off a victory on this one?"

"I don't," Cooke said bluntly. "From the second such an army hit our walls we would be doomed, and Lucy would have succeeded; we must see to it that such an army never comes."

"What's the first step?"

"We get the stones, we get armed, and we get ready to strike back."

"The NCC will be impossible to break into without some serious new bits of kit, James; it's swarming with new enemies."

"Good thing we've got some serious new bits of kit ready then, isn't it?""

"A little, but where the hell are they?"

"Ah, well..." With a great dramatic flourish, Cooke waved one hand across the table and the wood slid away, revealing a series of small compartments, each containing some manner of shiny silver device.

"These look like the things you tried out during the Faction War, James," McInnes whispered to his friend. "The kind that blew up after you used them once."

"Remarkable similarity isn't it."

Carter had, by this time, picked up the nearest device to him and slipped it onto his hand.

"What's this one for?" he asked, extending his hand towards McBride to show him it. The air rippled in the path of the shockwave that lifted the apprentice from the floor and slammed him bodily into the wall.

"Oops," Carter muttered apologetically to McBride as the apprentice pulled himself up.

"No worries, just point that thing someplace else." McBride brushed off his shirt.

"What works that thing?"

"In most people it'll work by a flexing of the fingers or stretching of the palm; some of the others work by pressing buttons."

"Most people?" McInnes asked.

"If they have a high enough concentration of hardlight within them it'll work automatically."

"Automatically?"

"At will." Cooke stood beside Carter and put one hand on the arm of the apprentice. "Raise your arm."

The apprentice did so and felt a tingling sensation spread outward from the point on his arm that the demon was touching. The device flared into life, the ripple of energy travelling out from it and striking an antique vase on the table. The vase went flying and Cooke removed his grip from Carter and pressed a button on the device to deactivate it.

The vase stopped in mid-air, directly in line with Cooke's outstretched palm. "Go through all of the devices and determine their uses, and then go and look behind the bookshelf in the study, examine the weapons there and find the most useful ones for wider scale production against our new foes."

"We have weapons that will kill demons?" McBride asked.

"We may do, and even if they do not they will still be useful."

Carter tilted his head, confused.

"How so?"

"Isn't it obvious?"

Realisation dawned in the eyes of the apprentices, as the horrible, inevitable truth swept over them.

"There will be humans among them?"

"Yes; humans are naturally weak creatures, and they are corrupted by power. It bends them to its will as easily as you would do a spoon. It is an unavoidable fact of our lives from here on in that some of the people we are fighting will not simply be foul creatures impersonating our former allies, but will be, in fact, our former allies."

"Well, that's a cheerful thought," McBride said, pausing for a moment to contemplate this. "We'll go check the study." The two apprentices left, and McInnes turned to face his old friend, slumped in an armchair in front of the fireplace.

"You didn't used to be able to stop objects in mid-air," he began.

"Hmm," came the noncommittal reply.

"Or teleport. Oh yes; I noticed that, and you could never have summoned the energy to kill two demons at once."

"Quite true."

"I am forced to wonder; how many more tricks have you picked up in the past month?"

"A few others." Cooke sat up and waved a hand at the empty hearth, summoning a roaring fire.

"You're becoming more powerful?"

"Not becoming; this would seem to be the extent of my power for now."

"What happened to you?"

Cooke pondered this for a moment. "They say that Hell is other people, but that is only if you hate people. It works upon a system that whatever the worst thing that could ever happen to you while you were alive, what you feared and despised more than anything else in the world, would happen to you, over and over and over again."

"And?"

"I spent my life fighting against the darker parts of my soul; the part of my mind that was created when I became a

Touched One."

"You fought against becoming a demon, so your punishment was to be made into one?"

"Yes; a lowly one, no more powerful than a hisa-me."

"But aren't demons evil?"

"Yes, and so I was. For what seemed like an eternity the part of my mind that could be called 'me', the conscious mind of what has always been known as Cooke, took a back seat to a demonic consciousness, evil beyond measure, but at the same time aware of what I had once been."

"What happened? How did you regain control?"

"Come along, Terry. You have a gift for predictions, for knowing things that you can't possibly know; what happened?"

"Eleanor."

"Good; what about her?"

"The knowledge she gave you; it was angelic knowledge. Somehow you used it to overpower the demonic part of yourself, and came up through a seal in place of a demon being summoned?"

"Very good." Cooke smiled. "Lucy doesn't know I'm here, but it's only a matter of time; she will eventually sense my presence, masked as it is, and she will come to this house and kill us all."

"Not very optimistic."

"I cannot see a way out of it."

"What about attacking first?"

"Just how powerful do you believe us to be, old friend?" Cooke sighed. "I am the most powerful creature on our side, and I do not have the strength to fight Lucy. She has an army, we barely have a platoon; she can crush us underfoot, unless a miracle comes before she strikes."

"Miracles are hardly rare in our experience."

"I fear we have used up our quota, Terry; however, there

may yet be hope, as it seems that even my clearest instructions do not get followed around here." Cooke got to his feet and looked around the room.

"What is it?"

"Hold on a second." He closed his eyes, a look of utmost concentration crossing his face. He span, waving a hand, and a patch of air glowed. "You can't leave, you know." The area that had glowed, formerly empty, was now exceedingly occupied by the figure of Eleanor Giles, a picture of absolute beauty in long white robes.

"And you can't keep that up forever," she smiled. "Drop it before you rupture yourself, I have no intention of leaving."

He waved his hand again.

"Thank you."

"I thought I told you to stay away."

"I like to keep an eye on my mistakes, make sure they come to fruition."

Cooke gave a short laugh.

"I must say, your transiting is much less advanced than I'd hoped."

"You knew this would happen?" Cooke asked, advancing on her angrily.

"No, but I had an inkling."

"How could you possibly have had an inkling? It's never happened before!"

"Well, it's exactly what needed to happen for this little crusade to succeed. And if there's one soul I've encountered that's belligerent enough to overcome the hellish reality that is—well—Hell, and not be driven absolutely stark raving mad by being ripped through different forms, different dimensions and having knowledge he's not ready for, it's got to be the first Touched One not to go stark raving mad to begin with."

"Thanks, I guess. Do you happen to have any useful

advice, or shall we just stand here all night and exchange long-winded and confusing compliments?"

"Regrettably, I lack any advice, and my side isn't sending anyone down. They don't even know there's a problem, it would seem."

"I'm sure that must have been a feat for a group of apparently omnipresent, omniscient people."

"Well, they do try hard to be quite as unaware as they are, but in fairness, angels are not omni-anything; that's just a way of scaring kids at night. I presumed you guys would have grown out of that sort of thing."

"We had," McInnes said quietly.

"And then?"

"An angel consulted us for help in killing a demon."

"Hmm, I see your point. Have you got a plan?"

"Well, I was thinking we walk in, kill everything that moves, then inform Lucy that she is required under the Society's Law to immediately surrender and return herself to the Hell from which she spawned, accompanied by any other demonic entities currently occupying this plain of existence." Cooke took in Eleanor's blank stare. "What? You don't think it'll work?"

"I think you may have a hard time finding clauses in the law designed to prohibit the seizing of your government by demons, or any instructions as to where they should go if turfed out."

"Ah, yes. Quite true. But I'm sure between us we can write a few clauses and slip them into the book?"

"Well quite, but I'm pretty certain that coup d'etats are in any case illegal and thus that Lucy is less than concerned with issues of the law."

"Oh well, it was good while it lasted." Cooke sat down. "Eleanor, you'd better go; we'll be summoned somewhere at some point, no doubt, to explain what the hell is going on to everyone else."

"Oh joy." The angel vanished.

"What's going on, James?"

"What do you mean?"

"The way this thing is supposed to work doesn't seem to be, well, working. From what you've always said, and the little I've been able to glean from Ellie, this isn't how things happen! Demons don't just start invading the earth! What's going on?"

"Lucy has broken every law, written and unwritten, and so desperate measures will have to be taken. When I woke up, took back myself, I knew this, but I didn't know how to do it. I still don't."

"Then we must pray that you figure it out."

"Hmm."

♦

David Short dived across the floor, swinging his sword up to meet Greenwood's as the Senator swung at him, and flipped to his feet as another man's sword arced down. He heard the door open and he leapt at the sound, lunging with his sword.

The blade buried itself deep in the floor as the target stepped aside.

"Master."

Short bowed to the two men.

"I was just—"

"Showing off, yes, we know." McInnes looked around the room at the assembled rebels. "Take some of the others, prepare dinner; I think everyone deserves a good meal."

"If you want a good meal, why are you getting me to cook it?"

"I'm not, I'm getting you to get other people to cook it.

Your job is to find all the pentagonal objects in the Hall and destroy them."

"That doesn't seem like a lot of fun."

"War isn't, Short."

"Yes, Master."

Most of the rebels were in the room as Short scurried off to do as he was told, and Cooke addressed them.

"I know that a great number of you do not believe that our battles involve creatures largely confined to mythology and theology, so I won't try and convince you; I will merely specify the following things about our new enemy."

There was a pause as everyone took this in, the silence broken by James Robinson sighing impatiently.

"Get on with it, then," he said.

Greenwood shot him a dark glance.

"A number of these enemies are immune to weapons like staples, bullets and swords; they can kill you from across a room without armaments, many of them can change form, and they are faster and stronger than any ordinary human being."

"How are we going to kill them, then?" Thatcher asked nervously.

"Mister McBride and Mister Carter have innate abilities to fight back, as do several others of our number, and we are working on weapons which will allow us to combat them."

"If Carter and McBride can kill them, why don't they just do so?"

"Their leader, a woman named Lucy, is beyond our power to remove."

"Hmm. Sounds awfully convenient; what evidence is there that they're immune to our weapons? That this isn't just some ploy by your people to gain power?"

"You're a paranoid son of a bitch, Robinson," Cooke snapped and the Senator snatched up his pistol, pointing it at Cooke. "Go ahead; it would, if anything, prove my point."

"What?"

"Fire. See if I can be killed by that."

Robinson didn't need any more instruction, and squeezed the trigger again and again until the clip was empty. Cooke jerked as each successive round smashed into his head and torso, blood beginning to spill from the wounds, but the Engineer was still standing, and as Robertson watched the wounds healed over and the blood evaporated.

"What the fuck are you?"

"Exactly the same thing as our enemies. Remember this! They are powerful, plentiful and completely without mercy; if you have an opportunity to kill one, take it. They will not stop. Ever."

"Right. So they're strong and fast and immune to our weapons. What are the rest of us here for then? If you're immune to weapons too, maybe you guys should just fight it out amongst yourselves?"

"Robinson."

"Yes, Cooke?"

"You're a dick."

"Hey!" Robinson began to get angry, then realised that the rest of the room had just taken this comment without objection, and that, when it came down to it, there was nothing he could do.

"We must raise an army to stop Lucy; when she becomes aware of our presence here we should have enough defences to discourage an attack on us to begin with, and then we can launch a strike of our own," McInnes said, clarifying their position. "Unfortunately, absolute secrecy will be difficult to maintain, considering the fact that our opponents can take on whatever form they want."

"What does he mean?" Greenwood asked.

"He means this." His own voice answered his question,

and the others watched as Cooke's appearance changed to that of Greenwood. "One of the neater tricks available to our enemy; they could take us one by one, and none of us would notice the difference."

"Except you and McBride; you can sense hardlight inconsistencies, can't you?" McInnes asked.

"Yes, powerful demons show up like a floodlight in the dark, but a weaker demon could be indistinguishable from a human if they're hiding their nature."

"Oh great," Greenwood commented, sarcastically.

"That should be enough doom and gloom for now, everyone. I'd practice with your swords and guns for a while before dinner, if I were you, but don't worry unduly; we've got the situation more or less under control for now." McInnes gave them all a comforting smile and the two Engineers walked from the room.

"Under control?" Cooke asked once they were out of earshot.

"Sometimes it's better to lie."

"Really? You think we should just tell them what'll make them feel better about themselves?"

"I think the moment's passed on that one, but they can't do anything with the knowledge that we're all doomed; they might as well think we stand a chance."

"Ah-so."

"You still think we should tell the truth? Resign them to their fate and to the abject misery that it must ultimately bring?"

"Yes, but I am a demon, so I guess suffering is kinda my thing."

"Well quite; though I think that may have less to do with being a demon than you think."

♦

The door to the weapons rack slid aside the instant

McBride put his hand on the battered old copy of Great Expectations, protruding slightly from the line of other books. Revealed now was row upon row of glittering weaponry; elaborate swords, complicated Tasers, rifles and a single, jet-black staff secured in its place by two powerful-looking clamps.

Carter reached for one of the guns when McBride put out an arm to stop him.

"No; that one." He pointed to the staff. "It's emanating power; gotta be something worth looking into."

"It's a little heavily secured, though," Carter remarked, looking ponderously at the clamps.

"Yes, quite. Now if only we had some way to get past that problem."

"Oh, all right." Carter put one hand around the staff and closed his eyes, allowing his body to become ethereal, taking the staff with it, and re-materialising with his arm a foot away, the staff now free of its moorings.

"Nifty." McBride took the staff and span it quickly through his fingers a few times, until he found the small raised panel on one end. He waved a hand at the window of the study, causing the glass to reduce to dust, pointed the staff through the hole, and depressed the panel.

A small ball of luminous green hardlight energy shot from the end and out of the window, like a lesser incarnation of the energy balls McBride was able to summon at will.

"Well that's probably worth having."

"Will it actually do anything against demons, though?"

"A good question; fancy a dry run?"

"Shouldn't we ask the master first?"

"Honestly Daniel; what's going to happen to us? The amazing vanishing boy and the guy who can turn bullets to dust?"

"Well, demons could happen to us, and if the Master

doesn't know where we are he won't be able to come and bail us out."

"Bugger that, Carter; let's go to the garage."

♦

Carter and McBride walked into the garage of Cooke Hall and looked over the two dozen or so cars assembled there.

"You'd better not be thinking about stealing the Aston, gents."

They turned quickly, McBride summoning an energy ball and then tossing it into the ground as he saw Cooke leant nonchalantly against one of the Jaguars.

"Borrowing it. And with every intention of returning it."

"You don't even know how to use it; shouldn't you try something a little smaller?"

"Of course we know how to use it, Carter's passed his test and everything. Key in, in gear, foot down. Simple, really."

"I wasn't talking about driving the damn thing." Cooke pushed back his hood and stretched out his hand. A small remote control lifted from the nearest workbench and drifted through the air towards him. "Did it not strike you as odd that we're the most technologically advanced group of people in the Society and yet our cars are completely unaugmented?"

"Well, you guys always say it's a travesty to incorporate weapons into items of beauty, and I know for a fact that Master McInnes refuses to do anything to his car, besides soup up the engine, of course."

"Yes, but those are our own cars. We've been preparing for a war with the SS for almost eight years; the cars we go to work in are a little more secure." At the push of a button the Aston Martin the apprentices had been planning to borrow revved up, its headlights turning on. He pressed a second button and long silver plates slid out from under the bonnet, moving over one another until the entire car was covered in the overlapping armour.

"Cool," McBride muttered.

"That isn't the half of it." Cooke drew his sword and began to use it as a pointer as he walked to the car. "Ablative adamantium armour will stand up to the force of a cruise missile impact."

"Okay—"

"Don't interrupt," Cooke snapped, before continuing his speech. "Instinctively modifying armour will adapt to absorb the blast of practically any weapon after around one hundredth of one second, reducing everything less powerful than a caesium bomb to a slight sensation of warmth and a bright glow. The best part, though; the modified atomic structure of the adamantium allows for this..." He raised one hand and loosed a small energy ball into the car, which impacted and spread as the car absorbed the energy of the blast.

"Well, that is cool."

"It'll be useless against a demon of any real power, but it'll give you a little bit more protection from the majority of enemies."

"Splendid." McBride pulled the door open and climbed into the driver's seat as Carter flipped over the car and got in the other side, the armour plates retracting as Cooke pushed another button, the car returning to its normal slick silver design.

McBride caught the remote control as Cooke threw it to him, and turned the keys in the ignition, slamming the car into gear and pushing his foot down.

The car shot forward and up the slight ramp that led from the garage to the driveway of the Hall, spitting up a hail of gravel as the it tore off into the distance.

"You let them go?" McInnes asked, stepping out from behind a Jeep.

"Yes."

"They'll be killed."

"No; Carter is learning how to use his powers now. Eventually he'll be able to use them properly."

"Marvellous: and if he dies?"

"The car is pretty secure, and their powers are fairly developed; they should be able to escape if the worst comes to the worst."

"'Pretty secure', 'fairly developed', 'should be able to'."

"This is a risky business, Martin, and the staff needs testing."

"Can't you predict how useful it will be?"

"It's a human device to be used against demons, it's unlikely a computer could create a model that would hold true in the real world."

"I'd rather you went with them, still."

"The clouds are gathering around us; the rain will fall soon," James said. "I will go in a moment."

"What will you do prior to that?"

"Let them have some fun."

♦

"The storm has begun." A man in black robes entered the Lord Protector's office without knocking. Richard Marlow, the room's only occupant, turned to face him without a trace of fear.

"Yes, it has," the new Lord Protector replied calmly; his own garment, a navy blue suit, rippling slightly in the breeze from the open door. "Is there anything you wanted, Fabian?"

"The ball is progressing well downstairs; the others are wondering when you will be joining them."

"Hmm," murmured Marlow, turning back to the window. As he did so, Fabian leapt with a sudden flash of metal, drawing a long gash down the Lord Protector's back, from which blood began to seep. The wound closed quickly, and the suit changed to resemble a more elegant version of Fabian's robes. The Lord Protector turned, his build changing and his hair extending as it turned from blonde to black.

"Lucy; I should have known the puppet human you placed in charge would be possessed."

"Then you should have known better than to try and betray me," she smiled brightly. "You're not going to the ball dressed like that, are you?"

"It is somewhat traditional, ma'am; I am a demon, and this is what demons wear."

"But you're not supposed to be a demon, Fabian, you're supposed to be a human; the District Commissioner of this society, in fact."

"What would you have me wear then? Surely you can't want me to dress like the wyrmkind?"

"Why not? They seem to do quite well for themselves."

"They're savages."

"Well-dressed savages," she corrected.

"Oh, very well..."

♦

The Aston rolled to a stop outside a bar and the doors swung open, the two apprentices in their casual clothes climbing out, Carter with a pistol drawn and McBride spinning the staff experimentally through his fingers.

"Now what? We sit here and wait for a demon to show up?" Carter asked, leaning against the bonnet.

"Don't be so ridiculous."

5

Figures in gowns, tuxes and robes waltzed across the floor with varying degrees of elegance and competence, observed by a figure standing on the balcony, looking down on the NCC's ballroom.

Under normal circumstances Alan Empter would be the kind of lurking figure to be described as shadowy—even dark—but as he stood above the ball he felt strange, his mind racing with thoughts that were not his own. It was quieter up here, away from the constant assaults of his captors, but there were still the voices in his head.

"Hello Alan."

He turned to face the girl walking towards him, Katie Hardy, garbed in a shimmering lilac dress.

"Hello, Samantha."

The attractive press secretary changed into the form of the late Samantha Kensington, shoulder-length bright red hair replacing the long blonde hair of Empter's friend. "How do you always know?"

"The numbness in my mind; can't think straight."

She walked towards him and he drew the pistol concealed within his tux. "I know this won't kill you, but it'll sting like a freakin' bitch, so don't even think about it."

"There are so many worse ways you could die than this; it's really quite enjoyable." She took another step. "Though I can see by the shape of your thoughts that even as you resist me out here you are trying to regain access to the part of your brain Lucy has closed off."

"Yes." The pistol did not waver.

"Then it seems we have something in common; we both wish to be rid of her influence."

"Then help me."

"I can't, and I won't; your way will result in your death and the death of countless souls I could feed upon."

"I would rather die than live any longer in this world where people like her control everything."

"Then give yourself up, and your wish will be granted."

"Never."

Lucy listened to the minds of the two on the balcony above as she stood to one side of the ballroom, watching the dancing humans and demons alike. She turned to face the door a millisecond before it opened, admitting a black-clad member of the new Civilian Guard.

"What do you want?" she asked as she reached the panting man.

"There's been an attack on a patrol in the city! They killed my entire squad."

"Which squad was that?"

"Third squad, first platoon, second battalion, third regiment."

"Were there any d— any of our people with that squad?" she asked Fabian.

"No ma'am; would you like me to take a group and find out what it was?" he answered.

"Yes. It was most likely just some members of the

resistance launching an ambush, but it is best to be careful."

"Indeed, ma'am."

♦

McBride looked up at the sound of footsteps approaching from the far end of the street.

"Here they come."

A single man in black robes sprinted ahead of the second squad of guardsmen, who were moving as slowly as they could sensibly afford.

McBride raised the staff, squinting along its length until he was happy that the target was going to be hit. The weapon fired as he squeezed and the energy collided with the sprinting man, knocking him from his feet.

McInnes and Cooke stood on the roof of the Hall, looking out over the grounds as the wind blew around them, unsettling neither of the men's balance.

"They are going to be attacked," Cooke said.

"Badly?"

"Yes."

"A powerful demon?"

"Several."

"You should go and help."

"I am trying to, but I do not know how."

"What?"

"I should be able to fly, but I cannot remember how."

"Oh," McInnes paused. "Well I'm sure it'll come to you."

The demon stood back up and McBride fired again, hitting his mark once more and knocking the man down, this time for good.

"So, two shots?" Carter asked.

"Two shots," McBride agreed, and squinted down the street; the rest of the patrol had vanished. "Guess we scared them off."

A staple bounced off of the wall.

"Guess not." Carter made two quick headshots and he moved onto the third target before realising that the second had shaken off the fatal wound.

"Killian!"

McBride needed no instruction, an energy ball already thrown before the yell had come; the green orb striking the creature in the chest.

Fabian felt the sting of the blow hit him as he flew back into the wall. He felt some mild discomfort from the impact, but returned immediately to his feet.

"Touched Ones? HERE?" he bellowed, raising a hand and hurling an energy ball at Carter, who dived aside.

"Car!"

The two apprentices leapt into the car, activating the armour plating, which slid across the hull just quickly enough to stop the next energy ball. Carter, now in the driver's seat, turned the key in the ignition and put his foot down hard on the accelerator. The engine turned over, the wheels turned via the axles, the CD player activated, but the car resolutely failed to move.

"Shit." McBride was looking behind at the sheet of adamantium blocking the back window, but he didn't need to be able to see to tell what was happening; the demon was holding on to the back of the car.

"Touched Ones, two of them," Fabian muttered to himself as the car's wheels span ineffectually in front of him. "What are the odds?" He heard the sound behind him, that of a wyrmkind landing, but didn't turn from his task. "About time you guys got here; I've got two Touched

Ones in this car."

"Yes. I know."

Fabian turned and looked at the faceless grey figure that had landed a few metres from him. The stranger struck out and Fabian flew into the wall once more, this time his pride injured at having been caught off guard. The car began to move away.

"Who are you?"

The robe turned white.

"I am the Flame." Another swirl of colour turned the white to black. "And the Shadow."

"Oh, thanks for being so clear." Fabian hurled an energy ball and watched with muted horror as it was deflected effortlessly.

Two light thuds on the ground behind Cooke indicated the arrival of two tuxedo-clad demons, the wyrmkind Fabian had been so scornful of earlier. As the black of his robe reverted to its original grey, Cooke looked around at the two newcomers. They were the hired muscle of the demonic classes, powerful demons without much ability to think for themselves, only at home in a fight, but well dressed nonetheless.

"Ah." Cooke span, drawing two pistols from the recesses of his robe and snapping off shots at the three demons. Fabian took a step backward as the rounds smashed through his face, instantly healing, astounded as ever by the ferocity of his comrades, leaping unhesitatingly towards their prey even as they were shot.

The leading wyrmkind smashed into Cooke, bearing him to the floor and pinning him there. He looked up at the face above him, its grasp on human form forsaken in the excitement, giving it decidedly feral features. Cooke gasped for air, trying to summon his strength to fight back, even though his limbs were all pinned.

Fabian spoke. "Foolish human; there is no escaping. You are powerful, no doubt, but can one of your kind hope to take three of us? I think not."

He addressed the demons. "Kill him."

The robed figure vanished from beneath the demon pinning him.

"Impossible," Fabian breathed, turning back. Cooke, leaping from a building, landed on him, bearing him to the floor. The wyrmkind ran to help, one of them meeting with a swift death as Cooke flung an energy ball over his shoulder, continually smashing Fabian's head against the tarmac as he did so.

The second wyrmkind lifted Cooke and hurled him away, allowing Fabian to flip to his feet.

"Good, I was beginning to get a headache." He followed the gaze of the wyrmkind to Cooke hovering some fifteen metres away, who had apparently managed to slow himself enough to avoid smashing into the wall. Fabian sighed and closed his eyes for a second, transmitting a message to Lucy requesting reinforcements, before nodding to the last demon. "Stall him, kill him; do what you want."

The wyrmkind took to the air, leathery bat-like wings sprouting from its back as it attacked the hovering figure with a series of fast clawing swipes, forcing Cooke to come to ground.

"Just stab him, he's only human!" Fabian yelled.

It dawned on Cooke that this wasn't true. He stopped, and doubled over as the five four-inch claws went through his stomach. The wyrmkind smiled, licking his lips as his wings folded into his back and vanished, his normal human features returning.

The smiling face of James Cooke rose in front of him, the claws still embedded in his torso, and brought one hand down on the demon's elbow with a satisfying crack as the arm broke. The right fist of the half-demon smashed into the wyrmkind's face, snapping it back, followed by a swift kick to the groin, fortuitously still painful to a demon while in human form. The wyrmkind fell to the ground after a few more vicious strikes, defeated by surprise and the speed of the other creature.

Fabian became aware that the only thing between him and Cooke was air. He raised both hands quickly, forming a barrier between him and the two energy streams shooting out of Cooke's hands. He felt his shield take the strain, and kept the energy flow up, content to sit behind the barrier until his reinforcements arrived, confident that he was more powerful than this creature, whatever it was. However, even as he bolstered the barrier's strength, he felt the gravel move under his feet as he began to slide, slowly but inexorably, backwards.

The pressure stopped suddenly, as something else took the brunt of the attack. In front of Fabian, the black robes and long hair of Lucy billowed as she stood unscathed in the path, her sword blocking both of the streams.

Cooke swore under his breath, funnelling his last reserves, already stretched dealing with Fabian, into the blade. The energy he was throwing out surged back and he flew through the front window of a store, crashing through the counter and out the back wall, raising a large cloud of dust and masonry.

Lucy leapt after him, found where he had stopped, crashed into a full water butt in a back garden, but the elusive man had himself vanished.

♦

"He's been gone a long time," Bishop remarked, looking anxiously at the clock as she and McInnes sat in the lounge, ostensibly relaxing after a hard day, though both concealed weapons, and neither was enjoying themselves.

"He can handle himself."

"He said he couldn't defeat Lucy, though; what if—"

"He wouldn't go after her. He just went to rescue the others, and they're back safely; he'll only be a little while."

McInnes, normally the ever placid, calmly reassuring figure of the pair, seemed strained by his own words.

Both of them were on their feet in an instant at the sound of a crash from the next room, guns drawn and sprinting wordlessly to find Dave Short, Becky Rossiter and Liam Cabot, who had been enjoying a game of poker, stood around the remains of their table. There were looks of panic on their faces, except for Cabot, who had managed to maintain his poker face and, McInnes noted, his cards.

"He just... fell, from nowhere."

Cooke's grey robe was torn in several places, and there were burn marks over much of his torso. He pulled himself up.

"If you wouldn't mind, Short, clear the room."

The three poker players left hurriedly while Bishop guided the wounded man to an armchair in the corner.

"He's not healing," she remarked, noticing the three long cuts along his face and the deep claw marks in his stomach. "Isn't he supposed to heal?"

"Lucy," McInnes said. "She did this."

Cooke nodded.

"Her sword is where most of her power comes from; it shines like a lighthouse in the dark. It's raw energy," he told them. "It's a sword that could kill me, Ellie, all of us, with a single swipe."

"She's using it to bolster her own power?"

"Yes; it's not hers though; the energy signature is very different."

"Energy signature?"

"It's like," he contemplated how to explain the concept, "energy has a shape. I can see it now, if I concentrate. All energy is individual and unique, it's like mothers being able to tell the difference between twins, and it's as clear to me as you're different to Siobhan."

"Okay, so the sword isn't made of the same thing that she is?"

"No, it once belonged to someone else. I can't tell who though; it's nobody I've come across."

"Okay then, what's our next move?"

"We wait."

"For what?"

"Her next move; I need to re-gather my strength, and she will know by now that our operation is being run from this Hall; that will lead her to one man."

"Who?"

"Someone I should have killed a long time ago."

♦

"Ah, Lord Cooke," Lucy said, greeting the man who stood before her desk.

William Cooke, the elder of the two Cooke brothers, had, as the undisputed favourite of their Father, become accustomed at an early age to the privileges that their family's immense wealth granted them, and, though they were around the same height, William was much stockier than his brother, even after several years deprived of luxuries, his expensive suit accenting a musculature developed and maintained through many hours a day in the gym. The gaze was similar though, William's bright blue eyes holding Lucy's gaze from beneath neatly cut jet-black hair in the same way as James' green eyes had from beneath his own brown locks.

"Why have you summoned me here?" he demanded, unabashed by the guards standing around the room and the calm radiated by Lucy.

"I am going to make you an offer you're not going to refuse."

"Surely you mean one I can't refuse."

"Well you can't, and you're not going to." Lucy rose from her chair. "Drink?"

"Scotch rocks, if you've got it."

Lucy nodded to one of the guards, who busied himself at the drinks cabinet.

"What's this offer then?"

"Tell me how to seize Cooke Hall without incident, and you can have it back."

"Why?"

"It is being held as a base for the rebels, who I believe are aware of how to use its security system. Tell me how to override that system and I will let you live there in peace, undisturbed by the changing of times."

"Now that's a tempting offer."

"You accept, then?"

"Oh yes..."

♦

"My jacket is covered in blood," McBride complained as he entered the cellar where Carter was waiting for him.

"I recommend vodka," Carter replied, leaning nonchalantly against the bar with a beer in his hand.

"Really? Does that actually work?"

"Well no, but you stop caring after you've had enough."

McBride nodded and went behind the bar, pulling a

bottle of cold beer from the fridge.

"Ah," he opened the beer and took a swig. "I've ruined more good clothes since I started this job than in the rest of my life."

"Yes, but you have a great many more clothes now," Carter reminded him.

"Good point." He took another swig of his beer. "Do you ever consider that perhaps this is just a trifle unfair?"

"What's that?"

"These gifts, talents, whatever you want to call them; the whole 'being a Touched One' thing. We didn't sign up for that, and yet we're lumbered with it, against our will."

"You signed up to serve the Society, Killian."

"Yeah, but I didn't know I was going to end up with a demon in my head, hurling energy balls across the room."

"I admit this is a little more intense than I'd expected, but it could be much worse."

"How, exactly? We're present for the downfall of humanity and we're supposed to stop it! Us! We're not made for this; we're ordinary guys, and we're going to fail, I know we are. How can I hope to kill Lucy when I keep atomising my bed-sheets every time I have a bad dream?"

"Hmm."

"Hmm?"

"Another beer, I think."

6

The study was illuminated by the pale orange glow of a single Art Deco light in the corner furthest from Cooke, its pale orange glow lighting the room as he stared at his hand, willing it to heal itself, but despite his best efforts the deep cuts remained. He sighed quietly, preparing himself mentally for what was about to happen. While he was alive, Cooke had shared his mind with another, far older consciousness, just as McBride did now. The alien mind had been able to occasionally seize control of his body, temporarily possessing him until Cooke had been able to reassert his authority. Of course, the perpetual voice had gone when he died, and he had believed it gone forever, but the voice had come back as soon as Eleanor had made him human again, and had dominated after his death before he had pushed it back once more and returned to earth.

Now the voice was gone again, and the consciousness was nowhere to be found in his mind. He knew better than to believe he had won.

There was a rustling from the shadows and he stretched out his hand to make an energy ball, but none appeared. The man stepped out of the darkness, chuckling to himself, clearly amused by the sudden impotence of the Master Engineer.

"What's wrong? Can't find it within you to kill me?" The voice was almost identical to his own, but colder, twisted. Evil. Cooke got to his feet and the man pushed back his hood, revealing a mirror image of Cooke's own face, before forming an energy ball in his hand.

"I thought I'd killed you."

"For as long as you exist, so will I, in some form. I cannot be disposed of now."

"That's why I wasn't healing; you're taking my energy, using it to reform yourself."

"Yes. I'm still very weak, but all it'll take is one strike and it'll be over, and everything you have will be mine."

"You'll side with Lucy?"

This brought a laugh from the demon in front of him.

"Don't be so ridiculous. With full access to the powers you haven't tapped into yet, abilities you haven't even dreamed of, I will overthrow Lucy's little regime; *I* will rule."

"I can't let you do that, then." Cooke leapt, spin-kicking the demon to the floor. "Go away."

"You're in no state to be making orders to me," the alternate version of himself said and leapt up, kicking back, the force smashing Cooke into the wall. He smiled triumphantly. "Always so weak..."

The gentle sound of a piano in the music room stopped abruptly and the man sat at the keys leapt up, snatching a poker from beside the fireplace. The cloud in the room was getting thicker as he ran up to it, swinging the long metal pole. As it came into contact with solid matter, Tom Gray stared briefly into eyes identical to his own, but filled with a look of surprise, before his double fell to the floor, vanishing in a haze of particles.

Gray looked down at the blood on his hand, which he knew to be his own, despite no weapon having pierced his skin, and broke into a run, knowing where he was going and what had to be done.

"I'll confess you've always been the stronger, but I kept you in check." Cooke seized a chair and hurled it at his own demonic self, who erupted into black matter, like a pile of leaves disrupted by a sudden gust of wind, before reforming as the chair smashed on the ground.

"No longer." The demon leapt towards him, ready to finish the weakened man. The door burst open and an energy ball struck the leaping form, atomising it in an instant.

"Is he dead?" Gray asked.

"No. He lives while I do." Cooke looked at his hand as the cuts healed over. "Thanks."

"I had the same thing, just sensed yours in time and expected the worst; he vanished too."

"Demonic?"

"Human, hit him with a poker and he went down."

"Ah-so." Cooke nodded; the two men had been linked by a strange bond since sharing the same demonic consciousness during the Faction War, so he wasn't particularly surprised that Gray too had been visited by a darker version of himself. "My brother is on his way to the hall; he has given us up in exchange for luxury."

"I thought he would. You should have killed him."

"He is family, Thomas."

"He *was* family, now he's a bastard in league with demons."

"Still, the same blood flows through his veins as mine."

In response to this, Gray swung the poker at Cooke's torso, embedding it within Cooke's ribcage.

"A little harsh, perhaps," Cooke said.

"No blood flows through your veins at all, James. William is a threat, and you must kill him."

◆

The doors were still not closed as the elder Cooke entered the house in his grey Armani suit, removing his sunglasses and looking around him with an expression of mild ecstasy on his face.

"It's good to be home," he sighed.

"I think you may have the wrong house."

The occupants of the Hall lined the staircase and the doorways, looking on as Master James Cooke stood in front of his brother.

"Not you again: she said you were dead."

"She believes me to be, yes."

"Look, I'm here to give you a choice," William said.

"Leave the house or die?"

"No; leave the house and die or stay in the house and die. Obviously I'd prefer you to pick the former, so that my home doesn't get damaged by the inevitable firefight, but it makes no difference, brother; I could have your corpse stuffed and made into a punchbag."

Standing to one side of the door, McBride cracked his knuckles angrily.

"And Annie, is she still here?" He scanned the stairwell until he found Annie Davies staring at him with contempt.

"Oh good. Still drooling over the Dalton girl, James? Or Julia, perhaps? Or has Annie been using her whorish ways on you too?" William continued taunting his brother. "Tastes good, doesn't she—"

McBride yelled, swinging his arm forward quickly with a flash of green light.

"No!" The ball stopped, held in place by James' will. "Mister Carter, get him out of here."

Carter put one hand on McBride's shoulder and both men vanished.

"I always knew you were a freak, brother, but I never imagined... why do you so habitually surrounded yourself with commoners, whores and weirdos when you are of noble birth?"

"There is more to life than who you were born as, William; I regret that you were never able to understand that, and that you will never have a chance to. Goodbye, brother." He closed his hand and McBride's energy ball blew his brother apart.

"Terry."

The Master Engineer approached Cooke. "Yes, James?"

"They will attack before the night is out. Put the civilians to bed, and get everyone else armed. McBride and Carter will need to be in the main hall; that's where I want the majority of our forces."

"How big is this going to be?"

"A skirmish, I'd expect; they have no idea what we're capable of yet."

"Neither do we, James."

"Then that makes it all the more likely that we'll learn something."

"You pick the weirdest things to be optimistic about."

♦

The doors to the Hall slammed shut behind the demons as they walked in casually, Fabian at their head.

"Kill every human you find. Kill the Touched Ones; locate, hold and kill the angel."

"Yes, sir."

"They're here." Carter picked up his staff. "Look alive, gents."

"Meh." Cabot put his cup of tea down gently on a coaster and snatched up a pair of thick goggles, pulling them over his eyes and flicking the switch on the side.

"Mister Cabot."

Cabot turned to face McBride, shielding his eyes.

"Yuh?"

"They're all demons; you won't be needing those."

Cabot tore the goggles from his head.

"Any reason you show up brighter than everyone else in the room?"

"They're Hardlight Goggles, they let you see higher concentrations of energy; may I advise against looking at Eleanor with them on, by the way."

"Whatev," Cabot replied.

One of the hall doors flew towards them and McBride waved a hand, evaporating it. He leapt forward, hurling an energy ball at a demon. The attackers spread out, energy balls flying at those wielding the hardlight staves as the counter-fire knocked a few from their feet.

McBride watched in horror as Samuel Mason took a sword to the chest and the demon he was fighting followed up with an energy ball, disintegrating his body.

"Fall back!" McInnes shouted over the sounds of combat.

The majority of the Hall's residents rushed through the back door of the chamber, leaving McBride, Cabot, Bishop and McInnes stood facing the eight demons who remained.

"Two to one? Yours odds aren't favourable." Fabian walked towards the four Engineers.

"We're up for it," McBride snarled.

"You may think you are, little mortal, but you know nothing of the ways of my kind; you will suffer for that."

Behind him one of the wyrmkind stepped forward, grabbing another by the neck and placing one hand against its chest.

The second demon exploded in a shower of fleshy globules and the first's tuxedo expanded into a flowing robe. A grey flowing robe.

"How about six on five? A little more even, don't you think?"

"A little." Fabian threw a burst of energy at Cooke, who deflected it, and the two men rose into the air, hurling energy at each other as they closed. As Cooke swung a fist at the demon Fabian raised a hand, forming a barrier between them which Cooke collided with and deflected.

Carter materialised in front of a demon charging Bishop, hitting him in the face with the end of his staff, and then bringing it round into the creature's stomach. The demon swung at Carter, long claws cutting his staff in two.

McBride ducked a swing from a demon and kicked it in the face. The demon began to fall back, being struck in mid-air by Fabian, who was trying to control his own flight, his hands outstretched towards the walls.

He stopped short of a collision and landed, facing off against Cooke again.

"Whatever you are, I doubt you are strong enough to withstand our full power..."

All the demons turned at once, as much strength as they could spare channelled into a single attack on their grey-robed enemy, streams of green energy crashing into him from all sides. The man vanished and Fabian breathed a sigh of relief, too soon as another demon exploded, Cooke leaping through. There was a sudden flurry of movement, incomprehensible even to Fabian as he let loose beams of light from either hand, the other demons not fast enough as a series of attacks tore through them faster than any mortal ever had before.

The dust settled, leaving Cooke and Fabian facing off once more. Everyone else who had survived the first round of attacks had already thrown themselves to the floor, to avoid the bloodshed and random bursts of energy that had torn so much of the room apart.

"You won't win; I saw you try and resist Lucy before, she's too strong for you."

"We'll see."

Fabian sensed Cooke's intention and flung out his hand, forming his protective barrier again as the energy ball flew. The attack was Cooke's most powerful yet, shocking Fabian as his barrier shattered, and Cooke's second energy ball tore the demon apart.

The muted silence of the aftermath was broken by the others getting to their feet, glass and plaster being crushed into still smaller chunks with each step. McBride kicked the smouldering remains of a chair over and a large portion of it crumpled to light ashen flakes, joining the thin layer floating around the floor.

"I think we may need to redecorate this room," he announced in a bid to be light-hearted.

"I think it can wait; we do have three other halls," McInnes replied. "Shame about the table though, it was an antique."

"Everything here's antique," James reminded him. "We ought to make sure the others are okay—"

"Did that not strike you as being a little too easy?" Bishop asked, expressing the logical sentiment that the others thought but dared not say.

"Easy? Ten people must have died, is that what you'd call

easy?" Carter snapped.

"Need I remind you, *Mister* Carter, that Doctor Bishop still outranks you, and that you know she's right," Cooke said quietly.

"Lucy could have sent an army after us," McBride muttered dolefully.

"Then why didn't she?"

"She underestimated us?" Cabot suggested half-heartedly.

"No; she fought me before, she knew I could take Fabian. I was expecting a skirmish, but this was too small for a serious attack. It was a diversion."

"But what's the other target?" Bishop asked.

McBride and Cooke quickly turned to each other, a look of understanding striking them both simultaneously.

"I sense it too," Cooke said abruptly, and vanished.

"Carter: Annie," McBride told his friend. Carter too disappeared in a flurry of particles and McBride broke into a supernaturally fast sprint, storming through the hole left by the explosion that had torn the doors off.

♦

Annie Davies was woken by the sinuous sensation of a cool breeze across her face. She was still half asleep, and so didn't stir as she heard a voice gently chanting in a language alien to her yet strangely comprehensible and bizarrely soothing.

Out of the darkness a barely visible male form began to take greater shape as he chanted, a body of no more than smoke becoming rapidly a tall, muscular man with thick black hair. He approached her bed in slow, cautious steps, making sure to continue chanting to keep her subdued and docile.

He turned suddenly but still gracefully, raising one hand to the newcomer in the room. Still chanting, he let loose an energy stream into the man, sending him sprawling, pinned to the ground by the energy and unable to rise or raise a barrier to defend himself.

Carter appeared and leapt into a kick at the demon, only to find his outstretched leg grabbed in one hand, and himself summarily thrown out through the room's open window.

The demon tilted his head curiously at the door, still focused on pinning Cooke to the ground and his lips still moving as he chanted. The ancient oak smashed, admitting McBride, already leaping with arms outstretched. He collided with the demon, wrapping his hands around the creature's neck and bearing it to the ground, slamming its head repeatedly into the ground.

Cooke flew to his feet as the pressure was taken from him, just as the demon—still chanting through the repeated smashings—pushed McBride up, sending the apprentice into the ceiling. The demon was on his feet in a second. As McBride hit the ground the creature waved a hand at him, muttering a different chant quickly under his breath. McBride's head hit the floor as he fell instantly into a dream-filled slumber.

The demon turned to Cooke and waved his hand at him, muttering the same syllables once again. Cooke mock-yawned, then grew suddenly serious again and glared at the demon.

"I do not sense any power in you; yet you do not seem to be killed by mine."

"That's easily explainable."

"How?"

"Balance. You have come to take her?"

"Yes, and the others within my influence."

"An ingenious plan; no doubt Lucy intended to remove our ability to fight long-term by taking our women?"

"That would be the gist, though I would ultimately have possessed one of you and killed your Touched Ones."

"And an impressive feat that would have been."

"But you knew I was here."

"The Touched Ones are not as blind as our kind would like to believe."

"Our kind?"

"Demons."

"An awfully crude word, do you not think? It just smacks of evil; almost a cliché."

"There are less evil things than wiping out a population of innocent women."

"You are no demon," the creature mused, ignoring Cooke's comment, "a demon would have succumbed to the energy I just pumped into you, and would never dream of siding against Lucy; she has the sword of the Morningstar."

"Oh, is that who it belonged to?"

The demon faltered, realising he had misspoken too late. Incandescent bands appeared from the air around him at a wave of Cooke's hands, quickly encasing the incubus with impregnable bonds of energy.

"Mister McBride," Cooke said softly and the apprentice jerked suddenly awake.

"Yes, Master?"

"Escort this gentleman to the room at the back of the wine cellar. Lock the door behind him and post two guards; he will not escape."

♦

An hour later McInnes, Cooke and McBride walked back into the wine cellar, striding with purpose towards the small room at the back, previously used for hundred-year-old Scotch but now occupied by the captured incubus.

Cooke nodded to the armed guards on the door and one opened it, admitting the three men to the room.

"What is your name?" McInnes demanded of the man, held against the walls by his bindings.

"Incomprehensible to your ears," he snapped back. "What is yours, mortal?"

"What is Lucy's plan?"

"How am I to know? I was merely sent to feed upon your women."

"Feed?"

"He's an incubus," Cooke explained without moving his eyes from the demon, "their energy is transitory. They need to kill other creatures in order to survive."

"And just how do you know that?" the incubus' attention quickly refocused on Cooke.

"What can I say, I'm special."

"You're an abhorrence."

"Thank you."

The demon screamed as his bonds tightened.

"Now let's try and be civil, shall we?"

"I make no parley with mortals."

"That's interesting to hear from you; if we leave you in here for too long you will become no stronger than anyone else, and if we wait long enough you'll become even weaker."

"You'd have to have plenty of time."

"I do," Cooke scowled, then straightened up, expression changing from menacing to gentle in a second. "Unfortunately, I'm also lazy." His hand shot out, pressed against the demon's forehead. Its face glowed brightly for a second or so before the hand was withdrawn, and the creature slumped.

"Is he dead?"

"No; worse." Cooke smiled. "He's mortal."

"Oh; and how do you intend to use this?" McInnes asked suspiciously.

"Well, it'll make him easier to interrogate."

"Why?"

"He can feel pain now."

The demon began to come round groggily.

"James..."

"If you have any objections to me torturing him, I suggest you leave quickly."

"James."

"Immediately, in fact."

McInnes nodded reluctantly and both he and McBride turned and quickly left the room.

"Has he lost his mind?" McInnes asked. "He hates torture; he despises eliciting information from people through violence. Why now?"

"He isn't torturing a person, he's torturing a demon, an enemy of all that we stand for: he is evil."

"And how, by doing this, is James any different? He said he was a demon; how is he not descending to their level? At this point, how is he any better?"

"He won," McBride said coldly, "and for the moment that's all that matters."

McInnes sighed, and a piercing scream erupted from the cell.

"What do we do if the James who comes out of that room is different from the James that went in?"

"He won't; have faith."

♦

The pistol whirled around Cooke's hand, snapping back into place the instant before he pulled the trigger. The high powered staple left the end of the rifled barrel spinning fast and smashing into the demon's kneecap, blowing apart the now-vulnerable bone with a crack that was muffled by the victim's screams of pain.

"What is Lucy's next move?" Cooke asked, grabbing the demon by the neck and holding its head up to stop it from slumping. "Tell me!"

"You're going to have to do better than that," The demon grinned at him. "I may feel pain now, but I'm still a demon inside."

Cooke gave a thin smile and waved his hand, sending a thin wisp of hardlight into the demon's broken kneecaps. The demon looked down with a sense of terror as he realised that the wounds had healed.

A moment later a second scream rang out.

♦

"He's been in there for six hours now," Carter said, looking lazily at his watch.

"Well, maybe he hasn't gotten any information."

"Maybe. I'm just saying; shouldn't we consider starting some kind of shift system?"

"I'll wait for him till he's done; you can go to bed Daniel," McBride offered. "I'll handle anything that comes up."

♦

The sounds from beyond the doorway stopped.

Inside, Cooke turned suddenly, facing the shimmering wall of green water in front of him.

"That's not actually water, is it." It was more a statement of fact than a question, but the incubus answered anyway.

"No," he replied mirthfully, a wide grin spreading over

his face. "It's a seal; someone's summoning you."

As he began to be sucked toward the green surface, Cooke flung out both arms, transforming them into sharpened metal poles and embedding them in the wall. His feet left the ground as he was drawn towards the seal. The masonry began to crack around his arms, the demon beside him laughing joyously at the futility. Cooke pulled one arm out of the wall and lunged at the demon, skewering him with the sharpened pole in the second before he plunged into the seal.

"What was that?" McBride leapt up, drawing his gun and running towards the cell door. He reached it just as the portal closed, wind blowing past him as the air rushed to fill the vacuum it had left.

"Shit."

7

Cooke lay prone on the floor in the middle of the pentagram, the only light in the room provided by the plethora of candles positioned around the outside of the arcane shape.

"I know you're awake," a taunting female voice said from the outside of the pentagram. "Arise and identify yourself."

Cooke remained still.

"You know how this works; you must do my bidding. I have summoned you."

Her captive got up, his face obscured by the dim light and the long grey hood, and turned a long, silent glare in the direction of the unseen speaker.

"Your barrier cannot hold me."

"Not indefinitely, no, but it is being maintained by my sword, so you will be stuck there long after your friends are dead."

"How unfortunate for me."

"And for them; my forces will now be able to take the Hall unopposed."

"There are still powerful people there."

"Powerful enough? Be honest now."

"No."

"Exactly. Now, who are you? I don't recognise your energy; it seems so weak at the best of times, yet you have thus far killed several of my best men."

"You wish to know my identity? Why not just finish me now?"

"Let's call it curiosity, shall we?"

"Very well." He reached up and pushed his hood back, revealing his face, smiling wryly in the candlelight.

"You?" Lucy stepped into the light, her reaction as he had expected. "I killed you."

"Twice, in fact."

"This is impossible!"

"Probable impossibilities are to be preferred to improbable possibilities." The energy barrier shone momentarily as his essence tried to fight its way out. The wall began to bend outwards, warping under the stress, but the light quickly faded.

"Insolent child; you are no more powerful than a Touched One. Do not presume you are able to stand against me."

♦

The centre of Lucy's operations was situated in the third of the three ballrooms of the NCC, the first being used for formal functions and the second currently housing the fuming Master of Cooke Hall. She strode into the third calmly, contentedly, and began to issue instructions.

"Prepare the Guard; they are to attack the Hall immediately. Their defences will offer no resistance any more."

Though everyone in the room was paying attention, Lucy was aware that many of them had covered over phones to do so, and that these same people were looking extremely nervous.

"What's wrong?" She demanded.

"The Guard are a little busy right now."

"What?"

♦

It had started off as one man, running down the street towards the NCC, and the Guard were waiting for him, preparing to open fire. Too late; his twin pistols and agility had made light work of the first squad, and as they had fallen, more people had taken to the streets in a clear defiance of the curfew, many of them toting weapons from the old wars. By the time the reinforcements had arrived, the Guard were facing a fully-fledged riot.

Now the riot moved quickly towards the NCC, the Guard falling back before them; some unable to fire, some still unwilling.

Inside the building itself the demons posted on the doors at high alert waited, watching as the figure in white at the front of the charge hacked down dozens of guardsmen with his swords. This would be a kill to relish.

♦

"This is definitely concerning." Senator Greenwood blinked a few times, attempting to wake himself as he gazed into his coffee. "They're both gone?"

"Yes, Senator," Carter said quietly. Assembled around the table were those members of the rebellion whom McInnes had instructed him to wake. After Cooke's abduction, McBride had gone straight to Carter, explained what had happened, then run through the secret passageway that led out of the Hall, locking the door behind himself and preventing anyone from following him quickly. This had left a troubled Carter to pass on McBride's report to McInnes, which had led to the calling of this emergency meeting.

"With them gone, do we stand a chance?" Greenwood asked earnestly; with Cooke vanished, apparently captured by the enemy, and McBride engaged in an unsanctioned and suicidal mission to rescue him, the mood among those assembled was serious to the point of morbidity.

"Without their power, perhaps, but their knowledge of the enemy would have been indispensable; we cannot afford to lose it."

"And Lucy will be here soon?"

"Not too soon; it seems McBride is making some headway, and the Guard is being forced to try and stop him," McInnes answered. "Really, we have three courses of action available to us."

"What are they?" Robinson asked; he too was looking tired.

"First, we sit here and do nothing."

"Not a good option."

"Indeed. Second, we follow McBride's lead, and launch an all-out offensive on the NCC."

"Will that succeed?" Greenwood enquired.

"No," McInnes answered. "Finally, we can send someone with a slightly less gung-ho attitude to retrieve our lost apprentice."

"And Master Cooke?"

"If he is still alive, he will find a way to escape; if he is dead, then he is beyond our help."

"Optimistic."

"Sirs," Carter spoke up, "I volunteer to take part in the third option; my abilities mean I can get to McBride quicker than anyone else and bring him home."

"Yes they do, but with all due respect Mister Carter, you're hardly any more responsible than McBride." McInnes turned to Kingston. "Go with him, make sure he comes back alive and with his quarry." Kingston bowed and left with Carter.

◆

The grey-robed demon knelt on the floor inside the seal, a deep and overriding cold permeating his unnaturally heated body. Lucy had left him for the time being, leaving him with only his memories, which provided more distress than comfort.

"Why did you abandon me?" he asked the floor quietly. "How did you take the warmth from me, leave me empty and without solace? There was more to your life than me, but nothing more than you in mine. I loved you, and you deserted me, left me to face the darkness and the cold alone. Did you not care for my suffering; for my loss? Did you even try to return to me, did you even look back? Or was the divine too important, more important than me? Look what I have become!" Cooke spat the last word. "I am demonic, the very thing I hate the most; because you left I am alone, and I will never feel warm again. Even if you return now your form is empty. You never loved me."

"I did," a voice said softly. A figure dressed all in white approached the seal from the outside and he rose.

"This is a trick."

"No trick."

He stared into her eyes.

"I did love you, but not as you wanted."

"That was enough."

"No, it wasn't. You could have continued pretending you

accepted it, even convinced yourself, but you never would have been free."

"Is this freedom?"

"No; you torture yourself over your new form, never accepting what can be done with it."

"I love you, Tina; I would give it up for you."

"That isn't an option. You have been dealt this hand. You cannot have me, you have this: you cannot trade one for the other."

"I hated you for so long, for your sadness. I couldn't stand it that I couldn't do anything, that you shut me out and acted like I didn't even exist. Then you went and died."

"You lost nothing when I died."

"I lost you. My best friend and the woman I loved."

"Do you still love me?"

"I always will."

"Then be happy for me when I am happy, mourn that I left, and move on. The girl needs protecting; she will be the same as me. You must help her."

"If she's the same as you then she won't let me."

"Let her know you're there; that's all it takes."

"I can't very well do that stuck behind this seal for the rest of my life! Help me escape."

The angel vanished.

"Thank you," he muttered under his breath, half sarcastically, half sincerely.

♦

"Wait until he is through the door, then seal it," Lucy ordered the guards standing in the main foyer of the NCC, looking out across the street to where the last tatters of the Guard forces between them and the riot gave up their lives. The mob's leader leapt out of the crowd, flying through the

304

air towards the building and coming crashing through the glass doors to land in front of her.

The demons around the door raised the energy barrier across it and several hisa-me moved in on McBride as he stood, lab coat splattered with blood, observing the room around him. With two quick flicks of his wrists energy balls had struck down the two nearest demons and the others halted, looking to Lucy for further direction as she and the apprentice, only a few feet apart, stared each other down.

"I've come for my master."

"Well, that goes without saying."

♦

Carter's atomised form reverberated off the mental wall in front of him and he reformed, Kingston appearing beside him, both facing the woman standing in front of them, garbed in casual, ordinary clothes.

"You don't look like a demon, Miss Kensington."

"And you don't look like the Gifted One, Melanie."

"Carter, go. I'll handle her."

"Handle me?" Sam cracked her knuckles loudly. "I'm not the same girl you once knew."

Carter vanished and Kingston leapt, kicking out at Sam, only to be met with two quick blocks and a counter-kick in the side.

"You're much faster than you were, I'll admit, but you still lack discipline."

Kingston feinted with her right leg and as Sam moved to block she leapt up, swinging her left leg into the side of her opponent's head. Sam flinched, and as she did Kingston put another three kicks in her opponent's side.

"Discipline is no match for power, Melanie; an asset you once possessed, when you were favoured, but the advantage seems to have switched to me now."

Kingston swung out with her fist, but not fast enough, and Sam's hand wrapped around her throat.

The demon lifted Kingston from her feet and slammed her bodily into the wall, forcefully enough for her to splinter the woodwork of the old building.

Kingston gasped for air as Sam tightened her grip. The young assassin placed one hand on the wall and put the other around Sam's neck, finding herself a purchase.

Gravity around Kingston altered, turning ninety degrees. She pushed herself off the wall into a one-handed handstand, lifting Sam from the ground before she could react and slamming her into the ceiling. Gravity reasserted itself and the demon fell to the floor again.

♦

"What are the security codes for the Hall's defence grid?" Lucy demanded, pacing around the pentagram-shaped wall of energy imprisoning McBride.

"I don't know," McBride answered passively, sat on the floor in the lotus position and staring straight ahead.

"How can the grid be disabled?"

"I don't know."

"How many people are defending it?"

"I don't know." McBride rolled his eyes and turned his head to face the demon. "Why don't you just kill me? That's what I was expecting, not the Spanish Inquisition."

"Nobody expects the Spanish Inquisition."

Two of Lucy's guards toppled forward, one of Carter's swords stuck through each of their chests. He slipped the swords out and the two corpses toppled. It was then that he became aware that the entire focus of the room was on him.

"Our primary weapon is surprise and fear—no—fear and

surprise. Sorry; our two primary weapons are surprise and fear. Oh, and a fanatical dedication to the Society..." Carter stopped, and grinned apologetically. "I'll come in again," he said, and vanished.

♦

Kingston flew backwards through the second-storey window, propelled by the kick she had just received. Around her the glass fanned out, so that none remained in her path when she hit the ground. Sam stood in the empty window frame, pointing a pistol down at the fallen girl. Kingston tried to rise, but found herself unable to move.

She watched the pistol muzzle flare as Sam fired, and the glass from the window lifted into the air again, forming a surface that deflected the bullet. The demon cursed from above and dropped down to the ground beside her.

"Any last words?"

"See you in Hell."

Kingston closed her eyes, feeling a flurry of movement above her, but her anticipated death did not come. When she dared look again she saw Sam, lying stunned on the ground from where she had been smashed forcefully into the side of the building they had just fought in. Her saviour had arrived.

♦

"Nobody expects the Spanish Inquisition! Amongst our many weapons are surprise, fear, a fanatical dedication to the Society and these two rather nice swords," Carter said as he reappeared, killing two more guards.

"Mister Carter," McBride turned to his old friend, "I don't mean to sound critical, but at the moment you don't seem particularly prepared to kill demons."

"Ah yes," Carter paused for a moment, becoming aware that the demons whose attention he had found were now walking towards him, "good thought."

"Yes." McBride hurled an energy ball against the wall of his prison and it was absorbed. "And, as you can see, I'm not really in any state to help."

"Quite." Carter vanished and reappeared behind a demon, running it through with his sword. The demon turned and pulled the weapon fully through its body. Carter vanished again, and reappeared when he hit the energy barrier in front of the walls.

"So, all three of those with power within the Hall have handed themselves to me on a silver platter," Lucy laughed as she drew her sword.

The door, and a large section of wall around it, exploded, sending a shower of rocks and glass, some two feet across, flying into the room. Demons were bowled aside as the rocks hit them; Carter atomised, avoiding one hurtling straight for his head. McBride remained calmly seated, protected by Lucy's energy barrier.

Lucy turned to face the door, the other demons pulling themselves to their feet. What came through the cloud of dust looked like a mass of sentient fabric; thick black silk snatching at the demons as it flew past, wrapping around each of them and knocking them back to the ground. Lucy swung her sword at the swirling shape as it moved towards her, slicing off shreds that evaporated like dew before they hit the ground.

The cloth span together into a single mass; a black, barely human form that took on more complexity as it turned into a smiling Master Cooke, his arms crossed in front of him. One demon began to get up from the attack and Cooke waved a hand, pinning the creature back down.

"Impressive." Lucy held her sword in one hand and began moving towards him. "How are you doing that? Making the air around him heavier? Or simply making his mind think it is? Either way, it's got to be hard; how many of us can you hold? Two? How about three?"

The rest of the demons began to come round.

"How about two dozen?"

"Put the sword away Lucy. Let us pretend there is honour among demons."

The sword was sheathed.

"Carter; McBride."

Carter leapt at his fellow apprentice, now in the open, and as he laid a hand upon McBride's shoulder, both men vanished.

"Are you actually going to fight me? Or am I going to have to imprison you again?"

Cooke leapt and she reached out a hand as he had done, holding him static in the air, unable to move or concentrate his mind to teleport himself.

"Imprisonment, then?"

♦

Alan Empter jerked awake. His thick sheets threatened to engulf him again, to drive him back to sleep, but he fought it, listening carefully in the dark; there was no noise, none of the subtle whispering of the past months, no heretical voices in his head.

He rolled out of bed, memories he hadn't been able to recall since the new rulers of the Society had arrived now surging through his head, each desperate to be noticed before the others. He pulled himself together and went to the bathroom. Turned on the cold tap, he splashed some water on his face before looking at himself in the mirror. He was Alan Empter, Colonel in the army of the PFS and Chief of Staff to Lord Stanford, the Lord Protector who was now dead. Katie was dead too; everyone was dead.

Not everyone. McInnes lived; of this Empter felt certain, and if he was alive, he'd be needing some help.

He pulled on a pair of black trousers and a white shirt, over which he threw on his black overcoat. The pockets of the overcoat were heavy; laden with guns he only now remembered were in there. He smiled and picked up the lamp from beside his bed, throwing it against the wall.

Outside the room, the two men assigned to guard his quarters heard the crash and turned to each other. Both of them quickly drew their pistols and one kicked the door open.

The room was dark, though the outside of the Society was quite well lit; an illusion created by the thickness of Empter's curtains. They moved further into the room. The light from the dimly-lit corridor poured in, but was insufficient to illuminate Empter as he swung the chair he had taken from his dining area into one of their faces.

Brief flashes of muzzle-fire brought Empter out of the shadow as he twisted through the air and kicked the second guard in the head, putting him to the ground swiftly.

◆

Cooke smashed through a wall, still unable to use any of his powers to defend himself or strike back. He landed amidst a pile of masonry and reached out, snatching up a piece of brick.

He felt Lucy's hold on him increase again and hurled the brick towards her. Her hand made the slightest of movements, shifting her power to stop the brick.

"A pathetic display of resistance, James: but I wasn't

really expecting more from a mortal."

He ran at her, fist striking her in the stomach. It was a blow to incapacitate any normal person, and she looked down.

"Interesting; how did you do that?"

"You are overconfident; you cannot control both the brick and myself."

The brick atomised and she thrust her palm into his chest. He fell to the ground but pushed himself back up into a spin, kicking out three times at her as he rose, then vanishing.

"Pursue them! Find them all and kill them; march on the Hall!" Lucy snapped, and the demons began to move.

"Covenant," Empter addressed the A.I. that ran the NCC's security systems.

"Voice Pattern Recognised, Colonel Alan Empter; good morning."

"Activate foothold scenario lockdown, initiate immediately, authorisation Empter Six Nine One Two Six One Two Seven Lock Hardy."

"Authorisation accepted, emergency lockdown initiated; securing control room and broadcasting emergency signals."

A few demons were already out when the large sheets of adamantium slid over the doors and walls, massive generators beneath the NCC, accessible only from the control room, roaring into life to charge the edge of the barriers with polarised hardlight energy. Automated machine-guns activated and began scanning the corridors for non-PFS personnel.

♦

Cabot wandered back towards his bedroom, a glass of warm milk in his hand, when he heard a muffled noise coming from one of the nearby rooms. He put the milk down on a table and slipped a pistol from the inside of his dressing gown before gently pushing open the door.

The room was dark, and he flicked the light switch on with his free hand, illuminating Doctor Bishop. She had clearly been preparing for bed when she had been captured, dressed as she was only in her underwear, tied to a wooden chair in the centre of the room with thick ropes that dug into the flesh of her arms and legs.

Thoughts began to spread insidiously and unbidden through Cabot's brain as he moved towards her, sliding a penknife from his back pocket and beginning to set to work on the ropes.

"Liam; step away," said Kingston, coming into the room behind him. He barely heard her voice as Bishop looked at him with a sense of urgency, a pleading look of helplessness.

"Liam; stop."

This pierced his foggy consciousness and he turned.

"This is no matter of yours, go bother someone else," Cabot said, groggily. Behind him Bishop strained against her bonds and the wood of the chair creaked.

"Liam, I'm warning you."

Cabot turned back to cutting the ropes. Kingston leapt at him, grabbing him by the shoulders and throwing him away from Bishop, but it was too late; as Cabot landed on the floor, rolling, the ropes were torn apart and Bishop stood up, batting the assassin aside.

"Stupid boy," she smirked. In a second Siobhan Bishop became Sam, fully clothed in tight black trousers and top, with a maroon leather jacket over that. She waved a hand at Cabot and he fell instantly to sleep. Stepping casually over

Kingston's unconscious body, she walked out into the hallway.

♦

Cooke sat in the great hall, a thick white bandage wrapped around his right arm.

"I'm fine I assure you, Terry; would you get her to just leave me alone?"

Doctor Lyons was just finishing tying the knot in the bandage.

"You're bleeding James; demons don't bleed."

"And I'm not totally demonic; I'm human with demonic abilities. Lots of them."

"And some angelic ones," McBride interjected.

"And some angelic ones." Cooke paused. "Miss Kensington has escaped. Killian, Dan, go get her; take guards with goggles and staves."

The two apprentices left calmly.

"Don't look at me like that."

"I wasn't looking at you at all," McInnes remarked, his gaze fixed on the organ.

"You were thinking it."

"Perhaps. Why did you bring her back here? She's a demon and she's working for the other side. Because of her you died."

"She's one of us," Cooke said succinctly. "She is not working of her own will."

"She has tried to kill us many times; she would have killed Mel."

"But she didn't."

"Because you intervened; if she was going to defect she would have done it by now, and she's trying to escape."

313

"She wants something; a promise I couldn't have given her two months ago, but which I will make when we get her back."

"Assuming we do get her back. And what does she want?"

"Peace."

♦

Sam turned, changing her body and clothing to the loose black silk and elegant grace of Rose Mendelson. Carter came around the corner in front of her at a run and stopped instantly.

"Rose, we're looking for Samantha Kensington."

"I thought she was dead."

"Long story; have you seen anyone suspicious?"

"No, sorry."

Five men came from around the corridor after Carter with hardlight staves and goggles.

"Mister Carter, it's her!"

Mendelson waved a hand at Carter and he grabbed one of the staves, swinging it by its end to knock out its former owner.

"Carter!" McBride arrived from the other direction, summoning an energy ball. "It's Kensingston!" He threw the energy ball at Mendelson and she caught it in one hand, throwing it back. McBride dodged it and threw another, which went wide.

Miss Kensington; desist! Come to the great hall, free my men from your illusions and we will talk.

The voice rang through the heads of McBride, Carter and the disguised Sam, who paused for a second before transmuting back to her true form.

"Lead the way, Mister McBride," she smiled at him.

"After you, Miss Kensington."

♦

"Ah, Samantha; you're looking well."

"James, you're looking... dead."

"Less dead than I have looked, though."

"What did you want to talk about? How I would like to die? Because given the choice I'd rather not."

"Curiously enough, that is exactly what I was going to talk to you about. If you come over to our side I promise to give you exactly what Lucy promised you."

"And what, pray, would that be?"

"Death by a level of hardlight high enough to end your existence permanently, thus prohibiting your ever returning to Hell, whilst ensuring that you needn't continue to eke out an existence on this plain."

"Impressive deduction, Master Cooke; and what would I be required to do here? What services would I be required to render?" She took a few steps towards him. "I can see into the minds of men, read their desires, and I know that the darkness in you always wanted something a little less wholesome."

Cooke' glare was stony.

"Something more..." she grinned slyly, "innocent, then?"

Her shape began to change to that of Tina Dalton. Cooke's grey robe changed quickly from grey to black and he thrust out an arm, sending Sam smashing into the wall.

"Ow, that really hurt." She pulled herself up. "I'm guessing you know I can't possibly beat you in an out-and-out fight."

"Indeed."

"So you want me to join you?"

"Yes."

"Why?"

"Because you're one of us; because you fought beside us before; because you believe in my cause and in the society; because Lucy's been playing you like a cheap fiddle for years. Because you want freedom and I can give it, and so you can undo some of the horrors you've caused."

"I don't think it was really that bad; no worse than any of the other wars."

"Demonic essence effects people, even when it's not inside them. They become twisted, the best of them can hardly stay innocent; you were living in a haze, seeing things through tinted glass." He closed his eyes and she felt his consciousness enter the room. Memories flowed through her head suddenly, memories that were not her own: stonings; corpses found by the roadside, flayed within an inch of their life; women branded with arcane symbols not understood by the men who had made them; medics and other neutral parties crucified. Finally, the image of Tina Dalton, Cooke's unrequited love, crucified by guards in Sam's service.

"This happened?"

"Yes."

"All of it?"

"This is only what I saw. There is bound to have been much worse; I read reports."

"Oh."

"Join us; make up for it all. Fight the demons that held you in the palms of their hands for years, forced you to Hell and then pulled you back when they needed you."

♦

"Kensington is dead," a demon reported to Lucy as she sat in her office.

"It was only to be expected; very unfortunate though, she

could have been useful. Summon another succubus, we may need one."

"And the howlers?"

"I think we have enough; dispatch them tonight to the houses with a team of hisa-me."

♦

You were tempted.

"I wasn't."

You were.

"Oh, shut up." The voice in Cooke's head was persistent, but weak enough for him to handle.

"Sorry, James?"

He looked up at McInnes. "Nothing. I feel there is much which must be explained to the others."

"That is undoubtedly true, but how much, and what is your motivation?"

"I don't know the answer to either of those."

McInnes rubbed his eyes.

"How's your sight?"

"How do you mean?"

"What's the weather going to be like tomorrow?"

McInnes was quiet for a second and when he spoke again his voice was distant, unfocused.

"A storm; lightning, some ten miles away, but relatively calm here. It'll pass us."

"Where are the documents to create more staves?"

"Your tomb."

"Who will lead the defence?"

"I don't know."

"Where is the stone?"

"The Sistine Chapel. Mister Empter is at the door; he is quite badly wounded. He has two shots to his torso and one

317

to his left leg. He requires medical attention quickly."

"I'll handle it." Cooke vanished and McInnes reverted to normal, playing a few bars on the piano in front of him.

"I didn't know you could play the piano, Terry."

Verity Robbins had entered the room while he was playing and was now pulling up a chair.

"I don't; it's just, er, a thing..."

"Oh, one of those. You don't understand because you think too much; you will learn in time, Terry."

"When did you get so wise, young lady?"

"I didn't; it's just, er, a thing," she parroted, and McInnes laughed for the first time he could remember.

"See; if you can still laugh things can't be that bad."

"There are bad people coming to kill us, Verity."

"There have been bad people coming to kill you since you were little more than a child. If they come for you again, you'll make them sorry they did."

"Thank you, Verity, but I fail to see how."

"Once again; think less."

8

The street around the Sistine Chapel was crowded, as always, with tourists taking snapshots of the building's exterior, before heading inside to stare in wonderment at the ceiling. Amid the crowd Thomas could hear no less than a dozen languages being spoken by the tourists and he knew them all, and all the others that had been spoken in six thousand years.

He listened to each of the conversations, each occupying a small fraction of his near-infinite focus as he patiently scanned the street below the roof upon which he was stood.

At last there was something of interest; a man who had just leapt a building and landed in the middle of the shocked tourists, drawing two pistols and shooting death at the hapless crowd before they could comprehend what was happening to them

Thomas stepped forward, falling from the building into the avenue. He hit the ground and carried on walking, not missing a step as he continued calmly, but with eerie speed, toward the man.

His cloak spread out, increasing in length and breadth and forming a barrier between the tourists and the man in black, who stopped shooting and dropped the guns in front of him.

"You are the guardian of this place?"

"Yes; it is my charge to protect it." Thomas was hesitant; this was not something that happened very often.

"I need to get a message to the Eight."

Thomas raised his hand and the area was engulfed in white light, blinding all but himself. The demon fell to the floor.

"Why did it have to be a Sentinel!" the creature screamed.

"Your kind have no place anywhere in this world, and certainly not here. You may not speak with the Eight; as you well know they are busy dealing with your master."

"My kind have a new master. I've come to warn them about her; she has the sword of the Morningstar!"

Another burst of bright light from Thomas' hand sent the demon reeling

"You are a deceiver and a falser; tell me your name so I may report my victory."

"My name is Sokar, I am Praetor of the Sixth; I have come to warn your kind of a great treachery, masked by a possession, in the Land of the Touched."

"There has been no activity there for ten years."

"You are mistaken."

Another burst of light.

"Would you stop doing that!" Sokar was on his feet faster than Thomas could react and had forced the sentinel angel back into the wall, one hand around his neck and the other restraining his arm.

"Impossible," the angel gasped.

"Allow me to reiterate," the demon said through clenched teeth. "My name is Sokar, I am Praetor of the Sixth, I have come to deliver a message to the leaders of your kind. You are a Sentinel of the Third Stair; you are here to guard the last stone of the Touched Master. The first, second and third seals have fallen, and your masters must be made aware immediately; a demon named Lucy is ruler of the Touched Lands now. She will be coming for the other seals soon; you must end her."

"Why are you telling me this?" the angel asked. "Why don't you do it yourself?"

"She has the sword of the Morningstar; she is the most powerful jinn to walk since the Manifest was tempted."

Sokar dropped Thomas to the ground and turned to go. As an afterthought he looked back over his shoulder and spoke again. "I bid you good luck on your quest; fail to complete it, and I will find you and kill you myself." He leapt high into the sky, far over buildings, until he landed in the business district on the other side of the city.

A tall man in a suit was walking by and Sokar extended a hand, touching his arm and possessing him in an instant.

♦

Back at the chapel, Thomas got to his feet and set about altering the memories of those who had seen what had happened. He had just finished doing so when he saw a man walking through the crowd outside the chapel. Everyone else was stood stock still, their concept of the passage of time halted by Thomas' influences on their mind. Shrugging off the strange occurrence, he waved a hand at the stranger to halt him, but the man continued walking.

Surely there couldn't be another one this quickly? Thomas thought, and teleported into the chapel. The crowds in here, still awake and alert, mostly peering at the ceiling, didn't see the angel appear in the doorway to an anteroom. Indeed, they couldn't see the ante-room itself, protected as it was by Thomas' power.

He walked into the room and stood between the doorway and the altar, on which a raised platform held the black, egg-shaped stone. The man appeared in the entrance and stepped over the threshold designed to prevent demonic access, the air around him glowing green as the hardlight barrier attempted, unsuccessfully, to stop him.

Thomas raised his hand and blinding light filled the room and poured through the doorway, incapacitating some more tourists with its glare, but Cooke continued walking, his casual clothes changing to more formal black robes. Thomas gave out a second burst of light, more powerful this time, but Cooke was unhindered, and teleported past Thomas as the angel drew his sword. He turned just as Cooke snatched up the stone, mouthed "thank you" and vanished.

Thomas sighed wearily; he now had no choice but to report in, as Sokar had instructed him to.

♦

"Twenty-four former members of our government were killed last night. No sign of a struggle; they died of natural causes, apparently," Bishop said, reading through a stolen paper in the living room.

"Fascinating," Robinson announced, "and the fact that our government is now totally controlled by Lucy doesn't make you sceptical?"

"It does somewhat." Bishop didn't look up from the paper as she spoke, and turned the page with almost painful slowness.

"Are you going to read that all that slowly?"

"It's always best to keep apprised of the news, Senator."

"Isn't there anything to do around here? How do you

people do it, sat around and waiting the entire time, waiting for death to come for us?"

"It is a foolish man who, sensing the end, runs headlong into his death; I would much rather sit here and wait for it in the uncertain knowledge that it may come, giving me opportunity to defend against it, than rush out and meet it early."

"Splendid. How is Mister Cabot recovering?"

Bishop's pointed silence was enough to make Robinson uncomfortable and he left the room in search of something more interesting and less dangerous to do.

♦

"It doesn't look good; there are around four thousand humans working for Lucy, and well over two hundred of her kind. When they come here I'm not sure we'll be able to hold them back."

"The time of this Hall is coming to an end, Terry; I don't think we can legitimately say it is powerful any more," Greenwood replied. "We may actually lose this one."

"I have no choice but to agree with the Senator." Cooke entered the room that was ostensibly McInnes' office and dropped the stone on the desk. "I don't know how to use it, and Eleanor can't find the knowledge in my mind."

"So the stones are useless?"

"Yes; we are doomed. The waves shall wash against us and we will be swept aside; everything we have fought for is lost."

The three men stood in silence.

♦

McBride's sword whirled through the air, cutting intricate patterns in the hardlight-enriched particles he had surrounded himself with. He focused his mind, fighting the voice that plagued him, struggling to fight the black figure that seemed to flicker on the edge of reality.

Turn.

I will not be turned.

Turn.

I am an Engineer.

The Engineers are dying.

I follow the path.

Whose path?

I guard the way of the Protectorate.

There is no Protectorate. Stanford is dead; his alliance had failed.

My heart is pure, and my blade is quick.

The pure of heart struggle not with darkness.

I serve my master and the Hall serves me; I am under its protection.

How much good will your protection do you when the Hall is as rubble and demons rule this land?

We are White, the truth is our way.

Your way has failed! What are you living for? What do you have to live for?

...

Turn.

"Annie, I live for her."

Then you will die for her.

"Killian!"

McBride turned, swinging the sword as hard as he could in his confusion. It was stopped between Kingston's hands. "You should watch yourself with that thing."

"You caught it, didn't you?"

"That's not what I was talking about."

McBride tilted his head quizzically, but already knew it was useless. The girl just stared straight through him; she could see the darkness flaring in his eyes.

"Don't let them get to you."

"I won't."

"See that you don't; stopping Cooke when he lost control was hard enough, and he didn't even know he had these abilities."

"Exactly; how would you stop me?"

"I would stab you through the chest, Mister McBride; not even Touched Ones can survive that. I came to tell you, James has recovered the last stone, but doesn't know what to do with it. He has gone to consult with the Master."

"The Master? He is the master, surely."

"You think he was born trained with the sword?"

"I guess…"

Kingston laughed.

"The mausoleum."

◆

Twelve creatures stood before Lucy in the old council chamber, awaiting her instructions. They were, unlike all of the others under her services, most definitely creatures; their natural form was fixed. They couldn't transmute, which was unusual amongst all but the weakest demons; they couldn't possess humans, defy the laws of physics, summon energy balls, or teleport. Indeed they weren't, strictly speaking, demons; they were creatures of mud, like humans, rather than fire or light. However, they had their uses.

The creatures were gaunt, but stood no less than six feet tall. They were bipedal, and had great powerful wings on which they could fly, but which they currently wrapped about themselves like thick black, leathery cloaks. Their heads were human, at least vaguely, with ears on either side and long flowing white hair coming out the back, two eyes exactly where you'd expect eyes to be, and a mouth, exactly where you'd expect a mouth to be, but also exactly where you'd expect a nose to be, and cheeks, and a chin; their long jaws stretched back past their small ears to let them fully open and shut a mouth that dominated over half of their faces.

The exact nature of the howlers was uncertain to Lucy, as it had been to most jinn and all but a handful of the angels, but she seen their work once before, in Venice during the Renaissance, and had liked what she had seen. They were utterly ruthless when it came to dispatching vast swathes of the human population, their hatred of which seemed greater than even that of the wyrmkind. Better yet they only had one request for payment; that they would be given the powers of Touched Ones if they succeeded in their task.

"This is your last task for me before you receive payment," she said to them in the hissing, clicking and snarling language she had once addressed Ellie with. "You will go to the Hall and ensure that everybody inside is dead. You will then return here with the bodies of the masters and receive your payment."

♦

The young Master knelt before the tomb of Danielle Entlis, his robe turning to white as he wept silently. His cause was lost, and he knew it. There were footsteps behind him.

"We've lost, Mister McBride."

"There's still a chance."

"Not one worth mentioning. We will be destroyed utterly by the onslaught; our powers cannot kill Lucy and we don't know enough about her to create a more human solution."

"So what are you going to do? Give up?"

"What else is there to do?"

"Fight!"

"Naïve; we will all die either way."

"Coward."

Cooke span to his feet and extended a hand. The force hit McBride as though he had been struck hard, and he was pinned to the wall of the mausoleum, his life being choked from him.

"How dare you, apprentice. I have given my life twice for this cause, without me you would be long since dead."

"That's not much use if I'm still going to die anyway, is it?"

"Insolence!"

"What does it matter? Unless you get off your robed ass and do something I'm just as dead as if you kill me now; maybe if you kill me you'll realise what a jackass you're being."

"There is nothing in my mind! We have searched it. The stones do not have any power in their current form."

"Then find something else! Or let us try to find something else, but we can't do either if you're not going to try and help. You're the most powerful one here, you've been fighting these things for longer than I have; you know more than me!"

He felt the pressure ease off.

"James." Ellie was in the doorway.

"Eleanor; what is it?"

"There are howlers on the wing; dozens of them. They're coming here. We need to get back to the Hall."

"Right."

They broke into a run, McBride struggling to keep pace, rubbing his neck.

"Howlers? What the hell are howlers?"

"Big flying bastards," Ellie said. "I had a run-in with one in the Andes a few years ago; it killed eight people before I took it down."

"It's a demon?"

"No, it just comes from the same place. A little bit of evolution gone astray with a little help from the Morningstar."

"Okay; let's start from the beginning. The Morningstar is..."

"The Fallen Seraphim. The great betrayer of my kind; the origin of your mortal sin, the Snake in the Garden. The jackal circling to swoop on the moral carrion of humanity."

"Lucifer," Cooke simplified.

"Right, and he created these howler things, why?"

"They have the ability to change a small section of the Plan; they can force a creature's time into the here and now,"

"They what?"

"Everyone has a time to die. They change it so that your time is now," she clarified.

"Right. How do they do that?"

"I haven't a clue, I'm afraid."

"How do we kill them?"

"They're effectively mortal, just really tough, so we just shoot them a lot."

"Now there's a plan I can get behind."

They entered the Hall and Cooke snatched up a speaker for the intercom.

"All hands, this is Master Cooke. An enemy force is on its way; grab what weapons you can. Engineers, meet me in the attic."

♦

The long-term residents of Cooke Hall, along with Verity Robbins, were gathered in the large attic that served as a dumping ground for everything that had been shifted to allow the WTDD to run their operations out of the rooms below.

"Okay, there are enemies on the way, things called howlers—"

"Howlers?" Cabot asked. "Never heard of them."

"Sure you have," Verity interrupted before Cooke could answer. "Banshees; they have evolved into a myth, a legend. Like demons."

"Well said." Cooke paused. "They are coming here, they will land on the roof and scream; when they do so the Plan will be changed to bring the death of someone in the house —the nearest individual—into the next ten minutes. However, it will have to be a violent death, so there will be troops coming to take us."

"We'll be ready."

"I know." Cooke smiled. "Liam, Verity, McBride; go down and help the others with the defence, we'll take the guys on the roof."

9

The first three howlers landed on the roof of the east wing with a series of quiet thumps. They crouched, preparing to scream.

From behind a chimney stack McInnes leapt, kicking the creature in its oversized mouth. It squealed at him as it got up, swinging one leathery claw which he ducked easily. He drew two pistols, already firing as he brought them to bear. The creature came quickly to ground, both wings shielding it from the accelerated metal better than a bulletproof vest. The clips ran dry and the banshee unfurled its wings, standing up with both claws raised, ready to strike.

It opened its mouth to scream but emitted only a foul guttural gurgling from the sword McInnes had quickly thrust through its neck.

On the west wing Cooke appeared in front of two banshees, who recoiled quickly. He reached out, snapped one of their necks and the other backed away, clicking, part angrily and part fearfully, but he couldn't understand.

"Whatever." An energy ball silenced it before he vanished once more, appearing near Bishop as she finished off her target with some quick staff work to the fragile neck area.

"Is it just me, or do very few of them seem to be landing?" Bishop asked.

Cooke pointed across the roof, and Bishop followed the line of his outstretched finger. Ellie, white robe glowing more noticeably in the dark of night, stood with her sword pointed into the sky, the remaining banshees flying around her, diving in to try and attack her before recoiling as she swung at them.

Three partially-dismembered creatures lay around her, and the remaining half-dozen were focusing all their efforts on her.

"Why aren't they attacking?" Bishop asked.

"They hate everything about what she is, as opposed to just feeling snubbed by us; they want to knock her down, land, then scream so she can be killed."

"They can do that?"

"I'd guess so; they change the Plan, and angels have to follow the Plan." He vanished and appeared alongside Ellie, knocking two of her attackers from the sky with a quick succession of energy balls, and grabbing one by the leg, hauling it down and wrestling with it.

"You can put the staff down, Liam." McBride scanned the people coming towards the Hall. "They're human."

"Thank God, an enemy I can kill." Cabot racked the slide on the shotgun he had slung over his back and examined the breech. "Let's get ready to give them a good old-fashioned Cooke Hall welcome."

Short sat waiting with an army officer for the attack when the doors to the drawing room burst open, admitting a gust of cold wind and a squad of guardsmen. Quickly the apprentice leapt to his feet, snatched a bottle of bourbon from the open spirit cabinet and threw it headlong at the invaders.

The sergeant laughed as he caught the bottle en route and began to unscrew the top with the thumb and forefinger of his left hand, the right keeping a pistol trained on the apprentice.

"Settle down, please. And you can keep your hands where I can see them."

Short's hands had been moving to his back, and he had just got a grip on his staple pistol when the man spoke. He brought his hands into clear view, placing his first shot through the bottle, igniting the alcohol within and setting the sergeant alight.

"Run; I'll handle them," Short said to the man who had been waiting with him, pulling another gun from under the table and firing a few more shots into the guardsmen as they recovered. He dived through the door after the young officer, smashing the alarm button nearby as he did so.

Cooke held the howler's mouth open with one hand and quickly stuck the other between the three rows of razor-sharp teeth. He wriggled his arm about inside the creature's mouth, visibly struggling, before retracting violently and releasing its jaw.

"Let it go," he instructed.

"Are you mad? It'll scream! You should kill it!" Mendelson objected, before she saw the long tongue in his hand.

"Let it go. Eleanor, tell it I'm letting it go as an example to its kind; if any of their number come here again then their entire species will be wiped from existence."

Ellie opened her mouth, and instead of the soft, heavenly voice they were used to, she spoke in a series of harsh clicks; the language the creatures themselves had been using. The banshee turned and flew away, but not in the direction of the NCC.

Cabot, sword in his left hand, shotgun in the right, worked through the Hall ahead of his squad, slicing at one enemy as a shell blew a hole in the chest of another. Cabot had never experienced anything that might be called bloodlust, and had never been a particularly enthusiastic killer, preferring to detain or capture an enemy, but he knew from years of experience that there were all too often situations in which mercy wasn't appropriate. In those situations, he was a cold, calculating killer, the voice in his head telling him to be good entirely ignored.

All at once there were no more enemies for him to kill. He relaxed, sliding the bloody katana back into its black sheath. One man rose from behind a damaged sofa and Cabot brought the shotgun quickly to bear, shooting the guardsman.

"And stay down," Cabot instructed glibly.

The man stood back up, an energy ball now in his hands.

"Shit."

McBride, standing silently behind Cabot, threw an energy ball to kill the demon. He patted the terrified Colonel on the shoulder.

"Remember; death first, gloating later," he said, reminding Cabot of one of Bishop's teaching doctrines. "You need to reload."

♦

"We won," Carter announced.

The Engineers were sat in the pool-house, one of a very few rooms not permanently occupied by members of the resistance.

"That's a relative term; nobody died on our side, and we killed thirty opponents, but there will be more. Lucy'll have finished playing games now; it's time for a siege," Cooke corrected him.

"I agree; it's long overdue," McInnes said. "Are we any closer to a working anti-demon defence system?"

"I confess that we're not; there still seems to be some fairly large gaps in my knowledge."

"That seems to be happening rather more often than is comforting. You didn't even think to associate the howlers with banshees," Sam said mockingly.

"I caught you didn't I?" he countered.

"You said you were sent to kill Lord Stanford?" Bishop asked Sam, trying to change the subject.

"Yeah, but I couldn't; before I could take his soul, my ability to hold the form of the girl I possessed failed. Then my energy ball failed to kill him," Sam answered with a hint of embarrassment.

"Why is that do you think?"

"Hold on a second," Cooke said quietly.

"I don't know; I should have easily been strong enough. I'd taken three souls that evening."

"Hold on," Cooke repeated, louder this time.

"What is it, James?"

"What did you say, Sam?"

"I said I'd taken three souls that evening."

"No, before that, about the howlers."

"I said that you'd had more gaps in your memory than just about the stones; you didn't associate the howlers with the banshees. Look, I didn't mean—"

"Eleanor; did you associate the howlers with banshees in human mythology?"

"I can't say that I did, no; though it does seem obvious."

"Who made the association?"

"Verity," McInnes said quietly, "but she wouldn't have known the exact nature of the howlers; would she?"

"Not ordinarily." Cooke got to his feet. "Keep thinking about why Rob might have been protected from Sam's abilities; I think we're onto something there. I'll be back in a minute."

♦

"Hello Mister James; why the serious face?"

Cooke had found Verity in her room, sat in an armchair reading Gormenghast.

"Verity, how did you know what the howlers were?"

"I must have read it somewhere—"

"Where, Verity? Where did you read it?"

"I can't remember." She seemed nervous, as if she was guilty.

"Verity; this is important. Where did you read it? I won't be upset."

"Alright; in the library. I got so bored of the normal books, so I went into the secret section and read one of the books in there."

"The secret section?"

"Yes, James; the section at the back of the library behind the Charles Dickens."

"Show me."

She led him quietly to the library and to the back, where she pushed a book on the bottom shelf in. The bookshelf slid backward and to the side, revealing a wall of black metal with nine raised pads on it, each bearing a glyph Cooke had never seen before. He reached out, dreamlike, as he stared at the panels, and pushed six of them in seemingly at random.

The wall swung aside, leading the way into a dark cavern that lit up as they entered. At the end of the cavern was a single pentagonal room filled with bookshelves. There was a raised dais in the centre, between the crossovers of lines going from each corner to the others.

"A pentagram," Cooke muttered, noticing the pattern on the marble floor. The walls were lined with books quite different to those in the main library; books of the occult, religious texts from hundreds of faiths, and a series of A3 notebooks in three colours—pink, black and grey—each organised neatly.

"Which book was the information about howlers in?"

"This one." She reached up and took down one of the weathered grey notebooks. He took it from her and opened it, flicking through the pages.

The pages were crammed with complex diagrams, each carefully annotated in glyphs similar to those which adorned the door to this room.

"Can you read this?"

"Yes. It's all quite clear if you read the introduction."

Cooke flicked to the first page, and found it covered in immaculate script that he had seen before, on the design for the staple sniper rifle, which he was vaguely aware was probably in one of these notebooks.

"I wrote this?"

"Yes, James; you wrote this."

"The introduction's all in Latin; do you read Latin?"

"I had to learn to read the introduction," she replied as if this was the most obvious thing in the world.

"I can't remember writing this; I can't even read the glyphs."

"But you opened the door."

"Yes, and so did you."

He turned the pages, and slowly, somehow, the meaning of the glyphs began to become clearer to him, until he understood what each of them meant. About half way through the book was a picture of a banshee and a description, in glyphs, of what they were. He noted the picture vaguely and was about to turn over again, then caught what was on the adjoining page.

Drawn on the paper were three ovular areas of shading, and the outline of some kind of altar, with no glyphs explaining what it was. Slowly, he turned the book around; and recognised the image. He walked to the dais he had noticed when he entered the room and ran his hands over the cold silver surface. A crystal dome covered the top of the dais, and was surrounded by ten pads, each marked with a different glyph.

Further down the dais, at one hundred and twenty degree intervals, were three circular wells, into which it appeared some round object could be placed.

"Do you know what this is?" he asked Verity.

"I thought it was some sort of machine; energy seems to be designed to emanate upwards from the crystal. We're underground, though, so I can't really see it doing any good down here."

"I had that thought myself."

"I'm sure you wouldn't have built it down here if you didn't have a reason."

"Well, let's hope, but I was somewhat crazy."

"No, just misunderstood; that's what Terry always said."

"That was very charitable of him, I'm sure."

♦

"How much can we throw at them?"

"Fifty hisa-me, twenty wyrmkind, the half-dozen howlers who didn't desert us, about a hundred jinn, and seven thousand humans in the Guard."

"It doesn't seem enough."

"Ma'am, with all due respect, there are at most three hundred inside the Hall, including one angel and one jinn; hardly an advantage."

"But the angel and the jinn will tear through the Guard."

"And you will finish them; you have the sword, Mistress."

"Eleanor also has a sword; I am not comfortable with the odds as they stand."

"What would you counsel we do then, Mistress?"

"Use the cannon design Rebecca sucked from the mind of the scientist, and instruct the jinn to convert a few hundred members of the Guard. Only slightly though; we don't want them going crazy."

"What purpose would that serve?"

"They'll blind the sight of the Hall; they will not be able to tell the difference between the actual jinn, and those that were just guardsmen."

"I can't say I'm comfortable using technology, either."

"I know it's untraditional—"

"It's not the fact that it's untraditional, it's the fact that we're becoming dependent on a human mind to fight humans."

"We are lying, cheating and stealing in order to gain victory over a lesser race. It's perfectly within our mandate as creatures of evil."

◆

"Open the forge; get blades made and keep making more of the staves. Everybody not being used in weapons production is to be training," Cooke demanded as he burst into the great hall, where most of the residents were eating their evening meal.

"James?"

"The Hall is defensible; we just need to be ready to fight them before they get here."

"McBride, Carter; take the Engineers to the forge. Siobhan; get the apprentices training with swords immediately," McInnes snapped and the Engineers went quickly to work. "What've you got in mind?" he whispered to Cooke.

"I'm not sure yet, but I'm almost certain it'll work." Cooke slipped the notebook to McInnes. "Read through the sections I've translated, do what you can with it; I know what to do on my end, just make sure the others are confident and ready."

"Can do. Good luck, James."

Cooke vanished.

"Right!" McInnes declared, turning to the room at large, where most of the rebels had looked up from their meals. "Everyone, I want you to finish your meals then get down to the firing range; we're all going to learn to use the staves before they get here. You'll have an hour doing that, then I want all the senators to go to the green room."

"Why?" James Robinson was on his feet.

"You'll find out when you get there, Senator; I still need to think about it myself."

10

There was a tenseness in the Hall as everyone scurried about, working on their tasks; they knew that the enemy was coming, and very few people felt ready, even though McInnes did his best to look confident and assured. There were currently enough staves for one between two and it was taking three fully-fledged Engineers an hour to produce each new one; it would take two days of non-stop work to make enough for the entire Hall.

In the metalwork forge, McBride and Carter were taking the short-cuts allowed them by their powers to construct swords quickly, whilst two steel cooling baths held the swords they had been making for themselves.

"We're never going to get enough done."

"Have some patience."

They turned and saw the young Verity Robbins behind them.

"Take a break; there's something you need to see in the dojo."

Neither man moved. They were slightly disquieted by the presence of the young girl in their midst; several years their junior and yet with a mastery and understanding of her powers that neither of them could match.

"I can handle your workload while you're gone," she added, and reluctantly they began to leave.

"What was that about, do you think?" Carter asked when they had moved out of earshot.

"I'm not sure, but did you want to argue?" McBride answered. "That girl scares me."

"More creepy than scary, I think, but I see your point; she's had these abilities longer than us, yet doesn't seem so affected by them."

"You think there are people naturally like that?"

"Perhaps not, maybe she's just got more used to it than us. She has had these abilities since she was very young, after all," Carter clarified.

"Either way; she's a little odd."

"You got that right."

They reached the balcony over the dojo and looked down; Doctor Mortimer was exchanging blows with Doctor Lyons, and around Doctor Bishop stood a crowd of apprentices and former soldiers with bokkens and staves.

"Ultimately, in order to be victorious in combat," Bishop said to the crowd, "you must be in tune with your surroundings; balanced, aware of both your enemies and of yourself. Nothing less than total harmony with the world is acceptable. Unfortunately, time is too short for you all to be trained properly in Eastern fighting principles, so I'll just set you fighting each other; apprentices versus regular army. Go to work."

The crowd began to disperse, but instead of beginning their training fell silent, turning to look at something at the far end of the hall. Suddenly they parted, creating a distinct corridor down the centre of the room, through which walked Colonel Cabot, dark green leather coat flowing behind him and maroon-sheathed katana in his left hand, held just below the guard.

No words were exchanged as Cabot and Bishop leapt at each other, the former lovers drawing their katanas and engaging. McBride watched, barely able to keep up as the master swordsmen fought, neither yielding any ground or tiring as they fought through now-practicing apprentices, parrying both each other's blades and the weapons of those they interrupted, lab coat and trenchcoat mingling in the air.

Cabot backed off and Bishop leapt, swinging for his legs. He jumped back, placing both feet on the wall and kicking off, gliding sword-first towards her. She side-stepped and he landed, rolled and flipped up, spinning his body to face her and his sword to meet hers.

"Now can you see?" Eleanor asked.

McBride and Carter turned quickly, shocked at having been caught unawares and saw the angel behind them.

"That is the true power of the Touched Ones, the true power of your kind; the speed, grace and balance even of Liam is the product of the human part of your blight. The other skills are the product of the inhuman."

"What do you mean?"

"Energy balls are nothing without control of them. If we cannot control the other mind within our own then it doesn't matter how good we are at using these gifts," McBride said, speaking softly, realising the lessons in both Ellie's words, and in the entire teachings of Bishop and Cooke since they had been touched.

"Why are you telling us this now?" Carter asked.

"You have both taken lovers within this hall, mortals who stand a high chance of dying when the winds that are coming buffet our home. Because of this, there will come a time when you have to choose between your heart and your soul. A time when the darkness that threatens this land comes to the Hall; at that point, your choice will either save us or ruin us. That is all I have to say; you may go back to the forge now, finish your blades, and be ready." Ellie swept away from them silently, her feet not touching the ground.

"Where is Master Cooke?" Carter asked. "I think we need his advice."

McBride closed his eyes for a second and then looked all around him.

"What is it?"

"He is no longer here; he left the Hall some time ago. We should get back to the forge."

"Where has he gone?"

"I cannot tell, but he will be back."

"How can you be sure? You said he was talking about giving up; maybe he went to Lucy."

"No. He will come back, and we must be prepared for him to do so; we should go to the forge."

♦

"Master McInnes, have you managed to work out what it is that you want from us yet?"

The Master of the Engineers was sat on the arm of a leather sofa when the senators entered.

"Yes." McInnes snapped shut the grey notebook he had been perusing and looked up at them. "Take a seat, please."

"I'd rather stand—" Robinson began.

"I said take a seat, please."

Robinson sat.

"Thank you. I expect this Hall will come under attack within the next twenty-four hours from Lucy's forces, and at the moment the defenders have nobody to look to as a leader."

"And let me guess, you want us to support you? Or

possibly Cooke?"

"No; the role of the Engineers has never been to lead. As senators, you were leaders of the people before this all started, and so you would be the logical choice to lead, both during the battle and potentially after, but during the fight everyone needs to know who they're looking to for orders; there can be no second guessing."

"And?"

"And you have two hours to decide which of you is in charge; have a nice day." McInnes got up and walked out of the room, pushing the door closed behind him.

♦

Bishop and Cabot didn't slow; to do so would show weakness to the others, though their faces were red and they could feel themselves getting tired. The others in the hall watched, stupefied, as they leapt from object to object, throwing what they could lay their hands on and kicking tables at each other.

Cabot leapt, spinning and loosing three throwing knives in quick succession at Bishop. She dodged one and her rapidly-darting sword deflected the others. He struck out at her, a succession of four quick attacks and a lunge pushing her back. She came forward again, batting his sword aside with a strength concealed by her slender frame.

McInnes and Cooke had trained them both. The first apprentice Engineers taken after the formation of the Society, with everyone else with any skill in designing weapons perished in the wars and the role of the Engineers changing rapidly, Cooke had decided to take in all those afflicted with the same disorder as himself, finding these two Touched Ones and training them to control the voices in their mind.

From the perspective of the apprentices watching them fight, their abilities were matched exactly, as neither struck the other or gained the upper hand in any visible way, but standing on the sidelines, Sam could see that Bishop was the superior fighter. Her stance and technique had a more practiced, honed edge, and she was occasionally tilting her blade away milliseconds before it hit Cabot, artificially prolonging the fight.

The young succubus turned away and stalked through the building, unnoticed. She came to an unoccupied drawing room, where she collapsed into an armchair. She licked her lips with her unnaturally long tongue, savouring the sweet flavour around the edge a moment before retracting it.

The taste did nothing, she knew, as her eyes grew heavier, and her entire body seemed to be itching. Her time was running out; she needed a soul, an innocent soul, and she needed it soon.

♦

"Darkness see me, hear my call," a single figure in black said calmly in a rasping voice, her features hidden by the cowl. The woman was short, barely more than five feet tall.

A shape gathered before her in the pentagram she had drawn on the floor.

"I bid thee rise, come before me."

The grey smoke turned to black, and dark particles moved away from the robe into the seal, the cloth turning to white as the form, its summoner's antithesis, appeared within the pentagram.

"Child."

The form of Verity Robbins, face scarred and eyes darkened, stared back through the barrier. Verity pushed her now-white hood back and gave the darkness a calculating, emotionless look.

"Where has he gone?" she demanded.

"Beyond the places I can see."

"But you still know where he is; you wander your realm unchecked. You know where he is, tell me."

"I will tell you nothing."

"Terry, who is in the clock tower?"

"I haven't sent anyone there, why?"

"There is immense power coming from there."

"Lucy?"

"Not enough for that, but a lot, nonetheless."

The girl is innocent; take her, she cannot resist you.

"Yes, the girl." Sam leapt up the staircase leading to the clock tower.

The windows of the tower exploded as Verity struggled to fight the energy of her counterpart, the room suddenly turning cold as the air rushed in. Verity closed her eyes as her counterpart created the illusion of fire rushing alongside her and raised one hand, beginning to chant an incantation to counter her enemy's power behind the seal, the force of the exchange burning the air around the seal and blackening the normally transparent barrier of energy between them.

The door burst open and Sam entered, almost knocked off balance by the current of power inside. She extended a hand towards the girl in the centre of the cloud of swirling hardlight, intending to make her fall asleep, but the girl turned quickly towards her, one hand still directed at the figure unseen behind the blackened wall of the seal, and waved her free hand dismissively.

Sam tried to move towards her, but found her joints unresponsive; she was unable to move, or even summon an energy ball. She was absolutely helpless.

Ellie appeared in the centre of the room and shouted something to Verity. The girl nodded in response and the seal vanished, along with whatever it had contained.

"That was most unwise," Ellie told Verity. "Where the hell did you learn to do that?"

"It was in James' book; I was trying to locate him."

"By summoning your own darkness? She knows all your weaknesses; nobody has ever fought their darkness in either metaphor or manifest and won. Why would you take the risk of losing yourself to it?"

"I had it under control."

Eleanor looked at the young girl and something about the young girl made the angel believe her.

"Don't do anything like that again without talking to me first; it's extremely dangerous. Now, what were you doing here?" Ellie turned to Sam, who widened her eyes in terror; it was about all she could do. "Answer me, Sam." Ellie created an energy ball in the air in front of her.

"She can't."

"Why not?"

"I suspended the hardlight energy around her; she cannot move."

"You suspended it? That's impossible—"

"It's easy enough; James can do it with objects to stop them in the air."

"Yes, that's an angelic Touched One ability, so you could have that, but there's no way you could have enough power to stop a demon in its tracks."

"She was a mortal, and now she's a succubus; she's only got maybe a day of energy left before she reverts."

"Even so..."

Verity opened her mouth and spoke again, in a language Sam could not understand; a soft and fluidic language that seemed to have no individual words, but was rather a stream of sound. Ellie listened to what had become her native tongue and nodded, pensively, the girl's use of this language clarifying some details in her mind.

"Where did you learn to do that?" she asked, leaving no indication as to what was said.

"I picked it up, you know, here and there."

"James' book?"

"There was a section written in different glyphs."

"Do you know what the glyphs are?"

"Most of them are deminine glyphs, taken from the darkness in his head, the others were not; I didn't recognise them; now I can."

"They were written in the language they explained, I would imagine, but how he came to know them I haven't a clue."

"Fascinating." Verity waved a hand and Sam began to move.

"How did you do that?" Sam asked Verity.

"Long story," Ellie replied. "You need energy, otherwise you will die."

"That's one way of looking at it."

Ellie loosed an energy ball at her, but instead of bringing a swift death, it melded with her, and she felt a sensation of warm rejuvenation come over her.

"Why didn't you do that before?"

"I wasn't sure I could trust you. I'm still not, but we'll need all the help we can get to win this. Just remember, I can take it back at any time, and if I die, so do you."

"The Lord giveth, and the Lord taketh away?"

"I wouldn't know about Him, but I certainly do."

♦

"He isn't here, Killian."

"He will be, Daniel." McBride bought the hammer down on the steel of his sword again. "Have faith; if anything, our experiences here should have taught us that."

♦

Cabot and Bishop finally stopped fighting as the evening turned to night, and the great hall was filled again with food. Most of the defenders ate solemnly, with the potential leaders eating separately from the others, still in the green room arguing about who they would choose.

McInnes watched quietly the mood in the Hall. Everyone seemed cautiously optimistic, which was always good, he thought; but they still had no word from of Lucy's arrival from the sentries, and James was still gone.

Where are they? he thought.

"They will come soon enough; you must rest, I'll keep watch tonight, you need to sleep." Ellie spoke as if reading his thoughts; he wondered if she could.

"I need to be awake in case they attack in the night."

"Do you think that's going to happen?"

"No."

Ellie smiled. "Then sleep."

"And what of the leaders? They still haven't decided."

"I think Mister McBride is handling that."

♦

Shards of door flew into the green room as McBride entered, blowing the door into small enough sections to negate the effectiveness of the lock.

"Some people knock," Greenwood reminded him politely.

"Our enemy could strike at any time and Master McInnes has told you to decide amongst yourselves a leader; why have you not done that?"

"It's not as easy as your Master McInnes seems to believe," Thatcher spoke up, her normally tidy hair slightly dishevelled and her face a picture of stress.

"How about this: if you haven't come up with a solution in three hours, I will walk in here and kill you one by one until all but one of you are dead, then that one will be the leader."

"That's hardly fair—"

An energy ball disintegrated a lamp and McBride stormed out of the room.

♦

Cooke finished his work and wrapped up his project in canvas. He looked out across the black and endless night towards where he knew in his head the Hall must be, and vanished.

Where he reappeared was not his study in the Hall, as he had expected it to be, but rather a small plateau atop a mountain, rain and lightning crackling around him.

"Do you know where you are?" The twisted voice he knew only too well spoke out of the darkness, its black form stepping into view.

"I'm guessing somewhere in the Middle East."

"Well done."

"There is much power here. You drew me to it by altering my transit path; impressive."

"I want the trinket."

Cooke glanced over his shoulder, casually noting that the case was still there.

"This?" He unslung it and the figure nodded. "Then fetch." He tossed the case out, away from the mountain, where it hung in mid air, a few hundred feet away.

They each threw off their robes, both men now dressed in loose-fitting trousers and shirts, only the colours of which differentiating between the real Cooke and his negative.

The black-clad Cooke moved faster, a fist striking his counterpart to the ground, but Cooke recovered quickly, legs spinning to force the other back as he got to his feet. He followed through, throwing a punch, but his fist was caught and he was sent hurling over the edge, willing himself to arc back towards the mountain, and slamming back into the demon, sending him to the floor.

Cooke bent over his counterpart, grabbing him by the neck. "You have haunted me for long enough, old man."

"You haven't seen the last of me. When you die, I will be waiting for you in Hell."

"No. You won't." Cooke leapt back off of the demon, who quickly got to his feet, loosing an energy ball at Cooke.

Cooke dodged the attack and extended a hand towards the case still floating a short distance from the mountain. The bag flew towards him and he caught it as it passed, sliding the blade of a sword from one end and swinging it, slicing the demon in half.

He watched as the enemy he had struggled with all his life collapsed, shedding particles as his body disintegrated. Cooke re-sheathed the sword, and vanished.

♦

McInnes woke at five o'clock in the morning and walked downstairs, still in his lab coat.

"Is there any coffee about?" he asked Bishop as he entered the kitchen where she and Cabot were playing cards.

"Just made a fresh pot."

"Excellent." He poured himself a coffee and drank a large sip of the thick black liquid.

"The senators came down a few hours ago; they've chosen Robinson," Bishop told him.

"Yes, I expected they would." McInnes sighed. "Anything else?"

"McBride and Carter have finished their swords and have been practicing for an hour; most of the Hall is awake but trying to relax, take their minds off of things—"

"And Master Cooke is back."

McInnes turned and smiled at Cooke as he entered the room, wearing his old lab coat coat, the canvas bag still on his back.

"James; I trust your little excursion was productive?"

"Most productive. There isn't much time before Lucy gets here, I expect the sentries will report in soon to tell us she's coming. Siobhan, Liam, I am proud to have had you as apprentices, go to your swords and get ready for the coming battle."

The two apprentices left quickly.

"Terry, do you know who you are yet?"

"I am Terry McInnes, Master of the Engineers and guardian of the Society." McInnes gave the textbook answer, not understanding the question.

"No, Terry, these are the clothes you wear, the role you perform here; but you are more than that."

"James—"

"Who told me where to find the stone?"

"I did, but—"

"How could you possibly know where it was, Terry? It was not hidden by anyone you have ever met; there was no way you could know. You fight demons and they can't hit you, a feat I cannot even manage. What is in the case on my back?"

"An angelic sword," McInnes answered without thinking, before he could stop himself.

"Terry, nobody in this house is what they appear, you least of all; you appear as a mortal amongst Touched Ones, but you aren't; Mel, Rose, they are gifted to protect you, that is their role, and you, as the hisa-me said when they first came here, are the Sighted One."

"The what?"

"Prophet, Terry; you can see the future."

"That's—"

"The truth; I've never lied to you about anything, why should I start now?"

"There's no good reason, but it's impossible."

"As impossible as angels and demons?"

McInnes looked pensive for a moment while he considered this.

"Yes; exactly that impossible." McInnes placed one hand on the phone and a second later it began to ring. "McInnes. Yes, I know; they're coming." He put the phone down as quickly as he had picked it up. "Lucy is two miles from the outer defences; they have war machines, and a large army. The sentry guards are returning to the Hall."

Cooke nodded, taking it all in. "Rouse the others, we will be ready."

♦

McBride and Carter met in the corridor outside their rooms—located opposite each other—white lab-coats on and swords over their back; a black katana for McBride and a white Tai Chi sword for Carter.

"Let's go to work."

The two men made their way to the great hall where the Engineers were assembling; apprentices, doctors and masters, all standing side by side, and all facing Cooke.

11

"My friends," Cooke began, "a little while ago I stood before you all as we were about to flee this Hall when the demons came. Now I am here to tell you the demons are coming again, but that this time we will not run. This time we will show immortal creatures of any and all kinds exactly what kind of threat mortals like us represent to them. We will form a critical part of the fighting force; your superior training and knowledge of the Hall will be indispensable at defending against this attack. Each of you will be assigned to one area of the Hall; stay there when the time comes unless the position becomes untenable or you are instructed to leave. We must fight to the last man if we are to stand a chance; now, General Robinson is addressing the others in the Dining Hall."

The Engineers filed into the dining hall just as Robinson's speech was winding up and the troops were being assigned rooms, and waited patiently until their names were called with room designations.

"Killian McBride; main foyer."

McBride nodded; he had been hoping for such an assignment.

"Daniel Carter; dojo,"

The apprentices exchanged a look of regret that they would not be posted together, but neither had really expected to be.

The names continued to be read out, until they reached the last name.

"Terry McInnes; great hall."

The group began to disperse, and McInnes put one hand on McBride's shoulder. The apprentice stopped and looked back.

"Yes, Master?"

McInnes was close to McBride now, so nobody else could hear what he had to say as he looked the younger man straight in the eye. They parted once he had spoken.

"What did he say?" Carter, on route to the dojo, asked.

"He said 'choose wisely'." McBride shrugged and went on his way.

♦

"Master McInnes."

"Master Cooke."

The two men smiled at each other.

"Confident?"

"Quietly; you?"

"I am... uncertain; the way forward seems a little less than clear."

"That's a good thing, I guess; two days ago I couldn't see at all a way we could win."

"What's changed?"

"We will see."

♦

"Master!" Lyons ran into the great hall as Cooke oversaw the drawing of a pentagram on the floor.

"Yes, Sofia?"

"There are war machines among their army; hardlight cannon, and H-Type walkers."

"Anna's devices." Cooke thought for a second. "They must have seized the knowledge from Richard; only he knew of their existence."

"That is correct," McInnes acknowledged. "They will take some time to compromise our defenses though; return to your post, Doctor."

"Yes, Master." Lyons bowed and ran out of the room.

"Are you sure of what you just said?"

"No; but it seems logical, and uncertainty will do us no good."

"True; how far are they?"

"They have stopped eight hundred metres from the Hall, just outside the gates."

"Excellent."

"It will take them about thirty seconds to destroy a large enough section of wall to advance through."

Cooke turned to the completed pentagram and muttered under his breath. There was a surge of hardlight energy and the floor glowed green before it dropped away, the large black marble dais taking its place. He waved a hand, lowering the seal, and stepped up to the device, quickly pressing a series of buttons on the surface.

♦

"Prepare to advance; get the birds in the air, target the cannon at the central wing, walkers to the east and troops to the west; see that they do not make it far." Lucy's forces were through the wall, and the cannon began to charge up, large grey crystals on the side slowly changing colour to the familiar green glow of hardlight technology. She turned to look at the Hall, her superior eyesight letting her see the building through the storm that blackened the sky and turned the ground around her to mud. "You may fire when ready," she instructed the demons around her. "Advance."

A great beam of hardlight energy burst from the top of the Hall, and began flowing down, forming a massive hemispherical energy barrier between Lucy's forces and the Hall, stopping a good five hundred metres in front of the demonic force standing in the pouring rain.

"Fire!" Lucy ordered, and the cannons burst into life, each of the six massive weapons firing a bright, crackling beam of hardlight at the shield, which swallowed the energy soundlessly.

"The scientist did not speak of this," a demon beside Lucy said.

"He did not know; this is Cooke's doing, but he cannot hold out forever."

Lucy turned to her forces. "Those that are able, take wing!" she bellowed. "Find a hole."

Along the roofs and windows of the Hall, the defenders breathed a sigh of relief as they saw that the shield was holding, but felt no real respite, knowing that their enemy would find a way through.

They watched in horror as winged shapes took to the sky in front of them, swooping and diving around the shield.

"The foul host is come; they will not go so easily," Cooke said sadly.

"Quite." McInnes grabbed his old wooden staff from the wall against which it leant. "I will go and make myself useful elsewhere; see you later."

"See that you do, old friend."

"The barrier is weakening," Lucy announced joyfully, staring at the shield protecting the Hall. "Soon it will fall, and with it the hope of their kind."

"Stand fast!" Ellie shouted above the noise in the entranceway. Two dozen guards with staves were behind her, more than in any other single room in the Hall. They knelt and pointed their staves at the door.

The shield flickered and faded, and one of the great winged creatures dived, down towards the ground. The staves fluttered into life, three-score bursts of hardlight in perfect unison tearing at the changing enemy, a few bolts striking the flying creature, but doing no damage. It fell through the doors to the entrance hall, slid along the floor for a few feet, then righted itself, rearing its massive, leathery wings.

The men began to move as the dragon roared, then fixed its large eyes on Ellie. She raised her sword and the bright light that had stunned Sokar tore from it. The demon reverted into human form and scowled at the angel, straightening its damaged tux slightly before taking a fighting stance.

"You will pay dearly for my life, angel."

Ellie smiled and raised a hand, palm towards the demon. Three tendrils of hardlight sprung from the centre of her hand, spiralling through each other as the powerful attack weaved quickly towards the creature, striking him in the chest before he could so much as scowl. His body was torn apart instantly, small fragments flying through the air for a few yards before they disintegrated.

As Lucy's forces rushed forward around her she bowed her head, aware of a sudden presence nearby, trying to gain access to her mind. She looked up and saw the angel that had destroyed her former self standing nearby, the army of demons moving conspicuously around her.

"A wyrmkind? Is that the best you can do?" Ellie called to her.

"There are plenty more!"

"So I see." Ellie looked around. "But they will meet the same fate; you will *all* meet the same fate, sword or no sword."

"We shall see."

Ellie vanished, and it was as though she had never been there; as, Lucy realized, she never had.

♦

Eleanor, the main entrance is breached. You must leave it; get the to the corridors of the east wing, they are too weakly defended. Cooke's voice reverberated around her head.

I can hold it a little longer, Ellie replied, looking out as the tide of enemies grew ever closer.

Go.

"Fall back!" Ellie shouted to the men in the entrance. They moved backwards, still firing their staves at the unstoppable horde.

"Mister McBride!" Ellie shouted at the Touched One on the balcony.

"Ellie, go; you are needed in the east wing. We're fine."

"Very well." Ellie turned to the men under her care. "You three; stay here, bolster the guard." The men nodded and she ran off.

A blast from one of the cannon blew apart the dojo wall directly in front of Carter, and the Touched One vanished from sight momentarily as he became gaseous to avoid the explosion. As he reformed the first guardsmen came through the hole.

"Fire!" he yelled to the defenders, swinging his own staff through one hand and shooting at the group.

The humans fell back under the weight of fire, bodies horribly burned, faces agony-struck and panicked as they fell, screaming.

One leapt from the ranks and over the twenty yards between Carter and himself, striking the young Engineer to the floor. Carter looked up at the man who was smashing his head against the floor, and saw in the man's eyes the same darkness that he had wrestled with these past months. He vanished and reappeared, behind the man. With a single motion, he plunged his long, straight Tai Chi sword through the man's back, releasing the man from his brief existence as a Touched One.

He turned as the charging guards struck his lines, swinging his sword violently into the skull of a woman. There were hundreds of them coming through to fight Carter's force of a dozen men, but he would hold them until he was dead.

◆

The barrier reappeared suddenly in the air between the two forces less than three minutes after it had failed, trapping hundreds of warriors without hope of reinforcement, doomed to death at the hands of the furious defenders. Lucy knew this. She didn't care. She turned to the last of the remaining wyrmkind outside of the Hall and issued them their orders, then unslung her sword from her back.

"Ma'am, cannon number three has stopped firing."

"What? Why?"

"I don't know, ma'am, nobody in the control vehicle is responding."

"Shit."

"Come get some…" McBride muttered, waiting until the enemy forces were fully inside the building before he began to hurl energy balls down at them from the balcony. Some tried to continue running into the building, but Doctor Mortimer's forces would deal with them, and the guards dealt with those that tried climbing the stairs.

The great hall was still devoid of activity as McInnes waited, leaning on his staff. He wanted to leave, but knew that the hardlight turrets in the corridor would almost certainly tear him to shreds.

They were coming through the walls. Doctor Lyons span, letting off a few shots from her staff as the demons continued to come from both directions, smashing through the bottle racks in the wine cellar. A demon reached out with long, clawed fingers and tore the face from one of her men, throwing what was left of him at the others, terrifying those the flying corpse didn't render unconscious.

The others ran up the ladder from the cellar and Lyons followed, taking the rungs two at a time and slamming home the door. She reached out and jabbed her fist into the emergency lock, causing a sheet of adamantium to slide over the wooden hatch built into the floor.

"This is Doctor Lyons," she said into the intercom as large fist dents began to appear in the panel, "I have three men down and demons in the wine cellar I cannot deal with; they are contained for now, but I need assistance urgently."

"Samantha, nice of you to join us." McBride looked at the succubus for a second, then returned to hurling energy balls into the hallway.

"Mister McBride; have you noticed anything strange down there?"

"Other than a demonic army attacking a centuries-old piece of architecture? No."

"There are reports of Touched Ones among the attacking force."

"I thought we were supposed to be a blight upon the face of the perfectly segregated universe?"

"Not as much, it appears, as James."

"Well, he is a blight, that's true."

Mister McBride.

McBride shut his eyes when he heard the voice.

Sam can hold the doors for now; get to Carter, his forces are going to be overwhelmed.

♦

Dan Carter's lab coat swirled around him, the reinforced material turning away the swords of his opponents as he struck out quickly, killing those who stood in his path.

He was the last man standing here, the others dead or fled. There were no targets in range of his sword, and he found that during the drawn-out sword fight he had been surrounded by figures in black trench coats; he recognized the same darkness in them all.

Carter opened his mouth to speak, hoping that he could form some dramatic and convincing speech before they killed him, and as he did so one of them was struck by an energy ball and vanished.

The others turned, swinging their swords at the incoming McBride, who leapt over the first wave and drew his katana. The broad arc he swung it in decapitated two of the new Touched Ones as Carter plunged forward, blade first.

"Uh, this is Doctor Lyons; we have a serious problem here at the cellars." The door dented again with another strike from below.

"This is Master Cooke; how long can you hold?"

"Not very long once they're through; two minutes tops."

"Very well." Cooke was consistently tapping buttons on the control system for the Hall's defenses, trying to stay one step ahead of the invader's shots and repeated attacks on the shield. "Mister McBride, Mister Carter?" He spoke out loud, and even though they were out of earshot they could hear his words directly in their minds.

Yes, master? McBride's voice came back.

"The shield on your wing is about to fall; the walkers will lead the attack, and Doctor Lyons needs help immediately in the cellars."

Got it.

"I'll take the walkers, you go help Sofia?" McBride suggested to Carter.

"Nah, there'll be demons there. I'll handle the walkers, you help Sofia."

"Right." McBride sheathed his sword and darted through the door. Carter leapt through the hole in the wall created by the hardlight cannon and looked at the walkers waiting on the far side. He grabbed his walkie-talkie from his belt and, after selecting the right channel, spoke into it.

"Rose, it's Dan."

"Hey Dan; what can I do for you?"

"When the shield falls again, I need you to kill one of the pilots of the large walkers, alright? Just kill the pilot; leave the machine intact."

"No problem." On the roof above him Mendelson snapped a clip into her sniper rifle and took aim.

Shield failure in ten seconds, Cooke's disembodied voice informed them and Carter braced himself, sheathing his sword. The shield fell and as the walkers moved closer to the Hall. Carter broke into a run, half-crouched to make himself a smaller target. He was halfway there when he heard the first crack of sniper fire from the roof behind him and saw the pilot of one of the walkers slump forward, his walker beginning to go out of control. When he was close enough, Carter leapt, vanishing as he did so, and reappearing atop the flailing walker, grabbing the pilot with one hand and disappearing again. He dropped the pilot out of the cabin and reappeared inside, quickly snatching up the controls.

He turned through one hundred and eighty degrees and opened fire on the advancing troops, cutting them down with the dual miniguns mounted on the machine's arms. Quickly the other walkers turned on him and he brought the guns to bear on them, targeting the nearest as they surrounded him.

"Leave. I'll handle this," McBride said to Lyons and her troops as he arrived. The cellar door was practically open by this time, and the guards gladly swarmed out of the room, closing the door behind them. The trapdoor burst open and a demon leapt out, waving its sword triumphantly for a second before it noticed the Touched One.

"Sorry mate; it's not your day." With a flick of his wrist he killed the intruder. More began to pour through the hole, some looking barely human in their anger; lunging out at him with metallic claws and writhing tentacles. He was quickly backed against the wall, swinging his sword one-handed to hack at the nearest tentacle or limb, whilst simultaneously hurling blasts of energy into the crowded and unnervingly overwhelming mass. He felt a brief flutter of fear run down his body; he hadn't anticipated quite such numbers.

Carter's walker leapt, one of its enormous metal legs swinging around and kicking another of the giant machines in the torso. As it toppled to the ground Carter span and opened fire with both arms at the second target running at him. He closed his eyes as bullets flew around him in both directions, some rocking the armour as they impacted mere inches away from his head, but eventually he heard the loud squelch as the last walker fell into the mud.

Carter turned to face the army surging towards him and tried to bring the guns to bear, but the damage to the walker was too great; oil poured from staple holes.

He heard Mendelson's voice.

One of the hardlight cannon is aiming at you; go.

The cannon fired and Carter vanished as he saw it, appearing a few feet from the walker as it fell, a neat hole punched straight through the middle.

"Thanks," he muttered, projecting the words to her. He turned to face the charging army, but seconds later the hardlight shield rose again.

♦

"Ma'am; they are destroying each wave of the attack separately, not allowing us any chance to press our advantage of numbers!"

"Yes." Lucy stood pensively for a moment, the rain

evaporating before it struck her head. "When the shield next drops I will lead the attack myself; all demons to the front, have the cannon concentrate their fire on the rooftops where the shooting is coming from."

"Yes, ma'am."

Both of McBride's arms were held now in the vice-like grip of a pair of tentacles, and he was thrown back and forth across the room, before being pushed back into and pinned against a fridge. The demon—one of the few remaining—walked towards him, limbs retracting into its body but still keeping McBride firmly in check as a third arm snaked from the creature's back and wrapped itself around the apprentice's neck.

"So you are the Touched One who has caused so much trouble for my kind?" the demon asked, pushing its face close to McBride's. McBride stared into the cold, black eyes and the demon blinked, eyelids moving in from either side rather than top and bottom.

"I am one of them, yes."

"The most powerful?"

"No, my master is far more powerful than me." For good measure, McBride spat in the creature's face.

"Good; I could use more of a challenge." A long forked tongue emerged from the creature's thin mouth and it licked its face clean. The demon swung around, releasing McBride and sending him flying through the parlour's huge bay window that led out onto the Hall's gardens.

McBride skidded across the gravel-covered path, bouncing haphazardly through the air before hitting the ground again, hard, and coming to a halt. He rolled onto his front and pushed himself up on his hands, only to cough up a mouthful of blood before his arms gave way again and he fell back to the ground.

"How long can you keep the shield up for?" McInnes said, arriving in the great hall where Cooke stood with both hands pressed against the dome of the shield generator, eyes closed as he focused on pumping every last ounce of energy into the barrier.

Hard to tell, Cooke replied, not even wasting his strength to communicate vocally.

"Lucy will lead the next attack." McInnes wasn't in the slightest bit put off by the intrusive thought.

Yes.

"Are you strong enough to fight her?"

That remains to be seen.

"Would you be stronger if you dropped the shield?"

Probably, but I would have to hold them all off at once.

"Let us handle the others, you just take care of Lucy."

Very well, Cooke said, before transmitting his thoughts generally to the Hall. *Cooke to all hands. The shield will fall for the last time in fifteen seconds; prepare to stem the tide as best you can. Good luck.*

"May God have mercy." Cabot racked the slide on his shotgun and stared out from the third-storey window as the wall of shimmering green light faded away for the last time and the demonic army surged forward.

"Open fire," he commanded of those around him, "stop as many of them as you can from getting to the doors!"

He double-checked the belt holding his scabbard to his side and leant out of the window again. His troops opened fire on the army below. Dozens of demons were hurled back, but not enough.

"I'm going to the reception," Cabot shouted across at a

junior officer. "You're in charge." He ran out through the door, snatching up his hardlight staff as he went, and made his way down the corridor. He was thrown forward a second later by a massive shockwave. Turning, he saw the room he had just left on fire, struck by a direct hardlight cannon hit.

"Shit." He grabbed his radio. "We have cannon fire directed at the third floor; without supporting fire we'll never be able to hold the Hall."

"Confirmed; I'm handling it," Master Cooke's voice came over the radio. "Get to the reception, we'll need everyone we can there."

♦

"The Hall is in flames, Mistress," a demon reported to Lucy. She turned to reply to him, when he was blown apart by a hail of hardlight staff shots.

Lucy strode forward at the head of the army, her sword deflecting or absorbing any munitions that were directed at her. The three remaining hardlight cannon fired again and great tendrils of energy flew from above the roof of the Hall, colliding with the beams and deflecting them harmlessly.

The crackling trails of hardlight altered course, tearing demons from the ground and throwing them down again before coming together in front of Lucy, condensing in front of the halted demonic line.

"Hello, Lucy."

"Master Cooke." She said, and curtsied sarcastically. "Impressively done; but you cannot save your Hall."

"It's taken a bit of a battering, I've got to admit."

"It was a valiant attempt though; I won't forget the efforts of your kind."

"How charitable of you. See you inside." He vanished.

◆

"Doctor Bishop?"

Bishop stood turned at the sound of her name. A man in a grey suit rushed her, and pressed a .45 calibre pistol barrel against her forehead.

"Take me to Master Cooke immediately," he instructed.

"Why should I do that?"

"Because I will kill you otherwise."

"You're a demon. I can only assume you're going to kill me anyway," she countered.

"Do you believe I can kill Cooke?"

"No."

"Then you lose nothing by taking me to him," he hissed, getting desperate now. "Please."

Bishop started to walk, as much curious about the demon's use of the word 'please' as scared for her life.

12

"Get up."

McBride rolled over at the sound of the voice and opened his eyes, admitting bright sunlight. He shaded his face with his hand and was just able to make out the bottom of a long white robe.

"Ellie?"

The light was obscured as the figure leaned across him.

"How do you feel?"

No, he thought; it wasn't Ellie, the voice wasn't quite right.

"Like all my bones are broken."

"Can you stand?"

"Yes, why? Where are we?"

"An in-between place; someone will be along shortly."

"Someone?"

She pulled him with unnatural strength to his feet and he saw her clearly for the first time. She was shorter than him by around four inches, with a minute figure and pale complexion, accented by long blonde hair.

"Who are you?"

"A friend of Ellie's, shall we say."

"I thought nobody knew what was going on?"

"Those who died for the Society have kept an eye open."

"You were in the wars? What's your name?"

"My name is Tina; surnames are more or less meaningless up here."

"Tina? But that means—"

"Goodbye, Mister McBride. Live well; you have another twenty years if you don't do anything too rash, but I cannot save you again."

The scene in front of him vanished and he found himself once again in the grounds of the Hall.

♦

"Master Cooke," Bishop announced herself quietly and he didn't bother to turn around.

"Doctor Bishop. You might as well let her go, Sokar."

The demon released Bishop and she moved away from him quickly.

"Sorry, James," Bishop apologised.

"Don't worry about it; I was wondering how long it would take for him to get here."

"No demon worth his salt needs an army to infiltrate an enemy stronghold," Sokar told him as the building shook from the assault.

"I guess not."

The two men stared each other down.

"You have to defeat her, Cooke."

"Why do you say that? Surely it would benefit your kind if she was in charge?"

"Difficult to feed off of human misery if there're no humans left to be miserable, I find."

"That's your motivation for coming here? To prevent your kind from being bored?"

"Also the high-ranking members of a deposed regime rarely stand to benefit from the rise of those who depose them."

"Of course; you want to lend your services to this endeavour?"

"I prefer the term 'expertise', but that's the general gist."

"Good; she will be here in ten minutes."

"Ten minutes? How can you be so sure?"

"We just are."

McInnes' staff snapped as it collided with the face of a Touched One and he quickly discarded the half that remained in his hands by thrusting the jagged, broken end into the chest of another assailant. He instinctively dodged a fist and a kick, then kicked out as he leapt back, gliding over to where the last remnants of his forces fought.

"Fall back to the great hall," he ordered and covered their retreat.

"Senator Greenwood!" Cabot stepped onto the dining hall balcony, shotgun in hand and staff slung over one shoulder.

"Colonel Cabot!" Greenwood didn't look up from where he was crouched firing down into the fray of invaders below the balcony.

"It's too dangerous here, sir; I must ask you to retreat to the great hall!"

"Doesn't that seem a little cowardly to you?"

"It is foolish to remain in a fight where victory is impossible."

"I will stand and fight here, if you don't mind; you are free to do what you want."

There was a lull in the enemy's charge, and the defenders began to take hope. Cabot peered over the top of the balcony, and saw that any jubilation was misplaced. Five demons, walking with arrogant slowness, had entered the dining hall in the space afforded them by the death of their more expendable allies.

Cabot took this opportunity to survey the scene. Bodies, of both defenders and attackers, littered the floor, piled three high in places. Cabot found himself slightly nauseated at the sight of so much death, but these latest demons paid little attention as they strode to the front of their troops and raised their hands, forming barriers between their men and the defenders.

Cabot quickly removed the staff from his back and took aim, squeezing three shots into the back of one demon, who collapsed, tried to rise, and was then destroyed by the fourth shot. He snatched up his radio. "This is Liam; we have powerful demons in the dining hall." He ducked beneath the balcony as two energy balls answered his attack.

"No cause for alarm, Liam, we've got you covered."

Mendelson's voice was closer than he had expected and, looking up, he saw the girl standing above him, shouldering her rifle and putting her eye to the scope. Her first shot obliterated a demon and before the others could react she had re-aimed and taken down another.

The doors to the garden flew open with the wind but the demons didn't turn, even as a beleaguered, sickly Engineer with torn and burnt robes staggered in.

"Ahem."

The sound echoed across the room and the fighting stopped.

"Engineer: kill him," one demon said to the other, and both threw energy balls at the apprentice. McBride raised his hand calmly and stopped both attacks.

"My name is not Engineer," he said, "it is Killian McBride, apprentice of Master Cooke, defender of this Hall."

He atomised the first demon. "Goodbye." The second fell to another energy ball.

McBride turned to his comrades. "Mister Greenwood, Mister Cabot; run."

There was a crash from above and the huge domed ceiling of the dining hall began to collapse, a human form falling in the midst of the shards of glass.

The man landed in front of McBride and adjusted the crimson bow tie of his tuxedo. "You're the Touched One?"

"Guilty as charged."

"You're scruffier than I expected."

McBride waved a hand over himself and the white fabric mended and cleaned.

"Better?"

"It makes little difference to me what you wear to die."

The demon flinched as a round from Mendelson's rifle struck him in the back. He laughed. "Human munitions are no match for true power." He extended one hand behind him and loosed an energy stream at the Gifted One.

Mendelson tried to move, tried to dodge, tried to become invisible, but her reflexes weren't enough and McBride watched her die, felt the hardlight in her dissipate.

"Hey, ugly!" he screamed and the demon turned. "Try picking on someone your own size."

"My size?" The demon exploded out, skin turning to armoured scales, face into a long snout, hands into claws.

"Ah." McBride stared at the dragon for a second. "Shit."

As the creature breathed fire he leapt aside and dropped into a roll, throwing two energy balls as he rose. The first went wide and the second impacted on the demon's snout. The dragon roared in pain and McBride threw two more energy balls into its exposed neck.

"Why won't you die, you mother-fucking bastard?" he growled and hurled another bright orb, not sure how long he could keep this up, but knowing for sure that if he stopped he was dead.

The dragon reared back further with every strike, but showed no sign of weakening until the eighteenth energy ball, as McBride was flagging, nearing the end of his strength; when it finally shrunk back to human form.

"An impressive display of strength, young one."

"Thanks."

"Not enough!" The demon reached out its arms; extending into long spikes, which expanded rapidly toward McBride. One went through the Touched One's left shoulder and he fell, letting out a yell as he loosed an energy ball straight at the demon.

The already weakened creature atomised, the blade withdrawing from McBride. The pain relaxed for a second, then sharpened as air hit the open wound.

"Mister McBride."

He looked up blearily.

"You're still alive; most impressive," Lucy congratulated him. "Very few mortals can claim to have defeated a wyrmkind."

"Tell me... that you don't have another."

"Regrettably not, but once this Hall is done away with there's no good reason for me not to summon more." She smiled. "I do, however, have something else you might be interested in." Past Lucy stepped the demon with the tentacles, that McBride had confronted in the parlour, holding Annie in its grasp.

"Annie!" McBride pulled himself to his feet. "What do you want, Lucy?"

"I thought that was clear? No? I want you all dead."

The demon behind her twisted its tentacles, snapping Annie's neck. She sagged in his grip and he tossed her corpse to one side.

"Bastard!" McBride drew his sword and simultaneously created an energy ball, gritting his teeth as he prepared to attack.

What are you waiting for? He felt the darkness well up inside of him. *Destroy them.*

"McBride!" Kingston yelled from the doorway. "Come with me! It's not worth it!"

"They have to suffer!" McBride yelled back, staring at Lucy, feeling his anger take control. The demon stood in front of him with her entourage, silently waiting. They were mocking him; he felt another surge of rage.

"You can't beat them! You'll die needlessly!" Kingston shouted again, but he didn't turn to look at her.

"What does it matter? What have I got left without her?"

"Choice!"

At this word he remembered McInnes' warning, and looked back, staring Kingston straight in the eyes and nodding. He turned back to Lucy, tossing the energy ball into one of the bystanding demons.

"This isn't over," he snarled as Kingston walked up behind him.

She took McBride's hand, and they both blinked into invisibility.

"A shame," Lucy muttered. "I had hoped his anger would destroy him."

She turned to another demon.

"Where is Cooke?" she demanded.

"The great hall, ma'am; it's still shielded."

"Very well; we will take it."

♦

"Gather round, children." Cooke turned to the door of the great hall as the forces on it began to increase. The surviving defenders of Cooke Hall were all here, everyone else being long since dead.

"This is it?" Greenwood asked.

"One way or the other." Cooke looked at McInnes, who nodded.

"Yes. One way or the other."

Cooke waved a hand and the door blew open. Dozens of black-uniformed soldiers ran in, quickly forming a circle around the defenders.

"Hold your fire," Cooke said calmly as the two sides eyed each other. Lucy strolled through the doors, sword case on her back, flanked by two demons.

"You have made a valiant effort, Master Cooke; but as you can see, my forces far outnumber yours. Your position is quite hopeless."

"We'll see about that." Robinson pushed his way past Cooke. "I'm the leader of this defence; you can deal with me, whatever you are."

"Very well, young mortal. Surrender this Hall immediately and prepare to die, or we will take both the building and your lives by force."

"No deal."

"Unsurprising; your kind have always been short-sighted."

Something caught Lucy's eye, and she sighed. "I expected as much from the angel and the mortals, but I have to confess to surprise seeing you there, Sokar." Lucy glared at the demon stood in the ranks of the defenders.

"When you are a little older, Lucy, you will see that this plain is not for us yet."

"That matters little now, it is already *mine*. The angels don't stand against me; all that is left is this ragtag collection of fools." Lucy paused, and for a moment the two sides simply stared coldly at each other.

"I guess we finish this now?" she continued, speaking now to Cooke. "See whose forces are greater? How much you have developed in the days since you last lost to me?"

"Something like that."

"Aha. I hope you don't take it amiss if I make the first move?" She span a pistol into her hands and fired two rounds, one through each of Cabot's kneecaps. The Colonel dropped, bravely attempting to stifle a scream.

"How unladylike," Cooke said calmly, though quiet anger could be heard edging his words.

"That's for the incubus."

"Ah, if that's the way we play it..."

A concussion wave spread out from the edge of the defenders, atomising the Touched One guards that it came into contact with. "That's for my Society."

"Ah, now you die," Lucy said and she leapt forward, barely leaving the ground but flying toward him with deadly speed, scimitar held in front of her at neck height, to decapitate.

As she moved she looked at him, their eyes locking, and she mouthed two words that echoed in his mind: *Goodbye, Cooke.*

As she closed the distance she turned her blade, making for the killing thrust, but stopped, without warning, mere inches from her enemy. Confusion flashed in her features, which Cooke did not fail to notice.

"Look down," Cooke whispered.

She did so, and caught sight of his katana, its blade locked against her own and preventing her from reaching him. He pushed forward and she flew back a few metres, landing facing him again.

"You have modelled one of our swords upon a mortal design? That is a travesty beyond forgiveness!"

"Not unlike myself." He smiled. "Though it does show

379

you just how far I've come since we last fought."

She leapt, striking, and he blocked effortlessly, batting her sword aside and lunging himself. She narrowly avoided the blade, but the hilt collided with her jaw as he twisted the weapon, knocking her back.

"When the playing field is level, who is it that is the better warrior? The mortal or the demon?"

She swung and he blocked again and again, putting up his guard with ample time to deflect her attacks.

"You forget you are a demon yourself, Cooke."

He leapt, striking out at her, sword darting this way and that, lunging at her with a strike she only just managed to avoid. "I confess you're a skilled swordsman, but that's to be expected." With a wave of her hand he was sent flying, landing forcefully on the floor with energy enough to create a small crater upon impact.

Ellie stepped in front of the fallen man. Seeing her do so, he flipped to his feet.

"Eleanor, stop," he said calmly. "I'll handle it."

"I have more experience—"

"I said I'll handle it," he insisted.

The angel stepped aside.

"How cute; now she can watch you die." Lucy waved her hand again and he was tossed into the wall. He vanished and reappeared alongside Lucy, swinging his sword with one hand. She blocked and his second arm rose, pointing a crucifix at her.

She reeled back and he struck at her. She dodged his sword swipe and swung up at the cross, removing the left T-bar and, her strength regained; she followed this with an attack.

They parted and began to circle each other, occasionally shifting their grip on their swords.

"Terry," Cooke said to his friend, who stood in the middle

of the room.

"James."

"Get the others out of here. Don't try and see why; just go."

McInnes began to funnel the others towards the rear doors, and the demons moved to stop them.

"Stand aside," Sokar growled at them and they hesitated. That moment was all that was needed and he struck, two quick energy balls clearing a straight path to the door.

"Run!" he commanded, turning as two more demons rushed him, one grabbing his arm and the other kicking him in the face.

"I remember when you guys didn't suck!" He jumped up, throwing the demon who had grabbed his arm off balance and kicking the other straight back into the wall.

"Sokar!" Cooke shouted. "Run!"

"I think I'll stay here, actually," Sokar announced as three demons pinned him to the floor.

"If you have some kind of master plan, Cooke, you'll have to kill Sokar too." Lucy told him. "Though I half expect you're just bluffing."

Cooke looked across at Ellie.

"James don't; it's against the rules."

"Rules be damned."

At these words, Cooke's body exploded in a burst of blinding white light. Where his human form had stood now was a spherical mass of pure energy, glowing with a light to blind or even kill any mortal in the room. Sokar shielded his eyes as dozens of sparking bolts tore from within the sphere, tearing the surrounding demons to pieces and colliding with Lucy's hardlight shield, trying to find way a way through.

Ellie vanished, leaving the room, and reappearing outside.

"It's begun," she said sadly to McInnes, and he sighed.

"We'll need access to the dais; can you transport it using a seal?" he asked, beginning to see the future unfolding before him.

"Not while that's going on in there; opening a portal would almost certainly tear this world apart."

"Ah."

♦

Lucy's shield gave way, leaving her with no choice but to follow suit and show her true form, her physical shell flying apart to reveal another sphere of energy. The two divine creatures merged as they duelled, tendrils of energy flicking out and striking at each other and the shattered room they were in, fragments of human form appearing in the maelstrom from time to time. Sokar, looking on, could discern no individuality in the chaos; they seemed not simply evenly matched, but looked almost as if they had become one entity. As he thought that, though, the unnatural storm pulsed brighter than before and separated, one beginning to condense into a material form.

Cooke swirled around, knocking Lucy down. She reverted to human form and, dazed, looked around for her sword, which lay across the room from her. The nebulous Cooke condensed into his human form, grey robe billowing behind him as he leapt and struck down at her with his katana.

She reached out and her sword began to fly toward her. Too slowly. His sword made contact with her and her weapon clattered to the floor as her body disintegrated.

Sokar rose, moving past Cooke and summoning his master's sword to his hand as he stood over it.

"Leave it, Sokar."

"This is the property of my kind; you will not take it from me."

"I'd like to say I'm surprised at you, Sokar, but it was a bit obvious you were going to betray me."

"What can I say? I'm a demon. Fancy your chances against me?"

"Actually..." Cooke vanished and reappeared behind Sokar, halfway through the lunge that plunged his sword into the praetor's back. "Yes."

He took the Morningstar's sword as it fell from Sokar's disintegrating grasp.

You can come in now, he thought to those outside.

The doors opened and Ellie and McInnes entered.

"It's over," Cooke told them. "She's dead. What comes next?"

"The demons will continue to pour through the seals they control," Ellie answered.

"We can stop them."

"Yes, but human casualties will be incalculable," McInnes told him. "We have made things better, but not good."

"I'm not so sure." Cooke broached an uncomfortable truth, "Lord Stanford is dead. The Council is dead. Mendelson is dead, Annie is dead, as well as countless others."

"What's your point, James?" McInnes asked.

"We have no resources, no government, no army, and very few troops left. We have little or no chance of being able to hold off the demons. Even with Lucy dead it is only a matter of time before they are able to regain a foothold in this world."

"Then we are lost. We either sit here and wait to die, or continue fighting to the death," McInnes summed up

Cooke's point glumly, and the three of them stood in silence, contemplating their fate.

"There is another course of action available," Cooke eventually said, tentatively, as if still unsure of himself. "Isn't there, Eleanor?" He looked to the angel for support, but she continued to stand silent.

"Ellie?" McInnes pressed her.

"We can reset the world to before this happened," Cooke answered for her, "prevent it from happening again."

"It is the last resort of the Choirs," Ellie told him. "It would take too much energy—even for me"

"How much energy? About three swords, a demon and an angel?"

"Even if we had enough energy, moving time around isn't easy; you'd need total knowledge of the Plan to pinpoint the place to stop."

"We have the Sighted One, Eleanor," Cooke reminded her, pressing through her objections. She looked at him, and saw the resolute determination she had learnt not to argue with when she was still alive.

"You actually want to try this?"

"The other demons have fled the Hall for now, but you know we're right; we would lose too many people to save a world that would barely be worth saving by the time we were done, if, indeed, we ever were. The dais can be used, can't it?"

"Yes," she admitted; having read those of Cooke's notes that even he couldn't read, she was more familiar with the device than he was.

Cooke took his sword and slid it through one of the three stones powering the dais, then walked around the side and inserted Lucy's. "Eleanor, if you wouldn't mind?"

"Very well." She drew her sword and slid it through the

last stone, offering a silent prayer that Cooke's plan was successful, though she was more aware than he was of the costs it would incur.

Cooke went to the centre and quickly tapped half a dozen buttons.

"Terry; if you could place both hands on the dome."

McInnes stepped forward and did so, his eyes closing instinctively as the dome lit up. An unnatural wind emanated from the device and light pulsed green for a moment before fading entirely. He slumped, sliding down the dais until he hit the floor, barely conscious.

"Terry?"

"Not enough energy," he panted, his words too quiet for the other two to comprehend, "only goes back a few years..."

"Why are we still here?" Cooke asked Ellie.

"The wave needs to get to the edge of the universe and come back," she answered. "It will take a few hours."

"So we just sit around and wait?"

"Yes; then the Plan will be restored."

"Will we remember?"

"Terry may have flashbacks, déjà vu, but nothing too major."

"Alright; we'd best tell the others."

"Tell them what?" Ellie asked. "There is nothing they can do."

As quickly as McInnes had been drained, he had recovered, and now Cooke turned to him.

"Terry, go and tell the others to take the rest of the day off to recuperate; tell them there are still demons in the Society, but that we're handling it."

"Good plan." McInnes left.

"Eleanor, you'd better go."

"Why?"

"My comeuppance is on its way; they'll take you if you're still here."

She smiled. "I don't believe that is true, but they may be displeased, and so I will leave you to your musings, my friend."

13

A cloud-like mass of small creatures flew as one, hundreds of thousands of tiny wings powering their flight as they moved in on the defenceless Cooke Hall. They descended, blocking out all natural light into the building.

"What's this? More demons?" McBride asked dully, looking around at the windows.

"No," McInnes said. "The other guys."

The darkness disappeared suddenly and McBride looked out of the window. A staggered line of white-robed entities now surrounded the Hall, scimitars in their hands.

"Didn't we save their asses?"

"They really stood to lose very little, I'm afraid, and we have broken practically every rule in the book."

"Every one?"

"More or less, yes."

"I'm going to tell Master Cooke."

♦

James Cooke sat at the desk in his office, an empty bottle of whisky lying in front of him. He bore the look of a man waiting for death, his expression sullen as he balanced his head on his hands.

"Master!" McBride entered the room at a run. "Angels have surrounded the Hall."

"There's nothing they can do now," Cooke muttered. "Go back to your quarters, they will not come any further."

"James." Verity stood in the doorway, her hands held placidly in front of her.

"Leave us," Cooke ordered McBride.

"Master!"

"I said leave us."

Anger flashed across McBride's face, but nevertheless he turned to go. As he reached the door, Cooke spoke again.

"Killian; I am sorry about Annie."

"Thank you, sir," he said without turning around, and left.

"You've been drinking?" Verity asked.

"Yes, heavily. The thing is, demons can't get drunk." He rose from his chair and sealed the doors with a flick of his wrists. "But you didn't come here to talk about my alcohol intake; this is about balance."

"Yes."

"I am the physical embodiment of its disruption, and therefore I must die."

"Yes."

"Do me a favour, would you; let me see you how you truly are once before I go?"

She nodded and transfigured, the youthful Touched One growing taller, into a five-foot eight woman in her early twenties, still recognisable as a much more mature form of Verity Robbins, wearing a long white robe.

"I guess I should have known; all that knowledge. When?"

"On the night of the second coup two hisa-me came for me while I was asleep, but I was dead long before that; I died the day you sent me away from this house, the day you betrayed my trust in you and forced me out into the dark."

"I'm sorry."

"It's a bit late for that, isn't it?" she snapped angrily.

"It's all I've got."

"As always. And it's never going to be enough. You killed me: it broke my heart to be sent away from the home and people I loved."

"Heaven hath no rage like love to hatred turned, they say, and you are now the physical embodiment of both."

"Yes."

"So why will you kill me, my dear?" He moved to the front of the table. "Because of your hatred of me, or for my betrayal of the Plan and its rules?"

"It is my duty as an Angel that drives me to this action, James."

"Good. I cannot resist you, so I will not even bother to try. Goodbye, Verity."

"Very well." She paused to compose herself. "James Cooke, jinn of the first seal, Master of the WTDD and of this Hall. You stand guilty of displaying your true form on earth, manipulation of prophetic visions for personal gains, expanding the range of human knowledge beyond human readiness, attacking an angel, disrupting the balance of mortal powers on earth, and raising an army capable of harming members of the Choirs. Your verdict is returned as guilty and your punishment is death."

As she stood there wind tore up around her, swirling forward and around the demon, tearing his flesh slowly from his bones. When no flesh remained, his bones disintegrated under the pressure.

James Cooke's emptied robes fell to the ground.

"It is done," McInnes said aloud, and a second later the hardlight wave hit the world, reverting the timeline.

14

Private Killian McBride felt his legs go weak, and he was lifted from his feet by the next blow from his opponent. He tried to rise but it was no good; the referee in the PFS army's in-house staff tournament had already called the end of the fight.

He slowly got to his feet and saw two lab-coated figures standing to one side of the hall, muttering to each other before turning away and leaving the gym. He span his staff idly through his fingers and cursed.

♦

"I think he had potential..."

"Maybe, Terry," Cooke looked pensive as the two Engineers walked to their car, "but something in my gut says it's not worth it; he'd be happier out here."

"You're certain then?"

"Yes; cross McBride off the list, we'll take Wilde as an apprentice."

"Alright; and the other matter?"

"Annie stays in the hall for as long as she wants, old

friend. Verity, however, will be taken from us in the next few weeks by the Civilian Guard."

"Will you resist them?"

"I wish I could, Terry; you know how much I care for her, but they might be right. Our lives are at constant risk, and she's still a little girl."

"So was Tina."

"And she died for her involvement with us: I'm not letting that happen again. If it is decided that she cannot live with us then we must accept the verdict and protect her from afar."

They climbed into their car, a large black off-road vehicle.

"Where are we now?" Cooke asked of their schedule.

"Meeting with the LP; he wants to know our progress on the MK. 9 programme."

"Of course. How is the Nautilus coming along?"

"Still in the planning phases, James; we haven't got clearance from Senate appropriations for a task this size, and an embargo has been put on you funding it out of your own pocket. They're afraid we'll use our possession of the most powerful warship in the Society for evil."

"Oh. Maybe they should try and get their hands on it." Cooke ran his hand across the steering wheel and the car started up.

"Tim's suggesting it this week."

"Again."

"You know how the Senate works." McInnes didn't flinch as Cooke cleared the facility's out-ramp already going at seventy MPH. "Everything has to be introduced six times before anyone warms to it; they only like old ideas."

"I know, I know. By the way, we need to start getting security ready for the Senate Ball next year. It's going to be troublesome, they insist on having more holes in their security network than a cheese grater."

"I'm sure we'll handle it, James."

♦

Seventeen years before the siege, Cooke Hall was still a place to grow silent late at night. Even the servants had gone to their quarters, save the skeleton crew required to stay in the kitchens in case his Lordship awoke and needed anything. At the far end of the east wing William Cooke slumbered, his father's snoring in the next room failing to disturb the heavy sleeper.

A figure moved silently through the house, illuminating the corridors as she went, though she carried neither torch nor candle. She reached the room at the end of the corridor, the Hall's smallest bedroom, and walked through the closed door.

She crossed silently to the bed and stood over the sleeping figure, a young boy with messy brown hair.

"Sorry," she whispered, reaching down and placing one hand upon his head. He writhed as his dream turned instantly to nightmare, and she removed her hand, taking a step backwards. Two more figures in white robes appeared beside her.

"It was the right thing to do," one said consolingly.

"We are angels; we're supposed to help people, not do that to them," the first argued. "Nobody deserves that."

"He will rise above the curse you have given him, and because of it will do a great many things."

"And he will need to be destroyed again."

"For the first time, my young friend."

"It doesn't feel that way."

"But it is that way; we have done what we have to do, the Plan's fracture has been controlled, now all that remains is to see what happens next."

The three angels vanished.

EPILOGUE

The kitchen was a hive of noise and activity. The back doors burst open and three men in black suits entered, quickly scanning the room. Behind them entered Lord Protector Robert Stanford and his entourage of aides, with, of course, Lady Emily Johnson.

They moved through the kitchen quickly in a haze of Secret Service agents, until they reached the doors from the kitchen to the main hall. Stanford faced the doors and composed himself before nodding to the men. The doors opened and Stanford stepped into the hall, free of his agents, to a burst of warm applause as everyone rushed forward to shake his hand.

More agents were positioned around the hall, he knew, but they did not surround him now. The only people at the party were friends and supporters; nobody here wished any harm on him, and for the first time in months there was no gun in his pocket.

"Hey, give a man some space."

The crowd backed away a little and Stanford looked around; the room was massive, and fully occupied by well-dressed members of the Society's glitterati and Senate.

"Honestly, anyone would think I just won the Executive Powers Bill."

The crowd laughed.

"Not very funny, but hardly surprising with a ninety-four percent job approval rating."

Another laugh rippled through the crowd. Stanford spotted the man he had been looking for, stood atop a balcony. He had messy brown hair and a gaunt face, and was wearing a long white lab coat. He thought for a second, and nodded to his old friend.

♦

Only one other guest at the party stood separate from the others, a muscular man of average height with neat brown hair. He wore a tuxedo but looked uncomfortable in it as he drank a glass of sparkling water. Why was he here? He was a Lieutenant in the army, and he had found himself excused from tonight's night shift in order to attend this little hootenanny, and he had no idea why.

"Enjoying the party, Mister McBride?"

He turned at the voice to face James Cooke, the infamous head of the WTDD.

"Uh, yes. It's very..." he struggled for any appropriate words, "well lit."

"Uncomfortable?"

McBride nodded slightly.

"Everyone is, don't worry; none of them have the breeding for it."

McBride smiled; the family history of the enigmatic Engineer was the subject of much speculation around the Society, where his imminent presence in any situation was always a possibility thanks to his carte blanche, and his general bizarreness lent him a certain air of mystery.

"I don't understand why I'm here."

"You were invited, and so you came."

"Invited may be too loose a word; two men came to collect me from the barracks, took me to a tailor where they made me this rather expensive tux, then they drove me here, and I got announced just like everyone else. I get the impression I wasn't given a lot of choice."

"You always have a choice; but this way works much better."

The party was moving on into the next room, a busy, throbbing ballroom that barely noticed the arrival of the Lord Protector's inner circle and richest supporters.

"We'd better go in."

"Who invited me, as you put it?"

"We did."

"The WTDD?"

"After a fashion. As you know, we are responsible these days for protecting the Society from itself, as well as from outside threats."

"I'd heard as much, but nobody seems aware of exactly what you do."

"With the Executive Powers Bill passed and the Nautilus project under way the ability of the Society to defend itself in the case of a crisis is more certain. However, control of the new military resources will no doubt be argued about by the two sides, executive and legislative, until the end of time."

"Yes, there is some talk among the officers of trying to gain control of the Nautilus program."

"I don't doubt it." Cooke paused. "A joint task force of CG and army officers and soldiers is being put together to ensure the security of the project. Officers whose loyalty is to the Society and not to their organisation, and who have no ties to the SS."

"Right…"

"As of tomorrow, you will be assigned to guarding the Nautilus development building, and eventually to guarding the Nautilus itself; you will be in charge of the army forces stationed there, answerable to Colonel Liam Cabot of the CG."

"Sir, I'm a junior officer in the army. I have no command experience and my rank isn't really enough to warrant this privilege—"

"It isn't a privilege, Mister McBride, it's almost certainly going to be hard work. Follow me."

Cooke cut his way quickly through the crowd, McBride following in the wake he left, and the two men walked up the staircase to a a door that, though it bore no markings, McBride felt certain was going to lead somewhere quite significant. Cooke opened it and the two men stepped into a lift, which began immediately to descend.

"Where are we going?"

"To show you what your life is about to become."

The door opened again and they stepped into a dark anteroom, where four guards with staple rifles stood alert.

"ID?"

Cooke quickly raised his hand, showing the guards the black metal pentagon clenched therein; the only identification that need be carried by Masters to grant them instant access to any building.

"He's with me," Cooke said as he breezed past into the larger room beyond. Men and women in gowns and tuxedos stood around peering at screens and poring over documents.

"Liam; what's the news?"

"CG patrols around the NCC have doubled in the past hour, Michael's dispatched three agents to that general area; looks like they're building for something."

"What do you reckon this time?"

"To be perfectly honest, I think the SS are going to try

and break into Councillor Andrews' office."

"How would the CG know that?"

"I expect they're there as a show of strength against the army trying to exert any influence over the Nautilus."

"Ah, so it's a coincidence?"

"Hopefully; the last thing we want is an open engagement between SS and CG."

"Right." Cooke thought for a second. "Liam; go up to the party and mingle, make sure Rob talks to Becky about how he hopes the spirit of cooperation will continue..."

McBride stood to one side, his mind racing as he put official titles to the first names.

"Sofia, call Siobhan and get her to put Bex in the NCC; let's try and get through this evening without body-bags."

"What's this room for?" McBride asked.

"Running the Society's defences while parties are on; the doors are fingerprint-locked, we're bombproof down here and we have access to the entire security network. While Lord Stanford wants to enjoy himself, his eyes and ears are here."

"And you want me to be part of this?"

"After a fashion. You'll be separate from this system—though we can help if the chips are down—but trying to get the same thing achieved; balance in the Society."

"Right."

"Agree to the job and you'll be promoted to captain immediately, the paperwork's already signed."

"That's awfully nice, but—"

"What if you refuse?"

"Yes."

"Never going to happen."

Cooke turned away. "The guards will let you out; I'll be at the party when you're decided."

♦

"My Lord." Cooke bowed slightly as he approached the Lord Protector.

"James; how's it going?"

"Alright; we have everything under control. Enjoying the party?"

"Yeah. It's nice to not be surrounded by agents, though I seem to have just exchanged them for bureaucrats."

"The twin curses of leading a modern society, I suppose, my Lord."

"Uh, Master Cooke."

Cooke turned to McBride.

"Ah, Captain McBride. Allow me to introduce Lord Protector Robert Stanford; my Lord, Captain McBride has decided to take up the position we were offering him."

"Thanks for helping us out of a tight spot." Lord Stanford extended his hand to shake McBride's, and in the second their eyes made contact all doubts McBride had were blown away.

"It's a pleasure to serve, my Lord."

"Excellent."

Cooke put one hand on the Captain's shoulder. "There's just one more person I have to introduce you to before you're free to mingle with whomsoever you wish." He guided him effortlessly through the party and over to a table where a young woman was sat.

McBride's eyes widened, taking in her every detail instantly. She was probably a couple of years older than him but ravishingly beautiful. She wore a long red silk dress, and her chestnut-brown hair fell down smoothly to her waist. She got to her feet.

"Annie, meet Captain Killian McBride; Killian, this is

Annie Davies, an old friend of mine."

"James—" Davies began.

"I'm sorry, I have to rush." Cooke quickly left the two of them alone.

"Uh, hi..."

"Do you have a clue what you're doing?" McInnes asked when Cooke joined him on the balcony.

"Have I ever? There are some things that are meant to happen, Terry; they are predestined."

"Since when have you cared for some great plan?"

"I don't, but if there is a way forward it is through acknowledging our humanity and that there are some things we cannot yet understand. The greatest things we do are those we do for love, so why shouldn't there be more of it?" He trailed off, his eyes meeting those of a woman in a black dress halfway across the hall. For a second he saw her differently, in a white robe, staring back at him knowingly, and then he blinked and she was as she had been, dancing with a senator.

"Yes, the greatest things..." he murmured and quickly rushed through the exit door. McInnes followed him, concerned for his old friend, but by the time he got outside Cooke had vanished.

"He has changed things," one of the two white robed figures, standing nearby but unnoticed, said.

"Yes, humans have a habit of doing that," the other announced, "with luck she will be happier this way..."

"The Plan—"

"What mortals do amongst themselves is their own business; we cannot interfere."

"Will she return?"

"We have lost the Morningstar's weapon, but she has not

broken through a seal yet; if she does return, it will not be for some time."

"And when she does?"

"We will be here, and so, I sense, will he."

"Someday he will die."

"Then another will take his place. That is the virtue of their kind; there is always another."

"And his apprentice?"

"He is following a new path, but the route will ultimately be much the same; everything, ultimately, ends up much the same."

The two women turned to each other, their faces concealed by the hoods they wore, despite the rain not being able to strike them. A common feeling of empathy for the humans, as well as relief that the job was done, radiated between the two.

"Until next time?"

"Until then."

ABOUT THE AUTHOR

Born in Bristol, and later moving to study Economics at the University of Reading, Michael T. Sanders is a fervent Christian and competent swordsman.

Conspiracy of Fire is his debut novel, having emerged from a years-long period of development of his war-torn vision of a futuristic Bristol; a reality he would happily confess to spending much of his life living in.

When not buried in paperwork or reading the Oxford English Dictionary for sport, Michael can be found sitting in the dark, surrounded by weaponry, attempting to produce green flames in the palm of his hand.